THIS STRANGER, HER HUSBAND...

Hallie stood frozen before her husband. She felt her hands clench, her lips quiver. If only she at least knew this tall handsome man...

"Relax, Hallie." His voice was a whisper, soothing her taut nerves inexplicably. His hands ran slowly down her back and then up again. He pulled her closer, her face nearly pressed against his massive chest. He smiled warmly at her, his voice intimate, making her feel as though she was the only woman in the world, the only woman he wanted. His own desires were raging as never before, making it a struggle to control the pace when he wanted to fairly ravage her.

His full sensuous lips lowered to hers gently. He found her lips, only to recapture them again and again, softly, sweetly, slowly, until Hallie relaxed a bit more in his embrace. His head lowered to her throat, kissing, nibbling lightly, breathing deeply of the scent of her, enjoying her as no other before.

He held her for another moment, feeling her body yield, become soft in his grasp. Again his lips met hers. She barely felt the cloak fall about her feet and did not care that she was un-shielded now, glad for the barrier to be gone, wanting her skin as close to his as possible...

WHEN LOVE REMAINS

VICTORIA PADE

AVON
PUBLISHERS OF BARD, CAMELOT, DISCUS AND FLARE BOOKS

WHEN LOVE REMAINS is an original publication of Avon Books.
This work has never before appeared in book form.

AVON BOOKS
A division of
The Hearst Corporation
959 Eighth Avenue
New York, New York 10019

Copyright © 1983 by Victoria Pade
Published by arrangement with the author
Library of Congress Catalog Card Number: 82-90549
ISBN: 0-380-82610-0

First Avon Printing, March, 1983

AVON TRADEMARK REG. U. S. PAT. OFF. AND IN
OTHER COUNTRIES, MARCA REGISTRADA, HECHO EN
U. S. A.

Printed in the U. S.A.

WFH 10 9 8 7 6 5 4 3 2

CHAPTER ONE

"Hallie! Hallie! He's back! He's home!"

Short, sturdy legs bounded up the stairs as fast as the small boy could push them. His excited voice rang throughout the house. Forgetting his manners, he flung the bedroom door wide, just as his sister knew he would, and burst into her waiting clutches as she stepped from behind the door laughing.

Hallie lifted her brother off his feet, though she was not a great deal taller, giggling with pleasure. Danny was not to be restrained. He wiggled out of her grasp, turning his flushed face up to her, his gray eyes shining. "Did you hear me?" he demanded, not even trying to contain his joy.

Hallie laughed, her own perfect features reflecting his pleasure. "How could I not? Are you going to tell me who is the cause of all this?" she teased.

"Adam's home! I just saw his carriage out front!"

Now it was Hallie's turn. Her face flushed with sudden excitement. For a moment she held her breath, then released it with a short exclamation of panic. She raced to her mirror, checking quickly to see just how untidy she must look, but did not actually see her reflection at all. Her thoughts were a jumble, her emotions raging.

Adam was back!

Danny laughed now, enjoying his sister's confusion. "I'll race you to the door! Bet I see him first!" He ran out, Hallie fast on his heels. Danny won, for at the top of the staircase, directly above the front door, Hallie stopped, suddenly in awe and unbelieving of what her eyes rested upon at the bottom.

Adam Burgess grasped Danny with an equal show of enthusiasm, then held him at arm's length. "Why Danny, you're nearly a man! I would never have known you," he teased.

"I'm seven now!" he answered proudly, then slipping back into his exuberance, "I missed you something terrible, Adam! I'm glad you're back!"

Adam smiled, pleasure evident on his handsome face. "I hope you're not the only Wyatt who feels that way!"

Suddenly remembering his sister, Danny turned to look up the stairs. Adam's eyes followed. More in control now, Hallie descended the stairs, much too quickly to conceal the fact that she was as pleased as her brother by their visitor.

Adam had not spent these past few moments controlling himself, and when Hallie reached the last step he scooped her into his embrace, lifting her clear of the floor. He kissed her, long and deep, as all of his starved passions surfaced; the years had been long, and his hunger for her had never abated. When his lips left hers he sighed deeply. "My God, how I've missed you!"

Knowing little more attention would be paid him now, Danny happily skipped off, leaving the two in the entrance hall, clinging to one another as though they could not bear to be separated. It was Hallie who finally broke the spell with words. "I don't know where to begin! I want to ask so many things. It's been so long!"

Adam laughed. "Too long! Did you miss me?"

She beamed, dark violet eyes sparkling. "You know I'm not supposed to admit that! Ladies are not allowed to be that brazen! Besides, I should still be angry with you!"

"You aren't, though," he said and smiled, the creases in his cheeks deepening.

"It was so foolish of you to go off to war just when you were ready to join Dr. Hathaway." Hallie pretended to be stern, a light frown creasing her features.

"I know it was! But I couldn't stay here! I was so angry I wanted to kill someone! How could I know your husband was going to die before you even set eyes on him? Besides, we had an agreement, as I recall. I considered us betrothed. I had every reason to be furious and to leave as fast as I could, regardless of what I left behind."

"And now?" she asked coyly, smiling so brightly Adam could hardly believe how beautiful she was.

He pulled her close again, holding her for just a moment to convince himself she was actually there. "And now I'm not the fool I was before. I start work with Dr. Hathaway next week. We won't be rich, but if you'll consent to marry me we can open the town house and you can decorate it in any way that suits you. Please, let's do it fast, before anything comes between us! Unless, of course, you're still in mourning."

Hallie's features exploded with joy. "You know that only lasts a year. Besides, I didn't love the man. I never knew him."

"And what about my proposal?"

She decided to tease him a bit longer. "I just don't know. Am I old enough now? That was your excuse before, wasn't it?"

"You know it was. I was stupid and I thought I couldn't marry a sixteen-year-old friend of my sister's, no matter how much I loved her."

"And now? Perhaps I've changed in two years."

"You certainly have from the looks of you, and all for the better." One blond brow rose as his brown eyes perused her slowly. "Stop torturing me now, Hallie. I love you and I want you to be my wife." His face grew serious.

"You're a fool if you think I'll even hesitate! Yes!"

Again Adam drew her into his arms, kissing her more tenderly yet savoring her with every sense. Hallie felt exquisite pleasure. It was as though she were in a dream, a wonderful hallucination she wanted never to end. So intent were they upon each other that neither Hallie nor Adam was aware of an observer. In his haste, Adam had not bothered to close the front door. Lounging there comfortably, one broad shoulder against the jamb, arms crossed over his chest, was a very interested, not so amused stranger.

"This is touching, but I must end it before it goes any further." The deep voice resounded with sarcasm.

Hallie jumped from Adam's embrace as though she had been burned, startled by the intrusion on so private a scene. Adam turned to face the man, angry at this interruption, yet when his eyes took in the sight he was more surprised and embarrassed than mad.

"Michael."

The tall, ruggedly handsome man bowed exaggeratedly, his own shock well concealed. "I hadn't a hint that this was the woman you talked about all those months, Adam. You must have enjoyed your joke," he said spitefully, astounded at the depth of his own anger.

"There was no joke. I didn't mention Hallie's name because I thought it in poor taste to be in love with your father's widow."

"My father's widow?!" the man nearly shouted in disbelief.

"You are Mr. Redmond's son?" Hallie asked in amazement, for she had never met any of the family she had married into by proxy. Their attorney had been her only connection to the Redmonds, and that was a brief meeting before the ceremony and again during it, when he acted as proxy for the man Hallie was to wed, Michael Redmond.

As Hallie stared at the tall man before her she began to recognize him. She had seen him before only at a distance, for a young girl did not travel in the same circles as an illustrious, sought-after bachelor. And even that had been two years ago.

All of the stranger's attention was focused on Hallie, a frown drawing his brows down over piercing blue-gray eyes. "Whom do you believe you married, madam?" he asked, his impatience audible.

Hallie's temper was spurred by his tone. Her chin lifted, her shoulders straightened. Her voice was commanding. "I married Michael Redmond."

"And do you recall the middle name of your husband?" he asked, undaunted by her tone.

"Of course. Michael David Redmond. Your father, if I am to believe you are the man Adam says you are.

4

Were you not aware that he died just two days after our marriage on the first day of May 1846?"

"I am well aware of my father's death. He was Michael *Anthony* Redmond. You may check his headstone if you are in doubt. That, madam, was your father-in-law. Michael *David* Redmond stands before you." Again he bowed, mockingly.

"How is that possible?" Hallie's voice was a whisper as the full impact of the news began to register.

"It is a simple fact that while the original arrangements were for you to wed my father, he became ill and I took his place. Surely Martin Chancelor explained it to you."

"He explained nothing! All his meetings were with my grandmother, except a brief visit when he informed me of the date and the ceremony itself."

"Then perhaps the fault lies with your grandmother."

Seeing Hallie's temper flaring and realizing Michael Redmond had no reason to lie, Adam pulled himself from his own unhappy shock. "The only thing we can do, Hallie, is speak to your grandmother," he said more calmly than he felt. "I'll get her."

Violet eyes locked menacingly with blue-gray as the two awaited Danny and Hallie's grandmother, a sprightly, smiling woman. She walked quietly to stand between Michael and Hallie, her features serene. "I do wish you had spoken to me first, Mr. Redmond. Didn't Mr. Chancelor give you my message?"

"No," he said bluntly.

Turning to Hallie, she sighed. "Well, dear, I wanted to break this to you more gently, but I'm afraid the younger Michael Redmond is your husband. I had to agree. You know how we needed the money, and I felt quite certain that you would never marry unless you thought it was old Mr. Redmond." She shrugged as though the matter were easily settled, kissed the stunned Hallie on the cheek, bade the men a good day and left.

"It's happened again, hasn't it?" Adam said, unable to believe Hallie had been plucked from his grasp.

"Sorry to disappoint you, but I'm afraid your plans were a bit premature, Dr. Burgess. You should have

5

taken my advice and used what was at hand instead of pining away for what belonged to another man."

Now Adam's anger was sparked. "It's hard to consider Hallie 'belonging' to someone who couldn't be bothered to come to his own wedding and then disappeared for two years without a word to his so-called wife," he shot back.

Michael shrugged nonchalantly, though a muscle in his cheek worked fiercely to belie it. "The fact remains that she is my wife, regardless of the tender scene I witnessed. And there isn't a damn thing you can do about it." Turning to Hallie, who was still dumbfounded by the whole affair, particularly her grandmother's deception, he said curtly, "You will have tomorrow to gather your belongings. I will send my man to bring them to my house late in the afternoon along with a gown you will wear in the evening. My family is giving a party to honor my return and to present you to Boston as my wife. Your brother and whatever servants you wish can come the following day. Your grandmother prefers to retain this house. I trust you will be ready to take your place as my wife tomorrow night?"

Snapped from her thoughts by his commanding tone, Hallie rose to the bait. "Have I a choice?"

"No, you haven't. You'll come with me whether you're ready or not. I have no aversion to carrying you out kicking and screaming if you prefer it." As though dismissing Hallie, he turned once again to Adam and said, "You'll be leaving now. My wife has too many things to do to entertain guests." Adam, feeling defeated once more, preceded Michael out of the house.

Just before he pulled the door closed behind them, Michael smiled back devilishly at Hallie. "You'll recover by tomorrow evening. After all, it's actually our wedding night, isn't it?"

6

CHAPTER TWO

Hallie sat back on the steps as though someone had pushed her. "How can this be?" she murmured in disbelief.

It had been over two years since it had all been arranged. Two years ago she had agreed to marry old Mr. Redmond, done the deed and been widowed, or so she had thought. All this time her grandmother had deceived her, knowing that her real husband would appear at any time to claim her.

Hallie's anger rose. She stood with determination, intent on confronting Etta Riley immediately.

Etta was calmly sipping her late-afternoon tea. She smiled sweetly and poured a cup for her granddaughter. "Come and sit with me, Hallie, dear. I know you have many questions."

"Will they be answered, or will you lie to me again?" she said angrily.

Etta sighed, suddenly looking all of her sixty-seven years. The lines around her eyes were deeper and more darkly shadowed, her mouth seemed pinched. It served to cool Hallie's temper a bit, for she was quite fond of the woman.

"I know it was horrid of me to hide the truth. At the time I viewed it as a good omen that the two Redmond men were both named Michael and allowed me to fool you so easily. It helped soothe my conscience to think a higher force was working with me, that it was all meant to be."

"But how could you? I trusted you!" Hallie accused, disillusionment apparent in her voice.

"It was necessary, my dear. I am an old woman who had nowhere to turn. Nothing of our predicament had changed because the groom had, we were still in dire need. Must we discuss it all now?" she said tiredly.

"Yes, we must! My entire life has been ruined, and I demand an explanation!"

"Oh, I do hope you're wrong about that. Perhaps because you were so young at the time you've forgotten just how desperate we were. I suppose that sixteen is too tender an age to take such matters seriously or to understand the importance of money. Your mother was not equipped to run the family's business when your father died. She knew virtually nothing about ship building. By the time she passed away after Danny's birth it was held together by the business of the Redmond shipping line and their orders for new vessels or repair of the old. I don't mean to malign your father, but he was neither frugal nor overly concerned with his wife, and he left your poor mother with an enormous debt and many other problems. I never understood exactly why the Redmonds took their business elsewhere, but when they did, our source of livelihood simply collapsed. The small amount I obtained by selling the business was barely enough to keep us going for those five years. When Mr. Redmond offered you marriage I had to agree."

"It wasn't your place to decide the course of my life!" Hallie nearly screamed.

"Perhaps not, but I did convince you, if you'll recall."

"Oh, I do remember that." Now Hallie's memories flooded back, quenching some of her anger with the return of the fear and desperation she had felt then. She remembered coming home one day and finding a horrid-looking man on the doorstep, staring up at the house. When she had approached, his assessment had turned to her, bulging eyes traveling her young body without hesitation, the thin nostrils flaring like those

8

of a hound discovering a scent. His smile was obscene. Hallie shivered with the same revulsion she had felt then. The man was a debt collector who relished his job. Hallie had been horrified to hear him speak of taking their home in payment for their debts. The ghastly smile remained as he spoke of placing Hallie as a bond servant for the remaining debts. The scene had grown grotesque as she watched him stare with a certain hunger at Danny and speak of taking the boy himself for the jobs that would be found for him as well. There had been no doubt in her mind that this was a grave emergency. After all, her grandmother was a helpless old woman and Danny a small child. She remembered feeling strongly that the responsibility was hers, no matter how unprepared she was.

Again Hallie spoke to her grandmother. "You assured me that Michael Redmond was too old to demand his husbandly rights. You said I was to be more a daughter to him. You even told me of his poor health and encouraged me to think he would not live long, though it seemed so cold to think about that. And all the while you knew he was not an old man, that he would surely come to claim me one day and that I would be expected to be his wife!"

"Please calm down, dear, and let me explain that. Mr. Chancelor came to me just two days before the wedding. By that time our creditors had been paid, we were well established again, in fact, we were in a much improved social position because you were marrying a Redmond. He told me that old Mr. Redmond had suffered another heart attack and he would not recover. I was devastated!" The gnarled hand pressed against her heart as if it again had begun to flutter with fear. "It was as though our only salvation had been pulled out right from under our noses. Then he explained that the Redmonds were committed to the agreement to join our families and that young Michael Redmond would be honored to marry you."

"He wasn't honored enough to come to me himself! Or to attend the wedding!"

"That was my doing, dear. I was afraid you would refuse, knowing how you felt about Adam and realizing that you had expected to be free, in time, to marry him.

9

I persuaded them that a proxy marriage would suffice and asked that you be allowed a few years to grow up before assuming a wife's duties."

"And you did this with no qualms?"

"Oh, Hallie! If only you knew the guilt I've suffered! Please try to understand. We were in such terrible need! I soothed my conscience with the fact that young Michael Redmond was an extremely handsome, desirable man. Every girl in Boston was after him, and he was choosing you!"

"But I loved...love Adam! You promised me that he and I would be together if only I would marry into the Redmond family to save us! You played on my naïveté and lied to me!"

"Perhaps you will grow to love Michael," Etta said sweetly.

"I love Adam!" Hallie answered stubbornly.

Etta sighed. "I was afraid of this. I do have only one suggestion then, dear." A small amount of Hallie's anger abated, as she regarded the flicker of pleasure in her grandmother's eyes. "You would have to be discreet, but you could take Adam as your lover," she said, clearly savoring the thought of a little excitement in her life as the accomplice.

"Grandmother!" Hallie said in half shock, half exasperation but not without a touch of amusement. "Do you know what you're saying?"

"Now, Hallie, I know you're young and idealistic, but there is no other choice if you intend to continue a relationship with Adam. You would be surprised at just how many perfectly respectable women have done the same. I would advise one thing, though. Wait a little while. Michael Redmond appears to have a great deal to offer a woman. You might find life with your husband more likable than you expect."

"I'm beginning to wonder if you don't have a bit of an attraction yourself for Michael Redmond," Hallie shot back, not a little shocked to hear her grandmother speak to her as a woman for the first time.

Etta Riley laughed lightly and for a moment there was a hint of the beautiful woman she had been. "I won't deny that if I were you I would feel quite differently about this matter. I know you have had a wicked

10

surprise today, dear. But try not to be hasty in your judgment of me. I assure you I did only what I had to and what I hoped would prove to be the best choice for you." She finished the last of her tea and smiled at Hallie, seemingly unperturbed by the predicament in which she had placed her granddaughter. "You had best run along and begin to pack your things. There is so much to do in time for tomorrow night."

Hallie rose to leave. "Well, at last I understand why there was no announcement of the marriage. It was not, as you said, because old Mr. Redmond wished to allow a bit of time for me to be old enough to assume my place as his wife. An announcement would have had the real name of the groom. Even at my young age I did think it strange that so prominent a family would not make an announcement of such a marriage. How very clever you are, Grandmother." Hallie's last words were full of bitterness.

Etta looked miserable. Then she said, "It wasn't all my doing, dear. The Redmonds have always been a rather strange family, staying far away from Boston's social world. As I recall, Michael's mother was said to have been descended from a very aristocratic family in England, but she made nothing of it. The Redmonds have never cared for society. I've no idea why—her background and the size of the family fortune would have made them welcome in almost any circle.

"Yes, my dear, they have always been somewhat aloof," she mused, though Hallie was quite sure she was only trying to stay away from conversation about her own treachery. "They have always preferred the isolation of Redland to the city's life. I don't know why they even keep that beautiful house on Beacon Hill; I've heard that they never use it, though I gather Michael's sister does live there part of the year."

"This is all interesting, Grandmother, but it does not change my feelings about what you have done to me."

Etta only shrugged. "I *am* sorry, child. But I had no choice. If I had, I would have seized it. I hope someday you will understand all this."

Hallie sighed in exasperation. It was clear she would

find no sympathy from this quarter. She rose and left her grandmother, her own thoughts a mass of confusion and dismay. A slight shudder took her by surprise as she began to realize that this was happening.

CHAPTER THREE

Sleep was impossible for Hallie that night. Well into the early morning hours she stood at her bedroom window staring out at the dark street. Directly across the street stood a row of ornate brownstones, the only variation coming in the bay windows that jutted from each. She knew well that inside they were all almost identical to her own. This particular home had been well taken care of in the two years since her marriage.

Hallie smiled slightly, remembering that two years ago she would not have been able to peer from this window, for the glass had been broken and boards had covered it to keep away the chill. She thought of the cracked plaster that had decorated the walls of every room, of the draperies that hung in tatters, hardly able even to catch dust. She remembered their furniture, cushions worn or split, and she smiled at the picture of a chair leg cracking when her grandmother pulled Danny to her lap for a spanking. Much of Etta's fine furniture had been sold; the rooms were sparsely furnished. The damp cold had permeated every room, and water seeped down the walls. Even the blankets were thin and worn. She remembered that her brother had grown emaciated, and her grandmother had taken on the look of a frail bird.

13

"So many things have changed," Hallie said to herself as she stared at the clear, star-filled October sky. The house was again lovely. All their wardrobes had improved, Hallie thought, as she fingered the fine lace that edged her soft velvet robe. Her old nurse Mercy no longer had to do household chores; she tended only to Hallie and Danny. Matilda, the cook, no longer had to invent ways to use carrots and potatoes; her efforts in the kitchen now filled the house with delightful aromas. Meat was plentiful again instead of a rare treat for the household. It was very different from the cold gruel or meatless soups and stale, hard bread of those awful days.

Their carriage was new, the horses a matched pair of black geldings. They were allowed a few luxuries, Hallie her sweet-smelling bath oils and her ribbons, Danny his toys and Etta her nightly snifter of brandy. Even Mercy was indulged daily with a crisp white apron and a small bit of her favorite sweets each week. Not really such great extravagances, Hallie mused, yet all provided for by the Redmond money, that sum which arrived with Mr. Chancelor's messenger each month like clockwork, free of questions or encumbrances or obligations. Until today.

The debt had come due. The price was her freedom and the future she had expected to spend with Adam. Hot tears filled Hallie's eyes and spilled down pale cheeks. For a moment it seemed difficult even to breathe, so great was the loss of Adam and that life she had planned. She had thought of little else in these past two years since thinking herself a widow. She had so many plans, so many dreams...now each one brought with it a fresh onslaught of anguish. She knew she would burst into hysterics if she didn't push it all deep down inside.

"What good does it do now, anyway?" she asked herself miserably. "None of it will ever be. I've sold myself." With that came a flood of worry about her new life as the wife of Michael Redmond.

When Hallie thought about it, there was very little she actually knew of the family she had been a part of for over two years now. She did not know any member of the Redmond clan and had stopped believing they would ever bother with her. She understood that her social class was not quite up to theirs and had concluded that the death of the senior Michael Redmond had allowed the remaining family to forget about her. It had never mattered to Hallie; her family's fortunes were assured, and she could look forward to the day of Adam's return and their marriage. There had been one occasion when she had seen Michael's sister at the dressmaker, but Hallie was just leaving as Lydia Redmond Kent was entering, and it was only by chance that Hallie had heard the seamstress call the woman by name. To her knowledge the family might not even know she had married Michael, though that seemed odd. But then the one thing she did know about the Redmonds was that they had a reputation for doing as they pleased, regardless of convention. Actually, she admired that. It was rather nice that Michael Redmond maintained one of the few remaining large colonial farms in Boston as well as their shipping industry. Hallie had never been one to conform herself. She appreciated free thinking and the courage to stand alone against the winds of time and progress. Certainly there was no question as to the enormous respect granted the Redmond family.

And what of her husband? How strange it seemed to think of him as that when she had spent all of this time believing herself a widow. Certainly he was well respected among men and sought after by women, just as her grandmother had said. Even at the age of sixteen, when Hallie had married, she knew of many young women who would gladly have given anything to ensnare him. What a disappointment it would be when they learned he was wed.

Hallie sighed. "What a horrible mess!" she said to herself, trying desperately to stop the flow of tears. "It does no good to feel sorry for myself."

There were so many questions in her mind. How did Adam and Michael know one another? And so well? Hallie knew they had never met before Adam had gone off to fight President Polk's war with Mexico. Did they meet then?

Hallie's thoughts went full circle to Adam with that, losing her tight grip over that which she wanted to keep

15

under control. The pain grew rapidly again, almost a tangible thing. She knew she must accept the fact that she would never be his wife. She and Amanda had made such plans together, thinking their friendship would become the more binding relationship of sisters. Her friendship with Amanda Burgess had been her introduction to Adam. Amanda would be disappointed. She had helped Hallie through that difficult decision two years ago, sympathetically understanding her predicament. She could not believe her brother's stubbornness. When Adam had refused even his sister's pleas, Amanda had advised Hallie to marry Michael Redmond. Hallie remembered her friend's hesitancy to repeat Etta Riley's words, speaking sheepishly, ashamed of the thought. "Perhaps if the man is so old you will be free of him in time and you and Adam can still be together."

How foolish it seemed now, Hallie thought, for deep down she had hoped it was true, herself feeling mortified to hope for such a thing. Two girls plotting what to do after the death of an old man, as though they were disposing of an old dress. The color returned to her face with that, embarrassed at her own heartlessness. Yet when he had actually died two days after the wedding, Hallie and Amanda had counted it as a stroke of good fortune, as though it were meant purposely to free her. How callous and cold and cruel two children could be. And how naïve, Hallie thought. But no more so than Adam. She had warned him that she needed a husband immediately even if he would not make an enormous salary as a doctor fresh from medical school. She was well aware of the money he inherited from his grandfather when he had graduated, and she knew it would stave off her creditors without depleting his savings. Still he had refused, saying she must grow up first, that her family could not possibly be in as much trouble as she thought. He had gone so far as to accuse Hallie and Amanda of devising this story to accomplish some girlish scheme.

In a way, her marriage to Michael Redmond had been tinged with a bit of rebellion. Angry with Adam's refusal to acknowledge her predicament, she had set out to show him she was no child.

Now Hallie laughed bitterly. "I certainly did show him," she said ruefully.

He was right, though, she thought. I was a child, a foolish child tricked by a clever, salty old woman.

Again Hallie sighed. Nothing was being accomplished with all of this, she told herself. She climbed into her bed, wondering how it would all end. Yet just as she thought she could finally fall asleep, her mind wandered to something her grandmother had said that afternoon. With every girl in Boston chasing after Michael Redmond, why, indeed, had he chosen her? And having done so, why had he run away until now?

CHAPTER FOUR

Michael was staring at that same clear, dark sky. The wide balcony reached far from the walls of his country house, escaping any of the warmth that might be given off from the interior. In the hot summer months it shaded the veranda below and now, as he leaned against the railing, it lent Michael the exhilarating feeling of the years he had sailed ships for his father. He would have preferred that it face the back portion of the estate, for it was from there that the fields stretched, away from the city.

Michael relished the air's crispness. He wanted a clear mind to contemplate what lay ahead. He wished that he were more certain of the future. Marriage and acceptance of his place as head of this household brought unwelcome obligations. He likened himself to a stallion he had purchased months before in New Mexico. It was a wild thing, willing to endure almost anything for its freedom.

Michael's mind wandered to the past. He had no reason for his free spirit, for his deep need to be unhindered by the conventions of society, rules his father had held so high, rules that kept a man tied to the duties of families and business, gruffly ignoring any pleasure, any adventure. But from boyhood he had rebelled. His father had sent him to sea at an early age, certain it would break his strong will, diffuse his wanderlust. Thinking about it now, he recalled the feelings of his boyhood strongly. He could see the huge man sitting erectly behind his desk; he felt himself to be that boy again, standing fearfully, awaiting the judgment of this stern patriarch.

"So you've done it again, have you?" his father boomed. "Swimming on the Sabbath like a heathen when you were to be in church, repenting for your laziness and disrespect! I've done with you! You'll leave tomorrow at dawn. A few years at sea will break you of these idle ways!"

Michael had begun to speak, but the heavy hand rose to silence him.

"Be gone now, boy! I will see you again when you can come to me as a man who deserves my name!"

Michael's life at sea had been tolerable. He admitted that he was not truly a sailor, but he did enjoy many aspects of sailing. The hard work had toughened his body and left him with a self-confidence he had not had before. It had been a good outlet for the energy that had previously served to get him into trouble. The tangy smell of salt water, the light spray against sun-bronzed face and chest as he had stood at the railing had pleased Michael, as had the lulling sway of the ship through the icy water below, the slow creaking of the hull. What had not been tolerable to Michael was the confinement. A ship, no matter how large, became a prison after a few weeks at sea, he thought, remembering how he had climbed the masts in desperation to see anything but the same flawless expanse of water, hoping to catch sight of anything else. He recalled almost welcoming the storms for the diversion they offered, regardless of the danger.

Old Farley had been his salvation. Actually, he thought now, had it not been for Farley he would most probably have jumped ship, for once the work was under control there stretched hours of uninterrupted idleness, time when he realized he could recognize every inch of the ship by the smell or feel, he knew it all so well. Farley was an enigma. On the surface he was a man of brawn and apparently no brain, for his size led people to believe he was doltish. Yet few could equal his knowledge and most of that gained from books. Farley's cabin had been a library. And that he had shared with Michael. There had grown a profound friendship between the two; Michael had found it odd that he could speak so freely to the older man, but never did Michael find judgment or recriminations. Merely a reasonable alternative possibility at times when Farley did not agree with Michael's boyish attitudes.

Michael's full lips smiled now at the thought of the first time Farley had patted him on the back in praise of a job well done. Michael had nearly jumped a foot with surprise and shock, for not only had his father never praised him, he also had not touched him in any way save to punish. They had been at sea three weeks when the older man had realized Michael was going mad with boredom as he ran laps around the deck, using the barrels and coiled ropes and boxes as an obstacle course. It was then that he showed Michael his books, volume upon volume stacked from floor to ceiling, piled on the desk, on shelves about the walls, even in the drawers beneath the bunk. A meaty hand had stretched wide. "Here lies your freedom, lad," he had said, placing a fatherly arm across the narrow shoulders and laughing boisterously at the look of disappointment on Michael's face. "I can see you've not been shown properly the contents of these packages. It's the whole of the world, me lad! Your mind can wander to places you never knew were there. You can taste the fruits you'll never find in the marketplace, hear the sounds that echo in another man's mind, see the land through another's eyes. You'll feel the wind or the snow or the kiss of a lass long before you've the courage to try it yourself. There's nothing quite like it, and then you won't chafe at a sailor's life—you'll thank it for the time it gives you to be somewhere else."

Michael had laughed at this rousing speech. Still, he had doubted his words and only began to read some of the volumes to please Farley and from lack of anything better to do. Michael had begun with *Gulliver's Travels*, then *Robinson Crusoe*, pretending indifference. By the time he began *The Last of the Mohicans* he was devouring each page, anxious to finish his work and seek

21

his book to arm himself with the knowledge he needed to discuss the story with Farley each evening. By the time he discovered *Moll Flanders* and *Don Quixote* he was well on his way to being impassioned with what awaited him in the next volume. He worked his way through the older man's library and began to make his own purchases in port.

At twenty-nine Michael had been with the older man for fourteen years. Farley was more a father to him than his own, spending time talking to him, explaining anything the boy asked of him. He had taught him so much, Michael thought, as he stared up at the small crescent of moon. And saved him in more ways than one as well. Michael knew he had run the man ragged with his wild ways, but always Farley was there helping, teaching, serving. In his gruff manner he had given Michael a better appreciation of his father, and that had led him to this current situation.

Three years ago Michael had returned to Boston and a father who was a shadow of what he had once been. Michael barely recognized him. The family had gone into near seclusion as a result of his poor health. Lydia understandably resented her withdrawal from her social life and all activities young women found important. Trent, then only twelve, was like a shadow, hiding in corners, not sure why his house was in the throes of maudlin despair, left entirely to his own devices yet being too timid to perform mischief. The house was dusty, for the servants did nothing without specific instructions. Drapes were left closed so that no sunlight entered, windows were never opened to air out the stuffy rooms. Voices never rose above whispers, and if the boy even ran he was reprimanded for the noise his shoes made on the wooden floors. The older Redmond had made it clear then that Michael was to take over. He had not found that terribly distasteful, for if his heart was in anything it was the land around Redland, and he had discovered with pleasure an aptitude for the business of shipping. The arrogance and innate air of command that his father had always disdained was to prove indispensable in taking over all that he was so soon to inherit.

Through Farley's eyes Michael had come to see his

father as a destructible man, rather than an immortal tyrant; a man like all others, holding beliefs that were not always rational. It was Farley who made Michael see that if he refused to understand his father's motives and feelings, then he was as narrow-minded as his father and as much at fault. Michael had come to think of his father as no more than human. And with his new vision came sympathy, compassion and not a small amount of pity. He found himself wanting to help him rather than continue the pain he had caused him by rebelling against his values. So when the elder Redmond confided his deepest secret to his son, Michael was at a very vulnerable stage and could not refuse his request.

Michael remembered that scene now. It had been his father's final coherent conversation. The elder Redmond's voice had been raspy and weak, forcing Michael to lean nearer to understand the words; long pauses fell between phrases as he fought to catch his breath. "Please understand, Michael!" he had begged. "I loved her. Your mother was gone from me. I needed someone! We didn't mean it to happen!"

Michael thought of his own shock at what the old man had unveiled and saw him more clearly as a real, flesh-and-blood man with weaknesses. He had listened intently to his confession of purposely destroying Hallie Wyatt's family, knowing that by taking his business elsewhere they could survive only for a short time before becoming desperate. Yet when the weak old man had told him of his planned marriage to the sixteen-year-old girl and the reason, Michael had still been shocked. His father had begged Michael to marry the girl in his place, to complete the plans to provide for the Wyatt family, asking but one condition and leaving the remainder of the relationship to Michael's choice. He had not been able to refuse, yet again the rebellion and wild streak in him had risen to the forefront.

Michael was more than willing to comply with Etta Riley's request for a marriage by proxy and two years to allow Hallie to grow up. It was his way of denying the deed altogether while still fulfilling his father's plea. It suited him tremendously to allow Martin Chancelor to take over. He had never wasted a second thought on his bride, relying on Chancelor to handle her and her family's financial needs. Michael shifted now, the wound stabbing at his side, his ribs aching with the cold October air; for a moment he grimaced and pressed his hand to his side.

"You needn't remind me, dammit!" he spoke to the still night air, his thoughts traveling for a second to the man who had saved his life, Adam Burgess. Pushing the picture of their friendship out of his mind, he forced his thoughts into the past.

Michael had not even told his best friend, Jason Curtis, about his marriage. Had it been shame, he wondered now, at the fact that he had cared for his father, done what he wanted and allowed the old man what he had attempted for so long, to rule his life? Perhaps. Or maybe it was another act of his immaturity at the time, he told himself, and his selfishness. He remembered feeling so trapped then, so much so that he would have preferred death to remaining in Boston, so he had joined President Polk's army to fight with Mexico for the right of Texas to be a member of the United States. That was a particularly unpopular action in Boston, for everyone knew that Texas and the territory into California were more sought after by the southern states to add more power to their strong hold on slavery. At the time it had not mattered. Michael had wanted only to be wild again, and he had wanted to vent this anger he felt. Texas was a long, long way from Boston and the staid society that contained a wife he had no inclination to claim.

Each time in the past two years that his wife had crept into his conscious mind, he had pushed her back again, as if refusing the thought made the reality disappear, too. Not once had he even wondered what his wife looked like, for they had never met.

Odd, Michael thought, how that war had changed him. A second grimace pulled his features, but now it did not come from physical pain. The first blood had been spilled on April 25, 1846. Michael had stayed in Boston, following the war in the papers, feeling nothing strongly about it, as many of his friends did. It was the cause of many a heated debate after their harness racing. Some felt that the President should be supported in his stand regardless of his methods, others argued that had he used a conciliatory policy it could have been avoided. Many saw the need for an expansion of the land in order for the country to grow, others saw it merely as a need for more slave territory. Michael had listened only halfheartedly until his need for rebellion arose. Suddenly he was very interested, though he still cared little for the politics behind it. The action fascinated him.

In August he had joined Colonel Stephen Watts Kearney in New Mexico, getting the first taste of battle by the eighteenth in the conquest of Santa Fe. He smiled ruefully now to think of it, for there had been almost no loss of life, and he had been disappointed at the ease of it all. Intent upon bloodletting, Michael had put in for a transfer to Veracruz and the forces of General Winfield Scott. He had stayed with him until he was wounded in the victory of Chapultepec, September 13, 1847, just one day before they entered Mexico City. Michael had had his fill of blood and killing by then, he thought now with distaste. After the first few battles his anger and need to prove himself were spent. He could not help feeling that it was a one-sided war, the powerful United States Army pursuing uneducated peasants. He began to think of it as sanctioned murder. It was an unfair contest, and the sight and smell of blood and dying flesh assaulted his senses. It still had the power to turn his stomach. There was the old man whose ancient hunting rifle had backfired into his face, blowing away the reflection of the fear as he watched his family killed. There was the small boy, not much older than Trent. The boy had charged the man in front of Michael with a blunt stick. The man had shot him in the throat and then moved away as if just annoyed. The wide black eyes of the boy had seemed to Michael to be staring in accusation at him, though he knew they were sightless. Michael's hands were clenched into tight fists, pressing hard into the cold wooden banister. Beads of perspiration dotted his forehead, and the cold breeze chilled them. He thought of the sounds of women screaming in horror as men he was ashamed to know raped and brutalized them. His gorge rose with the memory, feeling again the warm, sticky wetness of blood from the young girl who had run to him for protection

25

seconds before she died. It was as if a madness had infected men he had previously respected, and he despised his own powerlessness. The other aspects of his life as a soldier had worn thin as well, pulling at him as if taunting his mettle—the constant filth of his own body; the lice that had taken a home on him; the hard, dry meat with little to wash its lump from his throat; the scant hours of sleep on hard earth or in slimy mud. It was all enough to quench Michael's yearning for freedom, for the battle, to sprout a new fondness for all he had disdained before.

By the time Michael returned to Santa Fe, near death with a bullet still lodged between his ribs and his lung, he longed only to be back home, away from this death and destruction and depravity. Suddenly Boston's staid society seemed appealing.

It was then that he met Adam Burgess. The irony of that struck him now. Adam had performed the delicate surgery that saved his life. Afterward they had become friends, the sort of friendship that forms quickly, if not from mutual interest, at least from similar memories. Michael had recognized the difference in their personalities then, but it had never mattered; one complemented the other, at least until today.

A flicker of his earlier anger flared anew. He remembered many conversations with Adam when he had almost envied him his feelings for the girl he had left back in Boston. He did not doubt that Adam was as confused as Hallie about whom she had married. Etta Riley was a cagey old devil. Still it spurred his temper to think of Adam pitying him all those months, thinking he was sparing him the fact that he loved the woman he thought to be Michael's stepmother. What disturbed him most was the depth of the feeling he knew Adam possessed for Hallie, for he had never left that unsaid.

Michael was well aware of the intensity of Adam's love for Hallie. But did she have equal feelings? Michael wondered now. Certainly it had appeared so when he interrupted their reunion. Odd, Michael thought, how strongly that possibility stirred him. Why, he did not even know the girl, yet it bothered him to think that his wife loved Adam, and if it was even a degree of what

26

Burgess felt it would be a formidable obstacle in this marriage.

Michael again smiled wryly; perhaps it was his own punishment, for even after the months of recuperation in Santa Fe he had again become reluctant to return to Boston. Those had been months spent in camaraderie with Adam, yet now Michael did not even feel kindly toward this man whose skill had spared his life. He wondered if Burgess regretted the act now, for it could have left Hallie a widow after all.

Again the irony struck him; they had traveled home together, each returning to the same woman. Adam has returned just as he left, but I have grown up, he thought. He only hoped it was enough to accept this new role in life.

As dawn began to creep over the top of the huge house, Michael finally turned to go back in. His gaze traveled upward to the windows that formed the cupola on the level above the balcony, though it wasn't the house his eyes saw but the perfect features of the young woman he had seen for the first time that previous afternoon. He wondered if she was a person to accept her future so easily, or if she would be haunted by the shadows of the past. He shrugged, shaking off the picture in his mind of Hallie. He realized that before too long he would know well what he had gotten himself into, and he moved to enter the warmth of the house once again.

CHAPTER FIVE

Adam was barely aware that the day was dawning gray and cloudy, or even that he had been up furiously pacing the entire night. His long, lean body refused to feel fatigue as he continued to move around the room. Still his mind was racing with the events of the day just past, so much so that he had not even taken notice of his surroundings.

When he had taken these rooms at Tremont House he had been so certain that it would be a matter of a few days before he and Hallie were married and would open his town house again. His sigh was short and bitter. At least he would be comfortable in his accommodations; this suite was luxurious. It was to have been the site of his wedding night.

Michael Redmond had spoken of jokes; well, the biggest of them all was on Adam, he thought none too happily. Still, it was so hard to believe, he told himself for the hundredth time that night. He had been so certain it would work out this time. How was it possible that Hallie had been torn from his grasp once again and by the same family?

Adam's heart and mind ached with his love for her. He had loved her for what seemed like centuries. He remembered her as a little girl, playing with Amanda.

29

Their parents had been good friends, and Hallie and Amanda, being the same age, had become close almost immediately. Adam had been left on the outside, for not only was he a boy and ten years older, but also their friendship had brooked no intrusion. He knew that still they confided in one another.

Adam thought back now to the times he had watched them play, to all the years he had watched them grow. He knew that at first he had loved Hallie in the same way he did his sister. In fact, being so close, Adam had oftentimes simply thought of Hallie as another wild little girl in his family. But as she had begun to mature he had seen her differently; his feelings for her had changed. Adam thought back to times when he had been ashamed of his feelings for her, because it seemed ludicrous for a grown man to be enamored with a young girl, so much so that he had avoided all other women his own age. He knew that he had lost his virginity long after all of his friends, and then only with the thought that he did not want to come to Hallie inexperienced and inept at lovemaking. Always he fantasized that the woman was Hallie, and when he felt confident in his abilities as a lover he had stopped pursuing it, vowing a life of celibacy until he could have her.

In a way those years of Hallie and Amanda maturing had been a mixture of pleasure and misery for Adam. Any time he was allowed to spend with them or just watch them was bliss for Adam, his eyes never seeming to tire of the sight of Hallie, a beautiful young girl with curling black hair usually disarrayed, her deep violet eyes always sparkling with pleasure. Often he had wondered if she was actually flirting with him because she cared for him, or if she was merely practicing, as girls her age are wont to do. Then as she grew a little older he felt tortured to watch her flirt with boys her own age. Those times he feared she considered him simply an older brother, and he was miserable with the thought.

Medical school had offered him some respite, for it allowed him little time to worry over what would happen when Hallie actually did grow up. His obsession with Hallie allowed him to be a good student, for she was his sole distraction. He smiled now, thinking what

30

a coy little baggage she was. At first he had actually believed that her growing interest in medicine and his studies was merely for the knowledge. He knew now that it was only a portion. Her aptitude for medicine was like that of no one else he had yet encountered, but she had very subtly allowed Adam to know it was not solely his textbooks that interested her.

For a time her help with his studying had been a good excuse for them to be together. It had been Amanda who had pushed it farther. She had laughingly asked them one day why they were so afraid to spend time together without that pretense. After that Amanda had arranged to leave them alone often, until there was no question that Hallie loved Adam as much as he loved her. Those few years had been glorious for Adam, until he had finished his medical training and Hallie had turned sixteen. It seemed that within a matter of a few weeks his world had collapsed. Suddenly, when his life should have been just beginning, a series of events had changed its entire course.

Dr. Hathaway was an aging practitioner in Boston, looking among the newly trained doctors from Harvard Medical School to choose one to take into his practice. Adam had wanted the position badly, and when he was Dr. Hathaway's choice Adam's excitement had seemed boundless, his future glowing. He and Hallie had talked often of the day when he was a well-established doctor and she had finally reached her majority, that they would marry at last. All the world seemed open to them after the short space of two years. But when Adam had rushed to Hallie with his good news, she had been more than preoccupied.

It was such a vivid memory now. Adam had run wildly through Pemberton Square, leaping over the carriageway, ignoring the brick sidewalks to race across the manicured lawns. But when he reached Etta Riley's town house he had found Hallie sitting on the front steps, staring at the street and looking about as dejected as he had ever seen this lively, spirited girl. Still he had exploded with his news, hoping that it would brighten her mood. It had done just that, for Hallie's beautiful features had lifted as if from the depths to the heavens. He could hear again her exclamation of relief.

"Oh, Adam! Thank God! Then I can marry you!"

It had taken him aback somewhat, brought his pride to the surface, for he could not help but feel that she wanted him to marry her only for the support he could supply. How stupid he had been. After all they had shared, he had been ignorant enough and vain enough to think she wanted only his money. When Hallie had proceeded to explain her family's predicament and her grandmother's desire for her to marry old Michael Redmond, it had not soothed his dignity at all. Now Adam understood Hallie's feelings at the time; it was no wonder she was upset and her temper easily sparked. When Adam had heatedly refused to marry her right then, she had threatened to marry Mr. Redmond.

Adam laughed wryly, stopping for a moment to peer from the large window of his room at the dismal day. He had been a fool to think she was bluffing. Hallie did not make idle threats, no matter how her temper ruled her at the moment. By the time he had cooled off enough to apologize and offer the money she needed, the deed was done. Adam had no one to blame but himself. Amanda had tried to persuade him to marry Hallie immediately, but her pleas had only further incensed him. Then when he had heard of her marriage he had gone mad with the pain of losing her. How ironic that after all those years of fearing just that, it was his own stubbornness that had caused it.

In a fit of pure madness Adam had offered his services as an army doctor. It was not until he had received his orders that he heard the news of the senior Michael Redmond's death. By then it was too late. He reminded himself that it had not mattered; Hallie was not actually a widow even then. Still it had tormented him these past two years, feeling that they could have been married after all.

And so, Michael Redmond was Hallie's husband. How that thought infuriated Adam! He felt no friendship for the man, though he remembered well that it had existed before. Michael had been an adventure to Adam, who had always been practical, quiet—dull, if he were to be honest about the way he viewed himself. He admired

32

Michael in many ways. He knew him to be courageous, even fearless. He had seen his power, his intense will and strength, yet he had also been witness to his kindness to those very people he was to conquer. Michael was a man made for command of all situations and people. For the first time Adam did not admire that facet of the man, for now it would be Hallie and her life he ruled, and Adam feared or perhaps wanted to believe that Michael would not be a kind monarch. How, he asked himself, could he treat her well when in all of those months he had not even spoken of his marriage? In all the times he had spoken of this nameless girl he loved so deeply, Michael had not once even mentioned his marriage. Never had Michael felt the slightest qualm in going to the local brothels to satisfy himself, even when Adam had denied himself that comfort for the sake of the woman he had left behind. Michael had always acted totally unattached.

Adam fell with force onto the bed, staring at the carved ceiling. An evil grin spread his handsome mouth. What if he were to tell Hallie about her husband's escapades? Their marriage had not been consummated; perhaps he could persuade her to have it annulled. Yet only a moment's hope flickered. Adam knew Hallie too well. She had too much pride to take so much financially from Michael Redmond and then dissolve the union. His love for her rose above his need for revenge, and he realized that any knowledge of Michael's lack of affection and loyalty would only hurt her and cause her more problems.

So what was he to do? "Nothing," he said aloud to himself. That was the worst of it. He could do nothing honorable, at least nothing that would help Hallie.

Resigned for the moment to the situation, Adam set about forming a plan for his future. He realized that at all costs he must keep Hallie's friendship. If he could save that, then he still had a glimmer of hope, a continuation of his connection with her. If he must return to the time when she was a beautiful thing he could watch and enjoy but never touch, then so be it. Even then she had used their friendship, and what he needed now was to have her confidence. Perhaps, he reassured himself, if he could remain her friend, brother in a way, he could gain intimate knowledge of the relationship between Hallie and Michael Redmond. Then he would be the first to know when a rift developed in the marriage. It was unfair that the woman he loved to distraction and who loved him should be forced to remain with a man Adam thought had no respect for her.

In that moment Adam declared his own war on Michael Redmond. If determination were enough, then Adam Burgess would one day have Hallie for his wife.

CHAPTER SIX

Hallie slammed the lid to the trunk with force, venting her anger and frustration. After almost no sleep and a morning of packing her belongings to move to Redland to be with people she did not even know, her nerves were frazzled.

"I can't stand another minute of it!" she said aloud.

Mercy's moon-shaped face lifted from her task of emptying drawers. "You'd best calm yourself down, Miss Hallie. You aren't going to do any good that way," the old woman scolded. After a lifetime of caring for this family, she had no qualms about ordering anyone about, even Etta.

"I have to get out for a while, Mercy! I'm going to see Amanda!" she answered determinedly.

"And how do you think to have all of this packed by this afternoon if you go gallivanting around town?" Even after decades away from England, Mercy still retained her slight English accent.

Hallie's temper was up. "I don't care! Why should I have to do just as he orders without a question, especially when it is inconvenient for me?"

"Hmph! I'll tell you why? 'Cause Michael Redmond's your husband, that's why! It's for your own good; otherwise you'll go to your new home naked!"

Hallie could not help but laugh at that thought. She enjoyed the picture in her mind of regally entering the grand home of the Redmonds in the buff. Wouldn't that take them back a step! Still she needed some air, but sounding less like a spoiled brat now she said, "I promise I'll be back soon, Mercy. Have some lunch and a little nap and then we can finish when I come home." She kissed the wrinkled cheek carelessly, forestalling any further comment, and walked resolutely from the room.

Amanda had been hoping that Hallie might come by. After sending one of the servants for tea, Amanda fairly burst. "Both Michael and Adam were here this morning! I was afraid they would meet, and I wouldn't have known what to do!"

"They didn't meet, did they?"

"No, Adam left only minutes before Michael and Jason came out of the den. I'll tell you one thing: Your husband is a very attractive man."

Hallie laughed humorlessly. "I hadn't even noticed, as a matter of fact."

"Well, what do you think about the whole thing?" Amanda asked without hesitation. "I've been worrying about you since I heard."

Now Hallie paced, too nervous to sit still. "I don't think anything good, that's for sure!" she said emotionally. "I'm still in a dither, I suppose. I don't even know the man! There are so many things to adjust to."

"I've given that some thought since I heard the news. Amazing how naïve we were, isn't it?" She sighed and sat down heavily, tiring more easily as her pregnancy became more obvious. As much as she loved her brother, she could not help but feel he had caused his own problems. He had been so stubborn! And now he was paying a high price for that obstinance, but Amanda's deepest concern was for Hallie. Amanda knew her as well as she knew herself, and she could well imagine her friend's turmoil and fear. Amanda knew that she too had encouraged Hallie's marriage to Michael Redmond; she had known all of Hallie's problems and realized it was imperative for her to find some financial support for her family, even if Adam refused to recognize the severity of it all. It had seemed so logical then, when the possibility of Hallie's being pressed into service to pay her debts had been presented. Amanda could not bear the thought of Hallie being far away, their friendship separated by any number of miles' distance.

She unconsciously rested her hand on her abdomen as though the child there offered some comfort in this predicament. Amanda knew it was useless to dwell on what was past; they must now deal with the present.

"I just don't know what to do, Amanda!" Hallie blurted out. "How can I be a wife to a man I met yesterday, especially when you know how I feel about Adam? I love him so much! I have loved him for so long! And now I must make a life with Michael Redmond! My God, how will I do it?"

Amanda shook her head slowly, feeling every bit as forlorn as her friend. "There really isn't anything else you can do. Is it possible that he will give you some time to get to know him, do you think?"

Hallie laughed derisively. "I doubt it. From our short meeting yesterday I would say that Michael Redmond will have me and this marriage on his own terms. He does not seem like a man of patience." Hallie sat across from Amanda as their tea was served. When the serving girl left, Hallie asked,

"How is Adam? Is he taking this badly?"

"Yes, I'm afraid he is. I couldn't offer him much comfort. What could I say but what I've said to you? There is no going back. The worst of it is that you are suffering for his stubbornness."

"I know. I was awake all night going through the what ifs. What if Adam and I had just married two years ago? What if my grandmother hadn't deceived me? Even what if Michael Redmond had been killed in the war? Then I felt guilty for wondering about another man's death the way we had his father's. It just seems that everything got so complicated in so short a time. My mind is spinning. Sometimes I'm angry, at other times I feel nothing, but most of the time I'm just plain scared. What kind of a man marries someone he doesn't know without even bothering to meet her and then disappears for two years? Did Jason know about all of this?"

Amanda saw the torture in Hallie's thought, and her heart went out to her friend. "No, Michael didn't mention a word of it," she said quietly, knowing the fact would not ease her mind.

Again Hallie laughed derisively. "So he was that ashamed of me, was he?"

"No, Hallie, I'm sure it wasn't that! Jason has said that Michael was terribly preoccupied at the time. After all, his father was ill and dying."

"Even so, wouldn't he have told his best friend that he had been married? And then he left without a word, not even a note for the sake of simple courtesy! Obviously he never spoke of me in the past two years, for Adam was as shocked as I."

Amanda sighed wearily, looking more tired than usual. "I only know that I saw him today, spoke with him and he did not seem so horrible! He was kind and friendly to me, insisting that we use only our first names. In fact, I liked him. Jason assures me that Michael is a good man. Perhaps there is more to his story than you know."

Hallie saw the fatigue in her friend, realizing that she had totally forgotten about Amanda's condition. Pulling out a smile from deep within to hide her real feelings, Hallie said, "I'm sorry, Amanda. We've all worn you thin with our problems, haven't we? Do you feel as weary as you look?"

Amanda laughed lightly. "Do I look that bad? No, it isn't you or any of the rest, really. I find myself tiring more easily now. Some days I wonder how I will ever last three more months when I am so spent now."

At that instant the door to the den opened and Jason Curtis joined his wife and her friend, his bright red hair neatly framing a ruddy face. His smile for Hallie was warm, open, for he was fond of her and often thought of her as Amanda's sister. He sat on the arm of his wife's chair, placing her hand at his knee and then covering her hand with his own. The love they shared seemed to Hallie a warm glow that engulfed them. She knew well that her friend was comfortable in the knowledge that Jason adored her. It was obvious that their marriage was immensely satisfying to them both, and Hallie's thoughts tortured her, feeling she would have found the same with Adam but doubting that it would ever touch her with Michael.

"Amanda tells me you saw Michael this morning,

Jason." Hallie wished she could quell her curiosity about their meeting.

Jason chuckled lightly. "I can't believe Mandy hasn't told you every word of our conversation already."

Amanda's eyebrows rose in effrontery. "I haven't said one word about it."

Jason laughed, his face showing every ounce of his delight in his wife. "Then I must have come in too soon." He turned back to Hallie, and she saw the sympathy in his eyes. "To be honest, Michael didn't say a great deal. He paced the floor most of the time. He admitted that he is worried about beginning a marriage as two strangers. It won't be easy for either of you, Hallie, but I have known Michael all of my life, and I can assure you I've never met a better man. Contrary to Mandy's fears, you are not in need of a protector."

Hallie's smile was filled with her disbelief of his words. She was uncomfortable with this subject and sought a change. "Do you have plans for the Redmonds' party tonight?"

"You mean your party, don't you?" Amanda said. "Yes, I am planning on it, though I'll have to rest first. Jason is such a fussbudget sometimes, you know. I would never miss tonight!" she said, a spark of her anticipation shining through her fatigue for a moment.

"Then I will leave you to nap. Besides, Mercy will have my skin if I don't finish my packing. His lord and master Redmond has commanded that I be prepared to take up my place in his household by tonight," Hallie said facetiously, but a shudder of fear was evident to Amanda's knowledgeable eye.

"It will all work out, Hallie. You know that things usually do," she said, feebly attempting to console Hallie as she and Jason walked her to the door.

Jason patted Hallie's shoulder in a brotherly fashion, reiterating his wife's words. "It will, Hallie, and think about it this way: At least you two don't have to worry about your husbands despising one another."

Hallie's smile was unconvincing as she entered her coach and waved to Amanda and Jason from the carriage window.

CHAPTER SEVEN

The Curtis house was a Victorian-style suburban home with many gables and three verandas. It was not only beautifully elegant but it also sat in the center of well-tended grounds. It was ideally located, for though it was within minutes of the city it was set farther out of town than many residences. Hallie was grateful for that fact now as she settled back in her carriage. She relished the time out, away from the tension that seemed to fill everyone she knew, not the least of whom was herself. She inhaled deeply, willing herself to relax and think of nothing but the view beyond the window.

Hallie loved Boston, as did most Bostonians, a populace who prided themselves on their staid, conservative, aristocratic ancestors. Their pride in themselves was reflected in the city itself, for it was one of the cleanest cities in the world. Hallie passed bright, red brick houses, or a few of white stone, all sparkling with the care they received, nestling among grounds tended meticulously. Even the brass knobs and plates on the doors glistened with the sheen of polish. Again Hallie thought that Boston was a most beautiful place to live. The houses that bordered Amanda's were impressive. But even as they moved on to the business district and State Street, the buildings remained opulent. The public buildings and shops were handsome, the brick-paved streets nearly spotless, with tall gaslights of iron standing high enough for their glow to stretch far and wide. Hallie knew little of architecture, but even she was familiar with the name Charles Bulfinch, for he had been the most popular architect. Mr. Bulfinch had made Boston what it was, some people claimed, a town of beautiful red brick structures of the late Georgian style, all of which were shaded by huge trees and dotted with splendorous parks and squares, their peacefulness beckoning to all.

But still Boston was a thriving utilitarian city, with business obviously prospering. Hallie had heard many people praise even the waterfront, for as their ships docked, Boston had appeared as a sleepy English village overlooking a beautiful harbor dotted with small islands. Of course, Hallie realized there were seedier sides of the city, those sections barely whispered about among the women, and others that housed the poor Irish immigrants lucky just to feed their families from the salary paid for tedious factory work. Since the potato famine of 1845 the Irish population of Boston had risen tremendously, far faster than the employment opportunities for them. They were the most disdained citizens of Boston and the poorest. But Hallie felt more compassion. After all, her grandfather had been Irish, and he had shown great initiative and founded the fortune her father had all but destroyed. Still she preferred to think of her city in its most flattering terms, as the Athens of America or even as the metropolis of New England. Even though the codes of this society were often constraining, Hallie was a Bostonian to the core.

Her spirits descended again as she approached her home. She would be leaving this dignified row of dwellings soon, and she was not pleased by the prospect. If the facts were known, she was frightened half out of her wits by the imaginings of what might lay ahead of her as the wife of Michael Redmond.

The packing was complete, and now Hallie sat to rest for a few moments before joining her grandmother and Danny for tea. Hallie had requested that Mercy join them today; it seemed appropriate, since they would

42

no longer be living in the house. Hallie felt the need to mark her leavetaking somehow.

She sat quietly in a large pink chintz chair in her room, her slender hands folded in her lap, and for all the world she looked like a demure young woman, calm and dignified. What she felt was very different. It was as though rational thought or even anger had fled and all that remained was a fear. Suddenly she wanted to run and hide like a small child again. She wanted to refuse to perform this role, to deny it with vehemence. Only instinct was functioning now, and that pushed very hard for her to flee. She thought that she had not grown up enough for this yet, but she knew she was lying to herself.

What would he expect of her? Her heart raced with terror, her head felt light, her ears were ringing. She could not go through with it, she just could not help being a coward! Then the door to her room opened, again without a knock to announce himself, and Danny came to sit on her bed, his legs tucked beneath him. This entrance was far different from that of the previous day, and Hallie saw his fear plainly. Her own was somehow diminished in view of her brother's, for she was once again the older sister, responsible for the small boy.

Hallie's smile was gentle and kind. "It will be all right, Danny," she reassured him even before he had spoken his fears.

"How do you know?" he asked accusingly.

"Because I promise to do my best to make it all right."

"But we won't have Adam," he said petulantly.

Hallie fought the trembling in her lip. "No, we won't," she said as firmly as she could. "But we will have a new house and a lot of things we've never had before."

"I like this house! I don't want anything else."

"No, I don't suppose you do right now, but later on, when you get used to the changes, you might. Do you want to help me?" The small boy shrugged reluctantly. Hallie took it for an affirmative answer. "Well, what I really need from you for the next few weeks is a big smile and maybe a little hug every now and then and for you to try your very best to be a good boy. It is important to me that you be happy, and I promise I will do everything to help that be."

"Will we ever see Adam again?"

"I'm sure we will. Why, he loves you almost as much as I do. Now, come on. Grandma will be waiting for us downstairs."

She wanted to offer her hand to him, but she knew how offended he was at any hint that he was not a big, grown-up boy now, so she merely paused at the door and waited for him to leave the room with her. In that second she said a silent prayer that she would be able to keep her promise to him.

Teatime was unusually quiet after Hallie had informed Mercy and Danny that they would follow her to Redland the next day. Even Etta was not her cheery self as she watched her granddaughter closely. She saw through Hallie's pretended strength and hoped fervently she had done the right thing.

Their time was cut short by the arrival of the wagon that was to pick up the trunks. After the men had collected all of her belongings, one of them brought in a large box for Hallie, her first gift from her husband. Hallie was unable to share Etta's excitement. For Hallie it simply meant that the time of reckoning was upon her. She was truly about to become the wife of Michael Redmond.

CHAPTER EIGHT

Hallie heard the front door being opened to admit Michael Redmond. She sighed deeply, hoping she could summon some strength from the depths of her soul. She forced herself to leave her room and descend the stairs to greet her husband.

She paused at the top, much as she had the previous day, hidden in the shadows, to study him. Her first thought was that Amanda was right, he was a terribly attractive man. He was impeccably dressed in a formal tail suit of black over a silver brocade vest that fit tightly around his narrow waist. The suit coat fit perfectly across broad shoulders, the sleeves seeming to bulge slightly with the power in his arms. His shirt was white silk, lightly ruffled down the front, the collar points reaching toward his firm jawline. His cravat was a pale gray, tied in a half knot at his throat. Michael's features were accentuated by the bright candlelight in the entrance hall where he stood, tall and arrogant. His thick brown hair waved back from his face, slightly long around his ears and the back of his neck. His nose was slightly long and thin above full, sensuous lips. There was a deep cleft in his chin that Hallie had not noticed before; it made him even more handsome. He raised his eyes to the top of the stairs as though impatient, but Hallie knew he could not see her. She was struck by the piercing blue-gray of his eyes beneath thick lashes and the sharp planes of his cheekbones. When he lowered his glance to peer at the watch he pulled from his vest pocket, Hallie again breathed deeply and moved from the shadows.

She moved so gracefully that Michael did not hear her until she was nearly to him. A half smile of approval tilted one corner of his mouth. The gown he had chosen for her was beautiful, doing justice to her exquisite loveliness. It was mauve satin, the light shade deepening the intensity of her wide violet eyes. The gown fell gently off creamy white shoulders; its neckline had only a tiny ruffle of ivory lace, which extended over the top of her arms, then a second layer of ruffles formed the sleeve. Only a hint of soft skin showed between the elbow-length sleeves and her long lace mitts. A V-shaped inset of ivory lace descended the bodice; a deep violet ribbon encircled her tiny waist. The skirt billowed into three tiers of shining satin and was held wide by several lacy petticoats that quietly rustled as she moved. She was a sight to behold as Michael perused her, amazed that he had been lucky enough to falter into marriage with one so fair. His eyes rested on the alabaster of her throat and then lifted to her delicate, exquisite face, framed with glowing black hair. Her thick curls were caught above each ear and bounced past her shoulders. At both temples a few wisps had already escaped the confines of the style to feather her face softly in alluring disarray.

Michael wondered if these few wild fluffs refusing to be contained might be an indication of her disposition as well, for beneath the sooty black lashes was a challenging sparkle in dark violet eyes that quite intrigued him. Her nose was small; her lips curved slightly upward, even without a smile. She is a beauty, he told himself silently, there would be no man left without envy at his prize. No wonder Adam Burgess was devastated by his loss.

Michael saw the very becoming blush to Hallie's cheeks and wondered if it was caused by excitement or fear. He saw her thin shoulders straighten just before she spoke, her voice musical and pleasant.

46

"Is there something wrong with my appearance?"

A short laugh gave further evidence to his hand-someness. "No, I can find nothing to fault. You're very beautiful," he said matter-of-factly. "I see now why your Dr. Burgess pined away for all of those months."

The remark struck a very sore, extremely vulnerable spot in Hallie and Michael saw the anger and was not pleased by this evidence of his wife's affection for Adam. Hallie's tone was haughty. "In the interest of peace between us, it is best if neither of us mentions Adam."

One thick brow rose swiftly. "So you're setting boundaries already."

"In this I most certainly am."

"You will find, madam, that I am not a very tractable man. In the interest of peace I suggest that you not order what I am to do or not to do." His voice brooked no opposition, but Hallie was no less strong-willed and free-spirited than he, and her temper flared where Michael's was kept under cold control.

"I can see that there will be no peace between us."

A wicked smile curved his lips. "That will be more interesting."

At that moment Michael saw hatred in Hallie's face, and his instincts told him she was a formidable adversary. He laughed loudly at the thought, more pleased by her than he had expected to be. She had roused his interest, for he relished a challenge. Hallie was certain he laughed at her, and neither her temper nor her fear was calmed at all. Suddenly her emotions overpowered her rational thoughts and she turned to go back up the stairs.

"It's obvious this will never work. Either seek your freedom and I will repay what money I have spent, or be satisfied with an absentee wife."

One massive hand shot out like lightning to hold her wrist as her hand rested on the balustrade. But his voice was amused and his face mocking. "Running away? I had not taken you for a coward." He saw her spine straighten at his insult, pleasing him once more.

"And what are you? Our wedding was over two years ago, yet you chose to run away to some foolish war. Is that not cowardice?" she retorted.

Michael's handsomeness revealed nothing of the blow

47

she had struck. "I see. You would take my money and use my name while it suited you, but when the debt comes due you shirk your responsibilities. Are you a true example of the Wyatt family, or are there some with pride and enough honor to see through the bargains they make?"

Hallie's free hand bolted to slap his face, but Michael caught her other wrist. His voice was scathing, "Are you a child, or a woman who keeps her word?"

"Do you want a woman who hates you?"

His half grin was devilish. "I want you."

Silence reigned as Hallie stared vehemently at her husband. She knew she had no choice.

CHAPTER NINE

The large carriage moved swiftly through the icy night. The crisp sound of the horses' hooves was intensified by the chill, or perhaps they were loud because pure silence filled the interior. The air was so cold that Hallie's breath formed a light cloud in front of her. She found the cold more exhilarating than unpleasant, for it served to clear her anger-filled mind, to help her mind reign over her emotions.

When Hallie at last dared to break the tension-filled stillness, her voice was strong. "I would like to know what is expected of me before we reach your home," she said bluntly. Though it was dark in the carriage, Hallie knew Michael's face turned toward her.

His tone was courteous, but to Hallie it seemed he instructed her as he would a servant. "My home is now yours. You are mistress there. I expect you to perform all duties. To begin, you will be hostess of this party."

Still feeling that she had not received the answer she sought, Hallie persisted. "And what of being a wife?" A longer pause followed than she expected, unnerving her.

"Do you think I mean to bring you to my house as a glorified housekeeper and leave it at that?"

"I don't know what you mean to do. That is why I ask."

He chuckled softly. "Then let me explain it clearly. We are man and wife, you and I. I have every intention of complying with all of the allotted pleasures of that state, since I'm quite sure I will have to contend with all of the distasteful aspects. I expect you to be my wife in every room of our house, *especially* in the bedroom. I plan to enjoy a woman's touch not only in the arrangement of the house but also in all else. You, my lovely little lady, are expected to see to all of my needs, and I am determined to plant in you many Redmond heirs until our house nearly bursts at the seams with boisterous babes. Is that sufficiently clear?"

Hallie swallowed hard, hoping he had not heard, but knowing he must. "It's clear enough." Her voice was no longer strong. "I had not thought you to be a man wanting a wife and large family. I had rather expected you to place me as mistress of your home alone."

"And it disturbs you not to be placed simply as mistress?"

Hallie could not answer. Her throat was closed with fear, and suddenly she was very, very cold. How could she have been so naïve? she asked herself, yet still she could barely believe he asked this of her—no, demanded this of her. For one moment she thought of throwing herself from the carriage to escape the situation. As her silence stretched on, Michael's thoughts wandered, and his suspicions took root and began to sprout.

"Is it that you thought to run the household and keep a solitary bed at night? Perhaps you have made plans with Adam Burgess to fulfill the other parts of your life." His voice was no longer courteous or even instructive.

Still Hallie could not summon the courage to speak.

"I will tell you this, Hallie, and listen well, for I do not make idle threats. I will not tolerate infidelity. Your loyalty lies with me now, regardless of where your heart belongs. You have accepted my name and my financial support, and you owe me at least honesty."

Anger cleared her throat. "And what of you?" she

50

shot back. "Are you vowing loyalty as well?"

"It is not I who has made a spectacle of himself with someone else."

"Are you saying you have never been involved with a woman before?" she said sarcastically.

"I am saying that Adam Burgess is out of your life! I am your husband, and you will be faithful, or you will rue the day you stray. If you give me cause to suspect you I will go to very unpleasant lengths to ensure that the only children you bear are mine. I will not be father to Burgess's bastards. Is that clear?"

"You're making everything very clear tonight! It would seem I don't need to give you cause to suspect Adam and me."

"Take the warning, Hallie, and don't push my temper too far," he said tightly.

"Perhaps you should also be wary of the distance you press me."

Now Michael laughed aloud, his anger abated somewhat by this tiny waif's attempt to threaten him. "We shall see about that!" he said and laughed again.

Now Hallie held her breath and with it her temper. She would not stoop to his level, she told herself. The remainder of the journey to Redland was silent.

Hallie wished fervently that her destination was not so far away. She knew that Redland was fairly near Boston, yet still it seemed that this country house was much, much too long a distance for her immediate comfort. When at last they entered the grounds, she breathed a silent sigh of relief, but it was short-lived as she remembered she was in fact home and not just visiting for a few unpleasant hours. Hallie saw the huge mansion loom in the distance. It glowed with a warm, welcoming light. At the very top, in what appeared to be a cupola, one dim light shone. When the carriage pulled to a stop before the house, she saw that flicker and die into darkness. Hallie felt certain that their approach had been observed and that their arrival was now being announced to the remainder of the Redmond family.

CHAPTER TEN

Redland was one of the most beautiful country estates outside Boston. Hundreds of lanterns hung on strings draped between the branches of huge oak trees lining the drive that approached the grounds. It was an expansive colonial mansion standing three stories high with crisply whitewashed brick and a very steep roof. A wide veranda reached far from the front of the house, an ornately carved railing bordering it. Though it was late autumn, some huge vines still clung to the rail and the massive columns that supported a large balcony at the second level. Winter plants sat in large white vases at scattered points around the veranda, beyond which stood huge double doors, beautifully carved. There were six bay windows across the front of the house on the two levels, the third coming in the middle of the sloped roof, its windows reaching just beyond the slant between the eight chimneys visible there. The opulence was unquestionable, and Hallie was awestruck. She had never seen anything so grand, and suddenly her fear mounted. How could she possibly run a household of this size?

When she descended from the carriage, her violet eyes glowed wide in the light, her fear and doubts showing clearly. Michael saw it and felt a soft kindness for her in this predicament, chastising himself for his callous treatment of her and for his lack of consideration. After all, he reminded himself, she was very young, and he had been the cause of an onslaught of shocks and surprises for her in the past two days. He took her arm gently, moving with her up the ten steps to the veranda, but before he opened the doors, he turned her to face him. His smile was unlike any Hallie had seen from him before. His face was relaxed and kind. He is very handsome, she thought without volition.

His tone was soft. "There's nothing to be afraid of, sweet. I promise you I am not taking you into a den of lions. Jason Curtis told me you are very close to his wife, so I asked them to come early. They'll be here before too long, so you will have at least Amanda for moral support."

She had not expected this from him, had assumed that he had not given her a second thought after yesterday. Yet he had realized a bit of how she would feel and sought to provide what help he could. Her eyes were wide with wonder, and to Michael she was suddenly very desirable in her innocence.

"That was very thoughtful of you," she said almost in a whisper, for her eyes were held by the piercing blue-gray of his and she, too, was caught in the spell.

Michael's head lowered and his lips caressed hers softly. Hallie did not even consider pulling away from the kiss, as she easily might have. Instead it was so pleasurable, so unexpected, that she was swept into the pure delight of her senses and simply relished it, feeling even her tension ease slightly.

When the kiss ended, Michael raised his head only a scant few inches from her face. His smile was warmer now, more that of a man for a beautiful woman than before. "My pleasure," he said and opened the doors for Hallie to enter her new home.

With the sound of their entrance Farley appeared, a big, burly man with a red face and a large, bulbous nose. A graying thatch of hair fell to the side of his head, and bushy brows of the same color arched over hazel eyes that Hallie thought studied her closely while seeming not to. "We expected you sooner, lad," he said. His voice was gruff, but his affection for Michael was evident in his smile. "So this is the mistress, is it?" He turned to Hallie, whose face was still flushed from the cold and the kiss. She smiled at the man, thinking he had a kindness about him.

Michael's voice sounded, "Hallie, this is Farley. He is my friend and my right hand. Farley, this is my wife, Hallie."

A curt nod of his large head preceded, "Happy to know you, ma'am."

Before Farley could speak further, Michael said, "Where is everyone, Farley?"

It was a different voice that answered, a high, lilting tone from the top of the massive staircase. Half of the steps went up directly in front of the huge doors, then a landing changed the direction to exactly the opposite, veering sharply to the left. It was at that point Lydia Redmond Kent stood regally studying the scene below. She descended the remaining stairs, smiling sweetly at Hallie, but before the introduction was made Lydia moved away from them, again to a hallway beside the staircase. "Everyone is preparing for this party, dear Michael. You will have to excuse me for just a moment before we formalize this. I have one detail I must tend to first." She moved swiftly from them, and Michael stepped behind Hallie to remove the heavy cloak she wore.

As he handed it to Farley the two men spoke briefly, allowing Hallie the opportunity to gaze around her. The entrance hall was large. A claw-foot table stood in the center beneath an ornate crystal chandelier. To one side was a closed door beside which was a carved, walnut-framed mirror over a beautiful sideboard table with brass knobs at the drawers. On the opposite side of the entrance hall was a large double entrance beyond which she guessed was the drawing room, though it was difficult to see into. Beside the staircase, below a massive, well-carved balustrade was a small bench; beyond that stretched a long hallway. Hallie felt dwarfed as she raised her eyes to the top of the stairway, for it seemed to be high enough overhead to nestle among the clouds. The floor of the entrance hall was well polished; in fact, Hallie was certain she could not find a speck of dust if she searched for days. Apparently this house was already in very competent hands.

Lydia's return sent Farley off to check something, and Hallie wondered if it was only her imagination that he did her bidding resentfully. "I apologize for this, but I really was needed. I must say, I will not be the slightest little bit upset to hand over this household to you!" Lydia said, laughing gaily, her lovely features alight with pleasure. Michael's introduction was a simple formality that Lydia chose to ignore as she chattered on to Hallie. "I suppose I am exaggerating. I really could not be considered mistress even now. Michael returned to a very ill-kept house, let all of the people we had working here go and hired more ambitious servants. Really, except for the party, everything is his doing. I'm glad you will have to meet his standards and not I!" She laughed again, a pleasing sound. "I'm sure you would like to freshen up a bit after that carriage ride. There really isn't the time to show you the house now; we'll save it for tomorrow, when all of the furniture is back in place. I'll take you to my room. Yours is not quite ready yet."

"That would be nice," was all Hallie managed to say as Lydia ushered her up the stairs.

Lydia's room was large and decorated a bit too garishly for Hallie's taste, in cherry red. Hallie sat at the dressing table but was more interested in watching Lydia primp before a dressing glass. Lydia had Michael's same auburn hair, wavy and thick, and her eyes were the identical color but lacked the piercing quality. She was statuesque, her voluptuous breasts pressed high above the low décolletage of her shining red gown. Two dark moles spotted the side of Lydia's face, lending her an exotic look that Michael lacked but that enhanced her appearance greatly. Hallie was enthralled as she watched the woman. Lydia turned to the side, pulling the bodice of her gown a touch lower and then pushed both of her breasts higher above it so that even more of the pale flesh was visible.

Hallie was shocked by the procedure, wondering if many women sought to display themselves to this extent for the sake of men. In her short lifetime she had flirted mainly with Adam, and always it had only been a game. She felt her cheeks flush and averted her eyes to her own hair, trying unsuccessfully to catch the loose wisps at her temples back into the confines of the style. Her glance dropped to her own chest in an unguarded moment, thinking that in any event she did not have the right proportions for that kind of display.

Lydia saw the direction of her eyes and guessed at her thoughts. She laughed kindly and said, "Don't worry, Hallie. Michael is not that particular about the size of his women. I'm sure you have enough for him, although his last lady love was certainly well endowed."

Hallie's blush deepened to crimson. She was too embarrassed to ask what the woman meant or how she knew such a thing about her own brother but doubted that she wanted to hear her explanation, no matter what it was.

Lydia was unperturbed by Hallie's silence and said, "You really are an innocent, aren't you?" Then she laughed again, enjoying herself. "Somehow I never expected you to be like this. Michael's taste must have changed in the past two years." It was not said maliciously and led Hallie to wonder at just how much this family knew of the reason behind her marriage to Michael. She doubted that they knew anything at all. She would have to ask him what she was to tell his family.

Again Lydia spoke without a thought to the fact that Hallie had said nothing. "I suppose he is like all men. They play with one sort of woman but marry the other. Isn't it just like them to think philandering is acceptable for them but never for their wives."

"Yes, I suppose," Hallie finally answered, albeit halfheartedly, her thoughts more filled with her sister-in-law's previous statements about her husband's past.

"Well, we had best be going downstairs. I hear the music already. Our guests must have begun to arrive."

Before they reached the door, however, a knock sounded and a maid opened it to admit Amanda. Hallie smiled broadly, relieved to see her friend, particularly at this moment. When the introductions had been made, Lydia left them alone, much to Hallie's pleasure, for she wanted desperately to talk to Amanda about Lydia's remarks.

"Has Jason ever told you that Michael was a philanderer? I mean, I knew he had many women admirers, but is he a horrible womanizer?"

Amanda smiled, looking rested and very beautiful. "Jason has never spoken of it, but then he never speaks of his own reputation before our marriage. I wouldn't worry about it. The only thing that matters is what he does now, Hallie."

"But after listening to Lydia I'm beginning to wonder what I will face tonight after this party."

Amanda laughed, "I doubt if it will be anything different from what we all face. I assure you it is not at all what old spinsters would have you believe. Perhaps Michael will wait awhile until you get to know one another."

"I'm sure he won't, Amanda. I've never asked this before, because it's so terribly personal, and if you don't want to answer me just say so."

Amanda laughed, anticipating the question before it was asked. "I don't mind. Making love is a very pleasant pastime. Now, does that ease your mind?"

"Is it the truth, or are you just saying it to calm me?"

"Of course I'm not just saying it! How could there ever be so many people in the world if it was horrible?"

"Yes, but you love Jason. I wasn't so worried at the thought of Adam being my husband."

A shy smile curled Amanda's lips. "I believe I would enjoy it even if I didn't love Jason."

Now Hallie laughed, not really relieved but eased slightly all the same. "I certainly hope I'll feel the same way."

Amanda walked to the dressing glass to check her appearance. Hallie could not contain a smile at the thought of the difference between the two women who had stood in that same spot in the past few moments. Amanda was small, her pregnancy well concealed in a high-waisted burgundy velvet gown. She bore a great resemblance to Adam, though her features were more delicate. Her hair was a mass of unruly blond curls that she caught at the sides in combs and let fall past her shoulders in a splendorous golden mass. Her eyes were large brown pools set above high cheekbones and a thin, small nose. Pregnancy had increased Amanda's bustline, but she was well concealed, the neckline of her gown falling off her shoulders but not even remotely as revealing as Lydia's.

When she had finished, the two friends left the bedroom. Hallie felt more ready to face the evening and the announcement that she was the wife of Michael Redmond until Amanda stopped her abruptly on the landing dividing the staircase. She turned to Hallie, her eyes wide.

"I nearly forgot why I came looking for you! I had to warn you: Adam is coming here tonight, and he is not in a very polite state of mind."

CHAPTER ELEVEN

The lower level of the house was already brimming with
guests. Hallie knew only a few people personally, though
she recognized many of the others. The house was filled
with politicians and statesmen, and the wealthy and
powerful of Boston. Though Hallie had never lacked
self-confidence, she was not at ease in this gathering.
Her family had been wealthy, but it was money earned,
fought for at times, while these were people born into
enormous affluence, many choosing their life's work in
idleness. Hallie's first impression as she gazed around
her was that the people present were a snobbish group.

As Amanda stood beside her she must have guessed
Hallie's thoughts, for she whispered in her ear, "They
are not all insufferable. I have found a few truly nice
people, and I ignore the others."

Hallie smiled and asked, "Yes, but how do you wade
through these upturned noses to find those few?"

Amanda laughed. "More than likely they will find
you." At that moment Jason seized his wife, hurrying
her off for some reason and stranding Hallie.

Suddenly from behind she heard an unpleasant male
voice. Hallie straightened and drew away, judging this
person to be unsavory before she turned to view him.
Her first sight of him only confirmed that opinion. He

was tall, as tall as Michael, Hallie judged, but his arms and legs were so long that he reminded her of a spider. He was attractive, if one liked a rather effeminate look. The eyes that stared at her beneath puffy lids were pale green. His hair was white-blond and arranged very precisely, curling about his face and into the sideburns that grew down to his jawline in long whiskers at both sides of his face. Hallie stared at him unabashedly. His suit was of scarlet velvet, his tight trousers conforming to the newest style; his shirt was of pink silk, his vest black. The black cravat around his long, birdlike neck was tied so intricately that it was obvious he had followed the instructions in the old pamphlet *The Art of Tying a Cravat in Sixteen Lessons,* the bible to all dandies. Above the wide neckcloth stood collar points high enough to become lost in his albino whiskers. He reached into his vest pocket with a slender hand to pull forth a lace handkerchief, which he touched to his nose gently, as if sniffing some favorite scent from it. His mouth spread in a leering grin showing large teeth. Surely this could not be one of the nice people who had found her, Hallie thought, recalling Amanda's words.

Again the man spoke, his voice high, his eyes lowering to the neckline of her gown as though he addressed her chest. "You are a delectable little thing!" he said. "Why have I never seen you before?"

Hallie flipped open the lace fan she carried as an ornament, her indignation apparent. She held the wide fan over the section the man's eyes rested on before she answered him, her tone unfriendly. "This is my first party at Redland. If you will excuse me, I must find my husband."

The slender hand reached to her arm, detaining Hallie's flight. "You can't leave me before I know your name."

Hallie's eyes lowered to the hand that held her captive, her repulsion evident. "If you value your hand and the use of it I suggest you remove it."

The fop laughed loudly. "I love a woman with fire," he said, but he replaced his arm at his side. "I will plague you all evening unless I learn what to call you."

"My name is Hallie Wyatt...Redmond. And I hope we never meet again."

A more boisterous laugh rang from him, leaving Hallie to wonder at what amused him so. "That, my pretty, is virtually impossible!"

Hallie turned and left, feeling no need to stay and be courteous to this disgusting spectacle of a man. As she moved through the crowd in search of Amanda she could hear the man's laughter as he watched her retreat. She could not find Amanda, and since she did not know her way around this house she decided to remain near the stairway, feeling certain that eventually her friend would pass.

Instead it was Michael Redmond who spotted her. He moved quickly through his guests, his eyes never leaving sight of her, as though he expected her to run from him. "I've been looking all over for you. Where have you been?" he asked her, not impatiently.

"I have been accosted by some simpering fop!"

Michael smiled, amused. "I don't doubt that. You are very beautiful, and I know many a man here tonight who would want you. Lydia tells me we must go in to dance the first waltz so our guests will all see who you are. You can dance, can't you?" he teased her.

Hallie was hardly in the mood for humor. "Of course I can dance! Do you suppose I've been locked away in a convent waiting for you?"

"Perhaps that is where you should have been," he answered her sarcasm with his own. He offered his arm. "Then let's get on with it."

The ballroom was farther down the hallway beside the stairs. With the number of people in the room the only thing Hallie could determine was that it was huge. Four crystal chandeliers were needed to light it. The floor was highly polished. Michael led Hallie to the center, turning her into his arms.

The music began, soft, lilting, easily carrying them along with it. Michael danced as gracefully as Hallie had heard from many girls who had regaled her with his accomplishments. She wondered how many of those girls, her classmates at Chauncey Hall School, looked on now and how many would die for her place here. It was an odd comfort. Michael's powerful arms tightened around her. She lifted her head so that she viewed his face, trying to read the thoughts behind it.

Michael smiled down at her kindly, though not with any real feeling. He found Hallie attractive—desirable, in fact—but he was not a man to be consumed with love. He was not a man like his father, he told himself. He considered it his good fortune that Hallie was so interesting, amusing, and arousing. It would be very painless to make love to her, to father her children and provide the family for which he had decided it was time. He felt confident that she would prove an adequate mother and wife, and that was all he had ever expected. Long ago Michael had decided to separate the women in his life. There were those to ease his needs, but those he would not bring home to Redland nor allow to bear his children. Then there was the wife, and she, he had deemed, would be different, staid, probably prudish and ultimately very dull. Hallie was none of those things, but still she would fit into his plans. He told himself there was no threat of love or of any emotion save perhaps kindness and in time the loyalty of partnership and family interests. He knew himself well enough to be certain he would never fall into the trap his father had. Yet at the moment he had no thought of visiting his mistress. He assured himself it was the novelty of Hallie and marriage that urged his fidelity; it would only be temporary. It was all the better, he thought now as he held her in his arms, the music lifting them with it, for now he would make love to her until he was satiated and bored with her. Perhaps by the time he returned to Maeve, Hallie would be pregnant and his future well on its way. This thought soothed his image of himself as a free spirit, wild and untamed still. He saw himself fulfilling his desires and then moving on to the next challenge. Hallie would be a convenience, someone to return to when he wanted but never to hinder him in any way. His smile turned more introspective as he thought that perhaps marriage was not such a binding situation as he had feared. His life would not be changed, he felt sure.

As the music stopped, the crowd surrounding the dance floor clapped, for from a distance it appeared only that two very attractive people had just had their first waltz as a married couple; it seemed very romantic.

Michael bowed formally, his voice soft enough for

only Hallie to hear. "That was well done. I hope you prove as accomplished in other things."

Hallie's face changed almost imperceptibly from ease to fear and anger. She took the arm he proffered and let him lead her. As they reached the edge of the floor the crowd parted. Standing a few feet in front of them was Adam Burgess.

CHAPTER TWELVE

Michael stopped abruptly, staring into the face of the man who had saved his life. Adam Burgess stared at Hallie, oblivious to the heated look he was receiving from her husband. Hallie felt the tension between the two, herself suddenly on edge. She smiled fearfully at Adam, hoping he would not create a scene. "Hello, Adam," she said quietly.

"I've come for this dance," he said to her, then shifting his glance to Michael, he added sarcastically, "That is, if your husband can bear to free you."

Hallie's eyes widened at his remark, fearing it would be enough to set off Michael's temper. She breathed a deep sigh of relief when Amanda appeared, Jason fast on her heels. Her friend smiled sweetly at Michael and said, "I hope you don't think me too brazen, but I have heard of your ability as a dancer for so long I just must try you for myself, if you will, Michael."

Michael realized the tactic was diversionary but he did not want a spectacle. He saw that Adam was trying to provoke a confrontation, and Michael preferred to choose the time and place. After a long silence in which Amanda was afraid her plea would be ignored, he turned to her, his smile brilliant, though the muscle twitched in his cheek. "It would be my pleasure, Amanda, though

I assure you my dancing has been overrated." He turned to Amanda as though neither Hallie nor Adam were standing there and led her back to the dance floor.

Now Adam's smile was warm, loving as he took Hallie's arm. "I'm sorry to put you in the middle, pet," he said softly, "but I had to see you tonight." Adam held Hallie close, closer even than Michael had. Adam was feeling reckless this evening. What more could he lose?

"How are you?" Hallie asked, concern sounding in her voice.

"I'm miserable. How are you?"

"I don't know really. I suppose I'm too confused to feel anything except fear."

Adam's features were pained. "My God, I can't stand it! I can't let you go through with this!"

"It isn't your choice, Adam. There is nothing to be done. He is my husband."

"I could call him out."

"A duel?" She nearly shrieked, her eyes wide. "No, Adam! You mustn't! You would be killed! He has much more skill with a gun. Isn't it enough that we wished one man dead when we thought it was his father I had married? Look what happened to punish us for that!"

"Then what will you do?"

"I will be his wife," she said quietly.

Adam's teeth clenched in part jealous fury, part pain. "In every way?"

"It would seem so. He has already told me he wants a large family." It seemed so cold to be saying these things to the man she had thought to marry only the day before.

"Christ, Hallie! How can you say that?" he said, as though repulsed by her.

It hurt Hallie, and in defense she sounded angry. "What else can I do? I married him when you would not help me; my family used his money for over two years. Now he expects me to be the wife he has supported all of this time, and I must do it! You act as if I'm some—" Her voice broke.

Now he was contrite, seeing he had offended her. "I only meant that I know you love me. I know how hard this whole situation is, and I know I'm to blame! Leave with me now! Please, let's just walk out! I will do anything to have you, I'll pay back his damn money, I'll give him anything he wants, but please let's leave and forget this whole sordid thing!"

"Oh, Adam, don't!" she said miserably. "He won't agree to that. I tried to end it tonight before I came here, he made me so mad. But he is determined to hold me to this marriage, to this debt. We can do nothing! Except possibly be friends."

"You can't leave it at that any more than I can!"

"It has to be, Adam. We have to deal with what has happened. It can't be changed."

"I should have let the bastard die!" he said passionately.

"You could never have done that, even if you had known then. I know you better than that. How did you meet Michael?" She was purposely changing the subject, for Hallie could not bear the temptation to do as Adam begged.

He shrugged wearily. "I was with the army in New Mexico. He was wounded at Chapultepec and sent back to us because the bullet was lodged in his chest." He laughed mirthlessly. "After he recovered, we became friends. I actually liked the bastard! In fact, we came home together. He knew I was in love with someone, we talked about it often enough, but I never said who for fear of offending him. Isn't that ironic?"

"And he never said he was married, even though you were friends and spoke of a woman back home?"

"Not once. I have searched my memory for even one hint he might have given. And I chattered like a fool." Adam's bitterness was evident.

This news, though Hallie had suspected as much, was disquieting all the same. She wondered why that should bother her. If he was unfaithful, did that not leave her the option as well?

"You're thinking about him, aren't you?" Adam accused, his voice sounding hurt.

"I'm sorry! I was just wondering what was in store for me from a man who hasn't bothered to acknowledge my existence since our marriage."

"But it bothers you that he didn't speak of you! I can see it!" Adam stopped dancing abruptly, seconds before the music ended. Hallie could see the torment in his features but was powerless as to how to help. "You're attracted to him like all the rest, aren't you? Well, that's fine, Mrs. Redmond!" he said sarcastically. "Just remember your marriage leaves me a free man!" He turned and stormed off into the crowd, leaving Hallie to stare after him, her heart heavier even than before, her face pale with strain. She wanted to run away from this whole situation, to escape back into the time when her life was simple and uncomplicated by men and their tantrums.

It was Lydia who drew her attention from the retreating back of Adam, for Michael and Amanda had left the floor. The larger woman tugged at Hallie's arm. "Don't look so forlorn! If you look like you've lost your favorite lover, you'll set every tongue to wagging! Personally I think it's just fine if he is a little extra entertainment for you, but good Lord, don't show it so plainly! If nothing else, a man must be kept wondering."

Hallie stared at her for a moment, trying to grasp her words. "It really isn't like that," Hallie said feebly, following Lydia from the ballroom into the dining room, where a long table was set for a late dinner.

"Oh, honey, I honestly don't care! Why, I've had my little peccadilloes! Just don't let Michael know. He has quite a streak of jealousy if you're not careful. Now, take your place here at the end of the table. After all, as mistress here now you must be a perfect hostess."

Lydia disappeared and left Hallie to stare down a table that looked miles long. At the other end sat Michael, straight, composed, handsome, but even at this distance she could see the fury in the blue-gray eyes. Then he turned his head slowly and put his total attention on a very lovely woman to his left.

CHAPTER THIRTEEN

The meal seemed to stretch on forever. Hallie touched almost none of her food, for she had no appetite even if the food had been able to pass the lump in her throat. She felt very much alone, even though a nice older woman to her right tried hard to make conversation with her.

Amanda was only three seats away, but it was still too far for them to be able to have a real conversation. At the opposite end of the table, Michael appeared engrossed in whatever the woman next to him was whispering. Not far from Amanda was Adam, and his dinner partner was distressing to Hallie. He sat so near to Belinda Scott that they did not need two chairs, his head bent over her, smiling brightly as though he had not had another thought about Hallie or the predicament she was in. Her heart ached, and she was not just a little jealous.

Belinda Scott was a year older and had been at school with Hallie and Amanda. Belinda had always been a little snip, vain and unerringly contrary. She was very attractive, anyone had to concede that, her hair a thick, shiny, copper mass, her complexion flawless, her green eyes beautiful. Still, the fact that Hallie held only contempt for her and her conniving ways did not ease the fact that Adam appeared to be falling prey to her questionable charms. When at last the meal ended, the women gossiped while the men smoked cigars and drank brandy. At least Hallie was free of both Adam and Michael, though she did wonder what might happen in the other room, where the two most surely would meet.

Hallie sought a little peace with Amanda, ignoring her responsibilities as hostess and simply sitting quietly in the corner. She could have screamed when Belinda Scott invaded her seclusion, smiling wickedly. She spoke directly to Hallie, ignoring Amanda.

"I suppose congratulations are in order, Hallie. Your marriage was quite a secret. Is there a reason for that?" she asked insinuatingly.

"Yes, there is. We didn't want people to know." Hallie did not even attempt courtesy.

"How cute." Belinda's smile was taut. "Well, you may have caught the irresistible Michael Redmond, but you have freed delightful Dr. Burgess. He is more than adequate replacement, I would say. He has offered to take me home tonight." Her smile turned coy. Both Hallie and Amanda merely stared at her, not speaking until she sought another companion.

"My brother is a fool!" Amanda said passionately.

"I'm afraid it is my fault. You can't blame him too much, Amanda. He is in misery."

"And trying to make you feel even worse! Men are so selfish! I'd like to throttle him!"

"He has every right to find someone else," Hallie said dully. "What can he do? He can't wait for me to find some sort of freedom for myself, for he knows that can't happen."

"Still, he could have waited, and he certainly could have chosen someone besides Belinda Scott!"

In the other room men laughed at ribald jokes, their senses being dulled by further drink. It served as a good cover for the confrontation that Jason Curtis had the misfortune to be right in the middle of. Adam had been drinking heavily, and his self-control was almost nonexistent. Jason knew Michael well enough to realize he had avoided any liquor for that very reason.

Adam had approached Michael, his anger seething.

72

"How is it that I didn't realize what a bastard you are in all of these months?"

Michael was firmly in control, his tone cold, deadly calm. "Shortsightedness, I'm sure."

"You don't deserve her, you know."

"I presume you are speaking of my wife?" He paused only a moment. "I didn't expect you to come here tonight, Burgess, even though you were invited. The invitation, as you well know, was made before I realized you were in love with my wife. I didn't think you would have the gall to come into my home. But since you did, let's set this straight now. My opinion of you is no better than yours of me. Hallie is married to me now, and by tomorrow morning there will be no way in which she is not my wife. I have already warned her, and now I will do the same for you. I will not tolerate infidelity. The consequences for her would be severe, but you, Doctor, I will ruin if you so much as lay a finger on her."

"You're a hypocrite, Redmond! Your threats won't change the fact that she loves me or that I love her. She may be married to you, but she hates you for keeping us apart. Why do you insist on playing out this farce?"

An evil smile spread Michael's lips, his eyes glinting maliciously. "Because I want her," he said. He strode arrogantly to the door, opened it and spoke, his voice carrying easily throughout the room. "It is time we join the ladies. I for one cannot be separated for too long from my lovely wife." The large group laughed heartily, save one.

At last the guests began to depart. As Hallie watched Amanda prepare to leave, the last of the guests, Hallie had lost all courage. Her fear of the coming night spent alone with Michael Redmond was clear to Amanda's eyes if not to any others, and she had to admit she did not envy her friend.

Alone in the entrance hall Amanda spoke, her eyes misted. "I don't know what to say. I hate to leave you."

Hallie's smile was warm, if only a bit wan. "Don't worry about me, Amanda. After all, you assured me it wasn't so bad."

"Of course it isn't! I'm only concerned about you fretting over Adam," she lied.

"I'm too tired for that. Besides, I'm sure Belinda Scott will offer him a great deal of comfort."

"Michael really isn't a demon, you know. He can be very kind and compassionate."

Hallie laughed at the telling change in her friend's train of thought. "I know that. I only wonder if he's capable of showing it to me."

"I'm certain he will. Try not to antagonize him tonight. Perhaps if you try being patient, he will too."

Before Hallie could answer, Michael and Jason appeared from the library, where they had shared a nightcap. "I've tried to talk your husband into staying the night, Amanda. It really is a long drive at this hour, but he insists you must go home."

Amanda's eyes shot to her husband, who raised his brows as if in warning. "Yes, he's right," she answered. "I'll be fine." Amanda squeezed Hallie's hand as if it would impart a small amount of her own strength to her friend. "We'll talk soon!" she assured her as Jason nearly pushed her from the house.

The large double doors closed before her and Hallie stared at them, her fear suddenly growing like a tangible thing inside of her. She heard Michael's voice from behind her, tauntingly amused, adding to her trepidation.

"The time has come, madam. The debt is due."

CHAPTER FOURTEEN

Hallie was alone in the enormous master bedroom. Michael had at least allowed her the privacy to dress; he had gone into the connecting sitting room to have a drink. The bed chamber was a cozy room with a light blue brocade love seat and two matching chairs placed before an ornately carved fireplace. Several sideboard tables were around the room, its walls covered in a beige and light blue striped fabric. The same wall covering continued into the bedroom, which was dominated by a huge Chippendale bed, four tall posts nearly reaching the high ceiling. It stood on four massive claw feet, and the high, soft-looking mattress was covered in light blue silk. A candlestand stood on either side of the bed, ornate silver holders there with the candles already lit. The hearth in this room was identical to that in the sitting room, only before it stood two high, wing chairs. A day bed of the same blue silk sat beneath one large bay window, covered with richly trimmed light blue velvet draperies. Two large chests and wardrobes lined one wall, and Hallie assumed her clothing now resided in one of them. In one corner stood a dressing table, to the side of which was a large, elegant French dressing glass. Another corner had a washstand on which was a shaving glass, framed with drawers below it and to the sides. It was magnificent, and Hallie was awestruck once again.

Yet after her initial perusal her fear returned, for laid out on the silk bedcover was a gown and wrapper she was apparently expected to wear. She hurriedly undressed for fear Michael might return, but when she donned the nightdress her breath drew in a startled gasp. This gown was a sheer batiste, the front drawn down well between her breasts, which were clearly visible. Without hesitation she pulled on the wrapper, hoping it would conceal some of her exposed flesh, but found it to be equally transparent. She caught sight of herself in the French looking glass and knew that no man would have patience when faced with this; it was designed to add an alluring temptation she was certain Michael would not resist.

Quickly Hallie ran to the wardrobe, hoping to find her own velvet robe. The doors she threw wide revealed only men's garments. But just as she opened the tall double doors of the other wardrobe, she heard Michael's warning knock. She seized the first piece her fingers touched and ran to hide behind one of the tall wing chairs. It was not until then that she realized she had one of her heavy winter cloaks. Hallie knew only too well the ridicule she would suffer if she donned this. She remained behind the chair, the cloak held at her breasts to offer some sort of protection as Michael Redmond strode casually into the room.

At first glance he thought she had disappeared, for Hallie was not large, and her head and barely an inch of her shoulders were visible above the chair. When at last he caught sight of her, her raven hair in wild disarray around her flushed face, he could not help but smile. She looked like a frightened child hiding from a tormentor.

"What the hell are you doing?" he asked, one brow raising.

For a moment Hallie did not speak, for lack of a good explanation. Instead she stared at her husband, his shirt open to the waist, baring a hairy, muscular chest, his trousers his only other clothing. She saw that he carried a bottle of wine and two glasses and wondered how she was going to accept a goblet without revealing herself.

Again Michael spoke, less patient than before. "Are you ill?"

Shocked from her stupor, Hallie said, "No, I am quite well, thank you."

"Why are you hiding behind that chair?"

"I'd be happy to come out if you would only do me the service of finding me a robe among my clothes in the wardrobe."

"What is wrong with the night clothes I had Lydia set out for you?"

Hallie's face flushed. "They don't suit me."

"Well, those ugly things you had sent over didn't suit me. I burned them. I've already ordered new things for you, but for now you will have to make do with those. Come out from behind that chair. This is ridiculous."

Hallie debated and then decided she was only making matters worse. Hadn't Amanda warned her not to antagonize him? She sighed and threw the cloak about her shoulders, fastening it at her throat. When that was done and she stepped to face him, Michael roared with laughter.

"Are you deformed?"

"Of course not!"

"Then why are you so ashamed of your body?" he asked, pouring the wine and handing her a glass before he sat in the chair opposite Hallie. Suddenly another thought struck Michael and every drop of amusement deserted him, all of this evening's anger flared anew. "Is this some game to convince me you are innocent?"

Hallie's hands shook, nearly spilling the wine. She did not sit; her nerves were too taut for her even to move. "I am not playing some game. These clothes are indecent!"

"Are they? I have seen women in their nightgowns before. I doubt if it is that bad," he taunted. "You realize that no matter what you do now, in a short time I will know the truth."

"You speak in riddles! Just what do you think my purpose is?" Hallie's own temper was hot.

"I wonder if you're trying to convince me you are a virgin when in all actuality dear Adam has already plucked the fruit." He sipped his wine leisurely, appearing calm though the muscle in his cheek worked fiercely.

"You are insufferable! I wish to God that were the case! Do you know how it galls me to be forced to relinquish to you what I have saved for the man I love?"

Michael did not understand why he was struck so sharply by this, but he was, and his reaction was to strike back. "Even if the man you love is a spineless bastard?" he said maliciously. "Is he so deserving of that treasure, Hallie? You have strange loyalties. Your perfect Dr. Adam Burgess is the man who saw what trouble your family was in, who stood by because his pride was injured and watched you be married off to a total stranger without lifting a finger. He would have you his way, at his time or else not at all, regardless of what waiting would cause for you. That's an odd demonstration of love. It seems to me that if I were so consumed with love for a woman I would not even hesitate to help her when she needed me. Has it ever occurred to you that perhaps he didn't want you as his wife, that perhaps he had a less wholesome role for you in his life?"

"That wasn't how it was between us! He was only looking out for my welfare! He thought I was too young for marriage!"

"So he refused your pleas and let you marry a man who could very well not have paused a moment in deference to your tender age! He could have married you, supported you, as I did, and waited to claim his rights until he deemed you old enough. Perhaps it was more that he wanted you without the sanctity of marriage and hoped if you became desperate enough you would agree to that."

"You're wrong!" she shouted. "In fact, Adam begged me to go away with him tonight! He said he would give anything for my freedom, repay all of my debts! He would marry me in a moment! That was what he wanted even yesterday, before you intruded!"

Michael's anger grew as she defended Adam Burgess. "And when you refused he sought comfort in Belinda Scott. He didn't appear too distraught by your refusal to go with him."

78

"You don't know anything about him!" she fairly screamed.

"I know enough to realize that there is something lacking in any man who refuses to offer whatever he can when the woman he supposedly loves is in need."

"He would have! I rushed into this marriage before he had a chance to calm down and offer it!"

"And if I were to set you free? Would you run to him now, even after he deserted you when you needed him most?"

"Are you setting me free?" she challenged.

Michael paused as though weighing his decision heavily. "No, I can't."

Now Hallie's anger diminished slightly as a question returned to haunt her. "Why did you marry me?" she asked quietly.

Michael poured himself more wine, consciously calming himself, realizing this was not how he had planned this night. His gaze lifted to her, staring for a moment. "Don't you know?" he said snidely, as if she should feel shame in the lack of that knowledge.

"No!" she shot back in defiance. "I never understood why your father offered me marriage, and I certainly don't know why you took his place."

"He was dying. He could not go through with it."

"That doesn't explain why you did."

Michael's brilliant blue-gray eyes raised to some invisible spot above Hallie, one long, powerful finger tracing the contours of his lips as his mind wandered to something she could not know. When he spoke, it was with scorn. "Your grandmother is a sly lady. My father discovered some time ago that she had come to own fifty acres of land bordering Redland. It was a wise purchase, for our source of water originates on those acres. Of course, we offered her ten times its worth, but she refused. She said it was to be your only dowry." He gulped back his wine, his gaze lowering to Hallie's face. "Redland could have been ruined if that land fell to anyone else." He raised his empty glass in mocking toast. "So you see, Etta made it as imperative that I wed you as that you wed me."

Silence followed for some time as Michael seemed lost in thought and memories. It served to heighten

Hallie's fears. When she thought she could bear it no more she sighed deeply to draw courage and spoke, her voice soft yet strong. "I have a request to make of you about this marriage."

His attention drawn back to the beauty that still stood facing him, Michael lifted one brow in query.

"I would ask that we postpone the more intimate portion until we have time to know one another in other ways."

Michael was torn between compassion for her and her obvious fear of the coming encounter, and anger at the thought that she was stalling for time to end this marriage and go to Adam. His voice was level. "I can't allow that. It has been too long already. This marriage must be consummated. I am determined that you will be my wife in all ways by morning."

CHAPTER FIFTEEN

Hallie stood frozen before her husband. Even the heavy cloak seemed transparent as his eyes studied her. He drank the last of his wine and moved to blow out the many candles in the room until there remained only a dim glow from those on the bedside table. Hallie felt her hands clench, her lips quiver. She tried breathing deeply but found it did not help. If only I knew this man, she thought, trying to will away her nervousness.

When he came to stand close behind her, reaching around to unfasten the cloak, her hands moved to grasp it closed, to keep it around her shoulders. She expected him to pull it away, but instead he further unnerved her by kissing the nape of her neck, his lips moist, his breath warm against her soft skin. He smelled of wine and a faint hint of tobacco; Hallie did not find it unpleasant. When his hands touched her shoulders she stiffened further, for she was certain he would pull her cloak away. Instead he turned her gently to face him.

"Relax, Hallie. It will be much better if you just let me make love to you and don't be such a scared kitten. I promise it will be good." His voice was a whisper, soothing her taut nerves inexplicably, but still she clutched the wrap.

His hands ran slowly down her back and then up

again, into the silky mass of hair at her waist. He pulled her closer, her face nearly pressed against his massive chest. One hand cupped her chin, lifting her face until her eyes met his piercing blue-gray ones, kind and suddenly not the least bit intimidating.

He smiled warmly at her, his voice intimate, making her feel as though she were the only woman in the world, the only woman he had ever wanted. "You're beautiful. I've never known anyone as lovely as you. I've never wanted anyone as much as I want you." Even Michael was surprised to find that he felt this way, for his own desires were raging as never before, making him struggle to control his pace when he wanted to ravage her. He found her lips, only to recapture them again and again, softly, sweetly, slowly, until Hallie relaxed a bit more in his embrace. His head lowered to her throat, kissing, nibbling lightly, breathing deeply of her scent, enjoying her as no other before. Michael's lips again sought hers, only now it was a long, passionate kiss, his arms tightening around her, one hand bracing her head as it fell back to accept his lips. Hallie's eyes closed as she felt more of the tension ease from her body; she pressed herself against him. When the kiss ended, he pushed her face into his throat, inhaling the perfume of her curls.

"I'll be as slow as I can, my love."

He held her for another moment, feeling her body yield, become soft in his grasp. Again his lips met hers, though now his tongue teased lightly, his hands rubbed her back and neck like downy feathers, erasing the tension there. She barely felt the cloak fall to her feet, for she did not care that she was unshielded; she wanted the barriers to be gone, wanted her skin as close to his as possible. Now his powerful hands ran the length of her bare arms, sending tingles through her. He bent and picked her up, carrying her gently to the enormous bed. Hallie felt the wrapper and nightgown slip away as one piece. The sudden bareness of her skin brought her mind halfway back to reality, and her arms crossed over her chest.

Michael smiled patiently, pulling the silk coverlet down as well as the sheet and heavy quilt. "You can hide beneath the sheet if you must, Hallie, but it will be a great disappointment to me."

She did just that, for her desire had receded behind her fear once more. She watched Michael with wide violet eyes as he shed his own shirt, baring a broad, well-muscled chest. His right side was marred by a white scar, apparently left by Adam's scalpel. This reminder did nothing to ease her, though her treacherous body wanted the man before her. He stripped away his breeches, displaying long, sinewy legs and obvious proof that he wanted his wife even more than she wanted him. Hallie's eyes widened still further at his size, for she was totally innocent of a man's body. She quickly averted her gaze from the sight of his manhood.

Michael chuckled lightly. "Don't be so horrified. You'll offend me."

Hallie could not respond to his jest. "My sense of humor has deserted me," she managed.

"So long as the rest are well tuned," he said, his voice hoarse with passion. He sat facing her, his legs still off the bed. He leaned over Hallie, gently kissing her again. He teased her lips, biting them gently, then kissing her face, her ears, her throat. Hallie felt desire begin anew, stronger now, desire for something she was ignorant of. Michael lay beside her, pulling her close, his head bent over hers as his kisses became more demanding, and Hallie gave willingly. One powerful hand reached her breast, so lightly at first that she thought it was merely the sheet brushing against her; as his touch became more insistent, his fingers playing lightly at the taut, rose-colored tip, her breathing became much deeper. The feeling was divine as every inch of her flesh screamed out for him. His other hand lowered to the soft recesses no one had ever touched, sending a quick gasp of shock and exquisite pleasure as he massaged her lightly, teased, entered, and drew out again. His kisses were more urgent, his own need nearly unbearable. He spread her legs easily with his knees and rose above her. Michael lowered himself to his wife, teasing one last time before he entered her in a fast, surging motion to make the pain short. Hallie gasped and drew away, but Michael's hands held her hips so she would not destroy the perfect union. He lay still for a moment, kissing her gently, tantalizing her breasts with one hand.

His voice was taut with desire, "I'm sorry, my love. But I had to hurt you."

His face lowered to her breast, his tongue flicking the taut nipple until even Hallie forgot the pain, which had passed. Then he moved. Slowly. Filling and drawing away, again and again until her pleasure grew to a peak she had never expected, sending her mind sailing free, her body an exquisite chamber of delight. And then she felt Michael tense, heard him say her name softly and knew she had pleased him even through her inexperience.

Silence reigned. Michael moved to lie beside Hallie, pulling her close against his body, her head on his broad shoulder. He was as much awed by what had passed between them as she, for never had Michael felt what he just had, never had there been such perfect pleasure, and it threatened him as much as it fulfilled him. He could not help but fear the possibility that these were bonds he would never be free of, perhaps never want to be free of.

Hallie was consumed with something quite different, for in her mind she had betrayed Adam, and in betraying him she had also humiliated herself. It was one thing to submit to this man who was her husband because he demanded it in payment, but to enjoy it? To lose herself completely to this stranger? And worse yet, to want more of the pleasure she had just experienced? These things did not lend rest to her mind.

At last Michael broke the silence. "Are you all right?" he asked kindly.

"Yes," she answered simply, not knowing what to say.

Michael reached one long arm to his bedside table, pulling a small box from the top. Remaining as they were, he opened it and took from it a wide gold band. "I noticed you did not wear a wedding ring. I think this is an appropriate time to begin. You are most certainly my wife now." He placed the ring on her finger, kissing that spot lightly when it was in place. "Every time you catch sight of it you can remember when you received it and what preceded it."

"What will remind you?" she said, feeling like striking out at this man who had just caused such confusion
to her well-ordered senses.

Michael heard the underlying tone of challenge and
was himself too unnerved by the chance that he was
falling into what he considered the web of a woman not
to strike back. "It is you and not I who seems in need
of a reminder as to whom you belong. For make no
mistake about it, Hallie, after tonight you are mine."

CHAPTER SIXTEEN

The morning dawned gray, threatening an early winter
storm. Michael was awake but felt too warm and comfortable to rise. Hallie still slept soundly beside him,
turned to face the opposite direction, her small buttocks
pressed against his thigh. His thoughts were not on his
wife, for he felt that things had been settled between
them; his mind could concentrate on other matters that
had been neglected too long.

The Redmond family fortune had begun after the
Revolutionary War. Michael's grandfather and Jason
Curtis's grandfather had started with two merchant
ships that sailed to China, India, Europe and the West
Indies. They were among many who made enormous
fortunes there, allowing the initiation of the era of gracious living for them. Jason Curtis's grandfather had
begun to invest his profits in shipbuilding, fast losing
interest in a life at sea for himself. When that time
came for Michael's grandfather, he had delegated the
shipping to his son and built Redland. It had surprised
Boston's ever-interested gossips that the old man had
so successfully changed his interests to farming, but
before he died the Redmond name was on a large fleet
of merchant ships and also the most profitable farm in
all of the city.

Michael's father had been a man of the sea, spending as little time at Redland as possible until his later years, when he was more a burden aboard a ship than a help in the rugged existence. He had pushed Michael to follow his same course, but Michael found that he preferred the land to the sea. As the Redmond holdings passed from father to son, both the shipping business and the farm seemed blessed. Michael's father had liked to think their success was due to pious living, though Michael had great doubts about that theory. More, he realized, it was good business sense and pure luck. Still, he had to concede, their timing had been exceptional.

Their shipping business had prospered when many others turned to the slave trade. The Redmonds had steadfastly refused to truck in human flesh and had found their business increased when others changed their interests. Even Redland had prospered throughout these past years, when most colonial farms had sold out in favor of industry. It left the demand for what Redland produced that much greater.

There had been a few setbacks; no business was without them. The worst had come in 1844, the winter that the harbor froze from the wharves to the lighthouse; two of the Redmond ships had been docked there. Michael remembered watching the ice cutters at work, hardy men they had brought in from Cambridge, using iron saws to cut open the channel and free the many ships. There had been some bad crops, as well, but it always seemed that when times were poor for one of their businesses the other prospered to compensate.

But never had there been so little profit from the shipping business during the period Michael was away, and Lydia had insisted that her husband, Oliver, be allowed to take a hand in the business. It was to this that Michael turned his thoughts, staring up at the ceiling, his hands behind his head. When the senior Michael Redmond had died, leaving all holdings to his eldest son, Redland was doing well, but the Redmond shipping lines were better than ever. Michael had left for war feeling certain that the overseer of the farm could handle it and that even Oliver could not damage the profitable, well-run shipping business. He had set Farley the task of watchdog over Oliver.

Michael was not fond of his brother-in-law. Michael had never been close to Lydia, but still he could not fathom the reason behind her marrying Oliver Kent. To Michael's way of thinking he was a deceitful, conniving bastard in peacock dress. In two years he had wreaked such havoc that it would take a year or more to rectify it. He wondered how any man could be so inept. He knew the row that would be caused. He was often the recipient of Lydia's resentment for his having inherited everything. He supposed he would have to leave the pompous ass in some position of unimportance to appease her. He smiled sardonically at the picture of Oliver sweeping warehouse floors dressed in velvet.

Michael heard Hallie stir beside him, felt her soft, warm body snuggle close and then, realizing where she was, she stiffened and pulled away. "Good morning, Hallie," he said, his voice deep.

She rolled to her back, holding the sheet tightly at her bare breasts. The light of day only increased her shame. Her thoughts immediately ran to Adam, and guilt left her mood poor. "Good morning," she answered flatly.

Michael turned to his side, propping his head up on one hand. His smile was mischievous. "I preferred the reaction I received last night. Are you one of those women who awakens in sore spirits?"

"That depends on the situation in which I find myself."

"Sheathe your claws, madam. I don't care to argue before I've left my bed. What have I done to rouse this ugly streak in you?"

Hallie sighed resignedly, knowing he was undeserving of her attack. "It's myself I'm angry with," she answered sullenly.

"I see. No doubt it stems from last night's romp. My guess is you feel loyalty to the wrong man. I am your husband, and what we did last night is no different from what any married couple would have done. Has it occurred to you that dear Adam probably spent these same hours in much the same way with Belinda Scott?"

It had not occurred to her, but Hallie conceded that possibility, remembering well his attentions to the woman. "Adam would not do such a thing," she defended him feebly, her own doubts evident.

Michael laughed, yet his mood was not caustic; he was relaxed and enjoying the early-morning company of his wife. "Adam is a man, my love. A healthy, normal man who has led a celibate life for some time, if my guess is right, and who has just found himself denied that which he wanted so desperately. Don't you think it's quite possible that he seized last night for a little comfort?"

"Must we discuss Adam?" she asked, hurt by the thought yet feeling more certain by the minute that it was exactly the case.

Michael smiled, surprising Hallie with his amicability. "As a matter of fact, I would prefer never to talk of him."

Remembering the party and a vow she had made to herself, Hallie changed the subject. "What does your family know of this marriage? Lydia acted somewhat strangely about it yesterday."

"Lydia always acts somewhat strangely. But to answer your question, my family knows only that we are married. My father had not spoken of the arrangements, so when I fulfilled the plan I saw no reason to enlighten them. I told them only that it was our father's wish that I marry you to consolidate some holdings that affected the family's business. You may be sure that no one in this family has any interest in the workings of the business, and they would not question such a statement...unless, of course, it adversely affected someone's ability to spend endless amounts of money." His voice was harsh as he continued. "Upon my arrival here, I simply announced that I had a wife."

"But what are we to tell them when they ask about the date?"

"Whatever you would like. I really don't care what anyone thinks, so suit yourself."

"Well, I certainly don't care what your family thinks!" she said, affronted.

"Then should the subject arise we'll tell them the truth." At Hallie's silence Michael continued, reading her thoughts. "We can say that in a fit of passion we

90

eloped just before I left for war. Does that spare your humiliation?"

Indignant now to have been so transparent, Hallie said, "Well, it may save me, but it does little for you. It was not a secret that I waited only for the day Adam returned."

"Back to Adam, now, are we? Then we can say it was love at first sight and I swept you off your feet, snatched you right from under his nose. Is that better?"

"No, it isn't. I suppose I shall have to avoid the question, for there is no good answer."

At that moment a knock sounded at the door, followed by Farley's voice announcing Michael's bath. To Hallie's embarrassment he allowed the older man entry. She ducked beneath the covers, leaving only a blushing upper face visible. Farley was polite enough not to acknowledge her presence. He hurried to fill the tub and build a fire, then retreated discreetly.

Michael laughed. "I suppose I will have to change this routine, at least for Farley's sake. I think we embarrassed the old goat."

"I would appreciate it even if he would not."

Michael flung the sheet from his naked body, heedless of his state, and left the bed. Hallie stared up at the ceiling, not wanting to see her husband unclothed and particularly not in broad daylight. So she was surprised to see him standing above her at the bedside, grinning devilishly down at her. His hair was tousled from sleep, his features very handsome as they reflected the mischievous way he felt. Her deep violet eyes widened.

"I'm sorry, but we haven't really arranged for your toilette as of yet. So for today I believe the best way is to share our bath." He bent and grabbed her just as she moved to flee. Trying to keep herself covered put Hallie at a disadvantage as she fought Michael. He merely laughed, enjoying her struggle and clearly in command of the situation. A high squeal escaped Hallie as he lifted her up and strode to the large brass tub filled with steaming water. His long legs stepped easily over the edge, and he sat himself and Hallie down with a splash.

Mortified, her face flamed, and seeing it, Michael

again laughed. "I was just trying to be a thoughful husband! After all, you wouldn't want to go through the day without a bath, would you?"

"Do you find pleasure in humiliating me?" she said when at last she found her voice.

"Yes, as a matter of fact I believe I do. Your face turns such a lovely shade of crimson."

Hallie moved from his lap, where his rising desire for her was evident, and sank into the water, her arms folded over her breasts. Michael stared at her from the opposite side, one toe tickling her side in play. "Come now, love, let's see a smile! Surely you aren't always such a poor sport."

Hallie's lips pursed, still embarrassed but fighting an urge to laugh. She stared into his hairy chest, refusing to allow him to contact her eyes.

Michael splashed water at her gently, dousing her face and a long strand of hair that fell over her breast. Hallie could not resist this challenge, regardless of her modesty. She returned his splash in double force, drenching his handsome face. When she finally looked up to see how angry he was at her defense, she was surprised to see him grinning broadly, water dripping from his skin and his hair in wet strings down his forehead. He looked so ridiculous she could not help but laugh in return.

"That's better! I prefer my wife happy in the mornings, if you please."

"Why, certainly, Your Majesty!" she bantered, her words falsely high-pitched. "Anything you desire." When the words escaped her lips she wished she could summon them back again.

"In that case," he said much more seriously, moving toward her on his hands and knees in the water, "what I desire is an early-morning repeat of the night past."

Hallie pressed her back as far into the tub as she could to escape, for he was over her legs, leaving her with no other recourse. His tongue gently flicked away the droplets from her face, then her shoulders. Hallie's hands reached to his chest, hard and unyielding, feebly attempting to push him away. "The marriage has been consummated! You said last night that was what you expected!"

Michael merely laughed. "So it is. And now we shall begin to work on the other thing I expected, which is a houseful of babies."

Hallie gasped, for she had not thought him serious in that threat. But before his lips reached their goal, another knock sounded at the door, and again Farley's voice followed. "You'd best hurry, lad. The house is already chompin' at the bit to see your bride. I've nearly had to tie Miss Lydia to a chair to keep her from bustin' in."

"Damn!" was Michael's only comment to his friend and servant. He sat back in the tub, reaching fiercely for the soap. "A few things are going to be changed around here! It is time this household learns who is master and when not to intrude on our privacy!"

Hallie merely smiled victoriously, feeling she had been rescued. She dawdled in her bath, thinking Michael would leave her to dress. But as he rose from the water, unconcerned with what he displayed to her, he made it clear she was to leave the tub and go to breakfast with him. She managed to hide herself behind the large bath towel she used to dry her skin, but donning her clothes was another matter entirely. With her back to Michael, Hallie dressed as quickly as possible without Mercy's assistance. Hallie was not aware that her front half was well reflected in the large, full-length mirror. Michael neglected his own grooming to watch her.

Her body was as beautiful to look upon as it had been to touch. She was perfectly proportioned, slender and petite. Her skin was creamy alabaster, her limbs long and graceful. Before she donned her chemise his eyes paused at her breasts for as long as they were in view, small but perfect upturned mounds, their crests pink and taut. When she bent to pull up the many petticoats that would hold her skirt wide, he smiled at the view of her posterior and had the urge to pat it gently. The gown finally destroyed his pleasure at observing her dress, but as she primped and brushed the long, heavy mass of shining raven hair he was still mesmerized. Her hands worked adeptly until it hung free and smooth, and then she drew it back to the nape of her neck, gathering it there and allowing the re-

93

mainder to fall in a wildly curling disarray around her shoulders and down her back nearly to her waist. Then she pinched her high cheekbones and smoothed her brows and Michael was extremely pleased with the results of this quick toilette. Hallie turned, ready to leave the room, giving one last swat to straighten a wrinkle in her wide blue calico skirt.

"You're not even dressed!" she said accusingly, carefully keeping her eyes above his waist.

"Guilty as charged, madam. I was too engrossed in your work. And an admirable job it is," he teased.

He turned now to his own dressing, finally pulling on black trousers to free Hallie of the reminder of just how intimate they were. She too could not help but admire his masculine perfection, and again she felt guilty for her thoughts. As he carelessly brushed his hair back and finished the tying of his white cravat, she wondered if perhaps it would not have been better if he had been an ugly, offensive creature of a man, for then at least she could despise him as she thought she should and be free of this awful turmoil raging inside of her for the feelings she held for two men.

CHAPTER SEVENTEEN

Hallie and Michael descended the staircase. For the first time she noticed the many portraits that lined the wall there. The most recent two were apparently Michael's parents, for the man, though older, bore a great resemblance to her husband. The only difference was in the eyes, for the older Redmond's were pure gray. The woman was young and very lovely, her hair the auburn shade of Michael's, her eyes blue. It suddenly occurred to Hallie that she knew nothing of Michael's mother.

Hallie stopped now on the landing, staring up into the large portrait, admiring the woman it depicted. "She was very beautiful."

Michael's expression was odd, she thought, as he did not even glance at the picture. "Yes," was all he answered, offering no more.

"Is it painful for you to speak of her?" she asked, made more curious by his reaction.

"It is not painful. She has been gone many years. It simply does not warrant discussion."

Hallie shrugged, seeing no reason to pursue this. The woman was long dead.

The house had been put into order, a job Hallie decided was miraculous after the night's festivities. Fresh flowers decorated the large claw-foot table in the center of the entrance hall. "Where on earth did anyone find fresh flowers at this time of year?"

Now Michael smiled. "Our conservatory is resplendent with them. I retained only the gardener and cook when I returned. They were the only two worth their salt."

Michael led Hallie through the now well-ordered house, down the hallway to the large dining room. The walnut table was smaller than it had been the previous night, but still it was a massive piece. The chairs had ornately carved high backs with gold-brocade-cushioned seats. An enormous sideboard stretched the length of one wall, serving dishes abounding there. The remainder of the Redmond household was seated, enjoying the breakfast. Lydia smiled brightly, greeting Hallie warmly, while her brother received a somewhat less exuberant good morning. When Hallie's eyes rested on the man beside Lydia her spine straightened imperceptibly, her features froze.

Lydia rushed into the introductions before Michael could open his mouth. "Hallie, this is my husband, Oliver Kent."

The smile was as lecherous as it had been the previous evening, when Hallie had first encountered this popinjay. His pale green eyes peered from beneath puffy lids to assess her once again. The high-pitched voice grated on her nerves. "We met last night at the party, but I'm afraid I was remiss in introducing myself. It will be a pleasure having you here."

Hallie did not answer, wondering if any but she heard the insinuation in his words. Her eyes next rested on a thin, frail-looking young man sitting at the far end of the table, well away from Lydia and Oliver and obviously out of their thoughts. His cold blue eyes rested first on Michael, and Hallie wondered if it was contempt she saw there. When his glance moved to her she could detect only his sullen disposition. He was watchful, as though prepared to defend an imminent attack. Michael saw Hallie smile invitingly at his young brother and suddenly wondered if she might be good for him.

"This is Trent, Hallie." Michael's words were curt.

The voice that spoke was barely audible, the blue

eyes never losing their watchful gaze. Hallie much preferred his company, no matter how somber, to Oliver Kent. Taking the initiative, she sat beside him as Michael spoke to the butler, who stood in readiness to serve. Hallie smiled again, her friendliness evident. "I didn't realize Michael's brother was a grown man. I'm pleased to meet you, Trent."

His greeting was mumbled, but Hallie continued as though it had been warm and inviting. "My brother, Danny, will be arriving today, and I must warn you he is a bit of an imp. I hope he won't bother you too much; he has a bothersome penchant for practical jokes. Please feel free to come to me if he becomes a pest."

"I'll see that my room is changed so that I am nowhere near him." Trent's nose raised almost imperceptibly, but his voice cracked, belying not only the mature posture he worked to project but also the arrogance.

Hallie was undaunted. "I will leave it to you. I would not want you displaced from your own room if it isn't what you want. If you prefer, we can have Danny moved." Her voice was earnest, with no trace of condescension or anger.

When Trent's answer came, his tone was less hostile. "I have been considering the move from the nursery section anyway. I'll go to see to it now."

Hallie watched the slight young man leave the room, wondering what could cause such wariness and such a strong desire to be offensive in him. She hoped to find a way to ease his barriers down and allow a little lightheartedness into him.

Michael sat with Hallie, leaving Lydia and Oliver to their own conversation, which did not seem to bother them. Hallie saw Michael's brows furrow as he watched Trent leave the room, his head shake in what she thought was disgust. She hoped that Trent's surliness would not affect Danny's boyish high spirits. She thought it a shame to see a mere boy so sullen. Was this such an imposing, threatening place for a child? She suddenly had her doubts about bringing Danny here. As they shared breakfast she tried to broach the subject in an innocent way.

"You know, Michael, perhaps it would be best for Danny to stay with my grandmother for a time. After all, there is so much to get used to, it might be better all the way around. He could visit here occasionally, and he and Trent could get to know each other before we expect them to live together."

Michael's scowl was darker than she had expected, and his tone was calm but firm. "It has been agreed that Etta was to retain her house and for Danny to live here. The best way for Danny to get used to this place and Trent is for him to be here. Your brother arrives this afternoon for a permanent stay." Hallie opened her mouth to argue the point, but before a word was uttered he turned to Lydia.

"I would appreciate it if you show Hallie the house this morning. I have a few things to tend." With that he left the room, ending any rebuttal Hallie had planned.

Hallie was awestruck as she followed Lydia on the tour of the Redland manor. In her wildest imaginings Hallie had not anticipated such splendor. The rooms were enormous, the furnishings opulent and in perfect taste. Hepplewhite and Sheraton filled every area, the floors were covered in Aubusson and Persian carpets, the walls in fine silks or painted in colors to match the furniture. The drawing room was done in tan and burnished orange, as was the dining room. The ballroom had no actual color, for gilt-framed mirrors surrounded the room. The den was paneled in oak, the high-backed wing chairs in dark leather. The library was four walls of bookshelves, reaching two levels high, broken only by the large hearth on one wall, its furnishings all comfortable and warm-looking, beckoning a person to curl up with one of the hundreds of leatherbound volumes.

The second floor was all bedrooms, each decorated differently but all beautiful. The room that would be Danny's was a wonderland of toy soldiers, horses, boats and anything imaginable to occupy a little boy's time. There were so many rooms that were left empty of people, if not of furnishings, that Hallie began to wonder just how many children Michael had in mind when he spoke of filling this house. Even the hallway was grand, she thought. The handwoven carpet that lined it was too elegant for a mere passageway. The walls were divided by wainscoting, the upper half papered in a tan-colored brocade with many wall brackets decorating it, some holding vases or long-accumulated knickknacks. There were also enough ornate sconces to leave it well lit in the darkness of night.

The rooms of the third level were larger even than the rest, for here the ceilings sloped to accommodate the slant of the roof. All of the windows held cushioned seats at their sills. In the center of the front portion was an enormous cupola, its circular front extending over the roof to allow a wide view of the well-tended grounds that stretched to the main road. The entire semicircle was windows, all freshly washed, several of which had bench seats in front of them, others left to allow a person to stand directly in front of the glass. On this level was the classroom where both Danny and Trent would attend their classes and a second large, open space for Danny to play. The remainder was taken up in rooms for those few privileged members of the staff who did not reside in the small row houses behind the main structure. Farley had a sitting room connected to his, as would Mercy. The tutor was allotted only a bedroom.

Throughout the tour Lydia chattered incessantly, most of which Hallie did not hear nor respond to. When she had seen it all and they passed the cupola on their way back downstairs, Hallie's mind finally slowed its spinning.

"I wondered what that room was when we arrived last night. It held the only light on this floor until we arrived, and then it went out. I assumed someone was watching for us."

"Oh, yes. I'm sure Farley sent one of the servants to keep an eye out. He doesn't like surprises. I'll have to speak to him about not informing me of it, though. That man too often directs the servants as though he had the right. You had best make it clear to him that you are mistress here or he will undermine you with them as well. Michael gives that man far too much power and encourages him to believe himself far above his station."

"But it's such a small thing, Lydia. Can't you pretend I never said it?" Hallie had no desire to be the cause of more friction between this woman and Farley, who seemed warm and kind.

"I will not! The servants aren't that man's affair. He is always stepping in. It's Michael's fault completely. He has no business giving that old idiot the idea he can overrule my authority as if I were some guest here! He even tried to put the man above Oliver! Of course, these things would never happen had our addlepated father left things more evenly dispersed. As it is we are all at the mercy of Michael's whims!"

As she descended the stairs behind Lydia, Hallie wondered what she had done to spark this tirade in her sister-in-law so that she might endeavor to avoid it in the future. But hearing the vehemence in her voice, Hallie wondered just how much animosity existed between her husband and his opinionated younger sibling.

CHAPTER EIGHTEEN

"Carriage comin'!"

Hallie heard the announcement and ran down the hallway, colliding with Michael at the top of the stairs. His strong arms went around her, keeping both of their balance lest they roll down the steep stairs. When they were steady once more he spoke, smiling down at her but still holding her.

"I take it you heard? It might prove safer to walk to the front door to greet your brother."

Hallie moved from his embrace, too impatient to remain here and exchange banter with Michael. She held her wide skirts high, slender ankles showing as she floated quickly down to the front door, the calico flying out behind her. Michael followed, appreciating the sight of his new wife. Then he held his pleasure in check, reminding himself he must not become enamored of her. Hallie swung the doors wide just as the carriage pulled to a stop. She did not hesitate to dash across the veranda and down the front steps.

Danny jumped from the carriage, a wide smile on his features for his sister. "Is this where we're going to live?" he asked her, his eyes raising the full height of the three-story mansion.

"This is it!" she said and laughed, hugging him affectionately.

"Just calm down now, Danny boy!" came Mercy's reprimand as the heavy old Englishwoman descended the carriage steps. "You were fussing about coming at all, and now you can't wait to tear the place apart!"

"How's Grandma, Mercy?" Hallie asked as she helped her from the carriage.

"You haven't been gone but a day! She's the same as always. She says she'll see you soon." Then Mercy's eyes followed the same path Danny's had. "This is a fine home! Are you mistress to all of this?"

Hallie shrugged in indecision, but now Michael made his presence known. "She is." His voice resounded in the cold, open air. "Might we have the introductions in the house instead of on the porch?"

Once inside, both Danny and Mercy stared at their surroundings in as much awe as Hallie had. Since she was not rushing into introducing her husband, Michael took over. "I assume you are Mercy. Your duties here will be caring for your mistress and Danny. If you've been with these two for any number of years I'm sure you've earned a little time to yourself in between. We have enough servants to run the household."

Mercy granted him a friendly smile. "So you can tell already what hellions these two are? Well, you're right! And I thank you kindly. Of course, I'll be expecting some wee ones to be caring for. I wouldn't want to get lazy in my old age!"

Hallie saw clearly that these two would be friends and that pleased her, for she set great store by Mercy's opinions. Next Michael turned to Danny, staring down at the boy. "You have to be Danny. I can already see the mischief in you. I expect you to behave yourself. No pranks that would cause any harm to anyone. Is that understood?"

"Yes, sir," he answered quietly, clearly intimidated by the imposing man, very much aware of the fact that he had always lived in a household of women.

This beginning did not please Hallie, for she thought it unnecessary to frighten Danny before he had even done anything. Was this how it was to be for Danny, restrictions and controls as though he were a small

102

soldier? She would not stand for it. Hallie placed her arm protectively over his shoulder, pulling Danny close. "I have never known my brother to do harm to anyone purposely. He is not malicious," she said haughtily.

A frown creased Michael's brow as his eyes rose to her. "I didn't say he was. I believe a boy needs to know his boundaries."

"I have seen no evidence here of wisdom used in dealing with the raising of boys," she retorted heatedly.

"And I see no wisdom in allowing boys to be wild, unruly little devils."

"No, you prefer to stomp on their spirit and turn them into statues!"

"I hardly expect that! But I will not tolerate disobedience, nor will I stand for the boy to be undisciplined or coddled and spoiled."

Hallie's indrawn breath expanded her chest with fury. Mercy watched in amusement. She stifled a smile and was about to enter the fracas to stop it when Farley stepped from behind her with the same intention.

"This isn't a good way to welcome these folks, Michael, lad. Don't you think they ought to see their rooms before you two start arguing over them?"

After a pause in which Michael's expression told Hallie this would be continued in private, he turned to Mercy. "Farley will show you your rooms. I'll take Danny to meet Trent and see his room." He held out a large hand to Danny, his voice friendly. "Come on, Dan. I'm sure you won't be sorry to get out of this crossfire, will you?"

Danny smiled tentatively and accepted the hand, for he had taken far less offense at Michael's first words than Hallie had.

As the two moved up the stairs Mercy spoke to Hallie, her voice low enough for only her mistress to hear. "You'd best curb your temper, miss! Nothin's going to be made better by looking for fights with that man! Danny'll fare for himself. He can do his own battling, and it'll be good for the boy to have a man around him!" With that Mercy followed Farley up the stairs, leaving Hallie alone in the entrance hall to fume.

The door to the master bedroom slammed for the second time in just a few minutes as Michael followed

Hallie into their room. Her back had been to the door, but at the sound she whirled in fury to face her husband. "If you expect to rule my brother with an iron hand, you are sadly mistaken! I will not tolerate it!" she fairly screamed.

Michael's voice was lower, more controlled, but still his anger was evident. "*You* will not tolerate it?!" he mocked. "It is not your place to dictate to me!"

"And it is not your place to dictate to my brother!"

"Who is to do that? You?"

"Yes! He is my brother!"

"He is also a member of this household now. He has been pampered by a bunch of indulgent women for long enough!"

"I would rather see him pampered and indulged than have him cold and defensive like Trent!"

"For your information, madam, to my knowledge I did not cause either Trent's coldness nor his defensiveness. He has been this way since I returned, and I would not have it happen to Danny for any reason! In fact, I'm hoping something will affect my brother and turn him away from his arrogance. So far he is an insufferable little bastard! But I will not allow Danny to run wild! Is that understood?"

Hallie was surprised by this, and her temper cooled. Still, her pride was bruised and she felt protective of her brother, whom she admittedly spoiled. "Then perhaps you should revise your methods! I see no reason to be a tyrant with a small boy!"

"I am hardly being a tyrant, Hallie! I merely told him straight out what I would not stand for. Danny did not find that nearly as unacceptable as you apparently do. Would you have him turned into an undisciplined little brat, or would you have him taught how to behave and perform within limits?"

"I will not have the limits stifle him!"

"Nor would I!"

Knowing she had lost this argument, her voice lowered to a more normal tone. "You could be less harsh in the presentation of your demands! You would be surprised at the difference in the way they are accepted and responded to when you temper it with kindness."

"For you or for the boy?"

"Both!"

Now Michael smiled, conceding her this. "You could practice a bit of patience yourself. I'm new to this job."

CHAPTER NINETEEN

As Hallie passed the cupola in search of Danny she thought she saw someone move from the windows. Thinking that perhaps her brother was already playing games, she entered the large room only to find it empty. Before she could turn to leave and continue her pursuit she was startled nearly to death by two long arms grasping her from behind. Anger replaced fear as she stared down at the peacock blue sleeves and inhaled the overly strong scent of masculine cologne. She felt hot breath close to her ear.

"What luck! I have you all alone!"

Hallie broke his grip with effort, flinging herself from him. "In the future, Mr. Kent, you had best keep your hands off of me! I will not be pawed by you. Is that understood?"

His smile was a leer. "Let's not be coy, Hallie! I can do things for you that you've never even imagined."

"The only thing I want you to do for me is leave me alone!"

He dabbed at the corners of his mouth delicately, as though salivating at the prospect of such a delicious morsel. "You prudes are all the same, prim and proper on the surface, and beneath lies a hot little tart crying to be taken." He stepped closer to Hallie, his arms reaching to pull her to him.

She ducked under his outstretched arms and rushed toward the hallway. "I mean what I say, Oliver! Grace someone else with your questionable charms. You sicken me!"

She moved quickly to the playroom, where Danny sat atop a huge rocking horse, riding wildly, shouting encouragement to his steed. Hallie breathed deeply to steady her nerves. Before she stepped from the doorway she saw Trent enter the room from an adjoining portal. He eyed Danny angrily, his sigh impatient. "If you ride that thing so hard you will break it!" he said peevishly to the boy. Not seeming to care that Danny did not heed his words, he turned and slammed the door with a crash, at last gaining his attention. Hallie was pleased to see that her brother was undisturbed as his interest returned to his play for a moment before he realized she stood watching.

He ran to her, pulling her arm in impatience. "Come on, Hallie, come ride! He's the fastest horse in the world!"

"I can see that! But I'm not dressed for riding, I'm afraid."

"Isn't this a fine place?" he said, more a statement than a question.

"I'm glad you think so, Danny."

"When will Adam come and see it all?" he said exuberantly, not realizing the pain it caused his sister.

Her smile faded and her voice was quiet. "I don't think Adam will be coming here."

"Why not? You said we could still be friends!"

"Yes, I know, but this is Michael's house. Adam and Michael don't really like one another."

"Why, that's nonsense!" Lydia's voice interrupted as she entered the room. "I assume you're speaking of Adam Burgess. He saved Michael's life. Why wouldn't he be welcome here? He was here last night."

Hallie felt her pulse quicken. What would she say to explain this? She could think of nothing but the truth. "Their friendship has been altered slightly. Adam should not have come here at all."

"Oh? When did all of this take place? Just three days ago Michael expressly told me to invite him to our party.

Is some scandal brewing?" she asked, her eyes sparkling.

"It isn't a scandal. Adam and I were planning to be married before I met Michael," Hallie stated simply.

"And my boorish brother became jealous! Michael can be so archaic!"

"It isn't actually all his fault. I'm afraid Adam has no better feelings toward Michael. His coming here last night merely provoked him unnecessarily. I hope he will not return."

A conspiratorial look came over Lydia's face. "Or perhaps you would just rather play farther from home! I don't blame you. Michael is very dull. But then I imagine you know that after last night." She smiled, inviting a confidence. "Well, at any rate, I came to tell you something. I have a very talented maid, a young Indian girl called Sky. Originally I had only intended to offer her skills for your toilette. But it seems you may have other uses for her as well. She has a great many talents beyond the usual. I have found occasion to avail myself of her potions. She is irreplaceable in keeping me childless." A wicked smile lit her features. "And after hearing this news today you might find her to be a great help yourself."

"I have a maid I brought with me, Lydia."

Lydia laughed, a sound deep and throaty. "Well, she can do absolute magic with hair as well. If you ever want to borrow her, just let me know." The older woman left, leaving Hallie to wonder about her.

Lydia Kent seemed friendly, yet she also seemed capable of a very unpleasant arrogance. She was much like those Hallie had witnessed at the party the previous night and wanted to stay away from. Snobbery made her uncomfortable even when it was not directed at her. Besides, Lydia was a bit too open and candid about matters Hallie was not comfortable with in private.

Michael arrived late to dress for dinner, and Hallie was already finished. As he stripped off his clothing and prepared for his bath she decided to escape before her face became permanently suffused with color. Michael's deep, rich voice stopped her before she reached

109

the door. "I'd like your company while I bathe," he requested, though it was more an order.

Still, Hallie opted to remain rather than cause another argument. Searching for a topic of conversation to occupy her thoughts and keep her eyes from Michael's naked body, the muscles taut and bulging, Hallie said, "Has Lydia had Sky for long?"

Michael's brow creased, his jaw set. "She did not have her before I left. Why do you ask?"

"I was only curious. She offered me the use of her if I wanted."

"Do you?" he said, as though challenging her.

"No, I have Mercy," she answered quietly. "I hope never to have need of her services."

Michael stared at Hallie as she watched the floor, wondering what second meaning her words held. "Has she more to offer than your maid?"

"No, it isn't that!" Hallie answered too quickly. "I only meant that she is very experienced. From what your sister says, she must be a very knowledgeable woman."

"Apparently you haven't seen Sky. She is barely seventeen."

"Seventeen is hardly a child. I am eighteen."

"But you had the tutelage of Adam Burgess."

"I thought that was resolved last night."

"So were your virginity and childhood."

"And you know Sky well enough to know she is still a virgin?" Hallie shot back, offended by his offhand treatment of her.

"I know an innocent when I see one."

"That is hardly true, as I can attest."

"Don't fool yourself, my love. I was quite certain you were a virgin still. I was merely testing."

"Well, if Sky has had any dealings with Oliver Kent, you are probably mistaken about her."

Now his eyes rose to hers, his curiosity sparked. "What does that mean?"

"It means he is a lecher! He has pawed me twice now, and I shudder to think of what he would do to a helpless young girl."

Michael laughed. "One minute you're offended by my not including you in that category and the next you're

110

acting as though you're centuries older. Have you a penchant for harmless fops, Hallie?"

"He is most certainly a fop, but I have my doubts about how harmless he is!"

"I didn't take you for a woman who believes every word a man speaks to her is lechery."

Now Hallie's anger rose. "I know what I am speaking of!"

"Christ! You are an innocent! You are not Oliver Kent's style."

"And what is his style?" she asked sarcastically.

"My bet is you're the wrong gender, and certainly even in the instances when he uses a woman, you are hardly the sort. His tastes, or so I have heard, would curdle the stomach of the most stouthearted whore."

"I see," she said, quietly, embarrassed, though not really understanding what Michael meant. "Then he spoke the truth when he said there were many things he could show me."

"When did he say that?"

"This afternoon in the cupola."

"He is most likely toying with you, Hallie. I wouldn't take him too seriously."

To Hallie it seemed that Michael belittled her fears. She vowed she would never mention Oliver Kent's advances again. "If your opinion of Oliver is so low, what must that of Lydia be? After all, she married him."

"I told you before that Lydia is strange. Oliver makes very few demands on her and leaves her free to seek her own pleasures, whatever they may be. The last I heard she was bedding some seventeen-year-old artist. Her personal life is not my concern. I'm only glad that she spends very little time here. She prefers the town house most of the time; it allows her to be closer to her friends, shall we say."

Hallie's face was crimson. "I didn't realize." She heard Michael chuckle.

"Of course you didn't. Actually you are probably more innocent than Sky."

"I think that's how I'd like to remain. Has Trent been subjected to this sort of thing for the past two years?"

"I doubt it. I'm sure Lydia ignored him even on the few occasions she was here. Mostly he was alone with

111

servants who cared nothing for what he did or how he was taken care of."

"That's shameful! How could you have allowed it?"

Now Michael looked uncomfortable. "I'm afraid I was too involved in myself for it to occur to me, or I would not have. As it is, I hope I can reverse the damage. Had I been left with that kind of freedom at his age I'd have been an uncontrollable hellion, with a string of bastards to prove it. I find it impossible to imagine why he chose a snobbish demeanor more fitting for Oliver."

Michael stood in the tub, displaying his manhood without warning where the previous second Hallie had been staring into his handsome face. Her head jerked away in surprise. "Haven't you any modesty?"

"There is no such thing between a man and wife. I hope yours dies quickly. I don't appreciate it."

"There isn't much about me that you do appreciate," she said sharply.

"Now, there you're wrong, my love, very, very wrong."

CHAPTER TWENTY

The evening meal was served by three women under the butler's supervision. Hallie feared that Danny's table manners would not be adequate, but he surprised her by being a perfect gentleman, sitting straight in his chair as though he considered this a very important exhibition of his behavior. He intended to please Michael, for Danny watched covertly to be sure the man noticed. Hallie ignored Kent's stares, wondering if she would ever become accustomed to him. She wished fervently that he did not live in this same house.

Lydia's voice broke the silence and granted Hallie's wish. "We'll be leaving for the town house early tomorrow, as I'm sure you've guessed, Michael."

"Yes, I assumed as much."

"I do wish you luck, Hallie," she said, completely confusing her.

"What do you mean?"

A stern look from Michael warned Lydia. "I'm sure my dear brother will tell you when he's ready. At any rate, it will free you of having your sister-in-law in your home. I do run in and out at times, but we'll be in Boston for the most part. Feel free to drop in whenever you want; after all, that is yours too, isn't it, Michael?"

Hallie thought the tone of Lydia's voice was snidely

challenging, but her husband seemed unperturbed. "Yes, it is. You and Oliver are free to get a place of your own at any time, you know," he taunted in return.

"You would like that, wouldn't you?" Lydia's eyes narrowed, and coupled with the large moles on her face she suddenly seemed very wicked, but Hallie realized that was a result of the flickering candlelight. "I am still a Redmond. I will share in the wealth, whether you like it or not, dear. It is as much my due as yours."

"Unfortunately our father did not feel that way, Lydia. You share my wealth because I allow it, no other reason. You should curb your tongue, or you might find yourself in the streets. Or should I say *on* the streets. That might suit you better."

Lydia smiled tautly. "Oh, Michael, you really are such a wit." She rose, beckoning her husband to go with her. "You'll excuse us, Hallie. We have many things to pack for tomorrow. You have my full sympathy for being married to that man."

Hallie was very uncomfortable to have been witness to this family argument. "Does that sort of thing happen often?"

Michael's face was like a storm cloud, but with her words he held his temper in check. He shook his head slowly. "Lydia takes offense to the fact that I inherited everything. It galls her that I disappeared for two years and then came back to claim what she had been pretending was hers. She feels the need to be contrary. Don't let it bother you, for she seems fond of you in her way. Besides, her resentment is reserved for me."

The evening was late when Danny was at last tucked away and Michael and Hallie were back in their room, her trepidations growing strong once again. She hoped in her innocence that the last night's romp would satisfy her husband for some time.

Michael's arms drew up, his back arched as he stretched like a huge lion, pushing off the remnants of a long day. He tossed his jacket and vest over the back of a chair, pulling off his cravat and neckcloth and loosening his shirt until his muscular chest was visible. He moved to the sidetable that held a decanter of brandy and poured himself a snifter. "Would you like a drop of brandy, Hallie?" he offered.

"Yes, thank you," she said formally, needing something to soothe her nerves as well as to delay going to bed.

When he turned to her with the wide crystal glass he frowned slightly. "Why don't you undress and get comfortable?"

"I'm quite comfortable."

"And quite embarrassed. I was hoping that after last night you might be anxious for our lovemaking."

Hallie blushed scarlet. "I had hoped that last night was enough."

"For whom? Certainly not for me, and I doubt for you. Must we play games?"

"I am not playing games! If it's a harlot you want, I simply cannot be that! I suggest you seek one."

"I didn't say I wanted a whore." His piercing blue-gray eyes perused her as though he could see straight through her velvet dress and dozen petticoats. "I could seek out my old mistress, if that's what you want." His words were well calculated.

The color drained from her face. "I prefer anything to your approaching me."

"Do you?" He sipped the brandy, running one hand carelessly through the thick, waving brown hair. Why was she suddenly struck again by his good looks? Why did she find him attractive? He continued calmly, toying with her. "Do you prefer a celibate marriage? For we've already established that I will not allow an indiscretion with Adam. I could accommodate you. I know several very willing women. If you refuse me my rights and in that refuse to bear my heirs, then I will have to seek someone who will. Of course, then you would be expected to raise them, for I would not allow the product of my seed to be raised anywhere but Redland. Would that suit you?"

"You are despicable! I don't care what you do!"

"In that event you would be reduced to housekeeper. Perhaps I would even bring the mother of my children here to live. I don't care about conventions. She could share my bed, and you could serve her."

115

Hallie decided to call his bluff, seeing the desire in his eyes. "I can tolerate many hardships."

Michael laughed boisterously, realizing he had been bested at his own game. "You're quite a spitfire, aren't you? Adam Burgess would never have been enough man for you. Nor would he have appreciated you."

"And you do, I take it?" she bantered.

"Let's just say I find you amusing. Now, shall we go to bed?"

"No, thank you," she said caustically, turning her back to him.

"That is not wise, my love." His voice was conversational. "If you want a fight, I'll be happy to oblige. I was once in the company of a whore who wanted to be forced every time. I learned quite a few interesting things from her, but I doubt that you would appreciate them."

Hallie swallowed hard, fear rising in her throat, for his tone was dangerously calm. Was this the man who had been so gentle the night before? Was he the man she had seen show kindness and reason when she had been so angry this afternoon? Or was he a man who would take her against her will? As her thoughts raced, Hallie did not notice that Michael had moved to stand behind her. She became aware of it only when his lips caressed the side of her neck, softly, teasing.

His voice was low, filled with a passion that seemed contagious. "On the other hand, you could come to me willingly and let me be gentle and teach you some of the nicer ways of lovemaking." He nibbled lightly on her earlobe, his breath warm as he breathed deeply of the sweet scent of her hair. One massive hand ran down her bare arm, sending tingles coursing through her. "The choice is yours."

Why did she have to feel desire for him? Her mind raved. What was more, how could she want him, a man who was little more than a stranger, even if he was her husband? Her breath drew in as Michael's lips worked wonders at her bare shoulders, easing the straight neckline of her gown farther down her arms. And why must thoughts of Adam always plague her? Hallie felt her gown fall loose, the buttons down the back apparently having been unfastened. Her hands caught it at her breasts, barely covering her, yet still she fought for control of what raced through her blood to drive her mad.

Michael left her, dropped the remainder of his clothing easily, ripped back the bed coverings and lay down on his back, displaying his body in all its glory and waited. Hallie's mind fought with her body, yet even that battle was weak, for she still had the threat of Michael forcing her if she refused. Why cause herself unnecessary misery when even she desired only the pleasure? she reasoned.

She turned, deep violet eyes wide with wonder at her own feelings. Still she clasped the gown before her, and seeing Michael, her embarrassment increased, for the room was still brightly lit. He merely stared at her, his desire evident. She moved to blow out the many candles, and only then did he speak. "Leave them, Hallie. It's time to put behind that girlish modesty."

She hesitated. "I can't," she said simply.

"Leave them." His tone held just enough threat for Hallie to comply. Her face flushed scarlet. She walked to the bed, staring down at it as if in a trance, her eyes not raising to Michael, who once again waited silently. She turned her back to him. Knowing the next few moments would destroy all pretense of accepting Michael's lovemaking against her will, she dropped her gown, petticoats and chemise until she stood naked in the golden candlelight, her sleek backside facing her husband. She sat on the edge of the bed, unable to turn and display herself as he did and pulled the sheet to conceal herself as she slid into the bed.

When at last she looked at his face he smiled warmly, his rugged good looks enhanced with the desire for her. "You never fail to amaze me." His lips lowered to hers, softly yet demanding a response Hallie's body was only too willing to give. His tongue teased lightly, and then the kiss deepened. Her hands forgot the sheet as they reached around him, feeling the hard play of muscles in his back and broad shoulders. Suddenly she liked the feel of his skin beneath her fingertips, caressing him, exploring the ridges of bone and solid muscle. She felt the sheet slip below her breasts, but her eyes were closed, and to her it was dark. Michael's hand reached

117

one firm, round globe, kneading, teasing the nipple to tautness, sending Hallie's desire soaring. His mouth lowered to drive her mad with pleasure as his tongue teased lightly.

Hallie's hand moved to his chest, exploring the thick, coarse hair, feeling the hard ridges of scar at his rib. His hand covered hers, leading it slowly down his flat abdomen to the large, pulsating evidence of his need for her. He felt her stiffen, but his grip was insistent, keeping her hand at his most vulnerable spot, showing her what he wanted of her until she took the initiative of exploring him herself, enjoying the feel of her power over him as she elicited the same pleasure. His face rose to hers again, another deep kiss, less gently as his desires soared.

Michael's voice was hoarse with passion. "Open your eyes, love. It's time you watch and see the beauty here."

Her lids moved languidly open as though she could not resist his beckoning. Still her cheeks reddened, leaving her even more lovely as he stared down at her, grinning broadly. His mouth again lowered to her breast, then kissed her flat stomach. "You're lovely everywhere. There is nothing to be ashamed of."

He threw the sheet from her, leaving every part of her bare. His hand ran down her thigh, then back to the most intimate spot, caressing, teasing, driving her wild with a need for him as great as his for her. She was surprised to find that in her passion she forgot modesty, watching his perfect body beside her, reveling in the sight of his mouth and tongue and fingers working their magic over her flesh. It was like a well-orchestrated piece of music, perfect, lilting, lifting every sense on waves of perfect bliss, unequaled pleasure, culminating in an explosive climax of united ecstasy, floating back to comfortable sanity slowly, like a feather falling on a breeze.

Michael held her close, war raging within him. One portion shouted to be harsh and caustic now to prove she held no power over him, the other part wanted to concede that she did and enjoy it, let go of the controls he held over his emotions and let the tide of feeling he felt building flow free. He moved from her, lying once again on his back, his hands clasped behind his head, staring up at the ceiling. He said nothing and then rose and blew out all the candles, returning to the bed, as if anxious for sleep in the aftermath of the conquest.

Michael's actions were as strong as any words he might have spoken, cutting deeply into Hallie, increasing her guilt tenfold. Wasn't it bad enough that she betrayed Adam and her love for him? Why must that betrayal come with the degradation and humiliation of being treated like a used and discarded piece of cloth? Everything welled up inside of her until she could bear it no more. Tears spilled from her eyes unchecked, her breathing came in shallow gasps which she fought unsuccessfully to keep silent. She turned to her side, away from Michael, trying desperately to stop this flow of tears. She felt his hand at her shoulder tentatively, as though unsure of whether to approach her or not. Then without speaking he let a few of his controls over his feelings loosen and he pulled her into his arms, holding her closely as she sobbed inconsolably against this man who had caused her misery.

CHAPTER TWENTY-ONE

October can be a changeable month, one day threatening winter storms, the air crackling with freezing moisture, the sky obscured with dense gray clouds hanging low, ready to burst with drenching rain and sleet. The following day can dawn cloudless, the sky shining brightly though deceivingly, for still it gives off less heat than it appears to hold. Hallie had left the bed as the sun barely rose above the horizon, opening the French doors quietly so as not to awaken Michael, and stepped out onto the balcony. She had pulled a comforter from the back of the day bed and wrapped it around her against the early-morning cold. Her eyes stung from hours of crying, and her exhausted sleep had not allowed her a long enough respite. She stared into the distance, knowing that Boston lay there, just waking and preparing for another busy day. Her heart was a heavy weight in her breast, and she knew that if there were any tears left in her she could summon them in an instant.

Hallie felt cheap and shoddy, as though she had allowed herself to be used for some sordid scene. There was no longer even the thought that what caused her misery was a duty she owed Michael Redmond as his wife. She berated herself for being a fool, suddenly con-

121

vinced that she had been an easy mark, that her refusals and embarrassments had been only tokens. She was disgusted with herself for yielding to animal needs of the flesh. What a horrendous disservice she had done Adam! She had made him a fool, even if he did not realize it. She was convinced she was unworthy of him. Where was her pride?

Hallie's thoughts turned to Michael. How she hated him in that instant! He was a beast, using anything to lure her into soothing his needs, and when it was finished, forgetting she was even alive. How dirty it all seemed now. How ugly! And to make it worse, she had let him comfort her! She had actually allowed him to hold her, to cradle her in those treacherous arms. She could not bear the thought now. She told herself that her only salvation would be to leave. She could not stay and trust herself, she was too attracted to him, found him too handsome, her body enjoyed the pleasures he gave her too much. It all made her easy prey for his deception.

Hallie's thoughts were interrupted by the sound of the doors opening behind her. She did not move, her eyes never leaving the tops of the great trees that stretched before her. Her head was high; she was determined to salvage what she could of her pride. Perhaps then she could come near to deserving Adam and his love again.

Michael stood beside her at the railing for a long moment before he spoke. He was almost as heartsick as she, guilt-ridden for having taken this innocent and shattered her feelings. "You're thinking of leaving, aren't you?" he said quietly.

"No, I've already decided. I'm going to beg Adam to take me, even though I'm not worthy of him, and I hope he will never know that for a short time I was your whore."

Michael's firm jaw clenched as he controlled the fury her words erupted in him. This was no time for his feelings toward Adam Burgess to intrude and tinge what he now needed to do. "I won't let you do that," he said calmly, yet leaving no question as to his determination.

Hate-filled violet eyes turned on him, sparks of fury shooting out at him, the strength of her anger evident.

"Any whore can fill your needs. You don't need to destroy me in the process. Go to that mistress you spoke of last night. Perhaps she is no less animal than you, but I will not be a mere body with which you ease yourself!"

Michael let out a short, derisive, mirthless laugh. "If that were the case, what happened last night would never have been."

"Is that supposed to make sense to me?" she shot back.

Michael sighed, holding onto his patience with an effort, for he saw that nothing would be solved now if his temper rose to meet hers, seeing the stubborn fury that would equal his own and knowing she had more right to it than he. "I know this situation is difficult for you, Hallie, but it isn't all that easy for me either. I'm sorry about last night. I didn't mean to hurt you or offend you. I have discovered that when we make love it is a new experience for me, and I'm not adept at dealing with that fact yet."

"I have no way of understanding what you are talking about."

"I've spent my share of time in women's beds, probably more than my share. It was never as it is between you and me. It never meant anything to me beyond mere satisfaction of a physical need. These past two nights have been difficult, and it's hard for me to accept that what we've shared is important to me in a way I don't understand. I certainly did not expect it, and last night it put me in a state of turmoil for which I punished you. It was unintentional. I didn't turn away from you because I had forgotten your existence but because I couldn't, and that has never happened before."

"This is probably just another ruse to keep me from Adam. You are unscrupulous."

"Yes, I am. But this is not a ruse. Some new dimension is added to my pleasure when we make love. I can't define it, and it unnerves me. Probably as much as it disturbs you that you enjoy it to the extent you do while telling yourself you love Adam Burgess." The words stuck in his throat, the taste of Adam's name as bitter as bile in his mouth. "I can't take you lightly, as I have always been able to before." He did not add that he felt

123

certain the time would come when he could, but it eased his mind to believe it.

"How do I know you're not lying to me?" she asked suspiciously.

"I suppose it's difficult because you've never known another lover. But think of it this way." Michael steeled himself against his next words. "You are convinced that you love Adam, and yet what we have between us is so powerful it transcends that feeling, frees you, and in those moments you belong solely to me. Would a simple, uncomplicated act of sex be able to do that for you?"

Hallie thought it over carefully, wanting to accept this, for it cleansed her of a portion of her guilt. "Are you suggesting that because of that I should remain here and we should continue this?"

"There is no question about that. I won't let you go, and I will not refuse myself the pleasure we share in bed."

"How can you force me to remain, or make love to a woman you know loves another man?"

Michael's face grew tense with anger. Now his blue-gray eyes stared out at nothing, the muscle worked violently in his cheek. "I doubt the sincerity of this love you profess. Still, I can't say it pleases me. In time I trust you will give up that illusion and realize your future lies with me."

"Then you consider love an illusion?"

"I consider it a fleeting emotion, never lasting more than a moment at a time. Certainly never an enduring feeling, nor one to be trusted."

"And that is what you offer me? Practicality?" Her voice held disdain.

"My offer was accepted two years ago. It is now your place to fulfill your half of the bargain. Be glad that at least there is pleasure in it for us both."

"You don't believe it will become a shallow pleasure in time?"

"You're still young, Hallie, and romantic. In time we will share other things that will fill our lives."

"You have it all well planned, don't you?"

"Yes, I suppose I do."

She looked at him with eyes that suddenly looked wise. "I pity you, Michael. There is something very beautiful that you will never experience if you forbid yourself love. But don't expect me to do the same."

"Are you threatening me?"

"Merely stating facts. I cannot be ruled by my flesh and bury my feelings somewhere distant and obscure. I must feel to be alive. I won't refuse myself that."

"I warned you before, Hallie, I will not tolerate infidelity."

"You cannot control the way I feel or whom I love."

"Do you think that perfect feeling for Adam will last long while you're torn apart with wanting me, or while he seeks his solace with other women? Do you envision a holy love from afar, everlasting and pure?" he said sarcastically.

"I only know that I don't envision, nor will I accept, a life void of all feeling, of all love, of everything but carnal pleasure."

"There is something to be said for carnal pleasure."

"But not when that is all you have."

Hallie turned and left the crisp morning air to enter the bedroom again, now warm, for a maid had come in to light a fire while they were on the balcony. Hallie climbed back into the bed, feeling very tired now. She fell asleep watching Michael's back as he remained on the balcony and wondered if he gave her words any thought at all.

CHAPTER TWENTY-TWO

"Oh, Hallie, he's so pretty!" Danny nearly sang in excited praise. "You have to help me! Please!"

Hallie had been about to sit with a book and relax for the remaining hours of the afternoon. After the turmoil of the past night and morning, coupled with the tension-filled lunch during which Michael barely spoke, she felt the need for a little peace and time for herself. Still she smiled indulgently at her brother as he bounced up and down before her.

"I can't catch him by myself! I need another person to help! All you have to do is hold your skirts wide so he'll run my way!"

"Danny," she said patiently, "I don't know what you are talking about."

"A goat, Hallie! A beautiful black goat! I want to catch him and make him my pet, but he's too quick!"

Now she looked skeptical. "Where does this goat belong?"

"It's all right. Farley said if I could catch it I could have it! Oh, please, Hallie, please!"

"Danny, I am not dressed to chase goats through the mud."

"You don't have to chase him! All you have to do is wave your skirts so he runs to me!" he pleaded.

Hallie looked down at her gown. It was an austere brown muslin and not one of her favorites. She could not resist her brother, and she reasoned that it would be good for her, too. She sighed in mock exasperation.

"All right, just this once."

Danny shouted with joy, pulling her arm and racing with Hallie in tow down the hallway, through the kitchen and through the back doorway. Still he pulled her with him until they were well into the forest of trees behind the house. He stopped abruptly, studying the ground as though they were about to venture into a dangerous and vitally important act.

Hallie could see no sign of this infamous goat, but Danny searched among the trees intensely. She smiled at the sight, his enthusiasm infecting her. She was enjoying herself for the first time in days, she thought. Suddenly from behind the enormous trunk of an ancient elm she saw what was merely a flash of black as the billy goat fairly flew from behind the tree.

Danny's voice rose loud, urgent. "There he goes! Run, Hallie, run!"

They took off after the animal at a full sprint. Hallie lifted her wide skirt and innumerable petticoats and followed as fast as her garments allowed. The goat ran in and out among the trees, seeming to enjoy the sport as much as his pursuers. Danny shouted to his sister in complete seriousness, though thrilled with the game, sloshing through mud and fallen leaves, leaping over old dead tree trunks or large fallen branches. Even Hallie was engrossed in the pursuit, her skirts held as high as her arms could manage, her own feet soaked with mud, destroying a pair of brown kid slippers. The goat veered to the right, coming within a short distance of Danny, who lunged with all his might, his arms outstretched only to come up just inches short, face down in the muck of an autumn day after weeks of rain while the goat skipped past, almost gloating over his victory. But the boy was unperturbed by it, jumping up again as though his clothes were not caked with mud, or his face splattered with it.

"Catch him, Danny! He's coming your way now!" Hallie hollered in delight.

But the goat veered again, heading toward the front

of the house. Hallie ran out ahead, thinking to cut off his path, but instead in her hurry she lost her footing and fell backward, her hands sinking in the wet dirt of the drive leading to the house. She laughed, totally caught up in their play now, forgetting all but the goat. She stood again just in time to see Danny's arms close around the small black animal and then lose him as he jumped free, pulling the small boy with him into the mud. Still they had him cornered now. Hallie dropped her skirts and held them wide, flagging them at the goat to send him toward Danny. When the goat came within a short distance Danny jumped at the black fur ball, catching him in his weak grasp. Hallie saw him struggling to keep the animal contained, and laughing, she raced to help, adding her two arms to the fight, the goat kicking mud and muck in all directions, each face receiving what was not already being smeared on their clothes. The goat wiggled and fought to be free, brother and sister laughing as they struggled to hold their quarry. Danny lost his grip first, falling backward and giving the animal the opening he needed. He fairly flew out of Hallie's arms and raced away, far from the muddy scene of the boy and the lady laughing riotously as they sat amid the dirty splendor.

Hallie was the first to stand, pulling Danny up with her. "We had better get back to the house and clean this mess. It will take the rest of the afternoon to get you clean again."

Danny laughed. "Wait 'til you see how you look!" he said, pulling the mud-caked ribbons that had held her hair from their weepy position over her shoulder.

Still holding his hand, Hallie led Danny up the drive at a jaunty pace toward the house. She felt wonderful in spite of her condition.

As they walked, Danny raised large gray eyes to his sister, though the wide grin he was fighting to contain belied his words. "Are you sure you're my sister? You look more like a mud monster!" His laughter burst forward as he broke free of her hand, running like a wild deer for the house.

Hallie picked up her skirts once more and chased him, hooting and hollering as if she was indeed bent on a monstrous attack.

Both revelers came to an abrupt halt as they reached the front stairs leading to the veranda. Danny, having arrived first, stood staring up, his eyes wide with fear. Hallie was only a moment behind and was even less eased by what her eyes lifted to. Then she decided to make the best of it. Long black lashes framed deep violet eyes wide with innocence, and a bright smile spread her sensuous lips. "Hello," she said pleasantly, taking the boy's hand once more.

Michael stared down at his wife sternly, taking in every inch of her mud-splattered gown, torn at one side, her hair in wild disarray and her exquisite face dotted with brown spots. After a pause his voice sounded, low and unpleasant, his eyes turned to the austere-looking woman at his side.

"Emeline, this is my wife, just returned from what appears to have been a mud bath." Again his gaze fell to the two below him. "Hallie, this is my mother's sister, Aunt Emeline. She's come for a visit...to meet you."

Standing stiffly behind Michael and his aunt stood Trent, stifling a satisfied smile.

CHAPTER TWENTY-THREE

Mercy left Hallie to soak in the large brass tub, the water up around her shoulders, steam drifting all about her freshly washed head, her hair piled high and secured with a scarlet ribbon. Her thoughts returned to her husband and the afternoon's surprise. Hallie had not seen Michael since the encounter on the veranda. She had taken Danny to the back door, not wanting to track mud on the Aubusson carpets, leaving her husband and that woman to themselves. She would have been embarrassed had she met only Michael in that grimy condition, but to come face to face with a stranger, and a formidable-looking old matron at that, had unnerved her.

Hallie sighed. At least she had enjoyed herself. She reasoned that if Michael had warned her of his aunt's imminent arrival, she might have been more cautious. What does he expect of me? Hallie wondered. She was young and there was no reason she couldn't romp with her brother occasionally. Was she to become as somber as his aunt? She felt as petulant and defensive as a child. The door to the bedroom opened suddenly, and Hallie slid farther down into the water. Only Michael would enter without knocking. The time of reckoning had come.

Michael's eyes rested on his wife as she bathed, an inviting vision. He had spent the past hour with Emeline and that did not help his mood, but staring at Hallie's slender neck and the creamy white shoulders, his spirits lifted. Emeline had been berating him for marrying Hallie, fueling her ammunition by saying Hallie was an unruly child and not a woman at all. Michael smiled wryly at that thought. Emeline should see her now! He had been sent to deal with his wife's misconduct, but Michael could hardly find a reason for that. She had been alluring even in mud. He pulled a chair to sit at the foot of the tub and stared down at Hallie. "From the way you looked this afternoon I'd have thought a horse trough a more appropriate place for you to bathe."

Hallie lifted her chin defensively. "Why didn't you tell me your aunt was coming here?"

"I intended to. That was what Lydia hinted at last night. I fully intended to warn you, but you'll have to admit we were far from small talk either then or this morning."

"Is she so formidable that I must be warned?"

"I'm afraid so. She can be quite unpleasant."

"I don't suppose her first impression of me will ameliorate that, will it?"

"I doubt if it could have done any further harm to her opinion of you," he said enigmatically.

"Why would she already have formed an opinion of me?"

"It doesn't matter, Hallie. Just bear in mind that regardless of anything she says, you are my wife and this is your home. She is a sour old spinster who can count on one hand the people she has ever been pleased with in her life. Don't let her get the best of you. Now what the hell were you doing this afternoon?"

Hallie smiled sheepishly, refusing to be contrite. "It started out as an easy little game to catch a goat. But the goat outsmarted us."

"Apparently. Do you really think you should be frolicking in the mud with a boy and a goat?"

"I suppose not. But it started perfectly innocently!" she said, seeing he was not actually angry.

"You might temper your exuberance, Hallie. You're

a grown woman now and in time that kind of fun could be hazardous to you. Must I constantly watch over you?"

"No! I'm not a child!"

"Then don't act like one."

The woman who descended the stairs beside Michael Redmond bore only a faint resemblance to the muddy girl of the afternoon. Hallie's hair was piled into a mass of wild ringlets at the crown of her head; fluffy tendrils fell about her face. Her cheeks were flushed from her romp through the cold autumn air, her eyes sparkled. Her gown was a red plaid taffeta; the modest neckline displayed only a glimpse of her shoulders. The bodice was shirred to the waist, and the skirt fell to the floor in a wide circle, supported by ruffled petticoats.

Emeline Watson stood regally at the drawing-room window, her spine ramrod straight. When she heard Michael and Hallie enter the room she turned as though on a pivot, making it appear that her body never moved. Her prematurely gray hair was pulled into a severe knot at the back of her head. Her sharp features brought to mind a hawk, though she was large in stature and weight. Her gown was black, and its only adornment was a small watch, which hung from a black ribbon just beneath her left shoulder. Hallie smiled up at the woman, Hallie's discomfort only increasing as the narrow blue eyes traveled down her body and back up again.

"Hmph!" Emeline snorted derisively, "there is nothing to her! She is a mere child and not a very sturdy one at that. Why, I doubt she will even be able to produce an heir to carry on the Redmond name. But perhaps that is best." Staring at Hallie's face she said, "I suppose she bewitched you, Michael. You Redmond men are inordinately vulnerable to a beautiful face. Fools that you are." Speaking for the first time to Hallie, she did not even pretend kindness. "Well, miss, you resemble your mother in looks."

Hallie stared at her wide-eyed. "Did you know my mother?" she asked, not really certain how to deal with this woman.

"Yes, indeed! I'm sorry to say I did." She swept past them and into the hallway. "I'm quite ready for my evening meal now."

133

Hallie looked questioningly at Michael, who offered only, "I'll make dinner short. The evening will be over before you know it."

"I doubt that very much," Hallie said, as he led her into the dining room.

Emeline refused to speak during the meal. Her demeanor suggested that eating was a crude necessity of the body. When at last the meal was complete and they had returned to the drawing room, Emeline and Michael with their coffee and Hallie with tea, the older woman resumed the monologue she had begun before dinner, as though she had merely paused for a moment.

"I did not know your mother on a friendly basis. But enough. I wonder how much you are like her? How foolish of Michael to marry you, knowing well what we all do."

Now Michael broke in, "That is sufficient, Emeline. This serves no purpose."

"I am simply trying to understand this situation and get to know your wife. It is my duty as the oldest member of this family to question these things."

"Your duty ended at my door."

"Michael, I am only doing what is best. After all, you have married beneath your station." Turning to Hallie she smiled patronizingly, "I do not mean to offend you, of course, this is simply the truth."

"Enough!" Michael's voice rose threateningly. "Hallie is my wife, Emeline. You are a guest in her home. I suggest you use some of those manners you're so proud of!"

The narrow eyes widened at Michael's effrontery. "I will retire and allow you time to regain control of yourself," she said haughtily as she strode from the room and up the stairs.

Hallie was dumbstruck. She could not understand what had provoked such hostility in the woman. Turning to Michael she asked, "What did she mean by those insinuations about my mother?"

Michael sighed impatiently. "She's a bitch, Hallie, and a snob. I'm sure it was no more than her thinking your family is not sufficiently high on her imaginary social ladder. Don't give it another thought."

Hallie was persistent. "But what of her saying how foolish of you to marry me knowing what you all do?"

The brandy snifter he held shattered as he placed it on the tabletop with force. "How the hell do I know what goes on in that woman's mind? Now you know why Lydia leaves when she comes to visit. I will not be questioned about her rantings. Is that clear?"

"I can't imagine why that thought bothers you so. Is there something about my mother or my family of which I am unaware?"

"How would I know?" he said evasively. "Perhaps there is a hidden streak of insanity! Does it matter?"

"It matters to me! I am the one being maligned!"

"It's an old woman's foolishness! Leave it at that!" He strode to the doorway and then turned to Hallie again, this time more calmly. "After your afternoon of play I would think you'd be tired. Shall we follow Emeline's example and go to bed?"

CHAPTER TWENTY-FOUR

November brought snow and colder temperatures. Fall's remnants were hidden beneath a soft white sheet of snow. The ground was covered in a thin layer of glaring white; it was not deep enough to remain on the well-used road that connected Redland with Boston and its suburbs. The icy air was refreshing to Hallie as she sat beside Michael in the elegant brougham, a fur lap robe covering them both. She snuggled deeper into her mink cloak. To keep her hands warm, a prayer-book-shaped hot water bottle made of pottery was buried in the depths of her muff. Her hair was piled beneath a mink hat, leaving only her exquisite features showing, her high cheeks rosy with the chill, her eyes sparkling with pleasure. It had been two long weeks since Emeline's arrival, and Hallie felt as though she had just escaped from prison.

Michael's description of his aunt as *unpleasant* was a gross understatement. She was a venom-tongued battle-ax! She harped and berated and insinuated and insulted until Hallie wanted to hit her or scream or run away. Instead Hallie remained polite, trying to ignore most of what was said. Michael understood, but even his hovering presence did little to distract Emeline and so he had planned this day at the Curtis home, much to Hallie's joy.

Michael and Hallie rode in silence and for once she relished the peace of it, forgetting to feel uncomfortable. Amanda and Jason's home was located near the edge of Boston.

The large Victorian-style house came into view looking warm and inviting, nestled before a backdrop of tall, snow-covered elms, their branches reaching to the clouds like long, icy fingers. Within minutes Hallie was settled before a blazing fire in Amanda's drawing room, and Michael had gone on to join Jason in the city.

Amanda looked tired and drawn, but her eyes still sparkled with happiness so Hallie decided it was simply the strain of advancing pregnancy. The two sipped tea and relaxed.

"It seems like ages since we've seen each other."

"It certainly does! I've been dying to know what's happened to you, but Jason refused to take me to visit. He insisted that we wait until we heard from you— that way we could be certain your honeymoon was over."

Hallie laughed derisively. "It's hardly been that! Two days after the party Michael's Aunt Emeline arrived, and she has been there ever since."

Amanda grimaced. "Jason has told me about Michael's aunt. How long is she staying?"

"I don't know. It's already been too long. She's horrible! I spend all day long listening to her and she is absolutely hateful! I am her main target. For some reason she despised my mother. I am forever hearing her harp on whether or not every small thing I do is like my mother."

"I didn't know she knew your mother."

"Neither did I. Michael says it was a mere social acquaintance, but she talks as though she knew her very well. Or at least well enough to hate her. I can't imagine what my mother could have done to deserve all of this."

"Have you asked Emeline?"

"No! I barely even speak! It would only prolong the misery! I know it's silly, but sometimes I wonder if I am not meant to know what the reason is. Michael evades my questions, and he seems to hover about each time she begins another tirade, almost as though he's making sure she isn't able to tell me!"

Amanda's perfectly shaped eyebrows rose. "Do you think that's possible?"

"I can't think of any reason why. Surely no matter what my mother did to the old viper she deserved it!" They both laughed easily. "How are you feeling, Amanda?"

She shrugged. "I'm fine, I suppose. I just feel so tired all of the time. I'm sure Jason is sick of hearing me complain about it and then fall asleep instantly, anytime of the day or night. I never thought pregnancy would be so hard on a marriage. He's losing patience and there is still so much time left." She sipped her tea. "But I don't want to dwell on this! How are things between you and Michael?"

Hallie shrugged. "I don't know. We're polite. He can be very thoughtful. Today is one of those times. He realized I needed time away from his aunt. He's good to Danny, though he is still a little stiff with him. I suppose we're both trying very hard..." Her voice trailed off.

"But what's wrong?" Amanda saw it clearly.

"I probably shouldn't talk about this, but I'm going to. We were intimate the first two nights. The second night we had what I guess you would consider an argument. I was feeling guilty about being with Michael while feeling the way I do about Adam, and then Michael just turned away from me, as though I had satisfied my obligations and he had forgotten I was even there! I felt so cheap! And then the next morning he told me he couldn't deal with my being important to him, at least in bed. He said he didn't believe in love and that I was just a romantic, that in time we would share other things to fill our lives. I told him I pitied him if he never allowed himself to feel love. He hasn't come near me since."

"Have you come to care for him, Hallie?"

She thought for a long moment. "I don't love him. I still feel so strongly about Adam. But I don't hate him either." Her face flushed scarlet. "I did enjoy his making love to me, and then afterward I felt just awful about it. I suppose I feel more confusion than anything. Especially now, I don't understand why he has stopped wanting me, if perhaps he's found me repulsive in some way. I tell myself that if I truly love Adam I should be grateful that he leaves me alone. But then I reason that I want as normal a life as possible and it seems I can have that only with Michael, but not if I disgust him in some way. On the other hand, it was I who kept telling him I did not want to be intimate with him." She sighed. "You see how mixed up it all is?"

"I certainly do. I don't suppose you could just ask him what is going on, could you?"

"No!"

"Well, if he's still kind to you and he still shares your bed and doesn't seek someone else, I would guess that he isn't repulsed by you, though I doubt that he is in any case. Perhaps you injured his pride."

"I suppose that is possible. I was quite blunt about wanting to leave him that following morning and go to Adam."

"Hallie! Would you like to have Michael make love to you and pretend you were another woman?"

"I don't suppose I would."

"Well, he probably believes that is what you do."

Hallie shook her head. "I don't think so. His arrogance is awfully hard to shake. I guess I won't know what it is until he tells me." She sipped her tea, thinking of Adam. At other times she fought fairly successfully to keep him from her thoughts. "How is Adam?" she finally broke down, wanting to know, yet feeling it was unwise to ask.

"Should we talk about him?" Amanda asked.

"Probably not. But I can't help myself."

"He's all right," Amanda hedged, not wanting to add to her friend's already heavy thoughts. "He's working with Dr. Hathaway, keeping himself busy enough for two men. He works in the office all day and then offers his time to the hospital in the evenings."

"You're avoiding telling me something. Is he still seeing Belinda Scott?"

"Oh, Hallie, we shouldn't talk about this!" Amanda's tone was pleading. "It can only hurt you."

"Then he is."

"He isn't serious. She throws herself at him."

140

"It's all right, Amanda. He has every right to enjoy a woman's company. I must learn not to let it hurt me. I'm certain it is harder for him to think of me married. After all, there is no question as to what is happening in my personal life. At least I can fool myself by thinking he is pining away for me."

Hallie stood to stare out the bay window at the snow that had begun to fall. She wished that she believed her own words.

Amanda left the room to speak with her cook about lunch as Hallie remained at the glass, lost in her thoughts and fears. The rider she watched approach was unmistakable to her. Her mind quickly calculated how long it would be before Michael and Jason came for the midday meal. She realized they were courting danger even in just a short meeting, for her husband could return any moment. Still, she could not refuse herself even a minute alone with him.

Hallie didn't feel the freezing air as she stood in the open doorway, drinking in the sight of Adam as he dismounted, his own face red with the cold, his smile wide. He took both of her hands in his as they stood together in the entranceway.

"I knew you were coming today, Hallie. I just had to see you, to talk to you! I hope you don't mind."

She returned his smile. "Of course I don't mind! I've thought about you so often, worried about you, wanted to see you, too."

"I hope that means we can remain friends. If I can't have you as my wife, I would at least like to offer friendship and an apt listener if you ever need an ear."

"Let's sit down. I want so badly to spend some time with you," she said, feeling guilty even as the words left her mouth.

When they were seated on the sofa Adam leaned forward, pulling Hallie to him. His eyes searched her expression for some encouragement and he found what he sought, for she could not hide the love she felt for him, the longing, the pain. "I'm so sorry about my behavior at that party. My mind wasn't functioning."

"I know. I never blamed you. It was hard for me to watch you with Belinda Scott. I know it was no easier for you to see me with Michael."

Adam's face grew red, but now the weather had nothing to do with it. His own guilt over what had developed from that night was great. "It was cruel of me, I know."

Pushed by a need she did not understand, Hallie said, "Are you involved with her now?" She knew the answer before he spoke as Adam fidgeted uncomfortably.

"Not actually involved, Hallie. I need someone, don't you see? I'm so lonely without you."

"Yes," she said simply, the pain stabbing at her. "I understand it, Adam, and I certainly don't begrudge you. I have no hold over you anymore."

"But you do! My God, how you do! I still love you, Hallie, as much as before. I'm insane with wanting you! Have you thought about leaving him, of coming away with me?"

Now her smile was sad. Her eyes were bright with moisture. "I've thought about it a hundred times. I even came very near to doing it once. But it just can't be done, Adam. No matter what we feel for one another, I have a responsibility to Michael. I can't leave him."

"You're falling in love with him, aren't you?" he accused.

The raven curls danced as she shook her head rapidly. "I care for him as I would for any acquaintance, perhaps a bit more, but it is not love. My heart belongs to you, though I try to fight that."

"It isn't right, you know. We were meant to be together."

"Nothing is to be done about that."

"How does he treat you? Is he kind?"

"Yes. He has been understanding of many things. I was afraid he would be quite harsh, but he hasn't. In fact, my being here today is one of the thoughtful things he's done. He arranged this for me to be free of his aunt."

"Then he's trying to win you that way, is he?"

"Adam, he does not need to win me. I am already his wife."

"In every way?" he asked, not able to stop himself.

Now it was Hallie's turn to blush. "I am his wife," she repeated, her voice nearly inaudible. Then with more strength she said, "I can't talk about this with you. We must not ask personal questions of each other, if not because it is wrong, then because neither of us can bear the truth."

"You're right, of course. Can we meet again? Is there a time you can be free of him?"

"I will not be unfaithful, Adam," she warned.

"I don't ask that of you! I only want to see you, to talk, to know how you are. Is that so much?"

"I don't know how I could possibly arrange it." Hallie's teeth tugged at her bottom lip in indecision. She knew she should not, that it would not be fair to Michael, yet she was torn by her love for Adam. "Tomorrow," she said at last, her voice a bare whisper. "Michael is bringing me back into town. I'll be at the Old Corner Book Store at about this time. Beyond that I can't promise you anything, Adam."

"It's enough for now."

"Oh, my God! Adam! I thought I heard your voice!" Amanda stood in the doorway, her face ashen. "You must leave! Michael and Jason have just come up the back road! Please!"

Resentment was plain on his face, but in deference to his sister, Adam rose. His lips brushed across Hallie's hands quickly, his eyes reluctant to leave her lovely face. "I'll be there, Hallie!"

Adam turned and strode deliberately from the house, refusing to make haste. He would not run from Michael Redmond.

CHAPTER TWENTY-FIVE

Boston was bustling despite the cold of November. Businessmen and factory workers rushed through the cobbled streets to reach their destinations. Knitted caps pulled down over ears, rough-hewn clothes and makeshift coats differed drastically from the fine broadcloth suits, woolen cloaks and flare-crowned beaver hats of the prosperous. It was most often an accurate assumption that those dressed more for survival than for style were of Irish descent. Since the potato famine of 1845 and 1846, Boston had become home to thousands of Irish immigrants, docking in the harbor after fleeing poverty and starvation only to find much the same thing as they arrived with little or no money in a foreign land.

Hallie could not help but think of the unfairness of life as she rode through the streets in her husband's opulent carriage, tucked beneath fur robes. How many children are freezing? she wondered and could not help the guilt that came with the thought. Michael sat beside her pretending to listen to Emeline's monologue on those same Irish people. She viewed them as rodents invading her well-stocked pantry. Only a few even made good servants, in her opinion, they should be shipped out

West, it was wide open there, or so people said, certainly no one of any standing resided in the barren wastelands of the West, so it would be a perfect place for the Irish and their uncivilized ways.

As the Old Corner Book Store came into view, Hallie's spirits rose. She was to have time to browse among the books and to purchase one while Michael accompanied his aunt shopping for "appropriate" clothing for Danny and a new suit for Trent. It would be a glorious few hours to Hallie, who had always loved whiling away her time there. And today her anticipation was made stronger by the hope that she would see Adam again.

The atmosphere of the Old Corner Book Store pleased Hallie as much as the books themselves.

It was a place for the lonely to find company, if only in book form, a place where a person might discover all sorts of things, even that other people shared their opinions or experiences or reflections, perhaps ideals. It was a place to taste other lives, to find a bit of freedom from problems, to escape faults, to eavesdrop on conversations or even to join a heated debate about who best depicted the romantic experience.

Hallie thought that it was the richest place in the world and even hours spent there were not enough, but it helped to think of bringing just a tiny crumb of it home with her. Her time would be well spent as she searched the shelves and tables for volumes by Dumas or Dickens or Thackeray. She had her heart set on Charlotte Brontë's *Jane Eyre*, for Hallie was fond of works by the Brontë sisters, appreciating their imagination and insight into their characters. She would settle for *Wuthering Heights*, but she preferred the other. Her guilt at meeting Adam convinced her that she must not leave empty-handed, lest it arouse Michael's suspicions. She hated this feeling of deception, but her feelings for Adam pushed her on.

Hallie searched each aisle and table and chair quickly to be certain Adam had not yet arrived. Then she set about finding her book, hoping that at least would ease her tension.

So intent was she in the books, her leatherbound volume of *Jane Eyre* tucked beneath her arm, that she did not even feel the brown eyes that watched her, never

146

leaving her even when she moved to an odd angle. She did not notice that he drew nearer, slowly. Only when his voice sounded behind her, a low, soft whisper, did she forget her books.

Adam's smile was warm, relaxed, reveling in this that had not left his thoughts since leaving Amanda's house the day before. His tone was teasing. "If I didn't know better I'd think you had completely forgotten I was to be here today. You look for all the world as if you only came here for a book."

Hallie had to force her hands to remain clasped around her purchase as she wished to reach a loving finger to brush his blond hair from his forehead. It was obvious that he had run quite a distance in his eagerness to be with her.

Seeing two vacant chairs in a corner Hallie said, "Let's sit there." She knew her face was flushed. She had felt this same way at fourteen when she had feared her feelings for Adam would be discovered and ridiculed.

A light laugh sounded in Adam's throat as they sat facing one another. "My God, it feels good to be with you!"

Hallie merely smiled, wishing she could feel the same, unhindered by her treacherous conscience.

Adam reached into his vest pocket and drew out a small velvet box. He held it in his fist, pressed to his heart as though she were a child he was teasing with a prize. "I know your first reaction to this will be to refuse it." His eyes searched her face as if a clue could be found there for a way to convince her to take it. Then he continued, "Please, Hallie, if you still care for me at all, accept it. It is no more than a token, a small bond to remind you that I will always be here to help you if you need me. Perhaps as a small remembrance of what we have shared, as well."

Hallie's feelings raged within her as she opened the small box, finding a ring inside, a thin, silver band with a pear-shaped diamond in the center. There was no question that this would have been her wedding ring had she married Adam. She fought back tears. How could she take this? How could she refuse it? "Oh,

Adam!" Her voice was small and sad, echoing her torment. "It just isn't right! I know what this is!"

Adam's hand clasped Hallie's tenderly, closing it around the ring. "It is but a keepsake, a trinket. I don't expect you to wear it. I only want you to have it. I can give you nothing else. At least this can be kept easily. Please, Hallie."

The pleading tone magnified the pain Hallie already felt. "You know I shouldn't. You know we're not being fair!"

"Was it fair of him to do all he has?"

"The injustice was my grandmother's, Adam. I cannot punish Michael for that."

"I'm not speaking of punishing him! He need never even know you have it. Or if he finds it you can tell him it was a gift from long ago, or that it was your mother's."

"Lies and deceit! I can't do that, Adam!"

"It is the only thing I ask of you, Hallie. It is more for me, a balm to my wounds, if you prefer. Please keep it! I need to know you have it."

Hallie was torn. She knew it was wrong, yet she could not refuse this small thing. "I will keep it, Adam, but please don't do this to me again. I cannot bear it."

He smiled, watching her replace the ring in the box and then open her bag to put it away. "Don't look so sad. I wanted this to be a happy time."

Hallie managed a smile, though her doubts still glistened in her eyes. Before she could speak Adam rushed on, his voice and countenance no longer pleading, yet still she saw the intensity he felt.

"I spent all of last night thinking of ways we could meet again." His fingers pressed to her lips to stop her response. "I know! Only as friends. I want at least to be friends in the way we were before, a brother to you if you would rather. I have come up with an idea that is quite within the limits of convention. Do you think you could come to the office to help us with our paperwork? Even one day a week would be something!"

Hallie sighed in fear and frustration. "I'll try! Do you think you can arrange for me to do that?"

"You're certainly more qualified than most. Have

you forgotten all of those hours we spent together over my medical books?"

"Of course not! How could I forget? But I have no formal training."

"You'll be fine. Let me worry about that. You take care of convincing Michael."

"That won't be an easy task." She paused a moment. "You must understand, though, Adam, there can be nothing else between us."

"For now." Adam helped her on with her coat, his hands lingering longer than necessary at her small shoulders. He could not resist lowering his lips to her ear, softly, warmly caressing. His voice when he spoke was a breathy whisper. "I love you, Hallie. I will always love you. He can never say that to you."

Hallie moved from his grip, fearing she would lose her own control. Too many of her feelings for him had risen to the surface. She knew she was in danger of succumbing to anything he wanted of her. "Please don't! You do me no good this way, Adam!"

She hurried through the store and out onto the sidewalk, seeking the cold air to cool her own raging emotions. Adam followed, standing with her, fighting to keep his hands from her. "I'm sorry! I promise you it won't happen again!"

"Now, isn't that interesting." The change in the grating voice inside the carriage brought Michael's full attention to the scene on the sidewalk. His eyes widened, and the muscle in his cheek immediately began to pulsate. "I warned you, Michael. She is her mother's daughter! A trollop! Right on the street! For all you know she never even went into that book store! She probably planned this meeting. It's obvious he is her lover. Look at their faces! Why, it is obscene! Mark my words, young man, she is just as her mother was! She'll be putting off bastards on your good name!"

Michael's voice boomed through the carriage. "Enough!" He threw the door wide, banging it against the back side of the brougham so hard the entire coach shook. He lunged from the interior, his rage obvious in every inch of his body.

Hallie looked up with a start, and fear coursed through her. Michael's thick brown hair flew back from

149

his face, his blue-gray eyes sparkled with fury, his firm jaw clenched, his full lips were a thin line of anger as he bounded from the carriage. In that instant she thought that this must be what it was like to stare into the face of Satan himself.

CHAPTER TWENTY-SIX

Hallie felt Michael's fingers dig painfully into her arm, pulling her away from Adam to stand to one side and behind him. His voice had the ring of a steel blade. "You slimy bastard! What the hell do you think you're doing?"

"Michael..." Hallie's voice began, pleading for reason, but Adam interrupted her, seeming to relish Michael's anger.

"Unfortunately, I was merely talking to Hallie. I'd have done much more, but she refused," Adam taunted.

"You're pushing your luck, Burgess. The debt for saving my life cannot spare you forever. Don't tempt me further."

"You're a fool, Redmond. A blind, jealous fool. Hallie is loyal to you, though I can't imagine why. I suppose she had too much pride to be anything else. But then when that quality isn't a part of you it is difficult for you to recognize it in others. A bit hypocritical of you, isn't it? You could hardly be considered loyal to Hallie, could you?"

"It is none of your damn business! I'm concerned only with the present, and that means you stay the hell away from my wife!"

"Are you threatened by a mere friendship?"

151

"I'm not threatened by anything and certainly not by the likes of you. I would say there is a question as to your own scruples, dear Adam, or are you pretending that the little affair you're having with Belinda Scott is innocent?"

Adam no longer held control of his temper to taunt Michael. "You'll never win, Redmond. She belongs to me no matter what you do, and she always will."

A snide smile pulled one side of Michael's mouth. "Now, there you're wrong." He turned and pulled Hallie with him to the waiting carriage, pushing his way through the crowd that had gathered around them to witness the fracas. No one among them was brave enough to block the path of the large man, his face alive with a violence none would dare tempt.

Emeline sat with her nose lifted in the air. "Just like her mother," she said pointedly as the carriage jolted to a start again.

Michael turned his angry visage to his aunt, his voice low and threatening. "Keep your mouth shut!" For once the woman held her opinions to herself.

Hallie's temper grew with every step Michael pulled her. By the time they reached the master bedroom and the door was slammed with force behind them, she was as angry as he. Her cloak, hat and gloves were thrown furiously into a chair. Her violet eyes sparkled, her delicate features hardened as she lifted her pert nose in the air. "Must you always act like a jackass whenever you see Adam?"

"Pardon me! I didn't mean to behave poorly before your beloved Adam!" he mocked. "The next time I see him fondling my wife on a street corner I will simply beg his pardon."

"He was not fondling me! He was not touching me!"

"Wasn't he? Then the intimacy was thick enough to be evident without the contact."

"Intimacy? Two friends talking in a public place is hardly intimate!"

"I wasn't aware that your feelings had changed to mere friendship!"

"What do you want from me? I cannot change the feelings that grew throughout the years in a matter of

152

weeks because some perfect stranger strolls into my life and announces he is my husband. I am doing the best I can!"

"Well, it isn't good enough! I will not stand for your meeting with him!"

"You will have to. I have accepted an offer to work one day each week in Dr. Hathaway's office."

"What!" Michael's voice rose loud now, leaving no one in the house in any doubt that the master and mistress were at war.

"You heard me. They need the help, and I am qualified."

"Do you expect me to sit back and swallow this sham?"

"It is no sham! It is perfectly innocent."

"Nothing concerning you and Adam Burgess is innocent, perfectly or otherwise."

"Dr. Hathaway will be there the entire time, as well as a roomful of patients."

"No! Absolutely not! Your place is here, not working at some asinine job with Burgess! What do I have to do, keep you pregnant every year to keep you where you belong?"

"That's hardly likely at this point, is it?" Her words flowed through anger, not even tinged with common sense or inhibitions, suddenly letting slip that which had plagued her for the past weeks.

Michael stared at her for a long moment. When he spoke he was only slightly calmer. "Is that it? I haven't satisfied your needs, and you've gone to seek them with him?"

Now Hallie realized what she had done. Her face flushed scarlet beneath her rage. "Of course not!"

"He is a poor substitute, Hallie. He hadn't even the courage to stand up for himself and for you when I came for you that first day. I would never have given you up so easily. He's not man enough to satisfy you, if that's what you're planning."

"I'm not planning anything!" Now she shouted to the rafters. "Adam is my friend! Yes, I cared for him, still care for him! But that must be put behind me now! There is nothing to any of what you suspect."

"No? Then why were you with him today?"

"We met accidentally." Hallie hated the lie.

153

"Oh? What a coincidence! And you just happened to repeat the discussion of your leaving me, no doubt."

"What does it matter what we discussed? I didn't leave with Adam, nor did I arrange to have an affair with him." Hallie was calming herself with effort, realizing the direction of this argument could lead her to reveal more about her feelings than she cared to. Then she remembered Adam's words about Michael's loyalty. Her breath drew in quickly as her thoughts fell together. She turned to face the wall, not wanting him to see the effect it had on her. Her voice was soft, ultimately controlled, her slender back straight. "Perhaps you are so ready to believe the worst because you're guilty yourself."

"Now, what the hell is that supposed to mean?"

"You said you would seek your mistress. I can only assume after these past weeks that that is exactly what you've done."

The thought of Hallie being jealous eased a great deal of Michael's rage, and a wicked smile spread across his face as he stared at her back. "How do you like the thought, Hallie? Not terribly pleasant, is it? To think of being made a fool, of your own husband going behind your back to have an intimate relationship with another woman? Does that please you?" he taunted.

"No!" she shouted before she could catch herself.

"But you expect me to be tolerant of that possibility between you and Adam! Don't you think you're asking a great deal?"

"Is it true? Have you sought a mistress?" she asked defensively, ignoring his words.

"Is it true of you and Burgess?" he returned.

No anger was left in Hallie. She felt drained of all emotion, all rage. "No, it is not. He is a friend now and hè will always be, no matter what you want, but he is not my lover." When Michael did not offer the answer to her question, she persisted. For some reason she did not understand, she desperately wanted to know. "And you?" she said simply, her tone aloof.

Michael chuckled. "No, I have not been in touch with the woman since before we were married. But that does not mean I can't seek her out or find a replacement if you ever give me cause."

"Then what did Adam mean when he said you had not been loyal, if not that?"

"I was hardly celibate during the two years between the wedding and the day I returned."

"Proud of that, are you?" she said cuttingly.

"As proud as you are of marrying a man you hoped would be dead soon enough to free you for Adam, and then counting the days until you could accomplish that."

"I did nothing to be ashamed of. You know well that I came to you a virgin."

"Physically. What was in your mind was hardly pure, my love. I think it's best for us both to leave the past alone."

CHAPTER TWENTY-SEVEN

The evening meal was to be a family affair. Danny was dressed in his new black suit. The jacket was short, over a vest with lapels. He wore striped trousers and a black cravat, and his hair was parted severely to one side and slicked down with a great deal of oil. He fidgeted uncomfortably, pulling at the stiff collar and stretching his neck, his face contorted in a grimace. He grumbled to himself as he preceded Michael and Hallie down the stairs.

Michael laughed. "Now, that is a fitting punishment for a prankster if ever I've seen one."

Oliver sat in the drawing room, having arrived a short time earlier. After searching the room, Hallie addressed him. "Where is Lydia?"

He shrugged nonchalantly, his lecherous eyes on the bodice of her burgundy velvet gown. "She went upstairs to fetch something she had forgotten, I believe. I don't watch her every move."

Hallie was slightly surprised as Trent appeared beside her, shyly holding out a small glass of wine. She smiled warmly in thanks but then glanced apologetically at Michael, whom Trent had refused even to greet.

Moments later Lydia entered the room. "Hello, everyone!" she said brightly, scanning all the faces present before she went on. "Oh, good! I made it before Emeline could see I was late. At least we won't have to hear her tardiness lecture!"

Before another word was spoken Emeline's large frame filled the doorway. "It is about time you paid your aunt a visit, Lydia. I do not appreciate your leaving just before I appear. You should have been here to guard your family name." She glared in Hallie's direction.

Lydia laughed lightly. "Why, Aunt Emeline, Hallie is the model of propriety! What is there about her for you to distrust? It is absurd." She smiled at Hallie, clearly understanding what the younger woman was enduring. "I'm afraid I must apologize for my dear aunt, Hallie. She thinks too highly of us Redmonds."

"You needn't apologize for me, young lady! There is no shame in being cautious about your family's name and reputation. After all, you did enough damage marrying who you did. That alone should have made Michael think more carefully about the woman he took as his bride. Look at what has happened to you. Oliver hasn't a penny to his name!" It was apparently an old, oft-repeated refrain, for neither Lydia nor Oliver even flinched.

Dismissing the subject, Emeline turned to the squirming Danny. "Now, stop that! You have been left as a heathen for too long. You do not even know how to behave as a gentleman! Stand and let me look at you." She studied him seriously. "I suppose you look acceptable. Your appearance would be greatly improved if you would not slouch and hang your head as though someone were about to hit you." Turning to Michael, she continued her tirade. "You must take a hand with this boy. He needs a man's guidance, though perhaps that job should be left to Trent! He has turned out wonderfully in spite of you all." Trent's only response to her compliment was to turn to Michael with a self-satisfied smirk, as though some secret battle had been won.

Michael smiled understandingly at Danny and ignored Trent. Offering his arm to Hallie Michael said, "Shall we go in now? I've had a day that left me quite hungry, I find."

The dinner conversation was scant, for with every subject came a new flurry of comments from Emeline. Only Lydia seemed able to volley her aunt's unceasing harping, and Hallie envied her this talent and her obvious lack of concern over the older woman's opinions. Still Lydia and Oliver beat a hasty retreat when the meal was concluded, citing the weather as the reason. As they donned their cloaks Lydia smiled sympathetically at Hallie.

"I've spent many hours in the company of Emeline. The best you can hope for is a short visit."

"She seems to have settled in permanently," Hallie answered miserably.

Lydia laughed, the high, lilting sound floating throughout the entrance hall. "That's common. But she always leaves. You're welcome to stay at the town house with us. Why don't you come in for a few days of shopping? I have a new dressmaker who is divine! And the Thanksgiving parties will be starting soon."

Michael had overheard the conversation as he approached. Taking pity on his wife, he said kindly, "Would you like that, Hallie? I have some business to tend, and we could stay in the city for about a week."

Now she smiled brightly. "I would like that very much! Danny could visit with my grandmother, as she has asked. But what will Emeline say to everyone leaving her?"

"Nothing pleasant, but then that won't be a change. I'll take care of it."

The day had ended much better than Hallie had expected. Michael was downstairs giving instructions to Farley to prepare for their departure the next day. She had already asked Mercy to pack and now sat in bed with her new book, her raven curls falling down her back, the high lace collar of her nightgown framing her perfect features. The day's unpleasantness was put behind her. As she opened her book, she pushed away her painful thoughts of Adam.

159

Michael entered the room quietly, but Hallie paid little attention. The nights had fallen into a routine; each disrobed and donned nightclothes silently, then entered the bed, he to his side and she to hers, as though no one else were in the room. Sometimes they exchanged a comment, but most often they remained silent until they fell asleep.

Tonight Hallie did not take notice of the fact that Michael's blue-gray eyes never left her as he blew out all of the candles except the one on the table beside the bed. She did not even lift her deep violet eyes from the pages of *Jane Eyre* when he began to shed his clothing, though he stood very near the bed.

Michael slid into bed beside her, staring at her for a time as though feasting upon her beauty. He leaned over, kissing her bare arm lightly, the dark, full moustache he had recently grown tickling her arm. Hallie's eyes widened, but she did not look at him. She was embarrassed to think that he approached her because of what she had said that afternoon, as if she had demanded it of him. With the second insistent kiss she could pretend ignorance no more.

Hallie's voice was soft, sweet to his ear. "Michael, this is not necessary."

"Oh, but it is."

"I won't seek a lover because you no longer find me desirable."

Michael rolled to his back laughing. "What makes you think I don't find you desirable?"

She shrugged. "We don't have to discuss it."

"Yes, we do. Now, what on earth would make you feel that way?"

She blushed becomingly. "It has been some time."

"That it has! Did it occur to you that there might be another reason?"

"Yes, that you have a mistress."

"Has no other reason crossed your mind?"

"I hardly have a sophisticated knowledge of men," she said defensively, embarrassed.

Again he laughed, enjoying her innocence. "You have an adequate amount, my love. It has nothing to do with any of that."

"Then what is it?" she asked softly.

160

"I was waiting for you to be ready again."

"I don't understand."

"After the last time, for which I take complete blame for being a jackass, your feelings for me were far from good, were they?"

She shook her head, the light catching a sparkle in her eyes beneath dark, sooty lashes.

"Well, had I approached you then it would have to have been with force, I'll wager, and you would have submitted with no response whatsoever. I did not want you that way. It was too good before to have it destroyed by pushing before you were ready. I wanted that whole ugly mess to be out of your mind. I don't want it to stand between us." Now he moved to her again, kissing the side of her neck, brushing her hair aside to free her ear. "Do you think that can be now, love?" He breathed huskily.

"I don't know," she said, though he felt her relax, become more soft beside him.

Michael tossed the book to the floor and pulled Hallie to lie beside him, his lips hungrily finding hers. His hands played in the silken mass of her hair, his tongue teased gently. Hallie felt herself slipping into desire for him, realizing how much she had missed this intimacy. She breathed deeply, as though her exhaled breath washed the guilt and inhibitions from her body. She felt herself yield to the hard expanse of his powerful body pressed tightly to her; her mouth softened to return his kiss.

Michael felt her response. His hand lowered to one round breast, teasing, tempting, sending delight through every inch of her flesh. Hallie's hand explored his hard man's body, reveling in the sensations of his flesh on hers, the feel of his body beneath her fingertips. They searched one another, learning what pleased, what sent the other to new heights of enjoyment, lost for a time in the feelings aroused by the other. Theirs was a perfect pleasure leading to a perfect union of bliss and a mindless explosion of passion. They were swept higher and higher until their bodies locked as though fused together, no longer two separate people. When the waters of pleasure had stilled, Michael was reluctant to leave the warmth of his wife. He rolled, pulling her with him to his side, still joined. He held her closely, thinking of nothing but how good he felt, forgetting any worry about how much this small waif meant to him. His last thought before he dropped into peaceful sleep, his wife cradled in his arms, was how wrong Adam Burgess was. Hallie did not belong to the tall, lanky blond anymore, whether they knew it or not. Michael felt certain at that instant between full consciousness and sleep that given time she would belong totally to him, body and mind.

CHAPTER TWENTY-EIGHT

Redmond Shipping Lines occupied a large section of the buildings and warehouses on the wharves of Boston Harbor. Few lines equaled them. Their only real competition was from the Cunard Steamship Line. Since 1840 the Cunard Line had been sailing between Boston and England. That fact had spurred the senior Michael Redmond to convert to steam, though most of their ships were still equipped with sails for greater speed. The presence of sails left them a measure of security in case of a malfunctioning engine. Some of the ships were equipped with side wheels as well. The company had also begun to switch from hulls of wood to iron; these were supplied by Curtis Ship Builders.

Michael paced the office on the ground floor of the main warehouse, having spent three hours reviewing the records of these past two years. Now he waited for Farley to bring Jason and then plotted how he would handle the subsequent meeting with Oliver. Michael would have to appease his brother-in-law while taking him from any position of power. The warehouses were all nearly bare; ordinarily they were stocked high with quantities of tea, spices, sugar, nuts, silks, rice, bananas and anything else thought to be salable. Since Oliver had taken on running the lines the stocks could barely meet the demands; he mismanaged every aspect of the business.

Michael was pulled from his thoughts by a knock on the office door that announced Farley and Jason; both were brushing snow from their shoulders and immediately sought the warmth of the iron stove. Michael did not hesitate to broach the subject he had been mulling over for months.

"I'm going to need two clippers, Jason, as soon as you can get them in the water."

Jason's eyes widened questioningly. "What now, Michael?"

"I'm going to start shipping passengers to California. Rumors about gold there have finally been verified. There's money to be made just hauling Boston's finest. A lot of the Irish here haven't been able to make a living, and since the war things haven't been good for a lot of other people. The plight of Hallie's family is a common one; there just isn't the means for making money here that there was before. Most men will lose sight of everything but the thought of picking up gold nuggets on the streets. It's a juicy carrot in the face of a starving mule, and I mean to cash in on it."

Jason smiled. "You wouldn't like a partner in that venture, would you?"

Michael laughed. "As a matter of fact, I was hoping it would whet your appetite. I could certainly use those clippers at, say, half cash, half ownership to Jason Curtis?"

The slightly shorter, stocky man put out his hand. "You've got yourself a partner."

Oliver Kent pranced into the room without warning. He flipped his velvet cape from his shoulders and removed his hat with the same flare. He was dressed in a purple velvet suit, a yellow silk shirt and a black cravat. He sneered at Farley. "I suppose you have run to the master with tales of woe." Turning to Michael he said, even less courteously, "I did not appreciate your setting this watchdog on me, so I arranged it to be impossible."

"So I've heard," Michael said, not hiding his contempt.

"Well, let's get on with it. Someone awaits my charms."

Michael refused to rise to Oliver's bait. "I would merely like an explanation as to how you managed to put this business into such peril," he said bluntly.

Oliver shrugged, unconcerned. "A matter of circumstances and poor judgment. There were difficulties in buying from your usual sources, some stores were lost at sea to rot or poor care and there was Titus Lunt, a poor businessman and a fearful captain. He was afraid of overloading his ship. Of course, I fired him." He was obviously sure of himself and unconcerned with his mistakes. "I discussed all of this with Lydia, Michael. You will find she knows all of the problems and advised me as to what to do. And after all, she does deserve half of the Redmond estate. If you choose to control the land she should at least be allowed a portion of the shipping."

Michael breathed deeply, consciously controlling his temper and the urge to tell this fop what he could do with his opinions. "I don't agree with that, nor did my father, but this is not the time to discuss it. Be warned, Oliver, that I own this business and I will be in charge of it completely from this day on. Your job henceforth is simply to do the tasks I set for you. Is that clear?"

One eyebrow rose and an evil glint lit Oliver's pale eyes. "Very clear. I can't say Lydia will be pleased to hear it."

"I'm sure she won't. But that is how it is."

Oliver stood, flinging his cape back around his narrow shoulders. "Good day, gentlemen." He swept out of the room as though making a dramatic stage exit, leaving Michael, Farley and Jason staring after him.

CHAPTER TWENTY-NINE

Hallie sat before her dressing table gathering her toiletries as the last articles to be packed. She did not know what Michael had told his aunt about their spending a week in Boston, but Emeline had actually been quiet at breakfast, speaking only when absolutely necessary. Disapproval had been evident in every muscle of her hawkish face as she stared haughtily above the heads of everyone present.

Hallie had enjoyed a rare, friendly conversation with Trent in the silence Emeline left. Hallie did not understand what affected his moods, for when she least expected it, he actually initiated pleasant chats. Of course, they were few, and in the remaining times he was as sullen as he had been, but Hallie felt encouraged. What remained unchanged was his contempt-filled watchfulness of Michael. Regardless of what her husband ventured with his young brother it was never accepted. Trent seemed completely unwilling to make even an attempt at civility to his brother.

Downstairs Michael entered, his brow knitted as his mind continued the thoughts of business and Oliver Kent and his sister. Halfway up the stairs he encountered Emeline and forced his thoughts back to the present. She scowled at him but refused to speak further on the subject of Michael's imminent departure. "Well, what did you find out? Did that fool Oliver make a mess of things?" she asked bluntly.

Michael stared at her in surprise. "How did you know what I was doing this morning? I did not even tell Hallie."

"Hmph! You should know by now that there is never a secret from servants. That Farley man finally told me you were in town at the warehouses after I nearly had to threaten him. It was only a matter of common sense to figure the rest of it out. I can't imagine why you allowed that imbecile to oversee any portion of this business."

"Let's not be uncharitable, Emeline. He is Lydia's husband, after all, and you know how she feels about not having inherited anything."

"Well, the little twit should have married money! It is her own fault. How badly did he hurt the business?"

Michael considered whether to be honest with his aunt, but he thought better of it, knowing she needed no more subjects to rail about. He shrugged and said, "He did me no good, that's for certain. Still, he will have to do better under my supervision."

"The only thing that fop is capable of learning is the latest way to tie his cravat. But it is your problem, not mine," she said huffily, passing Michael to descend the remaining steps.

The French doors were opened wide when Michael entered his room; the cold air that entered negated the heat from the flames in the hearth. He moved to close them and then saw Hallie standing at the banister, her face lifted to the sky.

"What are you doing?" he asked, startling her into a shriek.

"Oh, Michael! You frightened me nearly to death!"

"I didn't mean to. Why are you out there?"

"I was merely enjoying the crispness in the air. Can we leave now?"

Michael laughed. "Should I be insulted that you wish to escape my aunt so desperately, or flattered that you're anxious to come away with me?"

She smiled brilliantly. "I hope you're flattered. I certainly would not want to offend you on behalf of your aunt," she teased.

Again he laughed at her, extending his hand for her to take. "You're a terrible liar, Hallie, but I will pretend I haven't noticed."

The Redmond town house was similar to that of Hallie's grandmother, but it was on Beacon Street and was considerably larger and more elaborately appointed. It was too dim for Hallie's taste; most of the rooms were done very masculinely in heavy woods and leather, the draperies all deep brown velvets. It looked as though a man had chosen it, furnished it and never allowed the touch of a woman. She was glad that this was not her home. She wondered how Lydia, with her penchant for bright colors, could tolerate this place.

When they arrived, only Sky was there. The young girl bowed her head shyly, her eyes lowered to the floor, saying she had been instructed to help them settle in. Suddenly Michael's hand went to her chin, raising her face to the light in the dim entrance hall. The bruise that darkened her cheekbone was in the waning stages, a green-gold glint the only remnants of what had to have been a severe blow.

Michael scowled. "Who did this to you, Sky?"

The Indian girl kept her eyes averted. "No one, sir," she whispered.

"You don't have to put up with this, you know. I'll find you another job where you would not be hurt. All you have to do is say so."

She shook her head.

Michael did not press it. He said only, "I'll help you anytime, Sky. You need only ask."

She left them without a word.

Hallie swallowed thickly. She knew Oliver Kent's lechery only too well, but this added a new dimension to his evilness. "You can't just ignore this, Michael! Speak to him!"

"It might not have been Oliver who hurt her."

"Surely you don't think Lydia would do such a thing?"

"I don't know what to think about my sister or her husband. But I can do nothing but offer the girl assistance. To be honest, I'm not too sure she would find a

169

better situation. And right now I have enough of Lydia's temper to deal with."

The evening was spent quietly as Lydia and Oliver never appeared. Michael was in such a hurry to retire that Hallie thought he must be very tired from the long day. She was surprised at herself and a little embarrassed by the disappointment that thought roused in her. She fought futilely in her mind, telling herself she could not want Michael so much when she still loved Adam. But the desire coursing through her waged a strong battle. By the time she had let her gown fall, leaving her in a transparent chemise and billowing petticoats, Michael was already in bed. She sighed silently, thinking he must be uncommonly fatigued.

His deep hoarse voice surprised her. "If you don't hurry, my love, I may not be able to wait, and you will find your petticoats torn to shreds."

She fought a smile, and her spirits lifted unaccountably. "I assumed you were tired," she said simply.

"Still so naïve?" he teased, then after watching her closely he laughed uproariously. "You have a very telling face, Hallie. I would bet my fortune on the fact that you were quite unhappy by the prospect of a night without lovemaking. Now you look positively anxious!"

She blushed deeply as he read her thoughts completely.

"Well, get those damn clothes off and get into bed! You won't find me having any difficulty complying!"

Hallie smiled. She decided it was time to acknowledge the fact that she enjoyed Michael's making love to her. It did not alter her feelings for Adam, she reasoned with herself, but still this aspect of their marriage was quite pleasant. She told herself to count her blessings. It would have been horrible to find this all disgusting. It was part of her duty, she told herself; she might at least enjoy it. With that she slid into the bed and into her husband's warm arms at the same time, and her mind immediately closed the discussion in favor of the pleasures that already lit flames in her blood.

CHAPTER THIRTY

Etta Riley was in the drawing room when Hallie entered her house. Etta's eyes widened at the sight of her granddaughter. "Hallie! I didn't know you were coming this early, dear! Come and sit down. I was just about to set out the tea service." The white-haired woman moved about the room, straightening a family portrait and centering a vase on the table. "I should be angry with you for not visiting me sooner! I send you off with a man you don't even know, and you don't have the courtesy to inform me of your welfare!" she reprimanded with a smile, mischief still in her eyes.

"It would be just what you deserved if Danny and I disappeared!" Hallie teased her.

"Tell me how you are faring."

"I'm doing well under the circumstances. This is hardly an ideal situation."

"Yes, but you're young, and there is more adventure this way."

"I don't know that I would call it adventure, but my life is definitely not dull. How have you been?"

She smiled, her wrinkled old face alight. "I'm doing very well for myself. In fact, I have a suitor."

"You do?! Who is he?"

"Now, Hallie, the field is narrow! There aren't many men my age still alive."

Hallie laughed. "Must I guess? Knowing you, it would not surprise me if the man were my age."

Now Etta laughed. "Men your age are too inexperienced and unworldly, my dear. It seems that Dr. Hathaway has taken an interest in me. I had him come around a week or so ago for a cold, and now he stops by almost every day. I quite enjoy it."

"I'm sure you do! Is this serious?" Hallie teased.

"My dear, at our age there is not time for frivolity. Still, there is nothing much to tell yet. I'd rather hear about your new life."

"There is not much to tell on that count either. We've just escaped Michael's aunt for a week."

Etta Riley raised her eyes heavenward. "Emeline Watson," she breathed. "Now, that is a rude awakening for a honeymoon."

"Do you know her?"

"Of course. I wish I did not."

"She despises Mother. Do you understand that?"

"Yes, I do, but there is no good in digging up old trouble. Is she punishing you for what she did not like in your mother?"

"She punishes everyone for everything."

"She is nothing like Michael's mother was."

"Did you know her, as well?"

"Only in passing. She was a lovely woman, kind and good-natured."

"Michael does not speak of her. I don't remember hearing how she died."

Etta thought a moment. "I believe it was soon after Trent was born. As I recall, nothing much was ever said about it. She was ill for some time before; in fact, the gossips could never understand how she could ever have had him at all."

A knock at the front door interrupted the conversation. Etta waved Hallie back into her chair as she went to answer it. Hallie's eyes widened at the voice she heard in the entrance hall, her gaze riveted in that direction in time to see Adam Burgess come through the doorway, her grandmother close behind him with a mischievous grin on her features.

"I invited Adam to tea."

"Hello, Hallie. I hope you don't mind."

"No, of course not. I was just unprepared."

Her grandmother smiled at her. "I have some things to tend for Danny. Please serve the tea, dear, and entertain Adam for me." She left the room quickly, leaving Hallie and Adam alone as she had obviously planned to do.

"I'm beginning to believe my grandmother has a bit of the devil in her. Did you know I was to be here today, Adam?"

He laughed, sitting across from her, though they were separated by such a small space their knees nearly touched. Hallie thought what a handsome man he was, his features well defined beneath striking blond hair. "She was very honest with me, as a matter of fact. She wondered if I would be willing to come today in case you were in need of my services. I believe she meant as a lover, but she only alluded to that portion of it."

Hallie blushed scarlet. It seemed Etta had put her in another uncomfortable situation. "I'm sorry, Adam. She doesn't realize what she is doing."

"Don't apologize to me. I was perfectly willing."

"We've already discussed this," she reminded him.

Adam laughed. He was not so intense today, more his old self, the carefree man she had fallen in love with so long ago. It made this all more difficult. "I am here as your friend, so don't worry about it. I came only to talk to you and have tea."

"I don't know what to say. Our subjects suddenly seem limited."

"It will pass. Did you speak with Michael about coming to help us at the office?"

"Yes. I'm afraid it is not possible."

"You mean he won't allow it, don't you?"

"It isn't that way, Adam."

"I see. Now you're defending him."

"You must be fair! He doesn't want us to be together like that."

"Not very sure of you, is he?"

"Things are fragile between us, Adam. Right now I have to keep things as uncomplicated as possible. Be-

173

sides, you have to admit it was hardly innocent on either of our parts."

Adam smiled wickedly, his brown eyes devouring her. "Certainly not on mine! Tell me, Hallie," he began, a confusing twinkle in his eye, "might we have an affair after all?"

"Adam!" she said, horrified.

"Well, really, Hallie, we wouldn't be the first. We love each other and there is only that one obstacle standing in our way. We could be very discreet. I'm certainly willing to take the risk."

"No! I could not do that!"

"Give me one good reason why not."

"Because I just couldn't! It's not right!"

"That isn't a good reason."

"I owe him!"

"And you are paying your debt by being his wife. You owe yourself something, too."

"If nothing else, Adam, I would die with worry over conceiving a child."

"That might be the answer to our prayers! If you carried my child, surely the proud Michael Redmond would free you."

"I have never heard you talk like this before, Adam."

"I have never been this desperate before."

Hallie was silent for a time, her mind racing. Her feelings for Adam were so strong and now, as he faced her, she was tempted. Yet something held her back— the reminder of the nights of bliss with Michael. Her cheeks flushed becomingly and Adam smiled, waiting, hoping she would agree. "I simply cannot do that! It is despicable! We could never live with ourselves, Adam, and you know it! I think you're teasing me."

"Never! I'm quite serious. I won't push you, Hallie, but if you ever want me, in that way or any other, I am here. I'll take you any way I can have you."

Adam stood, taking Hallie's hand and pulling her with him. "I love you, Hallie. You cannot go on forever pretending with him. And when you finally tire of it, I'll be waiting." He pulled her into his arms, his lips capturing hers in a fiercely passionate kiss. Hallie's head reeled; her senses were confused, pleasure, guilt, love, fear all flooded her being.

"Don't let me interrupt." Hallie lunged away from Adam's embrace, hearing Lydia's distinctive voice from the doorway. She looked into the amused face of her sister-in-law.

"I was slightly ahead of myself this afternoon. I didn't think you would mind if I came for you a little early, but I had no idea!" She laughed.

"It isn't what you think, Lydia!" Hallie was horrified, her face ashen.

Adam stepped in now, bowing gallantly. "Mrs. Kent, you have just intruded upon my forcing myself on Hallie. I assure you she is quite innocent and I accosted her."

The lilting sound of Lydia's laughter rang through the room. "Well, feel free to accost me at any time!" Smiling conspiratorially at Hallie she said, "Don't look so upset! Do you expect me to run to Michael with the news? It serves him right. Certainly you don't expect him to be faithful, dear, so why should you be? Why let yourself be tied down to one man and a passel of brats? A smart woman never lets herself get caught like that. Why, if I could not have my little peccadilloes I would positively die of boredom!"

"It isn't like that, Lydia! I have every intention of being loyal to Michael. I have just explained that to Adam!"

"How dull. Well, Dr. Burgess, perhaps if you are persistent you will convince her. Good luck." She sighed in exasperation. "Well, if nothing interesting is going on here, we might as well go on to the dressmaker." Lydia smiled at Adam enticingly. "Remember my offer, Dr. Burgess. What I walked in on looked very amusing."

Hallie was torn between resentment and mortification, but there seemed to be nothing she could do to rectify the situation save to remove Lydia from Adam's presence. Hallie prayed that this information would not make its way back to Michael.

CHAPTER THIRTY-ONE

Hallie sat watching Michael finish his grooming for the party they were to attend. He looked very handsome in his deep blue tail suit, with an ivory silk shirt and a black cravat. His moustache enhanced his good looks, lending a rakish hint to his features. Her desire for him rose even now, and suddenly the thought of having an affair with Adam seemed ludicrous. She had no desire to stray from Michael's bed or jeopardize that in which she found so much pleasure. She wondered if her love for Adam was becoming platonic, yet she realized with a blush that it had been far from that in the afternoon just past. Dragging her thoughts from that direction, she stood to check her own appearance.

Hallie's gown was a deep violet velvet, which accentuated the color of her eyes. The neckline was acceptably low, falling off creamy shoulders into long sleeves that ended in points over the tops of her mitted hands. The bodice descended to a narrow waist, where a white satin ribbon wrapped around her, dividing the gown just as the skirt billowed in a wide circle from there to the floor. She tried to tuck a few stray wisps at her temples back into the bunches of curls above either ear but found it impossible. She turned again toward Mi-

177

chael as he tied his cravat carelessly, but then she decided to await him in the drawing room.

Hallie descended the stairs, believing the lower level of the house was deserted. The only light came from one small candle in the drawing room, leaving the room engulfed in deep shadows. It was from one of these that Oliver stepped, blocking the doorway behind Hallie. "Have you perchance come searching for me?"

"I was hoping not to have the misfortune of seeing you all week, as a matter of fact."

"You're such a tease! But I don't mind. I always like a bit of a challenge."

Hallie decided the repetition of this conversation was futile. She moved to pass him and return to the bedroom and Michael's safe presence, but Oliver stepped quickly in front of her, again blocking her path, his face a mask of leering desire. "Excuse me," she said, mocking Emeline's best shrewish tone.

"Pure as the driven snow, are you?" he mocked. "Those are my favorite little temptresses. I love bringing them to their knees, hearing them beg." He laughed, showing his large teeth. His hands grasped her shoulders painfully, long nails digging into her tender flesh. Hallie struggled to be free of his grasp, but he held her tighter. She raised one foot suddenly and stomped as hard as she could on his instep. In that instant of surprise his grip loosened and Hallie ran to the opposite end of the room, hoping to draw him away from the entrance so she might dash through to safety.

Oliver Kent merely laughed. "I enjoy a little pain in my play. You will have to come near to get out of this room, my little dove. I can be a patient man." He drew a lacy handkerchief from the pocket of his pink vest, dabbing at his ugly mouth.

Hallie stood near the fireplace. She seized a poker, wielding it as she approached the man. "Move out of my way or I will skewer you!" she said dangerously, her eyes sparkling with a mixture of fear and anger. She knew she must make her stand clear or he would never leave her alone. Calling for Michael would only postpone this.

Taking her more seriously, Oliver sneered. "If it's a

fight you want, to be taken by force, I'm perfectly will-ing."

"I will not be taken by you in any way! Get away from that door and don't ever touch me again. I'll see you maimed or dead before I'll endure even your touch. Now, move!" She jabbed at him with the poker, leaving no question as to the seriousness of her intent.

From behind Oliver came a loud laugh as Michael stepped into view. "It appears my wife has bested you, Kent. Will you concede the doorway to her?"

Seeing his defeat he stepped aside, sneering angrily. Now Michael stepped up to face Oliver, and before the pink-plumed fowl realized it, Michael's heavy fist had landed squarely on his jaw, sending him sprawling to the floor, blood spurting from his mouth. The face that stared down at him was no longer amused. "The next time I hear of your bothering my wife I will leave you unfit for any woman—or man, for that matter. And I'll enjoy doing it. Don't think for a minute that being my sister's husband will save your skin." Michael took the poker from Hallie's grasp and threw it too close to Oliver for comfort. Then he smiled at his wife and offered her his arm. As he put the beaver-fur-lined cloak about her shoulders he said, "I really didn't know whether to step in or just let you at him. In the end I thought I had better save his neck." He laughed, his own raging anger dying rapidly.

Hallie was slowly recovering her composure. "That man is despicable! Where on earth did Lydia ever find him? And why did she marry him?"

"No one knows where she found him, and she ob-viously did not marry out of undying love. I believe he is a mere convenience."

Hallie did not speak, thinking that after all, she was no more than that. Then to herself, in what she thought was inaudible to Michael, she said, "The Redmonds have a penchant for that."

"I did not marry you out of convenience, Hallie. Lord knows it was anything but that." He smiled devilishly at her. "I would say it was more out of necessity."

The party was a dull affair, and Hallie was grateful that Amanda had come after all. She had not planned

179

to, but after Hallie's persuasion she had decided the change of scenery would do her good. She looked radiant, if a little weary; her pregnancy was becoming evident in spite of the billowing folds of her high-waisted gown. Amanda knew that the staid tongues of Boston would wag tomorrow about her being seen in public, but for tonight she did not care.

Amanda and Hallie sat together most of the evening gossiping and talking of their lives. Neither cared that they did not make an effort to speak with the others, for it seemed to each that they had not spent enough time together in recent weeks. Their friendship was a source of mutual strength and support.

At last Michael and Jason approached them, signaling that enough time had passed to leave without seeming rude. The two couples stood in a dimly lit section of the entrance hall where they were afforded a clear view of Adam Burgess and Belinda Scott being welcomed. Hallie stiffened beneath her husband's hands. Adam was being loud and boisterous, unlike himself, his hands nearly pawing Belinda Scott, who seemed to enjoy it all.

"Have to apologize for being so late, Stanley, old boy. We were tied up at Belinda's house and snuck away first chance we got."

Belinda smiled affectionately up at Adam, pulling his arm to her breast. "Adam has been imbibing a bit heavily tonight," she said, giggling.

Amanda was the first to step from the shadows, embarrassed for her brother. "Then perhaps he should come home with us. We were just leaving," she said coldly.

"'lo, Mandy. The party's just startin'! You can't leave already!"

When Jason, Michael and Hallie joined Amanda, however, Adam's high spirits plummeted. Ignoring everyone else, he spoke only to Hallie. "I didn't think you would be here tonight. You didn't tell me that this afternoon."

Hallie's features froze; she thought that her heart must have stopped. She felt Michael tense beside her. "We were just leaving, Adam. Good night," she managed, moving past Adam and a gloating Belinda Scott.

With no thought to anyone else Adam followed her,

his hands reaching her shoulders to turn her to face him. Hallie saw his misery in his features. "Don't leave! Please! Belinda doesn't matter to me! If I had known you were coming tonight I would never have brought her! Please! Just stay for one dance!"

"Oh, Adam! I can't! I hate to see you like this!" Lanterns hung around the porch, casting dim light, but it seemed to Hallie that she saw Adam's eyes fill with tears.

"I can't stand this!" Adam fairly shouted. Hallie knew his controls were drowned in alcohol. "I need you! I'm dying inside, Hallie! I'll do anything! Whatever he wants! Anything so we can be together!"

Michael's voice sounded as he stepped from the house and heard Adam's words. He pulled Hallie to his side, his grip tight and unyielding. "You've lost, Doctor, and you're dangerously near to being disgusting."

Hallie watched Adam as Michael nearly dragged her to the waiting carriage. She felt Adam's agony as her own; she could not bear to see him like this. She saw Adam's hand move to wipe the moisture from his eyes. The feelings it evoked in her to watch this were torture, and Hallie closed her own lids tightly, hoping to shut out the pain that welled up within her as well as the desperate frustration.

Michael waited only until the carriage door had slammed closed behind him to speak. "I thought you spent the day with your grandmother and Lydia?" he demanded angrily.

"I did."

"Then how did you meet Burgess again?"

"My grandmother invited him for tea."

"For exactly what purpose?"

Hallie sighed. Would these scenes never cease? "I suppose she felt guilty for her part in this whole thing and thought to offer me the opportunity to see Adam. She is an old woman, Michael. Sometimes she doesn't think clearly."

"It seems there is no end to the help you two receive in your deceptions."

"Please, Michael! Must we go through all of this again? I told Adam I was not interested, and then I made it quite clear to my grandmother that she was

181

not to do it again. You cannot keep me locked in a cage so that I never see the man again the rest of my life. You will simply have to find a way of dealing with Adam's presence in Boston."

"Or perhaps I will just have to brand you as mine and then follow you everywhere." He pulled her with force into his embrace, kissing her fiercely, passionately. Why do I hate Adam Burgess so violently? he asked himself. And why is his very exsistence in Hallie's life so maddening?

"You're mine, Hallie. And dammit, that will never change! If you care at all for Adam, you'll set him free, for he has no hope in this matter. I'll see him destroyed before I allow him a moment's pleasure with you."

CHAPTER THIRTY-TWO

The sun shone brightly the day before Hallie and Michael were to return to Redland. It was a beautiful fall day, the snow melting off the ground within the first few hours of warm sunshine. People strolled briskly down the cobbled streets, appreciating some of the last moments of autumn before being inundated with winter. Hallie was happy to be out about town, sitting beside her handsome husband. She loved watching the people, studying them all. She loved the sights, the sounds, the smells. Even the clattering tipcarts and drays were pleasing to her. Their first stop was Lydia's dressmaker, Madame Payne. Hallie had ordered two gowns that she wanted to take back to Redland. She was embarrassed when the woman returned to the front of the shop with six boys following her, their arms laden with boxes. Hallie did not want Michael to think she had been so outrageously extravagant with his money.

"There has been a mistake, madame! I ordered only two gowns!" she said hurriedly.

"It's all right, Hallie," Michael said from behind her.

Thinking he meant to show his generosity by approving this huge expenditure, Hallie was quick to explain. "I honestly did not order all of this! Two gowns will be quite enough!"

"But madame..." The dressmaker looked from one to the other in confusion. "They are yours!"

"No, they are not!" she said firmly.

Michael finally stepped between the two women, his hand restraining Hallie from her determined refusal. "They *are* yours, Hallie."

"I ordered only two dresses, Michael!" she insisted.

"Yes, but I ordered the rest."

"There is a fortune in clothes here."

"Only a small one. You lived too frugally these past years. I knew you would never take it upon yourself to order a suitable wardrobe. Knowing you, it would be another debt you felt you had to repay."

Hallie smiled brilliantly, her excitement mounting as her imagination raced with wonder at what might fill these parcels. She stood and kissed him lightly, surprising them both. "Thank you. It was very thoughtful of you."

The luncheon that followed was nothing less than elegant. They dined at a very elegant restaurant, a place nearly all in frosted glass, with large winter plants hanging from the ceiling and forming partitions for privacy between each table. The chairs were high-backed around tables covered with snowy linen cloths; china, crystal and silver glittered. Men in well-tailored, expensive suits escorted ladies in silks, satins and furs. The maitre d' hôtel's greeting made it clear that Michael was well known here. Hallie saw that many eyes followed them, the ladies smiling Michael's way while the gentlemen were appreciative of her beauty. She breathed a sigh of relief that she had taken such pains with her appearance this morning. What a haughty bunch it was, she thought, and how she loved being there at that moment, with the most handsome man in the room.

They dined on steaming beef and barley soup, chunks of carrots and potatoes swimming in the thick broth. Fresh lobster was the main course, boiled and placed before them with a draft of melted butter and lemon wedges. The bread was freshly baked and rivaled the best Matilda had ever made. By the time dessert was offered, Hallie was stuffed. She requested only tea and sat back, feeling like a glutton.

Michael smiled warmly across the table, his interest

solely on Hallie, as though they were alone in this splendid place. "Did you enjoy your meal?" he teased, knowing well that she did.

She laughed. "I will never fit into any of my new gowns if I come here often. It is a wonderful place."

Their eyes locked; blue-gray held tightly to deep violet. Michael was in awe of her beauty. His desires for her rose even now, and he fought to hold himself in check. This infatuation was lasting longer than he had anticipated. He had expected to have had his fill of her by now, but still he craved more.

The intimate glance was disturbed by a high, melodic voice. "Michael! I didn't know you were back!" the woman exclaimed, her face reflecting her worship of the man at whom she stared.

Hallie's eyes lifted to a beautiful woman in her mid-twenties, with eyes of sable brown and hair of flowing gold. Her features were exquisite, her skin like fine china. Hallie's spirits dropped markedly as she realized from the look on Michael's face that this was no light friendship.

Michael became slightly uncomfortable, "Hello, Maeve."

The woman clearly felt more intimate with Michael then his mere words indicated. Hallie noticed that the woman's breasts pushed well past the décolletage of even this day dress and suddenly had a good idea as to what had caused Lydia's initial remarks that first night. This woman was any man's dream, and Hallie suddenly felt as though she were living another nightmare.

"Why didn't you send me word?" the woman demanded. "You know I always spend this time of year in New York with my aunt; I've waited for you on pins and needles! How could you not let me know you were back?" she questioned, obviously feeling she had that right over Michael.

He cleared his throat, speaking hesitantly, "Maeve, this is my wife. Hallie, this is my friend Maeve Carson." The words fell heavily.

Maeve was clearly thunderstruck. Hallie could not quite gain control of her thoughts or her emotions as blinding jealousy coursed through her. The lovely woman drew herself back as though struck, her pain obvious. Tears filled her eyes, glistening there as she fought to hold them back. "I see." Her voice was a whisper. "I didn't know."

Hallie was intensely uncomfortable in the presence of the woman's misery. That was eased as Maeve Carson ran from the restaurant, nearly colliding with a waiter in her haste. Hallie suddenly felt as hurt as that woman must have. Not only did Hallie feel horribly betrayed and humiliated, but there was also a sharp pain at the thought that Michael had been seriously involved with a woman of this caliber. Never in her imaginings had she pictured the woman who might have been Michael's mistress as a woman of breeding and beauty. She had always pictured harlots, or women of easy virtue, at best someone of Belinda Scott's type. Maeve Carson was nothing like any of those, and she so obviously loved Michael. How must he feel about her? Surely such a woman as that had not allowed an intimate relationship to develop, had not let herself be mistress to a man who merely used her to ease his baser needs. Hallie's self-confidence plummeted with her spirits and she suddenly longed for the safe, secure love of Adam Burgess.

CHAPTER THIRTY-THREE

"Are we going to keep up this silence forever, or would you like to talk about what's bothering you?" Michael said as the door to their bedroom was closed behind them.

Hallie had not said a word since meeting Maeve Carson. It had been a necessary silence for her as she fought the raging emotions and held back tears of her own. She worried that once relaxed she would run to Adam and beg him to take her from this situation, protect her, for she was not strong enough to continue that which suddenly seemed a farce. She swallowed with effort, hoping she could speak without losing her control. "What do you suppose is bothering me?" she managed, her voice small.

"I'm certain I could not guess. We had a perfectly nice morning, shared a lovely meal and one introduction to a woman I have known for years sends you into some mood I cannot fathom."

Hallie's head shook, and she swallowed with difficulty. "Maeve Carson is the mistress you threaten me with, isn't she? And she is in love with you." Her tone was soft, matter-of-fact. "I can't help but question what feelings you have for her."

Michael's jaw clenched, and dark brows drew down

over steely blue-gray eyes. He preferred a tirade to this overly quiet response. She seemed overwhelmed with shock. He could not help feeling he had struck a vulnerable chord and left her in a daze of what appeared to be pain. After a long pause he spoke, his voice deep. "All right, Hallie. Maeve Carson was my mistress."

Again she spoke as if to herself. "My God, how cheap you make me. I feel more the mistress. She is no whore, that's obvious. The bond between you must have been deep. Instead you married me, wanting her all the time."

"It isn't like that, Hallie."

Her words seemed to ramble. "I could have been happy with Adam. He loved me. He would have cherished me. Instead I must be the shackle about your neck that keeps you separated from the woman you love. My God, what you've done to me." Her anguish was plain. Tears fell unchecked as she stared up at him, violet eyes wide, raven hair flowing to frame a face as ashen as any Michael had ever seen. What he had intended to be a pleasant day of courting to make up for that which they had both missed before their marriage had turned into a hellish scene of misery.

His voice was calm. "You're wrong in what you're thinking."

"Am I? I suppose you're going to tell me Maeve Carson is not in love with you. That she wasn't your mistress."

"No, I'm not going to tell you either of those things because they are both the truth."

Hallie's eyes closed as though she had been struck anew, the tears falling from beneath thick black lashes. Her eyes opened again and she walked to the door, the last remnants of her control lost. "I can't do this! I won't! I want to be away from this!"

Michael caught her before she reached the door, his powerful hands at her shoulders. He shook her gently just once. "Dammit! Don't do this, Hallie. I'll explain it to you if you will only listen to me."

"I don't want to hear it. I can't bear a life as a mere convenience to a man who loves another woman."

"There was no bond between Maeve Carson and me beyond the bed. I suppose she did love me, perhaps still does, but the feeling is not reciprocated! I had no intention of marrying her, regardless of what she thought. As for you, you are neither a shackle about my neck nor a mere convenience! Dammit! This is a marriage, as much as any you will find. You are my wife in every sense, and you will so remain until one of us dies. There will be children, my children, and a life together and it's time you accept that and forget what might have been with that bastard Burgess."

"Can you forget what might have been with Maeve Carson?"

"That, Hallie, depends entirely on you."

The remaining afternoon and evening were spent quietly as Hallie stayed in the bedroom alone, Michael having left the house. She ate none of the food Mercy brought up on a tray. Hallie's mind was in despair, her heart heavy with jealousy and concern. Could she believe him? She didn't know. But what troubled her most was how deeply it hurt her to think Michael was in love with another woman. Why should it matter? Because it did! Her mind argued irrationally with her emotions, and the result was misery. She wondered where he was now. Had he gone to explain the situation to Maeve Carson? Had he gone to console her? He had never left Hallie for so long a time without so much as a hint as to where he would be. Hallie's whole being ached. It was odd, she thought, that it was more painful to think of Michael with Maeve than it was to think of Adam with Belinda.

When at last Hallie heard Michael return, it was well into the morning. She stood at the window, staring down at the snowflakes as they hit the sill and melted with the heat that was retained there from the warm day. She pulled her robe closer about her body, as if that would aid her in facing her husband and her suspicions of where he had been.

Michael said nothing at first, only partially surprised to see Hallie awake. When he had shed his clothing and gotten into bed he spoke, his voice calm, quiet. "I have spent this afternoon and evening with Jason Curtis," he said in response to her unspoken question. Still Hallie did not turn, uncertain as to whether he spoke the truth or not. After a time his voice sounded again. "Come to bed, Hallie. This is doing neither of us any good."

"I can't," she said simply, thinking that if he had been making love to Maeve Carson these past hours she could not bear to share his bed now.

"Why can't you?" he said gently.

"It would do nothing but begin anew if I were to answer that."

"I would be a fool to tell you I had just spent so much time with the husband of your best friend if it weren't so," he said reasonably.

"Perhaps Jason would verify your story even if it were not so."

"I'm certain that he would. But I am just as certain that Amanda would not, and she was in and out often enough to know I was there the entire time. Your jealousy is not reason enough to send me to Maeve, Hallie. It will take more than that. If the truth be told, I am glad you're jealous of her. If nothing else, perhaps in the future you will show a little more understanding of my feelings about Adam Burgess."

Now Hallie turned to face him, her back against the cold windowpane. Her eyes, wide and beseeching, searched his handsome face. "Are you telling me the truth?"

"Yes. You may verify it tomorrow when you see Amanda."

"I thought we were leaving tomorrow?"

"I've made plans with Jason and Amanda. You are to spend tomorrow helping her pack while I take Danny and Mercy back home. Then in the afternoon Jason will bring you all to Redland. They'll be staying with us for a few days. We thought it might do you both some good."

"Thank you," she said simply.

"Now will you come to bed?"

Hallie blew out the candles and climbed into the high feather tick beside her husband. He pulled her to lie beside him, her head resting on his powerful shoulder, one hand on his bare chest. His lips lightly brushed the top of her head. "Sweet dreams, Hallie."

CHAPTER THIRTY-FOUR

The day was overcast but neither Hallie nor Amanda noticed. Both were in high spirits as they packed Amanda's belongings for her short visit to Redland. It was indeed just what each needed at that particular moment. They laughed gaily, teasing one another and gossiping, thoroughly enjoying their task as it brought back memories of other times they had worked together. Amanda had assured Hallie within the first five minutes of their visit that Michael had been with Jason the entire time he had professed; that knowledge eased Hallie's mind considerably. Hallie did impressions of Emeline to warn Amanda of what she would encounter, and both young women laughed until their eyes teared.

Suddenly Amanda stopped. Her face paled, her hand moved to her abdomen. Seeing her action Hallie, too, stopped, concern edging her voice. "What is it, Amanda?"

"A sharp pain. It's passed now. Probably nothing."

Hallie's brows furrowed. "Perhaps we should send for Adam or Dr. Hathaway."

Her friend smiled brightly. "No! I'm fine now! It must have just been a spasm." They continued their packing more quietly now as Hallie watched Amanda, worried over her condition.

"Do you think you will be all right to ride all the way to Redland?"

"Of course I will. It's early yet for the baby, at least two months. Jason says I'm bringing fatigue on myself by fretting so much. I'm beginning to think he's right. I feel wonderful today."

Hallie smiled her relief and they resumed their light chatter. The noon meal was a light repast, as only a young servant was left in the house. Jason had given all the rest a few days' vacation while they were to be away. They shared a thin broth and then a meat pie from the previous day, with cake and tea to follow. Amanda seemed uncomfortable, shifting in her chair, but her features were calm, so Hallie did not question her. No sense in alarming her for no reason, she thought. As they climbed the stairs to finish packing, Amanda suddenly doubled over, one arm clasping her protruding middle, the other grasping Hallie's arm for support so as not to fall back down the stairs. As quickly as the pain began it subsided, and Amanda lifted fearful eyes to her friend.

"Something is wrong, Hallie. It's too early!"

Hallie helped her up the remaining steps, trying hard to keep herself calm when fear coursed through her veins. "It will be all right, Amanda! I'll send for the doctor! Perhaps it's a false alarm; that sometimes happens, you know. Or maybe you just miscalculated." Neither woman was calmed by her words; each feared the worst was happening.

Once she had Amanda in bed, Hallie moved down the stairs at a full run, her skirts held high. Her heart beat rapidly, but she refused to acknowledge her darkest thoughts. She found the serving girl in the kitchen just preparing to leave for the day as she had been told she could. Hallie breathed a sigh of relief that she was still there. Her features showed her alarm and the young girl stared wide-eyed. "Mrs. Curtis is having her baby! You must go as quickly as possible to fetch Dr. Hathaway or Dr. Burgess. And then find Mr. Curtis! It's an emergency!" The girl stood dumbfounded until Hallie's voice rose an octave higher. "Go! There is no time to lose! Take a horse from the stables! Just hurry!"

As Hallie ran back up the stairs she counted in her

mind how long it would take before a doctor could get back here. Hallie retained a good working knowledge of all she had helped Adam study. If the books were right, a first baby took hours, and that was more than enough time for someone to get back to the Curtis house. She prayed that this baby was not impatient and steadied herself for the possibility that she might have to put her knowledge into practice.

As Hallie poured water into the bowl from the pitcher on the washstand she noticed for the first time that it was snowing hard. She saw that the drive leading to the house was still clear and again prayed, only this time it was for better weather. At Amanda's bedside she pretended calm control, assuring her that all would be well, although she grew increasingly doubtful of her own words.

The time moved slowly for Hallie as she talked to Amanda, helping her through each pain as they grew closer together and more severe. Hallie desperately feared that this birth was to be the exception to the rule of long labors. She gathered towels and fresh sheets, heated water and carried it up the stairs, hearing Amanda's groans as the pain racked her body. Where was Dr. Hathaway? Or Adam? Surely enough time had passed for someone to have gotten here. Had the young girl panicked? No, it was an easy task. What if she could find no one? What if nobody came? Silly! Jason would be here anytime to drive them to Redland. But what help would he be?

"Hallie!" Amanda screamed, her fear sounding plainly.

Hallie took her hand, gripped it tightly. "It's all right, Mandy! I'll take care of everything! I promise you!"

"I'm all wet!" Amanda said just before another spasm took hold, contorting her features into a mask of agony.

"It's the bag of waters, Amanda. It's normal. But I must look to see how close the baby is."

"Where is the doctor? Did you send for one?" she demanded angrily.

Hallie understood her friend's fear, her anger. She tried to sound reassuring but wondered how well she did. "I sent for them. They'll be here anytime." But as Hallie drew back the sheet that covered Amanda's bent knees she knew they would not be soon enough. "We

193

can't wait, honey. The baby's head is showing. We're going to have to do it ourselves."

Hallie breathed deeply and prayed as never before. Please God, help me! Help Amanda! But her voice held authority. "You're going to have to push, Mandy. I know it hurts, but it will ease when you bear down. But please only do what I tell you. When I say to stop, pant like a dog and don't push! It's important that you don't go too fast."

"Now! Now! I need to push! Please!" Amanda screamed.

"All right! Now easy, just a little." Hallie watched in awe as the circle of the infant's scalp widened, then receded again as Amanda's breath went out and she stopped. Then again she pushed, and the circle grew wider still, Amanda's tender flesh beginning to tear.

"Stop! Breathe!" she commanded, grasping the kitchen knife she had brought for just this purpose. Hallie had never applied a knife to human flesh before and she quailed at the thought, but she willed herself to do it, knowing she must. On the next contraction she cut a small slice in Amanda's skin, opening the way for the tiny head to pass into her waiting hands, the blue face turned to the side to allow its exit.

"Good girl!" Hallie exclaimed suddenly, caught up in the excitement rather than fear. This baby would be born! her mind shouted in pride. Amanda rested but a moment as Hallie steeled herself to help ease the shoulders out as she had read. Thank God for that knowledge, she thought. Another push and the shoulders were delivered.

Her voice held her pleasure. "The worst is over, Mandy. One more time and your baby is born!" Only seconds passed and the tiny boy was completely out, the thick purple cord still attached to his mother.

"It's a boy, Amanda! A son!" she exclaimed, laughing and crying at the same time.

Amanda lay back in exhaustion. Hallie held the tiny baby, smiling down in wonder. Her smile faded, as she realized the baby was dead.

"Dear God, no! Please no! Amanda!" The wail was an awful sound to the men who bounded up the stairs.

194

CHAPTER THIRTY-FIVE

"I did what I could, Adam! Was it me? Was it my fault?" Hallie asked for the fifth time, sobbing hysterically. She was out of her mind with grief, with guilt, and did not even realize she had asked the question before.

Adam held her, his own features contorted with sorrow. "It wasn't your fault, Hallie. The baby had been dead for days. There was nothing anyone could do! Not me, not Dr. Hathaway. You did the best any of us could do. At least you saved Amanda. She'll have more babies, healthy, happy ones. I'm sure of it."

"Oh, God, what I did to her!" she wailed. "I shouldn't have let her know! I should have let her think he was all right! At least let her recover before telling her her baby was dead! Oh, God, Adam! Will she be all right?"

"She's fine, Hallie, she'll be fine! You have nothing to feel guilty about. She would have known when he didn't cry!" Adam sat Hallie in a chair, going to pour her a snifter of brandy. His heart ached to see her so tormented. Why couldn't he convince her she had done well, that no one, no matter how much training and experience, could have done anything differently? Amanda's baby had been dead for some time. No one knew why these things happened. At least Amanda would live; often the mother was lost as well. "Drink this, Hallie," he said gently. "You need it."

Jason Curtis came into the room. He looked haggard, worn. He sat before Hallie, taking both of her hands into his own, smiling kindly into her tear-streaked face. "Amanda is asleep now. Dr. Hathaway gave her a sedative. She asked me to thank you before she fell asleep. She said she could not have gotten through this without you."

Hallie shook her head, unconvinced.

Jason continued, "And I want to thank you. You saved my wife's life, and that is the most important thing in the world to me. So please stop feeling guilty. We will be forever in your debt." Jason took the brandy from Adam. "Drink this, Hallie, and then we'll put you to bed, too. I think you need to rest as much as Amanda."

Hallie again shook her head. She suddenly had a need to be with Michael, though she did not understand it, could not explain it. "I have to go home. Michael is waiting. He won't know what has happened."

"I'll send a message to him."

"No, I want to go home. But thank you, Jason. Besides, this is a time for you and Amanda to be alone. You don't need me to deal with as well." Finally taking hold of herself, Hallie smiled warmly at Adam. He had been more comfort to her than he realized. "Will you drive me out to Redland, Adam?" she asked wearily.

He smiled his consent, relieved to see her more in control, but not so pleased to hear that she sought the solace of Michael Redmond and his home. Still, it was not a time for petty jealousy, he chided himself.

Adam sat beside Hallie in the carriage, tenderly holding her hand. He wished he could do more for her. After a time she peered up at him, her eyes dry. She looked exhausted. "Thank you, Adam. I could not have been alone this past hour. You don't know what a help you've been for me. I know it isn't easy for you. After all, Amanda is your sister."

He smiled warmly, the deep love he felt for her reflected in his brown eyes. "I know Amanda will be all right. It will take a little time for her to grieve, but she is in a place of her choosing with a man she loves. That will make all the difference. It's you I'm concerned with.

I wonder just how strong you can be after all the burdens heaped on your shoulders these past weeks."

"I'll be fine. I feel numb. I suppose that helps to deal with all of this."

"Why don't you let me take you to your grandmother's house for tonight at least? You need to rest."

She shook her head, not realizing what her determination to be with Michael did to Adam. "It's best if I go back to Redland. As I said before, things are tenuous between Michael and me. This is not a time to cause more problems, no matter what has happened. Like it or not, my place is there now."

Adam did not like it at all, but he held his opinion out of consideration for Hallie. "Will you be able to rest there?" he asked feebly.

"Yes. Better than at my grandmother's house. Mercy is already at Redland, and you know how she is. She'll probably confine me to bed for a week." She laughed weakly.

Adam gently brushed a stray curl from her forehead. "I'm so sorry for everything, Hallie. If I hadn't been so pigheaded we could have been married a long time already. I will never forgive myself for what I've thrust you into."

"No good will come of your guilt any more than mine will make Amanda's baby live. We were victims of circumstances, Adam, nothing more. I don't live such a hellish existence, at any rate. Redland is hardly a hovel. I have everything I could want, Danny is happy there and no matter what you think, Michael is kind to me. It could have been worse."

Adam pressed her head gently to his shoulder, caressing her temple. "I should not have brought it up now. Close your eyes and rest. I'll wake you when we near Redland."

Hallie slept peacefully nearly all the way. But as they neared the house she awoke with a start and a small cry of fear. Her eyes flew open wide and she studied her surroundings as though wondering where she was. The sun had nearly set, a red glow lent to the earth. Inside the carriage it was very dim, and it took a moment longer for her to discover she was with Adam. "I dreamed of Amanda's baby! I could feel his poor,

197

lifeless body in my hands again! How do you ever get used to that?"

"You don't really. I suppose a doctor's mind becomes trained to put such things behind in favor of more happy thoughts. Do you feel better now?"

"A little. Odd how drained this has left me."

"I don't think it's odd at all. The whole thing was a nightmare, and I imagine that right now most of your life qualifies as a bad dream." Adam paused, his face drawing into a frown. "I hate to bring this up again, particularly now, but I am tormented with guilt over it and I need to apologize for my behavior."

Hallie stared up at him in dismay. "I don't understand."

"The other night at that party. I was drunk and behaved badly. I didn't mean to embarrass you. I'm afraid I was out of control."

"The only harm you did was in letting Michael know we had been together that afternoon."

He grimaced. "I don't even remember doing that! I'm sorry. I doubt if that eased the tension between you. Did it?"

"It caused quite a bit more."

Adam was secretly pleased that Hallie had meant to keep their meeting a secret. "It won't happen again, Hallie, I promise you. There's no need to worry that I will ever let our seeing each other slip out again. I would never take another sip of liquor rather than cause you more problems."

"That, too, is past, Adam. I hope that the time will come when you and Micheal will not hold such animosity toward one another. I would appreciate it if you would hurry that along by not provoking him."

Adam smiled. "I'll try, for your sake. I really don't mean to make it all harder for you, though sometimes I'm sure it seems so. I doubt that Michael and I'll ever be friends, but I will try to control myself in the future."

Redland loomed ahead, large and imposing, the soft reflection of candles just visible in the first-floor windows. Hallie breathed a sigh of relief to be home, no matter what awaited her. She wanted only to relax and allow the guilt to ease from her sorely abused conscience.

198

Before Adam opened the door he turned to her one last time, sheepishly. "I also want you to know that there is nothing serious between Belinda Scott and myself. She eases the loneliness, nothing more."

Hallie seriously doubted that but smiled anyway. It was not her place to judge Adam, she reasoned, no matter how much pain his affair caused her.

Adam lifted Hallie from the carriage, his arm possessively at her waist as he helped her up the stairs. Once at the door she turned to him, smiling affectionately. "I really do appreciate what you've done for me this afternoon. Thank you." She rose and kissed his cheek, lingering a moment longer than necessary. She squeezed his hand and entered the house, closing the door behind her.

As she climbed the stairs the haughty voice of Emeline sent chills through her blood. "That was a touching scene on the veranda. I'm certain Michael will be pleased to have proof of the mistake he made in marrying you. You are the trollop your mother was."

CHAPTER THIRTY-SIX

Michael hurried into the house, knowing he was very late and that Hallie, Amanda and Jason should have been there for hours. He had barely handed his great-coat to the butler when a scowling Emeline appeared from the drawing room.

"Come into the library, Michael. I have something to discuss with you."

"I can't right now, Emeline. I have guests to greet."

"There are no guests."

Michael frowned, not understanding her. "Hasn't Hallie gotten home yet?"

"She arrived two hours ago. She was not alone, but the man who brought her is certainly not a guest in this house."

"I'm sure I don't know what you are talking about."

"We must talk in private, Michael."

She strode into the library. Michael followed, his curiosity roused. At Emeline's insistence he closed the door for privacy, then turned to her as she stood ramrod straight, her hands clasped before her.

"I know that your father coerced you into marrying that girl for his own vile reasons, but you have made a grave mistake, and it is my place to bring it to your attention."

This was a new tactic, Michael thought, more direct, but still he was impatient with the subject. "Emeline, I am in no mood to hear more of your railings against my wife. It is none of your business."

"As of today that is not true. It is my duty to tell you that you are being made a cuckold."

Michael's left brow rose in interest now. "Oh? Perhaps you would like to elaborate on that?"

"Your wife returned here this evening with a man the servants tell me is Adam Burgess. I witnessed a very intimate scene on the veranda. It is obvious she is no better than her mother."

Michael's temper rose, blocking out all thoughts of why Amanda and Jason had not accompanied Hallie. His jealousy overwhelmed his common sense. "Just exactly what did you see?"

"I saw them climb the steps arm in arm and then kiss quite passionately before she came in."

"Are you certain of this?"

"Completely. When I heard the carriage I looked out the window expecting to see your guests arriving with your wife. Instead I saw the culmination of an intimate afternoon spent with her lover, no doubt. Mark my words, Michael, she will try to pass off bastards onto your good name! Just as her mother did."

"Her mother did not do that!" he said, losing his temper with her repetition. "You know damn well what went on with her mother. She was hardly a whore."

Emeline drew back at what she considered the crudity of this attack. "She was a woman of loose virtue!"

"She was a lonely and unhappy person! Just as my father was!"

"Your father had no right!"

"I won't argue with you, Emeline. We view this differently and always will. Why would Hallie be so blatant about an affair?" he asked, his temper momentarily cooled.

"Because it is inborn! She is a trollop, I tell you! No good will come to you unless you rid yourself of her! I saw it with my own eyes!"

Michael threw the door wide, his fury once again raging. "I will deal with it!"

Hallie lay sound asleep on the high, fluffy bed, es-

202

caping her black feelings. She awoke with a terrible start when Michael banged into the room, slamming the door with force behind himself. His face was dark with rage. "I know your game, Hallie, and you can only be the loser!"

Hallie blinked the sleep from her eyes, her mind still fogged with it. "I don't know what you're talking about."

"You think by blatantly carrying on an affair with that bastard Burgess I will free you. Well, you're mistaken! I'll never do that, regardless of what you devise. All you have gained by that little show on the veranda today is a faithless husband. I warned you."

"Are you insane?" she asked in awe of the fury she saw in him.

"I suppose you have some explanation for it."

"A very good one! I can't believe you are so blind. I suppose the good Emeline has done this deed?"

"She means only to help me. She cannot forgive your mother and insists you have the same loose morals. I'm beginning to agree with her, though I at least understood your mother's reasons!" he railed wildly, forgetting he had avoided speaking of Hallie's mother.

Now her eyes were wide with shock and confusion. "I think it is high time you explain all of this to me. I would like to know just what I am being compared to!"

All restraint gone now, Michael exploded with the secret he had carried for so long. "Your mother had an affair with my father. Danny is my half brother," he blurted out.

Hallie was dumbstruck. "I don't believe you! This is more of Emeline's doing!"

"Hardly. That was why my father wanted to marry you. He knew that in doing it his son would be brought here to be raised as a Redmond, and he was obsessed with it. It was the only way without causing a scandal."

The deep violet eyes grew wider still. "And when he became ill," she finished, "he forced you to marry me and raise his son! It wasn't me whom either of you wanted, but Danny!" Her pride was struck a sharp blow, added to the shock of learning about her mother. A wild rage ran through her, pushing her to escape this sordid mess, to regain her self-respect. She was like a wounded animal, striking out at anything she could. "You Redmonds," she fairly spat, "you think so highly of your-selves. It never occurs to you to consider the feelings of others. Simply destroy what stands in your way and manipulate everyone until they comply. Is that how your father persuaded my mother into an affair? Per-haps he gave her no choice!"

"She had a choice!" he shot back in anger. "Appar-ently she was not satisfied with your father! In that respect you are a great deal alike, aren't you?"

"You're so ready to believe that! You come in here raging, asking for no explanations, just accusing and passing judgment without evidence! Well, go to your mistress! Do you think I care? She deserves you! A fool for a fool! I've been used for the Redmond family's pur-pose long enough! I only hope to God that my brother grows up as a Wyatt and never, never becomes anything like the man who sired him, if that is even true! I'm finished with you! This was not in the bargain, and that cancels it! You and your father should have tried hon-esty, but then I don't suppose that is possible for you! Go on! I'm sure Maeve Carson is waiting with bated breath! But before too long you'll learn just what an ignorant jackass you've been." Michael stared at her, his temper still raging beyond control, his mind held only onto the thought, irrational as it was, that Hallie was having an affair with Adam. He said not another word and left the room.

Within seconds Hallie heard the front door close be-hind him. She had no doubt as to where he was going. She fairly jumped from the bed, her own anger burying any thoughts of the past afternoon's pain, of anything but that she had been sorely manipulated, her circum-stances had been taken advantage of and all without one thought as to her feelings, her plans, her needs or desires. She had been merely a means for the Redmond family to claim what they considered rightfully theirs. She threw on her heavy cloak and bounded down the stairs, running through the cold night air to the stables. The coachman was surprised to see her but even more shocked to hear her order a carriage prepared. Hallie waited impatiently, the pain in her heart fighting with her fury. She tamped the pain down with an effort, refusing to let it cloud her decision. She would show

Michael Redmond that he meant nothing to her, just as she meant nothing to him. She would think only of herself, as she should have done two years past, she told herself. She would take what happiness and love was offered and to hell with bargains and agreements and honor and vows, to hell with this whole marriage and especially to hell with Michael Redmond!

Just before entering the carriage unaided she gave the driver the address of Adam Burgess's town house.

CHAPTER THIRTY-SEVEN

The key turned easily in the lock, allowing Michael entrance into the dimly lit town house. Everything remained as it had been two years ago, tasteful, elegant, much like the owner. He poured himself a brandy, noticing that the cabinet was still well stocked with his favorite brand. She had been very sure of him, he mused to himself. He loosened his cravat and sat heavily on a gray velvet upholstered chair, his long legs stretched out before him, crossed at the ankles.

So this is what it has come to, he thought. Odd how he had expected to return to this house because he wanted to, because he desired its owner. Instead he was here out of a sense of revenge. Perhaps I should leave before she returns, he offered himself. But his pride overruled that notion. He would make good his threats. He would teach Hallie, he would hurt her in the same way she had hurt him. He paused. Had she actually hurt him? Was he so vulnerable to her? Impossible! Michael Redmond was not guided by emotions and especially not those for a woman. So why did he feel so awful? And why could he not chase Hallie from his thoughts and concentrate on Maeve? Fool! he spat. Besotted fool! Had he allowed the little raven-haired minx to get into his blood? Impossible! Again he shouted to himself. He simply had not tired of her amorous attentions yet. Surely when Maeve arrived and he took her upstairs, touched that tempting body, gazed at that lovely face, he would find Hallie gone from his mind, lost beneath desire for another woman.

The door opened, diverting Michael's attention. Maeve smiled brilliantly at Michael, removing her short cape and hat. "This is a nice surprise," she said warmly, her voice melodic. She had decided on the day she met his wife that if he sought her she would not prove to be a shrew by ranting about the wrong she felt he had done her. She did not want him scared off, certainly not when he had a wife to run home to. At first Maeve had told herself she would not become his mistress, that she had only bedded him before because she was sure he would eventually marry her. Now she hoped to lure him from his wife. Divorce was scandalous, but she would endure anything to gain Michael Redmond.

At last Michael spoke, his tone clearly reflecting his black mood. "If you would rather I leave just say so. I wouldn't blame you if I am not welcome here."

"You're more than welcome."

"I'm not here for a little social chitchat."

Her smile turned sensual, "I know very well what you're here for. Would you rather just go upstairs? We can talk later."

Michael still scowled at her, but he led the way to the staircase. Maeve was unperturbed. She had dealt with Michael's temper in the past. He was always well soothed after lovemaking, and she was quite eager to offer him whatever balm he needed.

Michael drank the last of his brandy and discarded his clothing carelessly. He laid back on the bed, familiar with the situation, knowing Maeve enjoyed undressing slowly while he watched. Even now he could not keep from comparing her with Hallie, thinking how odd it was that he preferred his wife's slight modesty.

Maeve's back was to Michael as her slender fingers worked with a sensuality all their own. When the gown fell to her feet she dropped petticoat after petticoat until her well-turned rump bobbed in the air as she bent to remove the yards of fabric around her ankles. Then she turned, smiling seductively at Michael, her eyes traveling his naked body hungrily, appreciating his masculine beauty. She untied the transparent chemise but did not remove it, leaving it as an alluring veil over her full breasts. She stood before him now, posed, lace stockings still covering perfectly shaped legs, her chemise a soft whisper at her breasts.

Michael watched all she did, trying desperately to understand why he was not aroused by her. Maeve rolled her stockings down each leg and then moved to the bed. She knelt beside Michael and at last shrugged the lacy garment from her shoulders, her hands running the length of her own body before she lowered herself to his side. She realized it was to be a night she made love to him and knew that he was having difficulty leaving behind thoughts of his wife. But Maeve was confident of herself. She threw one leg over him, her thigh brushing up against his most private parts. Her hands explored his body, reveling in the feel of his powerful muscles. She kissed him slowly then ran her tongue lightly across his moustache.

Her voice was low, filled with sensuality. "I like the moustache. It makes you even more handsome."

Michael forced himself to touch her, gently grasping one large, round breast, feeling the nipple grow taut with response. Maeve groaned in pleasure, her own hand reaching below, between his massive thighs, disappointed by what she found. Again she kissed him, a hint of desperation rising in her.

Michael's mind raced. He had never experieced this inability he now found himself in. His thoughts kept betraying him. It was Hallie's face he saw before him, her body he wanted, and it all added up to a more disabling worry. Why couldn't he put her from his mind? He had always been able to put a woman from his mind if he chose to do so.

Maeve's voice broke into his thoughts, full desperation sounding as she realized he was lost to her in this endeavor. "I love you, Michael! Can't you please love me? Even just a little?"

Michael pushed her gently away, extremely sorry that he had done this to her. He knew she did not deserve such shoddy treatment from him. "I'm sorry, Maeve. There is too much on my mind."

"And none of it has to do with me," she said, hurt.

"On the contrary. It is unfair to treat you this way."

"Unfair? I love you and you speak of what is unfair."

Michael rose from the bed to dress, seeing plainly that this situation could only grow worse. "I never intended to hurt you, Maeve. It was just a bad choice of nights."

"What did you do, fight with her and then run here to punish her?"

"It's better if we don't discuss it," he said, finishing his dressing. "I apologize."

Suddenly realizing she was losing her tenuous grasp, she became contrite, hiding her hurt pride as well. "It's all right, darling. I don't mind. In fact, you're still welcome here at any time. You may feel differently another night."

Michael frowned deeply, worried about that. "Perhaps I will. For tonight I hope you can forgive me."

"There is nothing to forgive! I love you, Michael. We've known each other too long and too well for me to hold something like this against you. I only hope you will offer me another chance to prove to you how much you care for me as well."

Michael decided enough damage had been done without responding to that. He smiled at her and left. He had already decided that it was time for a private confrontation with Adam Burgess.

CHAPTER THIRTY-EIGHT

When Hallie saw the lights blazing in Adam's house she dismissed the coachman; she had no intention of returning to Redland. She drew courage from her anger and knocked on the door, her chin lifted defiantly.

Adam sat reading, a dressing gown over his shirt and trousers, when she was ushered into his drawing room. He stood, but when his eyes fell to Hallie his face registered his shock. "My God, Hallie, you are the last person I expected to see tonight."

She smiled timidly, suddenly unsure of herself. "I hope you aren't expecting anyone else."

"Of course not!" He moved to her, his love for her filling his warm brown eyes. Taking her hands, he drew her with him to the sofa, sitting to face her. His smile was kind, reminding her of days gone by, easing her fears somewhat. "What's wrong, Hallie?"

"Is it so obvious?"

"I would rather believe that you simply decided you loved me enough to forget everything else, but that is not what I see in your face. I told you I was always available for you, in any way you want me, and I meant it."

"In a way you're right. But I was aided reaching my decision by a few sordid facts I learned tonight." She

211

explained what she meant, feeling more relaxed as she spoke. Adam was, after all, her old and dear friend, the brother she had in a way adopted for her own before she fell in love with him.

Adam was not terribly surprised by her story. "I have to ask you just one thing, honey, because I don't want to misunderstand your being here. Did you come simply for a refuge as a friend, or did you come to me out of love, as a woman to a man? Either way I want you to know you're welcome."

Hallie's voice was soft, her hesitation as apparent as the fact that this situation was foreign to her. "I've come because I love you, Adam. As a woman to a man."

Adam's smile lit his handsome features like an explosion, his pleasure boundless. "I never thought I could hope for this. You've made me the happiest man in the world."

"I don't want you to take this the wrong way, Adam, but could we go upstairs and get it over with? I don't feel as though I will be able to relax and talk with you until that is out of the way." Her own words surprised her.

Adam laughed huskily. "I hardly need to be persuaded for that!" He gently took her hand and led her up the stairs, wondering if this was all a wonderful dream. How could he have been so lucky? He was willing to handle anything Michael Redmond dealt him just to have Hallie as his own. Knowing she was nervous, Adam showed her the room they would share and moved to leave her to undress in private. Before he reached the door, Hallie stopped him.

"Perhaps I'm not being fair, Adam. It is quite possible that Michael will try to destroy you for this."

He smiled warmly, as though it were the least important thing in the world. "I've already thought about that. If he does, we can always leave Boston. A good doctor is needed anywhere. The West is wide open; we can take Danny and start all over again. Just don't worry about it. He can't hurt me if I have you."

Hallie slowly disrobed, wondering at her own hesitation in following through with what she had set out to do. She stared at the room around her, thinking how odd that this was to have been her home, that she had expected to come here as a bride. Well, she was little more than a bride, she thought facetiously, but not Adam's. What a strange twist fate had taken. She wondered if she should be repudiating her marriage vows and coming to Adam in such a tawdry way. Still, she quelled her doubts; that was only guilt, and it would pass. Adam's love for her would give her strength, make it all right. But what of her love for him? she asked herself. She had lately come to wonder if that love hadn't returned to that for a brother, yet here she was, about to compromise herself, to fulfill Emeline's accusations. Hallie shook her head with force, as though that would clear it. She loved Adam! They belonged together!

Hallie slid between the sheets, pulling the top sheet up to her chin in modesty. It seemed such a short time since she had done all of this with Michael, first experienced his lovemaking and the pleasures he aroused in her. Why must he creep back into her thoughts? Would he never allow her any peace? Her hand reached to the ring Adam had given her. She had slipped it on her right hand before fleeing Redland. Now she turned it round and round her finger, hoping it would somehow chase away the image of Michael. Instead it reminded her that she still wore her wedding ring, and a fresh onslaught of pain flooded her.

Adam returned and blew out all of the candles before he shed his clothing, out of consideration for Hallie and the trepidation he knew she felt. He kept in his mind the thought that this was their wedding night, just as he had imagined it so many times before, she a virgin, fearing her first night in his bed. Adam laid down beside her, then pulled her to him, holding her close. "My God, how I love you, Hallie. I promise to make everything all right." He held her for some time to allow her to become comfortable with the situation.

Instead Hallie's doubts grew; her mind raced with guilty thoughts of Michael. She felt an odd longing for her husband, as though he symbolized home and family to her sorely abused emotions. She grew stiff in Adam's arms. He moved so she lay on her back and he loomed above her. He lowered his lips to hers, savoring the sweetness there.

Hallie did little more than endure his kiss, frustrated

with herself. Why must it be like this? she asked herself over and over again. How many years had she lain awake in her bed, wanting Adam to make love to her, wondering what it would be like? And now she could only wish for Michael. Wish that Michael's arms were around her, Michael's mouth embracing hers, Michael's body above her and Michael who whispered words of love. She was certain she had lost her sanity. She did not love Michael. She cared nothing for him—hated him, in fact. Didn't she? How could she care for or desire a man who merely used her? A man who at this moment probably lay in the arms of Maeve Carson?

"No! Stop!" she heard herself cry out at last, as if it were someone else's voice.

Adam drew away, at first searching her face for a sign that it was merely fear and tension that tore the exclamation from her throat. Then he fell back on the other side of the bed, knowing differently. His pain was excruciating. "You've lost your love for me, haven't you?" he accused quietly, his misery plain.

"It isn't that!" she said, sounding halfhearted even to herself. "I just can't do this, Adam. I feel so cheap."

"We can salvage at least our friendship with honesty, Hallie. Please allow me the dignity of the truth."

Hallie clutched the sheet to her bare breast now, staring at Adam, as hurt as he by what had just been revealed, for no matter how far out of love she was with him there remained the memory of a beautiful feeling, warm and bright, and still there was a different love, though it held no passion. Worst of all, there was such a strong wish for those old feelings to be there. "I'm so sorry! I'm so confused, Adam! Forgive me for this! I only meant to recapture what we had. I do love you, but I cannot do this."

Adam smiled sadly. "I suppose you wouldn't be the person I fell in love with if you could. Still, if ever that day comes when you've had enough of him, I'll always take you back, Hallie. I love you that much." He paused, a soft sigh of resignation and acceptance that his dream had been shattered, for the moment at least. "I'll wait for you downstairs and see you back to Redland. You can't solve your problems by running from them, honey. You'll have to face Michael." Adam rose, throwing his

214

dressing gown on and grabbing a suit of clothes to dress in the other room. Before he had opened the door to leave, an urgent knock sounded. When he opened the door a very nervous maid stood in the hallway. Hallie could hear her every word as she talked loudly out of tension.

"Sorry, sir, but there's a man downstairs to see you! Says he isn't leaving until you come down, and he means it! Name's Mr. Redmond."

CHAPTER THIRTY-NINE

Michael paced furiously, waiting for Adam. The realization that Hallie had become important to him enraged him. Still he did not entertain thoughts of loving her; in his mind it was simply a matter of desire.

Adam appeared several minutes later, his dressing gown over trousers and a shirt, his hair in order. "This is an unexpected visit," Adam said, echoing almost exactly the same words he had used to Hallie earlier. His tone was stiff and formal; for Hallie's sake he had no wish to provoke Michael.

"I want to know just what the hell is going on with you and my wife," Michael demanded, his rage barely contained.

Adam was relieved that Michael did not know that Hallie was in the house. Displaying a composure he did not feel, he responded quietly. "We've had this out several times. The answer is the same as always: nothing." The note of regret in his voice was genuine.

"Dammit! Don't lie! I know about your rendezvous on my veranda! Hallie was to have been with Jason and Amanda, so how did you find your way there instead?"

Now Adam was surprised. Could he know nothing of Amanda's baby? "My God, don't you know?"

"Know what?"

Adam turned to his sideboard and poured Michael a brandy. He turned and offered it to him. "Brandy still is your drink, I presume."

"I didn't come for a social visit, Burgess. Answer my question."

"I've already told you you're mistaken in your accusations of Hallie. There was nothing intimate in our parting on the veranda. Perhaps you should question your source more thoroughly."

"My aunt witnessed the display! She has no reason to lie!" Michael strode away from Adam and the proffered drink, pacing to vent his fury.

"Then perhaps her sight is not good, for what she saw was far from intimate. Did you bother to ask Hallie what had happened this afternoon?"

"I didn't have to! I had an accurate account."

Adam shook his head in disgust. "In all the time I have known you, I have never taken you for a fool. But Michael, that is just what you are." Before Michael could speak, Adam continued. "Sit down and drink this. You will need its support when you discover what you've done."

His tone struck Michael and he took the brandy, gulping it down at once, though he refused to sit. "Get on with your story. My temper is sorely stretched," he said dangerously.

"Where did you expect Hallie to be this afternoon?"

"Helping Amanda pack for a few days' visit," Michael said tightly.

"Well, that is what she was doing. Unfortunately, she and Amanda were alone in the house with just one serving girl when Amanda went into labor." Now Michael's full attention was engaged. "Hallie sent the serving girl to fetch me or Dr. Hathaway, but by the time we arrived the baby had been born. A baby boy, dead for some time before he was born, but Hallie could not have realized that. She was hysterical with fear and guilt, thinking she had done something wrong, that she had caused the baby's death. She was devastated at having blurted it out to Amanda in her horror instead of trying to keep the truth from her."

218

"Good Christ!" Michael exclaimed, disgusted with himself.

Adam continued, "It was not her fault. Hallie has a very good knowledge of childbirth. She did everything perfectly. But it was some time before Jason or I could convince her that she very possibly saved my sister's life. She was so upset Jason wanted her to stay there, to have a sedative and rest, for we were all as worried about her mental state as Amanda's. But she insisted, much to my disappointment, I might add, in running back to you."

Michael sat down, devastated by guilt. I am a fool, he berated himself silently.

Adam was feeling very little compassion as he gazed down at his former friend. "Don't you think she has had enough burdens heaped on her without your adding more? Do you believe she is as despicable as you are, as undeserving of trust because you cannot be faithful to your wife?"

Adam would never know what a raw nerve he had struck. Michael's cheek worked fiercely, his words as cutting as Adam's. "Do you believe it is easy for me, Adam? Do you think I like knowing my wife loves you? That she hates me for tearing you two apart? Do you believe it is comforting to hear her threaten to leave me for you at every turn and then to watch you do your best to lure her away? Do you wonder why I suspect you both in everything?"

Adam's features were contorted with pain, and his voice was low. "What I wonder is why it all should disturb you so much. How can you profess to have no feelings for her and yet be so obsessed with what she does or who she cares for? How can you be so jealous of a woman you say you married merely for convenience?"

"It's none of your damn business!"

"Interesting that each time I come close to the truth I'm told it is none of my damn business," Adam mocked. "Just to set the record straight, our intimate scene was composed of my helping a very weary, distraught girl from the carriage and up the stairs. She did kiss me, a light peck on the cheek out of gratitude for being with her in her time of need. Believe me, I wish it had been

219

more, but unfortunately your aunt saw passion where there was none."

Michael stood, moving to the entrance hall, knowing he owed his wife an apology. Before he strode from the house Adam's voice stopped him in midstride, deadly serious.

"The next time you're hell bent on hurting Hallie I won't be so generous. I'll seize the advantage, for her sake as well as mine."

CHAPTER FORTY

By the time Hallie reached Redland, snow was beginning to fall. She thanked the fates that allowed her to reenter the house unseen. Her heart had been beating apace with the rapid thud of horses' hooves through the night as Adam's carriage had raced to get her back home. She had gone down the back stairs of the town house, feeling even more guilty for having to sneak out the servants' entrance while her husband waited in the drawing room to speak to the man who had almost become her lover. Now she threw off her clothing, setting everything out of sight in case Michael came home. She pulled Adam's ring from her hand and thrust it into the top drawer of her bureau. She climbed into the bed and pulled the covers up to her neck. Only then did she allow herself a deep breath of relief, though her pulse still raced with fear. She prayed fervently that Michael would never learn what she had done this night.

Then her thoughts turned to his threat. Had he gone to Maeve Carson? If so, why had he been at Adam's so soon after leaving her? There had been enough time if he had not stayed long with Maeve, but would he have simply sought her favors and left? Perhaps. Hallie wondered if she would ever know the truth. Her heart ached, for surely if Michael had gone to Maeve, he had finished

221

the deed he set out to do, unlike herself. Her cheeks blushed crimson with embarrassment at her actions. It seemed that she had lost her wits today, and it was a frightening thing.

A knock sounded at her door. Hallie's heart leaped into her throat, but she managed to hold her voice steady. Mercy came in, a scowl pulling her moon-shaped face. "I'm ashamed of you, miss!" she blurted out, standing at the foot of her bed, reprimanding Hallie much as though she were a child again. "I heard your fight with the mister; isn't any way I could help it. Then I saw you tear out of here with that gleam of temper in your eyes. It doesn't take a seer to guess where you were off to. You ran like a gazelle to Doc Burgess, didn't you now?"

"Oh, Mercy, stop!" she pleaded. "You will never know all I've been through today and tonight. Leave me in peace!"

"It isn't in my mind to let you ruin your life like that! Mr. Redmond's a good man, he is. A wee bit heady and stubborn but a good man for you! And I'll be telling you another thing: I think you care more for him than you know, and I'm not all that sure he doesn't feel the same for you! But you can't be running off in a fit, or you'll ruin it all!"

"I know, Mercy! Please go to bed now!"

"Hmph!" Her hands were on wide hips, bushy silver brows drawn together as she scowled down at this woman whom she had cared for from birth. "I made excuses to that old harridan below so she doesn't know you left. For as I know, nobody but the coachman has any idea. You'd best hope he doesn't let on."

Hallie was grateful to her old nanny. "Thank you, Mercy! You've done me a great service. I promise you this won't happen again."

"Hmph!" was her only answer.

Farley was in the stables, checking on an ailing mare. He saw Hallie's return and shook his head. Farley had learned long ago that silence coupled with a watchful eye and an open ear taught a man much. He learned from the coachman where Hallie had gone. He had told the man that Adam Burgess was a doctor caring for an ailing relation of the mistress and that Michael had sent her to talk with him. He knew that it would keep the man from repeating his story. Farley was glad to see that Hallie had returned too soon to have done much with the man. Besides, he thought himself a fair judge of people, and Michael's wife was not the sort to be taking lovers. He liked the small raven-haired beauty; he considered her a good match for the man he thought of as a son. A much better match than that Carson woman, for he knew Michael cared nothing for her. It was different with this one, he mused, for he saw a new glimmer in Michael's eyes, saw a change in his treatment of her beyond mere courtesy. Farley only hoped that the lad was wise enough not to destroy this marriage by turning to the Carson woman in anger. He knew that was where Michael had been headed, but Farley still was gambling on Michael not to follow it through. When he heard Michael ride into the stables he knew he had won his wager with himself.

"I hope you've come back in a better temper than you left," he said without greeting.

"You see before you a jackass in man's clothing, Farley."

"Aye, I know it. You let your temper get the best of you. I could have told you your aunt was wrong about the girl."

"Then you know about it all?"

The massive man shrugged. "I saw your wife come home with Burgess, and I heard your aunt tell you how it was between them. She saw it different than it was."

"Why didn't you tell me?"

"There was no stopping you, lad. You didn't even see me waiting in the entrance."

Michael shook his head, still not believing what a fool he had been. How could he have believed Emeline when he knew what she thought of Hallie? "Did Hallie come down to dinner after I left?"

"No, she didn't," he answered, the truth if not the whole truth.

"She was upset; that was what Emeline saw on the veranda. She was with Amanda today when her baby was born. He was dead."

The wise blue eyes widened beneath raised brows.

"It's no wonder then. It makes your being so hard on her even worse, doesn't it?"

Michael sighed heavily. "It does. I told you I was a jackass. I hope I haven't done too much damage."

"I suppose that depends on how you've spent this night."

Michael smiled at the old man. "You know me too well, Farley. Fortunately, I was incapable of bedding Maeve. It seemed that my mind could not escape a raven-haired vixen."

The red face crinkled into a smile. "Aye, I've known that affliction myself a time or two."

Michael laughed, eased as always by Farley's understanding ear. "Well, it's time I face up to what I've done. Good night, Farley."

Michael loosened his cravat on the way up the stairs, his jacket and vest over his arm, and his shirt unbuttoned to the waist by the time he reached the bedroom. He went directly to sit on the bed beside Hallie, studying her beautiful face for signs of what she felt about him. He took her hand gently in his two huge ones, encouraged by the fact that she allowed it, not pulling away from his touch. He smiled at her, his handsome face looking weary beneath his wind-tousled hair. His piercing blue-gray eyes beseeched her understanding. His voice was tender. "I don't know what to say to you but that I'm sorry. I went like a wild man to Adam's town house tonight, and he explained it all to me. You were right before, love, I was an ignorant jackass. You should have forced me to listen to you."

"How could I have done that? I might have tried screaming over your accusations, but you wouldn't have believed me," she said gently, for her own guilt was too great not to forgive Michael his outburst.

"It was a harsh lesson for me, but in the future I will always listen to your explanations before passing judgment. I'm a jealous fool."

Hallie was surprised by his admission. She smiled weakly. "A little jealousy is a nice thing, but you mustn't get carried away," she half teased, lightening the tension in the room.

Michael watched her closely, as if to see into her

mind, to tell if she had actually forgiven him so easily. He hoped she took it for granted that he had been only to Adam's house and not fulfilled his threat of going to Maeve. He wanted her never to know. His voice, when he spoke again, was filled with concern for her. "Are you all right? Adam told me how upset you were."

"I was, but I'm fine now," she answered, grateful that Michael was so conciliatory. She, too, prayed that her minor infraction would remain forever a secret. Her features clouded with the thought of the afternoon's activities. "They told me I did not harm the baby, and Jason assured me that Amanda was all right. I only hope she can forgive me for the way I handled it. I lost all control when I looked down at that tiny, lifeless baby." Her eyes misted with the memory, the pain flooding back into her now that the anger was no longer present.

Michael drew her into his arms, holding her tightly, comforting her as he had not done earlier. Her voice was tiny. "I feel so badly about it! It was almost as though he were my own baby I held! I would give anything not to have hurt Amanda that way."

Michael cradled her, at last feeling as though he were where he belonged, doing what he needed to do. He did not question his feelings, merely took comfort in them. "I know, love." he whispered, kissing her head lightly. "But the most important thing is that she's alive. She will get over it and have more children, I'm certain of it." After a long pause in which each reveled in the solace offered by the other, Michael spoke again. "I have something else to tell you, Hallie, for I didn't do justice to anyone involved by what I led you to believe. Your mother was not a whore, nor was my father some horrible defiler of innocent women. They were two lonely, unhappy people who turned to each other out of desperation. Your father would have nothing to do with your mother; in fact, he lost her to my father in a card game. When my father refused to take her as payment, yours raised all hell, saying he'd been insulted. My father and your mother agreed to meet and do nothing more than talk, giving the appearance that she was paying the debt to appease your father. After

225

a time it turned to more. They loved each other, and from that sprang Danny."

Hallie pushed herself from his arms. "My father had little to do with me. I saw him rarely, for Mercy had orders to keep me out of his sight. I never realized how vile he was." She shuddered to think of what her mother must have endured. "What of the land and the water rights?"

"It was a lie. My father had purchased the land from Etta three years before our wedding. I seized the only reason I could come up with."

"Still, that leaves me as nothing more than the means to your gaining Danny," she said, pain evident in her eyes.

"At first that was true, Hallie. But you know as well as I do that we have more than that now."

"Do we?" she asked.

Michael stood. Uncomfortable with the change in subject, he began to finish his undressing. "We have a marriage, Hallie. As good as or better than most. We have a future and a life together."

But what if I want more? her mind shouted, but her lips remained closed. Instead she asked, "Is that enough, Michael?"

"Of course it is!" he said forcefully.

Hallie wondered if he meant what he said, for if he did, she did not know how she could bear it.

His voice interrupted her thoughts as he slid into bed beside her. His brow was furrowed as if he were confused by what he would say. "I have spent this past hour thinking of what we have together, Hallie. I don't want us to go on as we have, always on the verge of war. I wonder if we might agree to a truce."

Hallie stared at him. She did not know why this small thing caused lines to mar his face as though it were a monumental declaration. "Are you offering it?"

"Yes, I guess I am. We will never find even a measure of happiness if we remain suspicious and distrustful. What do you think?"

"Can you ever come to trust me?"

His smile was sheepish. "I'll give it my damnedest try! And what of you?"

"It isn't easy, is it?"

226

"No, sweet, it is almighty hard. But I believe we'll be better off for the effort."

Hallie fell asleep wondering if a semblance of happiness and trust was the best Michael had to offer.

CHAPTER FORTY-ONE

December dawned gray, the world swathed in dark clouds, the air filled with falling snow. For three days Redland was snowbound. Hallie worried over Amanda, not having heard anything about her since the day of the birth. The snow made it impossible for her to travel into the city to visit her friend. Instead Hallie was left to deal with a series of shrewish monologues from Emeline, a new aloofness on Trent's part that she did not understand and Danny's quest for mischief just to break the monotony. When the snow stopped and a spot of sunshine barely glimmered through dense clouds, tempers were all short. Hallie felt she would scream if forced to spend another moment with Emeline. Michael had left at dawn to tend to business that had been left undone with the snow, so Hallie set out in search of Farley. The large man smiled warmly at her approach and after some gentle persuasion agreed to forge the muddy roads to take her to visit Amanda.

The Curtis home was like a mausoleum. Everyone spoke in hushed tones and looked sorrowful. It was unlike anything Hallie had ever experienced around Amanda, for her friend liked happy, frivolous things and people. Jason appeared only seconds after Hallie had removed her coat, his haggard face lined with worry. He smiled weakly at his wife's best friend.

"I'm so glad you've come! We desperately need a bit of pleasant company! I hope you can help Amanda. I've never known her to be like this. She hardly speaks, she never cries, but she never smiles either. She seems only to tolerate me, almost as if she would rather I left her alone. Perhaps she will talk to you."

Hallie's face paled. "Does she want to see me?" she asked fearfully.

He shook his head slowly. "To tell the truth, I don't think she wants to see anyone. You must be prepared, Hallie. She sometimes is not very courteous."

"Has she said anything about my blurting out that the baby was dead?"

"Nothing at all. I wouldn't worry about it; I don't think she even remembers. I suppose that is for the best, but I can't understand the rest of it. I hope you can help her, Hallie. If anyone can it would be you."

Though the day was bright with sunshine, Amanda's room was dim; a single candle burned at her bedside. Heavy velvet draperies were pulled closed, blocking out any light. Amanda lay flat on her back, her blond hair flowing out around her ashen face. She stared blankly at the candle, not even turning to see who had entered her room.

Hallie sat in the chair pulled to the side of the bed, nervous in this first meeting with her friend since the birth of her dead baby. "How are you, Amanda?" she said hesitantly.

She turned slowly to face Hallie, never altering her vacant expression. "Hello, Hallie. I didn't know it was you. I didn't expect you."

Hallie smiled warmly, concealing the concern she felt. "Are you feeling better?"

"I suppose." The tone of Amanda's voice was expressionless.

Hallie took her cold hand. Hallie's first thought was that it felt as lifeless as the baby had in her hands. She suppressed a shiver. "Wouldn't you like the curtains pulled, Amanda? It is a beautiful day outside. The snow has finally stopped."

"No, thank you. I didn't know it had snowed."

"We've been snowbound for three days! I thought it would be spring before we could get out again." There was no response. Finally Hallie spoke passionately, for she could not bear to see her friend like this and did not know what to do. "Please don't do this to yourself, Amanda! You must bring yourself up out of the doldrums!"

Amanda's deep brown eyes closed slowly. "I'm very tired now, Hallie. Forgive me, but I must sleep."

Hallie stared at her for a long time, but Amanda's eyes remained closed. At last Hallie left the room, her heart heavy. She felt so helpless. She prayed that time would heal Amanda's heart as well as her body, but she wondered if that were possible when her friend refused to help herself.

Hallie pulled the bedroom door softly closed. Jason stood in the hallway, a vigil he seemed accustomed to. "She wouldn't even talk to you, would she?"

Hallie smiled, a feeble attempt to comfort her friend's husband. "It's so soon after the birth, Jason. You mustn't expect too much of her. Her wounds will heal, it will just take time. I know how much she loves you, and that hasn't changed; but she must find her own way back from this."

His own smile was weak. "I know. Adam tells me the same thing. I only wish there was something I could do for her."

"You might try opening her drapes and airing the room, even if she doesn't want it! No one can recover in a tomb."

"Hallie?" Jason stopped her as she moved to descend the stairs. "Adam is in the drawing room. He visits Amanda every day at this time. He's asked me to leave you alone with him. If you would rather not, I'll come back downstairs."

"It doesn't matter, Jason. I've been wanting to talk to him. But thank you anyway."

Hallie found Adam sitting in a chair that faced the doorway. His smile was full of love, of adoration, of wanting. It made her task all the more difficult, but her resolve did not waver.

Adam stood as Hallie moved toward him. "Mandy isn't any better today, is she?" he asked, seeing her

231

concern. At Hallie's shake of her head he continued. "I know she'll come to grips with this. It really isn't unusual for any woman to experience some low feelings after a birth. Under these circumstances, it is to be expected. It was good of you to come today."

Hallie could not allow him to go on; she needed to deliver her message, to remove a heavy burden from her own shoulders. "Adam," her voice shook with tension, "I must tell you something that will hurt you." She paused, hating what she was about to do. "Michael and I have called a truce. After the other night we agreed to make every effort to trust one another for the sake of our marriage. I must ask you, beg you to make no more arrangements to see me. Not in any way or any time or place that is not completely an accident."

Adam looked pale for a moment and then angry. "Has he threatened you, Hallie?"

"No, it isn't anything like that, Adam! Please! Don't make this more difficult. You and I know only too well that we have not been fair in this. We continue to meet, to see each other and pretend we have the right when we don't! We're playing a child's game, Adam, sneaking moments together and pretending it is our due. I have thought of nothing else these past few days and it has made me realize I had not made a choice, I had not completely accepted the end of our relationship, nor have I made a real effort to have a successful marriage. Always there have been thoughts of you, of being with you, even of some future with you. But it cannot be! Not in any sense. It is wrong for you and certainly it is a great wrong against Michael."

Adam stood now, pacing, pushing one fist into the palm of his other hand. "Dammit, Hallie! Don't you see that this will never work? You can't simply put away your feelings for me as though they were old clothes, any more than you can conjure up new feelings to make this sham a success! There is more between us than that! At least if we meet on occasion, if we have a small amount of contact you can weigh the feelings you have for me, you can test whatever you feel for him! To stop seeing me and pretend you feel nothing is absurd! It is not any more honest, or any more right! You are cheating us and it will not help the damned marriage succeed. It was doomed from the start!"

"It is what I must do, Adam!" she fairly shouted. "I can't live with this constant turmoil! I can't float back and forth between the two of you! It's tearing me apart, don't you see that? When I'm with Michael I always think of you—and God knows after the other night, I proved to myself that I can't leave Michael behind to be with you! I must find a place to settle, a future that is certain and not always torn between the present and the past! I am married to Michael. He must be my future. If you love me as you say, then allow me to move securely into the present. Don't keep luring me back into something that can never be!"

Hallie saw his shoulders slump and she knew he would honor her wish. "I hate him for this, Hallie! I have never despised another person as I do now."

"It isn't Michael's fault, Adam. It has simply happened, and there is nothing to be done."

The pain in his eyes was bright as he watched her don her cloak to leave. "I'll do as you ask. I won't seek you out again. But please tell me you will know I'm always here for you, that you will never hesitate to come to me for anything."

Hallie's eyes filled with tears, her lips quivered with the fight to still them. "It doesn't need to be said, Adam. That knowledge wraps me like a warm blanket when I most need to feel that I am not alone."

Adam moved to her, his hand raising her chin gently. His lips lowered to hers, first softly, then more desperately, until he knew he must stop or reach a point where he could never pull back. For a moment his lips rested in her hair, breathing deeply to calm himself, to find something he could seize in himself to allow her to leave.

Her whispered words rang with pain. "Please, Adam, please," she begged.

He stepped away from her and turned as though the sight of her leaving was something he could not endure.

CHAPTER FORTY-TWO

It was only three days until Christmas, but Hallie had no spirit at all. She hoped the holidays would not be a repeat of Thanksgiving; that holiday had been marked by enormous family arguments. Lydia had badgered Michael incessantly about her lack of power and ownership in the Redmond holdings, Trent had found many opportunities to vent his hostility toward his brother and by the time the turkey was carved, a tension-filled silence descended over the table.

Hallie's thoughts were anything but festive. Since her visit to Amanda, she had been worried about her friend to the point of distraction. From all accounts she was still in bed, making no effort to regain her health. Hallie had sent message after message asking if she could come to visit, but each reply was the same: Amanda was too tired.

A new worry had occurred to her. She worked hard to convince herself it was not so, that the human body often malfunctioned; certainly her emotions had been affected by the shock of Amanda's baby and all the tension she had felt since then, not to mention the past two months with Michael. Still, it had never happened before and her fear that she was carrying a child grew with each passing day. Hallie refused to think about it, telling herself that if the new year had not proven her wrong, she would worry about it then.

Lydia had ordered the town house decorated for her Christmas party. Silver and gold ribbons, bows, tinsel and streamers seemed to hang everywhere. Somehow the effect was cold; it was totally unlike the warm, homey feeling that Hallie had created at Redland with red and green and white ribbons woven up the banister, a large pine wreath on the door and boughs over every mantelpiece. Hallie had expected to see an abundance of red, if only because it was Lydia's favorite color. Instead it appeared only on Lydia. The neckline of her velvet dress was so low all but the very tips of her large breasts were pushed into view. She relished the lurid stares she received, bending slightly forward as if to hear every word spoken to her by every man.

Michael's moustache tickled Hallie's ear as he whispered, "I thought a party might brighten your spirits, my love, but it appears this is to be more a display for Lydia's questionable taste."

Hallie forced a smile, knowing that in recent days her mood had not made her easy to live with. Even Danny had berated her for being a scrooge. She turned deep violet eyes up to Michael and said, "I would rather not stay long, if you don't mind. I'm not much in the mood for a party."

Michael looked around him and did not wonder why. Lydia had had the audacity to mix the cream of Boston society with a rather bizarre and seedy assortment of her friends. It was assumed that the worst of the fops and dandies, all looking much like outlandishly plumed peacocks, were friends of Oliver. They stood off to one corner, their chins lifted higher in the air even than those members of the upper class they were offending. Several women present made Lydia seem modest in comparison. A few of the men were of a rougher cut, looking very out of place in formal suits that did not fit well. These reminded Michael more of the toughs he had come into contact with as a sailor, dangerous men who lived by their wits and fists.

As Hallie's eyes scanned the crowd, she was suddenly struck by the difference between the way things appeared and the way they were.

It seemed an odd dance as staid matrons and respected gentlemen stood in formal postures mouthing accepted courtesies while eyes wandered to paramours and lovers, bespeaking secret intimacies. She thought that it was sadly ludicrous and wondered if she were naïve to hope and wish for fidelity from Michael.

"You're looking sweet tonight, dear." Belinda Scott's tones were condescending. "Lavender is such a good color for a matron."

Hallie returned a smile as insincere as Belinda's. "Thank you, dear," Hallie said derisively. "That girlish pink frock is terribly becoming."

Belinda laughed shortly. "Adam requested I wear it this evening. I was just about to put on a different gown when he insisted on going through my wardrobe to choose what I would wear. It's too bad he was called away on an emergency just before we were to leave. He had promised me such a lovely evening. Of course he'll make it up to me later. I do hope you did not make the mistake of playing the virgin when you knew him," she continued, heedless of the drastic change of subjects, her voice mockingly concerned. "You really missed quite a wonderful lover if you did."

Hallie's face turned scarlet not only for the woman's words but also with the reminder of the occasion when she very nearly discovered the truth in this particular matter. Belinda laughed maliciously. "Can you still be playing the prude?" she asked. "Some women never get past that, do they? Well, let me tell you this, Hallie. I've had Adam and I've had Michael and I would pick Adam every time! How foolish of you to tie yourself to Michael! Unless, of course, you really didn't try them both out before deciding."

At that point even Oliver Kent was a welcome rescuer as he bowed before Hallie and begged for a dance. She gladly allowed him to lead her away from Belinda without a word. A few moments later she wondered at the wisdom of her choice as Oliver worked to catch a glimpse down the décolletage of her gown. It took only seconds to decide not to continue the dance, and she attempted to extricate herself from his suddenly tight grasp. "I only agreed to dance with you to be free of that viper, Oliver. And now I will be free of you as well. Let go of me!"

His face above her was reminiscent of a rapacious animal. "Not so soon, my little nymph. You allowed me this dance, and I mean to finish it. I have something to tell you to whet your virgin's appetite."

"I'm not interested!" she said forcefully, seeing the lurid gleam in his eyes.

His arms became a vise around her, nearly crushing her ribs. He spoke as though he had not heard her last words. "There is a place I can take you to give you the pleasure you deserve! It is a wonderful house, made to tempt the flesh with every delicacy imaginable. There is one special room in which I would awaken you to the delights I know you crave, fine leathers and strong chains and other treasures, all to be used and enjoyed by those who know the better methods of love." Beads of perspiration formed on his forehead, his pale eyes lost in the sordid vision in his imagination.

Hallie's contempt and disgust rose. It seemed that everyone's worst instincts were brought out by this crass environment. She raised her hand to the side of Oliver's face as though to caress it, then grabbed a firm hold of his long whiskers. Tightening her fist around them, she pulled just forcefully enough to distort his cheek. "Let go of me, Oliver. You will stay away from me with your vile stories, or I will tear this bit of fur from your face and half of your skin with it. Do you understand me?"

As Oliver feared disfigurement more than anything else in life, his arms dropped to his sides.

Hallie released his whiskers. "That was very wise of you, Oliver," she said, her contempt showing clearly. "Please try to remember it in the future."

Hallie moved regally through the crowd in search of Michael. Just as she caught sight of him in the distance she saw his head lower to hear something being said to him. Hallie's heart lurched as she saw the recipient of his warm grin. Maeve Carson's lovely sable brown eyes shined up at Michael. She was dressed in shimmering white satin; her low-cut gown displayed a tantalizing view of her creamy breasts. She looked exquisite, and it seemed clear that Michael was enjoying the sight.

As she watched, Maeve took Michael's hand and

238

pulled him toward the dining room, out of sight. Hallie pushed through the crowd, moved by a horrible need to witness what was happening between her husband and this woman she so feared. Hallie swallowed the lump in her throat with difficulty as she eased the dining-room door open just a crack. Michael's back was to her, but it was obvious by the angle of his head that he was deep into a passionate kiss; Maeve's arms were around his broad shoulders.

Hallie closed the door silently. Her head was pounding and she felt faint. When Michael found her several minutes later she did not have to explain her need to go home. It was very apparent that she was not well.

CHAPTER FORTY-THREE

Mercy insisted that Hallie stay in bed, but after two days Hallie was determined to be up and about. Mercy stared at her as she dressed, her eyes knowing as she watched the girl carefully.

"Now, dress warm! It's not a time for catching a chill."

"I know, Mercy," Hallie answered quietly. She realized that Michael had planned the day's outing to bring her out of this mood, but she was quite certain it would not help. Sometimes she felt that Amanda's misery had somehow been transmitted to her, though she knew the reason behind hers was far different.

The sled was a large structure, four rows of seats nestled between two ornately carved sides. Smooth iron runners were meant to glide across dry, hard-packed snow as a well-matched team pulled it to the light ring of sleigh bells that enhanced the feeling of Christmas in the air.

On the seat beside Trent, Danny fidgeted impatiently, his face bright with cold and the excitement of Christmas Eve. Michael and Hallie shared the driver's seat, a heavy fur lap robe tucked firmly around them. Michael flipped the reins across the horses, called to them and they were off, floating along the icy road, traveling through a world of naturally beautiful crystal and glass. The sleigh raced through Boston heading out Beacon Street past less elaborate sleds loaded with hickory and walnut, drawn by huge oxen. The drivers were all dressed in hand-knitted neck wrappers that were pulled up over their mouths and noses to warm the air before it filled their lungs. Matching caps were pulled down over their ears, leaving only eyes to peek from their swathed heads. Their hands were covered in buckskin mittens as they urged their teams in a slow parade to the wood market.

Once past these slow-moving sleds, Michael went over the Mill Dam to Brighten Road, where many people skated on a small pond. Danny was eager to get on the ice, though he was not an accomplished skater; Trent joined him, although he was considerably less skilled than Danny. Trent slipped several times; with each fall his eyes raised in embarrassment to Hallie. She began to call encouragement back to him and gently teased him from his discomfort.

Michael sat with Hallie, his arm around her, drawing her to rest against him as they watched the boys. Mercy had given him strict orders to keep Hallie warm and to make sure she did not skate. As he was not particularly agile on skates, he was more than happy to comply. It did occur to him that it was odd that Hallie was content to sit quietly; he had expected an argument from her when he suggested they stay in the sleigh.

For a short time Hallie forgot her problems, forcing herself not to stiffen beneath Michael's touch. Lately she could not stop the dark thoughts that cropped up whenever he came near her. Belinda Scott's hateful words rang in her ears. How could Michael have had anything to do with her? And she could not stop thinking of the sight of Michael bent over Maeve Carson in the dining room. Did he think his wife too stupid to suspect that he had resumed his relationship with Maeve? These thoughts were particularly unbearable when Hallie had to confront the possibility that she might be carrying his child. But she forced herself not to dwell on her own pain or Michael's deceptions.

She watched the boys play on the ice. She was pleased that Trent seemed to enjoy himself, putting away his

242

usual somberness. He was even making some effort, albeit awkward, to be friendly to Danny. But no matter how much Trent seemed to unbend, his hostility toward Michael remained. He ignored any comment his older brother made to him and refused even to acknowledge Michael's attempts to praise him.

After about half an hour the boys were ready to leave the pond and head for Etta's house and steaming cups of Matilda's hot chocolate.

After they had warmed themselves, they all piled back in the sled and went on to Lydia and Oliver's. The Kents would join them at Redland for the holiday season. The sled made its way back slowly, for it was fully loaded. Even Trent joined in singing carols.

The tree that Michael, Farley, Danny and Trent had dragged into the drawing room was immense. It was the most perfectly shaped pine tree Hallie had ever seen, and suddenly she was able to put her worries behind her and join in its decoration. Popcorn was strung with berries and wrapped around the wide tree. At the end of nearly every branch was a small candle in a golden holder. Hundreds of carved and painted ornaments were hung on the boughs and on the top was a golden star that twinkled brightly with glitter and beads, a small candle at its center.

When they were finished Danny stood back in awe, as did Hallie, Michael and Etta. Trent stood off by himself, but his face showed his appreciation of the sight. Emeline, Lydia and Oliver remained unaffected as they sat together in a far corner of the room engrossed in conversation.

On Christmas morning Danny roused all but the Kents before dawn. The candles on the tree were the only light in the still, dark house, and Danny gaily discovered one treasure after another. When at last he had depleted his supply of gifts and thanked everyone ten times over, it was Etta's turn. From Danny she unveiled a picture he had painted of himself standing before her town house. The painting was proof that he would not grow to become a great artist, but it touched and pleased Etta. From Hallie she received embroidered handkerchiefs, which she was fond of wearing pinned behind her watch from her shoulder. She thanked her granddaughter with a kiss and then smiled at Michael.

Emeline received soaps from Danny and similar handkerchiefs from Hallie and Michael as well as a fine bottle of sherry, which she liked to sip before bedtime. Trent's gift to her was a small gold brooch, and this she immediately pinned to her robe.

Hallie was next, opening first a box of rocks from a laughing Danny. When he finally contained his laughter he produced a box that was hidden behind the tree. Inside was a fur hat Hallie had admired in a shop. From her grandmother she received a lacy chemise, the delicate stitching coming from the old woman's own hand. Emeline's gift to her was a bottle of scented bath oil, which she appreciated as well. The last package she opened was from Trent. It was a small ivory fan, a beautiful red rose painted on the center. She raised warm violet eyes and a brilliant smile to him. His face blazed crimson with her thanks. His pride seemed to increase when he opened a shaving mug and brush from Hallie. His shoulders squared, his head rose as his hand went involuntarily to his still smooth chin. It was a gift for a grown man, and that in itself made it special.

Last of all came Michael. His gift from Danny was a new razor strop, which he good-naturedly threatened to save and use only on him. From Etta he received a gold watch chain and from Emeline a fine set of handkerchiefs. Hallie's gift was a silk shirt she had spent hours making. Her handiwork was as delicate as her grandmother's, for she had been well tutored.

Before he proceeded, Michael pulled a small box from his pocket and presented it to his wife. Hallie released the ribbon and opened the lid to find an exquisite brooch of diamonds clustered like a rose petal set amid a silver splendor of leaves. She fingered it breathlessly, unable to speak. Deep violet eyes glowing with candlelight stared up at him, and her voice was soft, touched. "It is more beautiful than anything I have ever seen," she said. "Thank you."

"It was my mother's, and hers before."

Emeline's indrawn breath broke the spell woven around them. Her disapproval was obvious though she said nothing. Ignoring her, Hallie pinned the lovely piece to her robe, smiling up at Michael.

Only one gift remained, and that carried Michael's name. When the beautiful paper was torn from it he lifted the lid to reveal an expensive black velvet dressing gown. A card was tucked into the breast pocket.

Michael's frown drew everyone's attention, but only Emeline bluntly questioned it. "Well, who sent you that fine gift?" she demanded, seeing his reluctance.

Michael's blue-gray eyes looked apologetically at Hallie. "It will have to be returned. Maeve Carson sent it."

Hallie felt as if she had been struck. The joy of Christmas was washed away in the humiliation that she felt.

"She has good taste, I'll say that for her. She obviously knows you quite well, Michael." Emeline's voice grated even more over Hallie's already frayed nerves.

Michael folded it back into the box and replaced the lid, pushing it to the back of the tree. It mattered little to Hallie what he did now, for the damage had been done. What more blatant proof did she need than an extremely personal gift waiting for Michael beneath the tree on Christmas morning?

CHAPTER FORTY-FOUR

The day had been long for Hallie. She was relieved when at last she climbed the stairs to her room, alone, for Michael had stayed to share one last cup of cheer with Farley. Her heart was heavy with thoughts of Michael's peccadilloes—past and present. She felt certain that his talk of coming to trust one another had merely been a clever ruse. She unpinned the exquisite brooch from the bodice of her dress, staring down at its luminous glimmer in her palm. So this is how it is to be, she thought. I am the figurehead wife, hostess and bearer of children, while Michael is free to carry on his life just as before. Would marriage to Adam have been like this? What a miserable lot was the life of a woman, she thought now, her depression clouding everything. She tucked the brooch away in its velvet-lined box. Her nerves were stretched taut, she knew; it was best to seek the warmth of her bed and hope she felt more like herself in the morning.

The bed was downy, the clean sheets warmed from the pans Mercy had placed between them. The room was lit only by the fire in the hearth, casting long shadows from the corners. She watched the flames, mesmerized by the popping and crackling as the fire engulfed the wood. It took only moments for her eyelids to become heavy, and Hallie did not fight the blessed comfort of sleep.

Michael had not expected his wife to be asleep. He stood quietly, staring down at her small form in the large bed as he disrobed. He had held his passions in check for too long a time, and the sight of her peaceful profile was enough to arouse his desires boundlessly. Michael's long, lean body pressed closely up to Hallie's back, curving to meet her at every inch, his need for her evident. He kissed the side of her neck, pulling the high, lacy collar of her nightgown down to reach the soft, sweet-smelling flesh there. He nibbled lightly on her earlobe, whispering her name softly, merely a warm breath brushing it. His hand was at her shoulder, caressing the soft batiste there.

Hallie responded to his touch in her sleep. As she came awake her body stiffened and she drew away from her husband. "Don't touch me." Her tone was icy.

"Why not?"

"Please just don't!" The level rose an octave.

"I want you, Hallie."

Since it seemed that she could not escape his persistent caresses she rose, standing before the fire to keep herself warm. She could not control her rage. "Pretending to return your gift will allow you to visit Maeve tonight. Spare me," she said bitingly.

Having his passion thrown back in his face did little for Michael's pride and spurred his own temper. "Christ! I hoped we could just ignore that. It was a foolish gesture on Maeve's part. I have told you that she is in the past."

One finely arched brow rose over a flaming violet eye. "That is not what I observed at Lydia's party."

"Oh? Perhaps I should be informed as to what I am guilty of."

"My eyesight has always been good, Michael. Even from a distance I saw the look in your eyes. I followed you into the dining room and was the unfortunate witness to your touching and tender embrace. Quite frankly, I have no inclination to keep you two apart. Or perhaps you would rather have the company of Belinda Scott. She gave me a lecture on the relative merits of your lovemaking and Adam's. Pity she did not send a gift as well. We could have had such a full tree!" Her tone was derisive, her eyes bright with anger.

"Belinda Scott?" he shrieked, sitting upright in the bed. "I have never touched that woman and would refuse if asked!"

Now Hallie's voice was more calm but still snide. "What an adept liar you are."

Michael exploded. "Dammit! I'm tired of this! Do you expect me to be faithful to a shrew? I've tried to be patient, I've done everything I know to brighten your shrewish spirits, and what do I get for my trouble? A slap in the face, a refusal in my own bed and an attack for something you have no cause to believe! Well, I am finished with it! This house has far too many peaceful rooms to remain here! I told you that I wanted you. Now you can keep your lonely bed until you can say the same." He lunged from the bed, not bothering to put on a robe, strode through the doorway and slammed the door. Moments later the sound of another door was heard.

Tears fell from Hallie's eyes as she collapsed on the floor, feeling utter despair. She was certain she was going to have his child and in that instant made her decision. She began to cry harder, for that pain was more difficult to bear.

CHAPTER FORTY-FIVE

Hallie stood before her bureau, staring down at the small bottle she held in her hand. She had remembered Lydia's words about Sky's unusual talents. Hallie had approached the girl early in the morning, at a moment when Hallie could be sure no one would overhear her request. Hallie hated the way she felt. She had spent the day on the verge of tears, arguing with herself, a persistent lump in her throat. Her stomach was in knots and her voice quivered with each word she was required to speak. She remembered Sky's words as she explained the effects of her potion in vivid detail. The young servant's disapproval sat heavily on Hallie's already weighty doubts and fears.

"What's that you're looking so solemn about?"

Hallie jumped with fright at Mercy's words, hiding the blue vial beneath her nightgowns in the dresser. "It's nothing. I thought you were going to arrange for my bath?"

"Doesn't take that long. I did it already. Now, what was that you hid?" Mercy pressed.

"An empty bottle. I've kept it for storing something in later. It is of no importance."

"Looks pretty important to me."

Nervousness spurred Hallie to turn on this dear and

trusted friend. "I said it was nothing, Mercy! It is not your place to question me!"

The bushy brows rose with surprise at her words, for never, even as a child, had Hallie raised her voice to the old woman.

Hallie was instantly contrite. "I'm sorry, Mercy!" she said, her tone begging forgiveness. "My mood is just not good lately. I have a great deal on my mind, and I don't feel well."

Mercy shook her head, knowing what ailed her. "It's time you let some of us help with your problems."

Hallie closed her eyes against the tears that threatened to flow. "There isn't anything anyone can do." Her voice was soft, quivering with the effort to hold her emotions in control.

Mercy's suspicions rose. "Sometimes things aren't as black as they look. Try thinking about the good, and before you know it that's how it is." The heavy old woman moved to Hallie's side and pulled her close. "It's a horrible thing to feel alone with your troubles but worse yet to act against them before you've thought about it for a long, long time. It isn't the way for us to take God's work in our own hands, love. Be careful what you're about." She led Hallie to the bathroom, then left her alone.

Hallie sank deeply in the steamy, scented water and closed her eyes. After a few minutes she felt some of the tension disappear. Her mind again wandered to the morning's visit to Sky. One thing the girl had said had been plaguing her; she could not put it from her mind. Did she want to kill this baby? What a horrible way that was to put it. Up until this day she had not thought of ridding herself of this problem as either killing it or of it as being a baby. It is a baby, she thought, my baby. Regardless of how unhappy her marriage had come to be, she wondered how she would live with herself if she swallowed the concoction in the blue vial. Would it be so bad to give birth to Michael's child? she wondered. She was becoming increasingly certain that she could not follow through with a plan that had been formed in anger. If she could not have Adam's love, and surely she would never have love from Michael, at least she would have her baby to love and fill her life.

Her spirits lifted as she resolved to go to Michael that night when the house was quiet and tell him the news. Perhaps it would bring some happiness to their union as well, for he had told her often of his desire for children. Maybe this would be enough to bridge the gap that had grown between them. She could not help hoping that it would give Michael cause to be loyal to her and their vows. She smiled now, thinking that Mercy was right. Sometimes when you thought about the happy aspects of a situation it became so.

As Hallie closed the bedroom door and moved down the hallway to dinner she hummed a light tune, suddenly feeling pleased with the fact that she and Michael would have a baby.

Michael stood staring out at the frigid January night, a light snow falling once more. Oliver Kent sat in a corner, engrossed in the *Boston Evening Transcript,* paying no attention whatsoever to the other man. Both faced Hallie when she entered the drawing room, but she looked only to Michael, a warm smile for him on her lovely features. Michael returned it tentatively, wondering why he should be so blessed after all this time of coldness. It took only this small indication for his blood to quicken with desire.

She crossed the room to her husband, her voice so soft only Michael could hear it. "If you would not mind, I would like to talk with you later tonight, in private, please," she said sweetly, feeling unexpectedly anxious to break the news to him.

One dark brow arched in question. "My pleasure," he said, his voice thick with insinuation.

The entrance of Lydia and Emeline with Danny in tow forestalled any further conversation. The older woman's grating voice resounded through the house. "Michael, you must speak to this boy! Cook has been complaining about him wreaking havoc in her kitchen. Lydia and I just met her chasing him down the hall to get him out of there again. Will you please lecture him on his manners?"

"I believe you have done that already, Emeline. I doubt if Danny needs a second warning. Do you, Dan?" Danny shook his head negatively, though it was apparent he fought to contain giggles. Michael suggested they go in to dine before more could be said on the subject.

Steaming bowls of soup waited at each place; Oliver and Trent were already seated and did not bother to rise as the ladies entered. Michael eased Hallie into her chair, lingering close for a moment to enjoy the sweet scent of her hair. Seconds later Danny broke into wild giggles that betrayed his mischief.

Michael picked up his water glass to find a large goldfish swimming in its depths. He studied it leisurely. "I see your fish has found a new home. Do you think he will be happy in my stomach?"

The small boy laughed gaily until Michael raised the goblet to his lips. "No! No!" Danny shouted seriously, fearing Michael would do what he threatened.

Michael lowered the glass slowly. "I suggest that if you mean to save your fish you had better remove him from the table."

Danny rose swiftly, whisking the glass to a safe place on the sideboard. Hallie twittered lightly, trying not to show her amusement, but her mood had lifted so much she found it all quite funny.

Emeline's voice reprimanded her. "My dear young woman! I find nothing amusing about these heathenish displays. Your laughter encourages defiance of the rules this boy should follow. What will become of him if you allow such behavior?"

Michael did not want his aunt to destroy his wife's sudden high spirits. "He is a mere boy, Emeline. A harmless prank is hardly unusual."

"Mark my words, Michael. You will rue the day you did not take a firm hand with him."

Instead of responding he simply said, "This soup smells delicious. I suggest we enjoy it before it cools."

Hallie felt her husband's eyes on her as she slowly ate her soup, thinking it did not taste as good as it smelled. She had consumed at least half of the bowlful before she realized it had a strange flavor. "Does this taste all right?" she asked.

"Mine is very good," Michael answered her. "Is there something wrong?"

Hallie took another large spoonful, wrinkling her nose at its foul aftertaste. "Yes. It is quite odd. Perhaps it's just me." Still she had felt more hungry tonight than she had since she had begun to think she was pregnant. With that thought she felt her stomach lurch as though rebelling against the foul-tasting soup. Her face paled.

"Are you ill, Hallie?" Michael asked in concern.

"She looks positively ashen," Lydia offered.

"Oh, dear! I do hope she hasn't brought some horrid disease home," Emeline said in disgust, drawing her head back and holding her napkin before her nose and mouth.

Hallie paid little attention, for her stomach was churning. She felt severe cramping in her abdomen.

A snide sigh sounded from Oliver. "She looks quite awful and is ruining my appetite."

Michael rose and moved to his wife, his brow creased with concern. Before he could question her, Mercy burst through the door from the kitchen, the blue vial in her hand. Her face was nearly as white as Hallie's.

"Lord God, you didn't do it, did you?"

But Hallie could manage no reply as she fled the room.

CHAPTER FORTY-SIX

Michael turned to Mercy, his eyes wide with surprise. "What the hell is going on?"

Mercy sniffed Hallie's remaining bowl of soup, holding the blue vial close to her breast as she raised her eyes skyward. "It's there! Oh, Mr. Redmond, you'd best send for a doctor. Miss Hallie is in terrible trouble!"

"What is it?" he shouted impatiently.

Mercy only shook her head and gestured to Michael to follow her to the next room. She did not want the others to hear what she had to say. As soon as they were out of earshot, she whispered, "She's going to have a baby. The poison was to get rid of it."

"Christ!" Michael's deep voice boomed throughout the house as he ran into the next room, Mercy fast on his heels, pleading all the way.

"She didn't know what she was doing! She's been mad with worry!"

Hallie stood bent over the sofa, doubled over with excruciating pain. Her face was a mask of anguish. Michael picked her up into his powerful arms quickly, shouting as he carried her up the large staircase. "Send for Dr. Hathaway! Now!"

To Hallie his tone was low, almost as though he

spoke to himself. "How could you have done something like this?"

Hallie could not speak; her body was racked with a pain more intense than anything she had ever endured as it tried to rid itself of the contents of her womb. Once on the bed she curled herself into a tight ball against the misery. At last she managed to speak, though the words were barely audible. "I didn't do this!" But the large man merely shook his head, still too shocked to grasp what she said.

Mercy moved to the bedside, loosening Hallie's gown, futilely muttering the same words of comfort she had used for all of her childhood illnesses and accidents. Michael returned to the dining room, where he retrieved the blue vial Mercy had left on the table. His stormy countenance warned Lydia, Oliver and even Emeline not to venture one word. Danny was more worried for his sister's health than afraid of this imposing tower of anger.

"What's the matter with Hallie?" he demanded, though the fear was in his voice.

Michael paused for only a moment, suddenly remembering the boy's trick and the cook's complaint against him. "It is very important that I know," he began seriously, trying not to frighten the boy. "Nothing will happen to you, but did you pour what was in this bottle into Hallie's soup?"

"No, sir!" Danny exclaimed at once, his eyes round with fear. "I only did the goldfish! I wouldn't hurt Hallie!" he said emphatically.

"Did you see anyone else do it?" Again a negative reply.

"Will she be all right?" Trent ventured, for that question had yet to be answered.

"I don't know. She is very sick, and I just don't know." He saw the tears well up in Danny's eyes, but Michael could not stop to comfort him. He stormed into the kitchen to confront the servants. The response was identical: No one had seen the bottle. Mercy alone had seized it from a corner table near the dining room.

A moan from the upper-level bedroom brought his attention abruptly back to his wife. He took the stairs three at a time, not knowing whether to be worried or raging mad but following his instincts to be with her in this hour of misery. Beads of perspiration dotted Hallie's forehead, her teeth clenched to keep from crying out against the pain. In her mind was only one thought—a plea to keep this child. Surely, she thought, this was punishment for her earlier plans.

It seemed like hours passed before the front door was opened to admit the doctor. Adam Burgess's own face was tense with concern. He did not await instructions but ran up the stairs toward the moans that echoed throughout the house.

Michael looked up from his wife's twisting form to see Adam in the doorway. He charged like a wild beast, pushing the doctor out into the hall, his face etched with worry. "What the hell are you doing here?"

"Dr. Hathaway is ill. I'm all there is. What have you done to her?" he demanded, his own fury clear.

Mercy's voice interrupted them, her old features drawn. "This is no time for that! She needs a doctor, not a fight over which of you is to blame!"

Adam pushed passed Michael, speaking to Mercy as he rushed to the bed. "Keep him out of here. He's done enough to her."

Mercy looked up at the worried visage left in the hallway, her eyes beseeching. "It's best. Let him do his work." She closed the door and moved to Hallie's side, watching Adam at his task.

"What happened here, Mercy?"

Tears ran down the old woman's moon face. "She's going to have a baby. I thought she was planning to be rid of it; I saw that poison in her drawer. But I knew she wouldn't do such a thing! Then I found it in the kitchen, empty. Somebody put it in her soup. By the time I went to warn her, it was too late."

Adam shook his head sadly. "How far along is she, do you know?"

"No, sir. But I think it's not very long."

His cool hand went to Hallie's burning forehead. "Well, it cannot survive this. Whoever gave her that poison left no opportunity for a baby to live through this. I only hope she can!"

The pain grew worse as the night wore on. Hallie was mad with it, having no idea where she was or who was at her bedside. Adam did what little he could to ease her pain, caring for her as she retched violently, murmuring words he only hoped she heard. It was torture for him to watch her suffering; he felt utterly helpless. He prayed for the skill and knowledge to save her. Mercy wept and watched, adding her own prayers. Hallie's moans faded only when she lapsed into unconsciousness.

Outside Michael paced, unaware of Farley's presence. Michael's emotions were a riot of confusion, his concern and fear only somewhat greater than his anger at having Adam Burgess at her bedside while he was relegated to the hall. He wanted to be there, to hold her hand, to do anything but this walking up and down like a caged beast. The muffled sounds of her suffering tore through him like a knife. Did she hate him so much that she would endure this rather than bear his child? As the night drew on, Michael swore he would offer her her freedom to be with Adam if only she would live.

Adam moved to the foot of the bed, knowing the end was near. Only minutes passed before the bloody mass was expelled. He worked swiftly to stop the bleeding, perspiration blinding him in his frenzied work to keep Hallie alive. When at last he had succeeded, he dropped his head in silent thanks for her life. He moved to her bedside once again, taking her cold hand in his own.

Hallie was lucid now, exhausted, but aware of what had happened, at what had now passed. Her face was ashen, and her mental anguish was clearly as great as her physical pain had been. Her voice was so weak Adam had to lower his ear to her lips to hear her. "I didn't do this, Adam."

He smiled sadly, wearily. "I believe you," he reassured her, somewhat buoyed by the fact that she cared what he believed.

"Thank you, Adam. I could not have survived without you."

He squeezed her hand gently. "Rest now, Hallie. We'll talk in a day or two when you're stronger. I promise you I won't let any more of this horror happen to you. If it takes my last breath of life I will see you happy again."

Her violet eyes closed, long, sooty lashes shining with

tears against her ashen cheeks. Adam left Mercy to tend to Hallie, then moved to face Michael in the hall-way. Had it been anyone else Adam would have pitied what he saw, for he was a compassionate man and Michael was clearly tormented.

"Is she all right?" Michael demanded.

"Yes. She is weak and will be for some time. She needs to be pampered and cared for and above all not upset. Do you think you're capable of that?"

"Of course I am! I don't need this from you, Burgess!"

"I think it's obvious that someone needs to step in for Hallie's sake. Certainly she has suffered enough at your hands."

"I had nothing to do with this, dammit!"

"Was the child not yours?" Adam asked sarcasti-cally.

"Of course it was mine! I would never have harmed her and certainly never would I have endangered her life or that of my own child."

"And what do you consider causing her so much tur-moil and strife that she seeks such a thing as this?"

He struck a raw nerve with that, for Michael had asked himself a hundred times in these past hours why he had allowed his own temper to rule him. Why had he not realized the reason she had been so upset lately and eased her fears? He could not counter Adam's ac-cusations, but his pride would not allow him to ac-knowledge them. "I appreciate your coming, Doctor," he said coldly. "Now I must see my wife." Michael walked into the room as though Adam had been effectively dismissed.

The doctor moved to follow him, but Farley's massive hand stopped him. "It's a time for them to be alone." It was an echo of the words Hallie had said to him of Jason and Amanda when their baby had died. "It was their babe who was lost tonight. And no one can intrude on that, Dr. Burgess. Their grieving has to be done to-gether and alone for it to heal them. They shared in the making by themselves and now they've got to do the same with the losing of it."

Adam conceded to his words, though it was a torment separate from the horrors of the past hours and he did not know how he would survive the pain of it.

CHAPTER FORTY-SEVEN

A cold January wind shook the shutters and the glass in every window. It howled and whistled and pushed its way into every crack and crevice of Redland, chilling it despite the roaring fires in the hearths. Though it was long past noon, Hallie still slept, never moving, her breathing so shallow that Michael was afraid to take his eyes from her lest she slip away in that instant. Michael had not left her bedside since Adam had departed. Michael could not stop questioning himself in those long, empty hours, wondering why he was so devastated by the thought of losing Hallie. He still fought the notion that he loved her, insisting it was something different. He cared for her, desired her, he admitted, but love was still a word he disdained.

Hallie stirred slightly, as if uncomfortable after so many hours in one position. Her eyes fluttered open slowly, her lashes like a butterfly's wings. She stared at Michael as he watched her; each wondered what the other's reaction would be.

Michael spoke, his voice husky, his face lined with fatigue. "How do you feel, love?"

"Not as bad as you look," she said kindly, wanting to caress his rough, bewhiskered cheek but fearing it would not be welcome. Michael appeared uncomfortable

263

beneath her scrutiny. "Michael, I must explain this to you."

"Not now, Hallie. It's important that you rest."

"I cannot rest until you know the truth. I did not do this! I was upset before, when I first realized there would be a baby. I was angry and hurt and I wanted to strike back at you, so I bought that potion. But last night I realized that I wanted the baby, I was suddenly happy to bear our child. That is what I intended to tell you. I don't know how that horrible stuff found its way into my soup, but I swear to you that it was not my doing!"

Michael saw the anguish in her eyes, saw the tears that fell from the corners, heard the regret in her voice. He did not doubt it. He wanted to hold her, to ease her suffering, but he, too, refrained, feeling she would not accept it from him. "I believe you, Hallie, though I realize it is my fault that the thought occurred to you." He paced, as if his next words were difficult to speak. "I think this has all gone on long enough. I know I've been unfair to you in demanding that you forget your past and forcing you to be a wife to me. I see now that I have driven you too far, and so I will tell you this, when you are well again, if you so desire, I will not stand in the way of your freedom. Perhaps you are right in saying that nothing can come to good between us under the circumstances of this marriage."

His words were sharp blows to Hallie in her weakened state. She had just told him she wanted to bear his child, and his answer had been only that she was free to seek Adam. It seemed obvious to her that he no longer wanted her in any way. Perhaps this incident had brought to light the fact that if there were a child he would owe her an allegiance he could not feel. Hallie closed her eyes in answer, too weary, too filled with agony to speak.

Having done what he had vowed he would if she lived, Michael returned to the lonely guest room, feeling desolate.

Only Michael and Emeline were present at the evening meal. Emeline made no mention of Hallie until they were served coffee. "Well, how is she?" she said. perfunctorily.

"Weak, but she will be fine."

"You know, Michael, I hate to bring this up, for I can see how weary you are, but it is my duty. I cannot let too much time pass and chance your forgiving her. Certainly you must realize that she did such a horrid thing because she carried another man's child. She no doubt thinks you cannot turn her out in such a weakened state."

Michael's blue-gray eyes shot daggers of contempt at the woman. His voice was icy. "The baby was mine, Emeline."

"That is just as bad!" she broke in abruptly. "Do you want a woman who murders your heirs before they are born?"

"Enough!" he shouted, his fist pounding the table. "She did not do this to herself!"

"Has she duped you so soon? You heard her maid tell you what had happened!"

"She was mistaken!"

"Who would do such a thing if not she?"

"I have an idea. But I can't prove it. So help me God if I ever can, they'll rue the day they were born!"

"Michael!" she said, horrified. "You don't believe that young boy would do such a thing to his own sister!"

"Of course not!"

"Well then, whom do you suspect?"

"The only people who would benefit from my never having heirs."

"Certainly not Lydia and Oliver?" she said in disbelief, her eyes wide.

"As I've said, I have no proof."

"To think such a thing of your own sister! Why, that little tart has fogged your vision! Lydia may be jealous that you inherited the Redmond holdings, but she could never do such a thing. If it is true that your wife did not do this to herself, then I suggest you look among your servants for the culprit."

Michael said no more. There was no point in discussing Hallie with Emeline. He would pursue his own suspicions in his own way.

CHAPTER FORTY-EIGHT

Hallie lowered the flaps over the carriage windows, not wanting to see Redland as she and Danny left it. Her heart ached and, though she had not thought it possible, she was more despondent than she had been when she had first realized she was pregnant. The weeks of convalescence had healed her body but not her spirits.

The time had been spent in her room almost every day, with Mercy fussing about her constantly. Danny had visited each morning, entertaining her with his antics and exaggerated stories and regaling her with descriptions of his practical jokes. Trent had come several times, always in the early evening. Though he was obviously uncomfortable and found conversation difficult, Hallie appreciated his concern. She was sorry that his feelings for Michael were not improved. His visits always ended when Michael appeared in the room. Emeline had entered her room only once, out of courtesy, but Lydia had come often to keep her informed of the latest gossip.

The most difficult part of it all had been Michael. He had come every evening, formal and polite, often standing with his hands held behind his back the entire time. She could detect no warmth in him. She would have preferred a show of hatred to this cold courtesy; at least that would indicate he cared about her.

But nothing in his manner encouraged her to stay.

As her strength returned, Hallie decided she could no longer live at Redland. She sent her grandmother a message requesting an invitation for an extended visit. That would give her time to sort out her thoughts and form a plan for her own future as well as Danny's.

They had settled into their old rooms within a few hours of their arrival. Mercy set about tasks as though she had never left, although her expression indicated that she felt Hallie should have remained with her husband. Etta voiced no opinion to her granddaughter, but Hallie saw her disappointment and sadness and knew the old woman felt responsible for her unhappiness. The atmosphere was not a happy one, and Hallie's spirits remained low.

On the second morning of her stay Hallie was pleased by a visit from Amanda. She had not seen her friend since she had visited her bedside. It had taken Amanda a long time to rise out of her depression, but with the help of Adam and the love of Jason she had at last realized she must go on with her life. As she entered the morning room, Hallie could see the signs of strain in Amanda's thin face. Still Hallie saw the familiar enthusiasm was back in her friend's eyes, so she was convinced Amanda had recovered.

"Oh, Hallie!" Amanda's voice came in a sigh, "I'm so sorry all this has happened to you."

Hallie smiled weakly. She knew there was strength and comfort to be drawn from the silent, unquestioning understanding of her friend.

Amanda sipped her tea slowly. "Michael spoke with Jason yesterday." She saw a glimmer of interest spark in Hallie. "Michael was very upset about your leaving. I felt sorry for him."

"He could have stopped me, Amanda; but he didn't. Besides, what kind of life can we have? I can't bear his affairs."

Amanda shook her head. "He is not having an affair with Maeve Carson, Hallie. I'm sure of it."

Hallie shrugged. "He will never love me, Amanda."

"Do you love him?"

"I don't know! I was beginning to think I did. I wanted our baby. I missed him in my bed. I couldn't think of anything but how to make him care for me. I know that my feelings for Adam have changed." Her face blushed crimson at the thought of the night she had gone to Amanda's brother. "I love Adam, truly I do, but not as I did before Michael. The night I thought Michael had gone to his mistress I went to Adam. I could not go through with what I had planned, and I went back to Redland. I knew then that it was really Michael I wanted, that my feelings for Adam had altered. It is all so confusing! Still when I am so unhappy I wish to be with Adam, I want his comfort. I've hoped so many times that he would come to me and just take me away. But this feeling for Michael is always there, though I wonder at my own foolishness, for he will never love me as Adam does."

"I hope you're wrong, Hallie. I believe you have fallen in love with Michael, whether you think so or not. Why don't you just go and talk it all over with him? I honestly believe this is only a terrible misunderstanding." Amanda paused, hesitant to speak of her brother. "Perhaps I should not tell you this, but Adam came to me the day after you lost your baby."

Violet eyes widened. "He promised he would visit me, but I have not seen him since then."

"I told him not to come, Hallie. And he knew deep down that he shouldn't intrude. He was upset at what he saw in Michael; it was evident that night how much Michael cared for you, how he suffered to know you were so ill. It was a harsh lesson to Adam, Hallie, but it made him decide to go on with his own life, because he realized there was a strong bond between you and Michael. Perhaps you are simply too hurt by what you thought was going on to see it as it is."

"If he cares for me, why hasn't he come to me, said a single word to show he wanted me to stay?"

"Did you make any attempt to show him you wanted to?"

"No, of course not! I will not beg to remain with him!"

"Is it not possible that he feels he would have to beg for you to stay as well?"

She shrugged. "I just don't know what to do, Amanda."

Her friend smiled warmly, reassuringly. "For now I think you need rest and a little time to think. Perhaps Michael will solve it for you."

"What about you, Mandy? Are you all right now?"

Amanda smiled. "Yes, I am. You know now how hard it is to lose a baby. But we must go on, Hallie. It's just part of what life deals us. If nothing else Jason and I are closer now than before." She reached for her hat and gloves. "I'll leave you to rest, but I'll be back in a day or two. If you need anything before, just send me word, Hallie." She squeezed her friend's cold hand in encouragement. "It will all right itself, I know it will."

As Hallie awoke from her nap the next day, she heard Adam's voice in the entry hall. She roused herself to go downstairs, wondering at her own unwillingness to see him.

"Are you feeling well, honey?" he ventured quietly.

"I'm fine, really, Adam. You saved my life."

"If I had saved your life two years ago, it wouldn't have been necessary now. I feel responsible for everything."

"You shouldn't. You're not to blame."

"Hallie," he persisted, "I know you're heartsick now, I can see in your face the torment of what you're feeling. But I must ask this of you: Is there any hope for us now?"

"Oh, Adam." Hallie's teeth tugged at her bottom lip, her eyes moist.

Before she could speak, he continued. "I know it's too soon to make any commitments. All I ask is for a chance. If I can do nothing else, I need the opportunity to try to bring a little happiness back to you. I feel that I have taken so much away from you."

"You haven't, Adam. You have given me more than I could ask in your loyalty and love." The tears she fought welled forth, falling unhindered down pale cheeks. Adam leaned forward, taking her hands in his, though he wanted to grasp her in his arms and quell all of her agonized emotions. Hallie continued, her head bowed so as not to confront the raw passion in his gaze. "I'm so confused now! My mind is tired and I can't think.

270

I can't give you what you ask at this moment, Adam! I must have time to gather myself back into a whole person again. You must give me time!"

Adam saw clearly that his words had added to her burden. He knew he must allow her what time she needed. "I understand. I'm sorry I came with this today, it was selfish of me." He placed the back of his hand against her moist cheek. "I want only for you to be happy, no matter what that takes."

As Hallie heard the door being closed behind him she dropped her face into her hands, sobbing uncontrollably. She felt such utter despair, for it seemed that happiness would never be within her reach.

CHAPTER FORTY-NINE

Michael paced the warehouse office waiting for Oliver. Michael did not understand why he felt tormented by the loss of Hallie, yet he could not rise from it. After talking to Jason these past days he still could not admit to himself that what he felt for Hallie was love, yet he was ready to swallow his pride and do anything, offer her anything to persuade her to come back to Redland.

Michael stopped at the small window which was the only break in the wooden wall. He drank from the steaming cup of coffee in his hand, staring out at the harbor. January was usually the coldest month of the year in Boston, and this was no exception. The air was thick with condensation, leaving a foggy blue mist lying heavily over the icy water. Billowing puffs of smoke came from the docked ships as the remaining hands warmed themselves on deck. The lighthouse in the distance was barely visible, the huge lantern lit even though it was the middle of the day. Ice crystals formed at the corners of the window, the cold air seeping in here enough to chill the warm lungs it filled.

A freezing gust of wind swept into the room as Oliver made his dramatic appearance, his wide cape flying around him, a ridiculous purple feather standing well above the hat of black silk and polished beaver. Michael did not delay his purpose in being here, working hard to conceal his fury at this fop. "Those last shipments were greatly improved, Oliver. All but *The Swan.* Why was there only half a cargo of tea, spices and molasses?"

Oliver shrugged negligently. "Did you expect perfection so soon?"

"Even the rest are hardly perfect. They are all shorter than they should be. But I am asking about *The Swan* now."

"There was a crack in the hull of the hold. Nothing too serious, but enough to destroy half of the cargo."

"Where is she now?"

"Being repaired, of course."

"I don't see a requisition for that, nor has Jason mentioned it."

"That is because he is not doing it. I decided that with your new partnership he would be too busy to do it in the time Mahoney's could. I sent it there."

"And the order?"

"I must have misplaced it." Oliver's confidence had not wavered.

"Dammit! You don't make those decisions anymore! Why wasn't I told about this?"

Oliver shrugged nonchalantly. "I didn't see the point. You've been so preoccupied with your little wife that I doubted you'd want to be bothered with business details."

Michael gritted his teeth in frustration, knowing if he fired this cocky imbecile Lydia would never let him rest. "This is your last warning, Kent. Next time you're through."

Oliver's cape flew out as he turned back to the door, a mocking sneer on his face. Michael's coffee cup hit the door as it closed behind his brother-in-law.

It was well past dark when Michael finally closed his ledgers and gathered his papers into one pile. He stretched back in his chair, running his large hands through his hair. At first he thought the smoke he smelled came from a downdraft in the chimney of the old stove. It was only moments before he realized the room beyond the door was a roaring blaze. He moved swiftly, but as he reached the door he found it locked from the other side. Michael heard the timbers crash and flames crackle as they swallowed the lofts and shelves in the outer room. He moved from the door, raising one powerful leg to kick the old wood free of the frame. Once down he jumped back, seeing the flames spring through the opening. He pulled a handkerchief from his pocket, holding it over his mouth and nose as he made a wild dash toward the warehouse door. His lungs burned with the smoke he inhaled, his vision blurred, his head grew heavy. When at last he reached his destination he found that, too, securely locked from the outside. He pushed and kicked, but his strength was fast deserting him. He felt his shoulder snap as he threw himself into the door, using the last power he could summon.

Michael fell to the floor as the heaviness in his head overwhelmed him, turning the bright orange and gold flaming room into a pit of darkness.

Hallie sipped her morning tea, sitting near the hearth in the drawing room. She had not slept well the previous night because of the clanging fire bells. Her thoughts had turned to Michael, and she had been unable to sleep, wondering if they would ever find a solution to their problems.

Her attention was drawn to a commotion at the front door. Setting her teacup down, she moved to the entrance hall to investigate, a deep frown of curiosity pulling her features. She heard Amanda's voice and stopped. She knew that her friend would never make a social call at this early hour. Something had to be wrong. Hallie's breath drew in sharply, and her eyes widened as fear took hold. Seeing her, Amanda moved quickly to her, leaving Adam in the doorway. Cold talons of panic closed around Hallie's throat. Amanda's eyes were red-rimmed, and her voice quavered.

"Hallie! Oh, my God, Hallie!"

"What's happened?" Hallie shouted, raising her eyes to Adam in horrible query. "It's Michael, isn't it?" she whispered.

"There was a fire in the warehouse last night!"

Amanda's words rushed out. "I'm so sorry, Hallie. Michael was caught in the building. He's dead!"

The sounds all seemed to Hallie to be coming from a long distance. Her head spun wildly before her knees turned to water and blackness took her senses.

CHAPTER FIFTY

Hallie stared at Adam's handwriting on the note she held in her hand. Her sigh was deep. The short missive brooked no denial; Adam would come for her in one hour. The weather was unseasonably warm for late February, and he had decided they should spend the afternoon in a carriage ride in the country.

In the weeks since Michael's death Hallie had learned too well the agony Amanda suffered after the stillbirth of her baby, for she was plunged into an inescapable grief. She realized now, when it was too late, that the feeling she held for Michael was indeed love, stronger and more haunting than any she had felt for Adam. She moved about in a daze, her thoughts wandering. She did not hear all of what was said to her and rarely felt compelled to answer. Sleep each night came quickly, only to bring with it horrible nightmares of Michael's death by fire, or worse still, vivid fantasies that he was alive, in the bed beside her. She was tormented by the fact that their last time together was coldly polite, that so much had been left unsaid.

Amanda visited every day, but it seemed to Hallie that no one could offer comfort. She saw Adam often, for all of Etta's efforts went into bringing the two together as her conscience pricked with the feeling that she had caused her granddaughter this misery. Adam was kind, gentle. He never pushed his suit, offering only warm solace. Still, Hallie knew he was biding his time. She realized what he expected of her, and she feared she could not give it.

Hallie felt chilled as she sat beside Adam in the open carriage. She knew the chill originated somewhere deep inside her own body, and she wondered if it came from her heart. They rode in a companionable silence. But when they went onto a little-used country road, Hallie sensed a change in his attitude. When he brought the carriage to a halt in an open glen, she felt uneasy.

Adam turned to her, one arm resting across the back of her seat, very near to her shoulder. His smile was filled with his love for her, though his eyes showed anxiety. "I was hoping the sunshine would put a little color in your cheeks, but instead you are deathly pale."

Hallie managed a tremulous smile but could offer no comment.

The back of Adam's hand brushed gently against her cheek. "Oh, Hallie, I want so badly to help you! Please let me."

"You know you've helped me, Adam." Her tone was quiet, apprehensive.

"I love you," he said softly, pressing his fingers to her lips before she could answer. "Let me say what I brought you to hear. I have to tell you first that I realize what I say can only be my honest feelings because Michael is dead. I could never accept them if I thought he could ever walk back into your life. I'm not being as magnanimous as I sound."

Hallie stared at her clasped hands resting in her lap. She wished fervently that her feelings would stop their wild spinning so that she might be able to judge them.

"I want us to be married as soon as possible."

Hallie's eyes closed. She had been afraid that was his purpose.

"Please hear me out. I have seen clearly these past weeks that what you felt for Michael was more than I ever let myself believe. I have even begun to understand that there was a certain amount of love for him. I know your grief is real, and I know that what you felt for me has been lessened, or perhaps merely locked away. I can accept that now."

Hallie's eyes raised to him, her heart heavy. "It is too soon for this, Adam," she whispered.

"But I'm so afraid, Hallie! I can't help feeling that I'm on the brink of disaster. I can't bear to lose you again. I know it isn't rational. I know Michael is dead and you need time for your wounds to heal, time to mourn. Yet I am obsessed with this fear. I want you to be my wife, Hallie. I want us to be married! As soon as possible! In the next few weeks!"

"Adam, please!" she beseeched.

"Just listen, honey! I know it's too soon, I can see in your eyes that your feelings are confused. What I ask is only that we marry. Afterward you can have all the time you need before you become my wife in any other sense. You needn't live in my house. You can stay with your grandmother if you would rather. I'm willing to allow you anything in the world you need, Hallie, even years. But marry me now and put my fears to rest. I swear to you I will not pressure you to do anything else. I won't even court you until you're ready, and even then we will begin all over. I'll woo you and do my best to win you again. I know you love me, Hallie. It only needs time and care to bring it back out."

"It sounds so simple, Adam, but it isn't!"

"Are you saying that you're certain you have no love for me?"

"No, that isn't what I'm saying. I suppose it's just that I can't quite believe Michael is dead. I don't feel free to give you hope, let alone marry you. My feelings are still so filled with him." Her eyes misted.

"He's gone, Hallie, you know that," he said gently.

"Of course my mind knows that. But my heart is not so easily convinced. It would be unfair to you, Adam. I need more time just to accept his death."

"It's all right, honey! I don't care how long a time it takes, only marry me now! Please, Hallie! Don't let what's happened before happen again! We must marry, we must join ourselves legally before anything else can pull us apart! I'm begging you!"

She saw the anguish in his features. She hadn't the

strength to refuse. "I don't think it's right, Adam," she said weakly, but he knew she had capitulated.

"It's exactly right, honey. It's the best way. I've done you so much harm already, I promise you I never will hurt you again."

CHAPTER FIFTY-ONE

Hallie peered at the light snow through the carriage window. It had taken all the will she possessed to tend to some things that had to be done before her wedding to Adam. It was only three days away, and she felt no excitement or anticipation. She would go for the final fitting of her gown, and then she would meet Lydia for tea. She had no idea why Lydia had insisted on this meeting; they had not been in contact since the funeral service for Michael, which was held even though his body had never been recovered from the burned warehouse. Hallie's mind was always full of memories of him, but seeing people associated with that short marriage brought a surge of pain that was almost unendurable. How cruel was fate, thought Hallie, to keep from her the knowledge of how much she loved Michael until after his death.

Madame Payne's shop was warm and inviting. Hallie was several minutes early for her appointment and stood off to one side looking at a new arrival of exquisite French lace. Her mind suddenly flashed to the nightgowns Michael had ordered for her after that first night. All seven had been trimmed only in this fine soft lace. She recalled his hand, warm and strong, running softly along the plunging neckline, pausing so that the backs of his fingers rested against the side of her breast. As she stood lost in this painful memory, trying to control the welling tears, a voice sounded behind her.

"Well, if it isn't the Widow Redmond." Maeve Carson's words held no compassion for the misery apparent on Hallie's face. "Shopping for your second trousseau?"

Hallie turned, slightly disoriented by the abrasive intrusion. "If you'll excuse me, I have an appointment," she said, moving to pass the larger woman.

"What kind of woman are you?" Maeve said, blocking her retreat. "Michael gone barely two months and you're remarrying! It's disgusting! You've certainly shown us all what you thought of him!"

Hallie could manage little force in her voice. "What I do is not your concern."

"It is my concern because I loved that man! He was mine before you worked your wiles to trap him! Now you haven't even the decency to mourn him properly!"

"The grief I feel is something you will never know, Maeve. Believe me when I tell you I wish to God I could share it with you, but I doubt you are as willing to take part in this as you were in other things."

"You took what was to be mine! And I am the one who mourns him now, as you do not!"

"You will never understand what Michael and I had together. Now excuse me." Hallie pushed the woman lightly to the side to pass. As she moved past this other woman, Maeve's final words fell hard onto her sorely abused senses.

"Don't be such a fool, Hallie. I was privy to everything that was between you. I would pity you if I did not hold you in such contempt."

As Hallie entered the Redmond town house she could not help being overwhelmed by memories. Lydia swept into the drawing room where Hallie awaited her. Lydia flung her coat and hat on a chair, leaving no doubt that she meant this tea to be brief.

"How have you been?" she asked, her tone friendly but hurried.

"I'm well, thank you. And you?" Hallie accepted the half-filled teacup.

"I'm marvelous, as always. I must admit I quite like not having Michael around to bicker with! I was never fond of him, as you must have known, and his constant tyranny grew tedious. He should never have been allowed all he was, and I will not pretend grief."

Hallie felt anger rise at Lydia's cold pleasure in her brother's death. "What did you want to see me about, Lydia?"

"I'm glad you don't object to going right to the point. Don't take offense at what I am going to say. I would like you to return the brooch Michael gave you at Christmas. It belonged to my mother, and since you will no longer be a part of this family, I think it is only right to return it."

"You can't be serious."

Lydia sighed in impatience. "I really don't care about it. I have my own jewels, and the last thing I want is some old trinket. But Emeline fancies it, and she is driving me mad with her insistence that I get it back from you. After all, she has more right to it than you."

Hallie stood, her temper overcoming her sorrow. "I will credit you Redmonds with one thing, Lydia: You have more gall than any one group of people I have ever encountered! The brooch was a gift from my husband to me. It was his to give, and it is no less mine because Michael is dead! I would not part with it under any circumstances, and nothing in the world could make me surrender it to Emeline!" Because she could not bear for Lydia to witness her sobs, Hallie ran to the front hall, snatched up her cloak and went to her carriage. Gasping for breath, she settled into her seat. When she had regained her composure she was surprised to hear herself order her driver to take her to the dock, to the site of the warehouse where her husband had died.

Snow was falling heavily; a white blur softened the harsh roughness of splintered wooden walls of the warehouses that lined the wharf. To Hallie's eyes it could not ease the sight before her. She stared at the charred ruins of the office of the Redmond Shipping Lines. The iron stove stood alone near the edge of the dock, its chimney gone.

Hallie had stanched the flow of tears and steeled herself to come here, though still she did not know what had driven her to come at all. She had not felt compelled before, even to visit the empty grave which bore Michael's name. She supposed that she had needed to see for herself what had been described to her. Perhaps it would allow her mind to lay Michael to rest, though her heart never could. It did not help. Somehow it did not seem possible to her that Michael was dead.

Hallie was startled by the sound of Farley's voice beside her. "This is no place for you to be, missus."

She smiled warmly up at the older man. "Hello, Farley, it's good to see you."

"Go on back home. There's nothing here."

Her gaze moved back to the rubble, "Where is he, then, Farley, if not here?" Her voice was small.

"Depends on what you believe, I suppose." His voice was soft, almost as if he spoke to himself.

"I'll tell you what I can't believe. I can't believe he's dead."

Farley sighed, a deep, ragged sound. "Aye. I understand that feeling, I do. But no matter how much we hate it, it's the truth."

"Tell me, Farley, does it go away in time, this not believing? Does there come a day when you stop expecting to see him at any moment walk through the doorway or call to you? Do you stop waking with the thought that he's where he was before? Do you stop forgetting it's happened when he's in your thoughts so strongly that you know it must be real?"

His meaty hands reached to pull the hood of her cloak up over her head, clasping the frog at her throat to protect her from a chill she did not feel. "I hope so," was all he could answer her. "But it doesn't do any good at all to stand here and stare at this mess and will it not to be. Go on home. That's where the healing comes."

Hallie remained in silence, staring until she lost track of the time. Farley kept his arm around her shoulders in an attempt to comfort her, or perhaps himself. Her eyes lifted to the water beyond the dock, the thick fog that drifted like smoke across the wide expanse. Her voice was a whisper to herself. "I don't think it will ever heal."

Farley turned her now with gentle force, pulling her with him to her waiting carriage. "I'll not have you here like this, missus. It can only do you harm." He lifted her up into the carriage, and now her eyes rested on the old man. Her hands clasped his in silent thanks as he took them from her waist.

"I know this sounds silly from me, Farley, but if you ever need anything at all, please call on me."

He smiled shyly, clearly touched by her words. "I'm content working for Jason Curtis. He's a good man. If ever *you* need me, though, missus, I'll be near."

She kissed his cold cheek softly, knowing that only here was there an understanding of the depth of her grief.

CHAPTER FIFTY-TWO

The first day of March was gray and cold. Hallie sat stiffly before her dressing table as Amanda wove satin ribbons through her hair. Her wedding gown of pale peach satin and lace awaited her on the bed. She had given up pinching her cheeks to color them, for her skin always paled again. Even Amanda's high spirits were subdued by her friend's sadness.

"I hope you're doing the right thing, Hallie." Her voice was soft, comforting.

"I hope I am too. I feel as if I will wake up someday and find this is all some dream, that we are still girls in school giggling over a smile from some swain."

Amanda smiled kindly. "We're far from that, aren't we? I have some good news, though; maybe it will brighten you up."

"I could stand a bit of brightening."

"I'm going to have a baby."

Now Hallie's smile was genuine. "I'm so glad, Amanda! It's just the thing for you now, isn't it?"

"Yes, it is. Jason and I couldn't be more pleased. I only wish I could give you some of my happiness."

Hallie patted her friend's hand as it rested on her shoulder. "You deserve it all, I'd say."

"What about you, Hallie. Haven't you earned some?"

She shrugged. "I'll have it. This is always what I wanted. I only need some time to gather my wits, and then I'm sure Adam and I will be as happy as you and Jason."

Mercy's moon-shaped face peered into the room from the hallway, her eyes large, her voice high with excitement. Hallie knew that both her grandmother and her trusted old nanny hoped she had finally found her way to a happy future. "Miss Mandy, come out here a minute, will you, please?"

Hallie and Amanda's eyes met in the mirror, smiling companionably at the old woman's tone. "Just a moment, Mercy, I must add one more ribbon, and then I'll come down."

"I'm sorry, Miss Amanda, we need you right this second!"

Amanda shrugged. "I'll go and see what the problem is." She left to follow Mercy as Hallie sat staring at her reflection.

She was sorry that she would be such a sad-looking bride for Adam, but there seemed to be no remedy for it. She sighed deeply, hoping to summon enough strength to carry her through the day, for she wondered how she would ever keep up this show of a semblance of happiness. Even though only her grandmother, Danny and Mercy would attend the ceremony that Amanda and Jason would be witness to, Hallie felt that for Adam's sake she must not be a mourning bride; she must at least appear happy at her own wedding.

In the mirror she saw the door open slowly until it stood wide. She watched in interest, for she knew that Mercy or Amanda would have opened it only enough to allow them to slip in. Instead a man stepped through the doorway. Hallie's eyes widened in unbelieving shock. She stood quickly and turned to face him, fearing this was some apparition or a horrible trick of her mind. Hot tears welled up with the surge of emotions she could not control, and her cold fingers pressed tightly against her lips.

Her voice was a whisper. "My God! Michael... is that you?"

Perfect teeth showed in a sheepish grin from the center of a full beard and moustache. His cheeks were sunken, and he was gaunt and pale. "I didn't think I was so fearsome-looking, Hallie. You look as if I've frightened you to death."

Tears fell from wide violet eyes as she grasped the back of her chair for support. "They told me you were dead," she said blankly, overwhelmed and lost in a tide of emotions.

Michael moved slowly to her, his blue-gray eyes seeming to drink in the sight of her. One hand raised to caress her wet cheek gently. His voice was a husky whisper as he saw the pain in her features and knew this awful trick to be the cause. "I'm not dead, love, though someone tried hard. I am no ghost." He pressed warm lips to her forehead, lingering to breathe in the scent of her. He sat her tenderly back in her chair and then seated himself on the very edge of the bed so he could lean forward and clasp both of her hands in his. He saw that Hallie was in a state of shock as she stared at him, unblinkingly. He only hoped she would understand his words.

"I have seen only Farley since I arrived in Boston this morning. He told me all that has happened in these past three months. I would have done anything to spare you this, Hallie, but I had no way of doing that."

"They said you were dead, Michael," she repeated, a bit of realization just now dawning. "They said you were burned in the fire."

"I know, love. I nearly was. Someone locked me in that warehouse and then set fire to it. I would have died, but just as I lost all strength someone pulled me free. I don't know who it was, I only know that as I passed out, someone dragged me out. When I awoke I was on the deck of a ship bound for New Orleans. My shoulder was broken, and no one believed I was anything but a stowaway. I worked until we reached port, and by then I had pneumonia. One of the crew took pity on me and took me to a hospital. I spent nearly a month there. It's taken me until today to work my way back."

"Are you all right?" she asked feebly, searching for signs that he was not.

"I'm fine now, Hallie. A little less meat on my bones, but fine. What about you?"

The present crashed in on Hallie's mind suddenly. "Oh, Michael! This is to be my wedding day," she blurted out before she could stop herself.

"I know." Michael's back straightened and he released Hallie's hands. "In the past months I have thought of nothing but our marriage, Hallie, especially these last weeks. I doubt that you'll believe me, but before that damned fire started I had made up my mind to come here, to persuade you to come back to Redland. I have been tortured with the knowledge that I made your life unhappy, that I drove you to want to destroy your own baby, and I told myself I owed it to you to give you your freedom." His breath drew in as if to strengthen his resolve. "I will tell you honestly, Hallie, I want you as my wife. It has nothing to do with Danny or our families. It has only to do with you and me. I care for you, I need you, I will do whatever you want if you will only come home." He paused, and his reluctance to continue was plain. "But I made a vow to myself, and I will keep it. If you tell me right now that you love Adam Burgess, that you want to be his wife, I will do nothing to interfere with that. I will give you your freedom without another word, unconditionally. All you need do is tell me."

Through the confusion that spun inside of Hallie's mind and heart she was sure of one thing. She thought of the pain she would cause, and she hated the agony her decision would bring. But she had no choice at all.

Her eyes grew misted, her teeth bit into her bottom lip. "I cannot tell you how happy I am that you're alive, Michael. I care for Adam, I always have and I always will, though I know you can't understand that." She paused, breathing deeply. "But I am already wife to the man of my choice. I don't want the freedom you offer. I didn't want it before. I want only you."

Michael pulled her into his arms in a grasp that nearly crushed her, but she felt no pain, only overwhelming joy as his lips met hers in a kiss that seemed to meld them into one.

CHAPTER FIFTY-THREE

A pleased smile spread Hallie's features as she first caught sight of Redland that evening. It was the final sparkle to the already glowing happiness that had engulfed her along with Michael's arms. She fought back thoughts of Adam, knowing they would mar this moment, hoping that the message she sent with Amanda would help him understand.

Her happy feeling at returning home was somewhat short-lived. Emeline walked into the entry hall, took one look at them and fell to the floor in a dead faint. Trent had been right behind her; his face became ashen and for a moment it seemed that he might join Emeline on the floor. A moment later he recovered and helped Michael carry the older woman to the sofa in the drawing room, calling for her salts and sending the servants into a flurry of surprise and confusion. Trent said not one word to Michael and ignored Hallie as he applied the acrid smelling salts to his aunt.

When at last the older woman regained her senses she sat upright, pulling on her stiff, formal demeanor as though it were a protective cloak. "I can't believe you're alive, Michael. Why didn't you send word? Where have you been all of this time? Good gracious, what a

291

thoughtless thing to do! You should have done anything to get word to us!" She wasted no time berating him.

When Michael had answered all of her questions and finished the story of these past three months, Emeline turned to Hallie. "I thought you had taken up residence elsewhere. In fact, I believe I heard you were to marry that doctor." Her contempt and disapproval echoed in the now quiet house.

Michael spoke before Hallie could open her mouth. "I persuaded her to come home, Emeline."

"Then you're a bigger fool than your father."

Michael's face turned threatening. "You take too much for granted here, Emeline. You are a guest in our home and no more."

She stood stiffly, taking Trent's arm to steady herself. Her head raised and her voice knife edged she said, "That is something I can never forget, Michael." She moved stiffly with Trent to her room.

Hallie was more than surprised when Michael kissed her lightly on the forehead and left her standing in the doorway of the master bedroom. She stood for a time, disconcerted as he moved toward the guest room down the hall. She had assumed that Michael's wanting her back at Redland meant that this reunion would be the beginning of a new life together, a marriage like all others even though he had spoken of caring for her and not exactly of love. How could that be if Michael retained his separate bed? As Hallie donned a lacy nightgown she pondered the situation, remembering the reason her husband had taken that other room in the first place. He had told her then that he would not come back until she said she wanted him. She sighed in resignation, knowing that she had no option if she wanted to win his love.

Hallie brushed her hair into a long-flowing black mantle. Her violet eyes glistened with anticipation, her cheeks were rosy with the excitement and trepidation she felt. The high neck of her nightdress was of lace; it fastened at her throat with purple satin ribbons. She undid the ribbons, allowing a hint of the velvet skin of her breasts to show. She hoped it was all enough to entice her husband back to her bed.

Michael had shed all but his breeches as he paced the guest room. This was not where he wanted to be. When he swung the door open fiercely he expected to see Farley standing there with a line of servants carrying the equipment for his bath. Instead his blue-gray eyes widened to see Hallie staring up at him. "Is something wrong?" he asked, afraid to hope she had come for what he wanted.

"Yes, there is something wrong. My room is half empty."

One well-curved brow rose. "Is it? I don't recall ordering any furnishings removed."

"It isn't the furnishings. I believe one of the occupants has been misplaced. When I took up residence there was a man in my room, and now I seem to have lost him."

"I see. Does that disturb you?"

"Perhaps not if it were summertime. But for March I find I am in need of more than a warming pan for my feet. The chill is quite uncomfortable."

"I can't say I'm flattered by this need for my services. I had rather hoped you might want me as more than a bed warmer."

Hallie blushed slightly, seeing that he wanted an outright admission of her desire. "Must you torture me, Michael?" she said seriously.

"Am I torturing you? I think it is more that I want to be sure of you."

"A test then."

"Perhaps." He studied her, aroused by what he saw. "Or perhaps just a plea for honesty. I want only that, Hallie. I will have no more of duties or of force. I made up my mind on the ride here that I would come to your bed only because you want me."

"All right." She conceded defeat. "I would like you to come back into our room. I didn't come back home just to continue with the way things were before."

"Why?" His handsome face broke into a pleased, one-sided grin that hinted now at teasing.

"Because I want you, Michael." Her voice was almost inaudible. She gazed up into a handsome, seductive smile, eyes glinting with anticipation. He smoothed his moustache unconsciously, as if his smile were wide enough to muss it. He bent and picked her up into his arms and strode down the hall to the master bedroom, kicking the door wide to admit them.

Farley had stopped at the top of the stairs and watched Michael carry his wife back to their room. The big, burly man let out a whooping laugh of pleasure and turned to order the bathtub and buckets of water replaced until the morning.

Michael placed Hallie gently on the bed, dropping his trousers and climbing in beside her quickly. He drew her into his arms. His voice was hoarse with desire for her. "Are you well, love?" he asked, concerned yet hopeful.

She laughed lightly, "Well enough. And you?"

Michael's lips found hers in answer. He had been too long without her. His senses were overwhelmed by the sweet smell of her hair, the silky feel of the long, thick mass, the velvety softness of her flesh, the taste of her lips, of her skin as his mouth traveled her face, her throat, her shoulders. His tongue found the pink crest of her breast, teasing lightly as his hand traveled below, down the flat belly to a soft spot, warmer, inviting and driving him wild at the same time. His senses rushed, wanting more and more, needing to consume her in the warm cloak of passion.

Hallie reveled in the feel of Michael's muscular back beneath her hands, teasing fingers tracing patterns around his sides, lingering at the jagged scar at his ribs. She tickled him lightly, pressing deeper into the hair at his chest to the hard play of muscle and bone. Her tongue met his as they kissed again, a sensual delight all its own as warm, soft lips caressed hers, his teeth gently tugging at her lower lip. Hallie explored his body, for still she was inexperienced and unsure of that which offered her so much. Her own desire for him rose quickly with each kiss, each caress, each teasing of her taut breasts, every gentle stroke of her most intimate parts. She knew he paced himself for her, pushing her to the limits of her endurance until she begged him to join his body with hers, wanting more than anything in the world to feel his hard manhood filling that portion of her which screamed out for him. He moved slowly, at first teasing, tentative, careful in this first time since her illness. But when it was complete each found a new surge of desire, an overwhelming sense of perfect pleasure, a flawless union. Instinct prevailed as they soared together into the nether lands of exquisite satiety, a peak of unequaled perfection, gliding back to reality on graceful wings of air until each breathed deeply again, relaxed and welcomed the return of sanity.

In that moment Hallie wanted to tell him, to say the words that explained her feelings, but she could not, as though the mere sound would shatter the beauty of the bliss that had just passed, that they had shared together as one. Instead she floated into sleep, certain that never before had there been a more love-filled act.

CHAPTER FIFTY-FOUR

Early April brought cold temperatures but no snow. The past four weeks had been rapturous for Hallie as she basked in Michael's attentions. They had spent a good part of it in bed, for it seemed that neither could ever get quite enough of the other. No words of love were spoken; indeed, the subject was much avoided. Hallie readily admitted to herself that what she felt for Michael was love, but she feared letting those feelings be known. She did not wish to frighten him away with the intensity of her emotions, nor did she want to do away with the challenge she thought she presented and make him bored.

Hallie wiggled deeper beneath her lap robe against the cold, thinking that ugly reality had crept back into her life. She had sent word to Adam, asking him to meet her at Amanda's house this afternoon. They had not seen one another since the night before they were to be married.

Amanda's house loomed ahead; Hallie could see Adam's horse tethered outside. Her stomach lurched and she wondered why life must be so difficult, so complex. She wished that she could feel nothing for Adam, and he for her, but she knew better. In spite of the strong love she held for Michael, there was still love for Adam, a warm fondness that she no longer tried to believe was only friendship. It made this meeting harder for her, and she dreaded it.

Amanda opened the front door; her expression warned Hallie that all was not well. She indicated to Hallie that Adam was in the drawing room and left them alone.

Hallie stood in the doorway for a moment, watching him, seeing his jaw clenched as he leaned with one arm on the mantel and stared at the fire below. She knew that she had earned his anger and steadied herself to receive it as she walked toward him.

Hearing her, Adam turned slightly, his eyes cold and hard, though his pain was reflected in the brown depths. He did not speak as she removed her hat, muff and coat.

The violet gaze she lifted to him was beseeching. "Will you sit and hear me out, Adam?"

"I can't imagine what you want to say, Hallie." His voice was not as cold as his expression, and that lent her hope.

"I'm not really certain. It would be easier if I were."

Adam moved to the chair across from her, his body rigid. He said nothing but remained staring at her.

"I would like to tell you that Michael forced me to return with him that day, that he refused me my freedom as he had before, but it would be a lie. I care too much for you to lie."

"Thank you for that, at least."

"I'm afraid the truth is more painful. I chose to return to Redland, to be Michael's wife when he offered me my freedom." She saw that her words were like the thrust of a knife, even though he must have known. "I would do anything to make all of this easier, Adam!" she cried suddenly. "There is nothing simple about it. It's hard for all three of us, but I know it is worst for you."

"I don't need your pity."

Hallie was struck by the harsh tone of his voice. "My God, Adam, it is not pity I offer you."

"What do you offer me, then, Hallie? Shall we become lovers?" he asked facetiously.

"No." Her voice was small, she was defenseless against his attack.

"What then? Tell me!"

Hallie's eyes filled with tears, for she could offer him nothing he wanted, she knew. "Don't do this, Adam, please! Try to understand!"

"I understand it all now. You love the bastard, you wanted him and you've got him. Now what the hell do you want from me?"

"Nothing," she said softly. "Forgiveness, perhaps. Friendship?"

"Dammit! I can't be only a friend to you!" He screamed, causing her to sit back in her seat. His voice remained loud, his fist hit the arm of his chair with force. "I'm in love with you! I will always be, no matter how much I wish it weren't so! I'd kill him with my bare hands if I thought it would solve this! I'd do anything! Don't ask me to feel differently, because I can't! I've tried! You are in my blood, a part of my being. I can't rid myself of you any more than I can rid myself of my heart. Don't you see what this does to me? I must receive your sympathy, see your tears, die to hold you, to have you and know I cannot. Don't torment me with explanations!" He pushed himself from the chair and strode out of the house, grabbing his coat on his way but never looking back. When the door slammed behind him Hallie dissolved into inconsolable sobs.

It was well past midnight when Michael arrived home. He was surprised to see Hallie sitting wrapped in a quilt staring into the fire in their room. He saw that her eyes were red and swollen and he judged her meeting with Adam had been difficult. She managed a sad smile for him as he sat beside her on the settee, his arm across her shoulders. He kissed her chastely on the temple, sighing into her hair.

"Your meeting didn't go well, did it?" he asked quietly.

"It was a nightmare," she said, her voice quivering anew with the thought. "I hurt him so much, Michael. It was horrible!"

"What did you expect, love?"

"I don't know. I deserved all he said. I knew he would be hurt. Somehow I thought he still might ask for friendship and pretend it all hadn't happened, I suppose. It was so ugly! He thought I pitied him!" Now the tears fell slowly, and Michael pulled his handkerchief from his pocket to wipe them away.

"I'm sorry, sweet. Are you having second thoughts about your choice?"

"No, it isn't that. But I would have given anything not to have hurt him like this, and then I could do nothing, offer him no solace. I try never to harm anyone, Michael, yet today I felt as if I had set out to do him mortal damage."

"There was no other way, Hallie. He'll find his way back. I'm sure of that."

"Perhaps, but it is so awful to have to inflict those wounds."

Again Michael's lips rested on her temple, pulling her closer into his embrace, as though he would protect her. "You know, I believe that in any instance I would have wanted you as my own."

A small chuckle sounded from beneath her sore spirits. "Why is that?"

"You're quite a lady, Hallie. I'm proud to have you as my wife."

They sat in silence for a time, staring at the fire, reluctant to leave this warm moment. It was Michael's voice that sounded again. "I had a row with Trent today," he said, his own tone disturbed.

"What happened?"

"He wanted me to ask Emeline to stay on permanently."

"And what did you say?" she asked hesitantly, fearing his answer.

"I refused, of course. This is our home, and she works to cause too much trouble in it. I won't have her here forever. I told him I would not ask her to leave, but I would not invite her to become a permanent resident."

"Poor Trent. I believe he is more softhearted than he wishes anyone to know."

"I only know that I can't seem to find any peaceful ground with him, and I'm damned if I understand it. No matter what I do, he rejects it."

"Perhaps it's just his age, Michael. It seems hard for him to enter manhood, and maybe you seem to be his adversary in that passage. Sometimes it seems that he feels in competition with you."

"That's ridiculous! But you're right, he does do that. He seems to have warmed to you, though. I'm glad of that."

Again silence reigned. Hallie snuggled nearer.

"How is Amanda? Is she happy about this baby?"

Hallie was reticent to discuss this subject, fearing where it would lead them. "She's very well and very happy."

"I know Jason is thrilled. It seems to have been the perfect way for them both to resolve their grief."

Hallie said nothing, hoping the subject would change.

"What if it were you, Hallie? Would you be happy?"

A heavy silence fell before Hallie spoke. She hoped that she could lure Michael into returning her love for him before she conceived a child and lost her appeal to him. In her mind becoming pregnant would leave her a dull, unattractive matron—surely he would never grow to love her that way. All she could manage in answer to his question was, "I just don't know, Michael." Her pensive voice led him to believe only the worst.

Hallie stood then, moving to their bed. "It's late," she said evasively. "I think it's time we went to sleep."

It was several minutes before Michael joined her in bed, wondering what plagued his wife.

CHAPTER FIFTY-FIVE

Hallie peered in the mirror one last time. Her gown was pale yellow poplin, the neckline wide to reveal her shoulders but high enough to be demure. The bodice was pleated at her breasts and cinched at the waist, with a wide yellow satin ribbon slightly uncomfortable for Hallie. The wide skirt had flounces of the same pale yellow poplin. She wore white mitts to protect her hands from the June sun and carried a small yellow parasol to guard her face and shoulders. Her hat was a wide-brimmed piece tied at her cheek with a large bow of satin ribbon to match that at her waist. For all the world she looked as though she intended nothing more than a visit with her grandmother and a ride through Pemberton Square or Boston Common, as any other young woman might do on an idle afternoon. She intended to do both of these in order to prove herself honest, but the true purpose for this outing was to see Dr. Hathaway. Though she tried hard to deny it, Hallie could no longer delude herself. She had decided to have her fears confirmed medically before dealing with the worry consciously. It was good that she had prepared her deception so well, for at the bottom of the steps she encountered Emeline, her expression suspicious and disapproving as always.

"Where are you off to dressed like that?" she demanded haughtily, as though she were the mistress of Redland and not a guest.

Hallie sighed, drawing once again on her limitless store of patience with the harridan. "I am going to visit my grandmother," she said. "And then I intend to have a pleasant ride through the park."

"No doubt to meet some swain and cuckold your husband," Emeline returned bitingly, having long since stopped any attempt at civility.

"Emeline, I have no swain, nor have I ever been unfaithful to Michael." She wondered how many times she had repeated these words.

"He may be fooled by that innocent guise, but I am far too wise to accept things at face value. There will come a time when he sees his error."

"Good day, Emeline," Hallie said simply.

Waiting in front of the house was the open victoria she had ordered for her journey. A silk-hatted coachman held open the side door of the carriage. His coat matched the carriage sides and the Turkish tufted and buttoned upholstery of black broadcloth. It was a shining black vehicle with four wheels and a collapsible top that for this day was down. Twin carriage lamps adorned each side, and a long black whip rested in a leather socket on the dashboard. A matched pair of black geldings waited patiently to pull this ornate vehicle to its destination.

Finding her grandmother not at home, Hallie left a note. She then ordered the coachman to drive through Boston Common, legitimizing her journey before she sought her goal. The Common had been made into a park in 1830 and had since become a popular place for the townsfolk to enjoy a casual promenade along the shaded paths. There were grassy areas and marble benches where a weary person might rest, or simply sit and enjoy the quiet splendor, the fresh scent of sweet flowers, the lilting notes of birds among the treetops or just the picturesque view of statues or fountains or the lush greenery.

In this peaceful scene Hallie felt no tranquillity. Of late she feared that when Michael discovered she was to have another child his interests would wander, having accomplished his purpose for having her as his wife. She wished desperately that he loved her as she did him, but she could not convince herself of it. If only he would tell her, she would be ecstatic with the thought of this baby, for she loved Michael intensely. But she felt too insecure, worrying that for him she was merely an amusing distraction for the time being, and once an heir was on the way he would find someone else more amusing.

She ordered the coachman to go to Dr. Hathaway's office. It was near Massachusetts General Hospital for convenience, in a quiet section of the city. The house looked deserted, and Hallie was afraid Dr. Hathaway was not working today. She hoped he would see her, for it had not been easy to arrange this deception. She had made certain through Amanda that Adam had hospital duties for she was reluctant to see him after their last disastrous encounter.

The front door was ajar, so Hallie knocked and then pushed it open. She saw no one but decided to go in, thinking perhaps he was in the back of the house. The office was empty, though a woman's reticule and gloves were there and a man's jacket, giving evidence that people had just been there. She moved through the house and examining rooms, calling for Dr. Hathaway, realizing it was odd for the place to be empty in the middle of a working day. Finally she heard a man's voice upstairs and standing at the foot of the staircase, she called to the upper level. Expecting to see the old doctor descend the stairs, Hallie was surprised to see Adam Burgess.

"Oh, Hallie!" he said, sighing in displeasure. "I wish it weren't you!"

She was somewhat taken aback by this greeting from Adam, even under the circumstances. "I'm sorry if I've come at a bad time, but I need to see Dr. Hathaway," she answered him quietly, guilt reddening her cheeks.

He shook his head wearily. "He isn't home and hasn't been for two days. I don't suppose the news has traveled to Redland yet."

"What news."

"Asiatic cholera has broken out in the city. It looks to be the start of an epidemic. Dr. Hathaway is quarantined down at the docks treating it. I've got Maeve Carson upstairs with it. You'll have to stay now. I can't let you leave after you've been exposed."

Hallie's eyes widened. "I can't stay!" she shrieked, thinking of the implications of her being alone in this house with Adam, even with Maeve Carson, of all people. Michael would never understand.

"There is a five-day quarantine, Hallie. I'm sorry, but you shouldn't have come in. Didn't you see the sign in the window?"

"No! I saw nothing! I have to go home, Adam!"

"Not for five days. I only hope you don't come down with the damn thing."

"Why is Maeve Carson here?"

He shrugged. "She came because she had felt ill; she had no idea it was cholera, and I put her to bed."

Hallie's violet eyes were wide with horror. "Adam, you don't know what this means! Michael will never understand!"

"No, I don't suppose he will. Are you ill?" he asked, a note of worry sounding clearly.

Hallie's face paled with the memory of why she had come here in the first place, now fearing for the life of her child. If she were to contract the disease and lose the baby, she might as well die herself. "No, I'm not ill," she said softly. "I think I'm going to have a baby, and I wanted to see Dr. Hathaway."

Adam's blond head shook slowly, "That makes it worse. Pregnant and exposed to cholera—God, I'm sorry!"

"Are you sure that is what Maeve Carson has?"

"No doubt. Are you sure you're pregnant?"

"Almost. I wanted Dr. Hathaway to confirm it."

"I can do that for you, you know."

"I think it better if we keep this as proper as possible, Adam."

He laughed derisively. "As proper as living here together for five days can be. We had better send a message to your husband."

Adam opened the door and called out to the waiting coachman. When the man got within a few feet of the house Adam stopped him from coming nearer and gave him the message for Michael Redmond that his wife would be quarantined for five full days...and nights.

CHAPTER FIFTY-SIX

Hallie stayed in the lower level throughout the day and evening, hoping that by avoiding Maeve Carson she would not contract cholera. She arranged for a place to sleep in the den and then paced, her mind filled with the damage this would do to her marriage. Every sound caused her to stand, fearing Michael would come here regardless of the quarantine. She could hear Emeline's voice for the next five days harping on the situation. How could the fates have been so cruel? Just as she was gaining ground with Michael, earning his trust and she hoped his love, all of his suspicions would be raised anew.

Adam interrupted her pacing as he entered the kitchen, moving slowly, as if his legs were too heavy to lift. He sat to enjoy the coffee she proffered, smiling weakly.

"Are you all right, Adam?"

"Yes, just tired. I've been at this for two weeks now with little rest. I had four cases here who died."

"How is Maeve?"

"I think she is past the danger stage. It is usually fatal within the first twenty-four hours. She's made it past that, so her chances are good. Then again sometimes just as it appears to be getting better, they die anyway. It's a horrible disease. The mind is alert while the body deteriorates in a matter of hours."

"How long does it last, if she lives?"

"There is a three-day incubation, Hallie. But I don't want you upstairs during any of the five days. Is that understood?"

"Yes, but you look as if you need to rest or you will do her no good."

He sighed. "I'm fine. I get a nap every time I can." He paused, changing the subject. "How far along do you think you are?" he asked sadly, shaken by the news.

"I've suspected for about two months."

"When is it due?"

"I would guess about Christmas or the first of the year."

"And does it please you?"

Hallie saw the pain this caused Adam, and her heart ached with being the cause of more of it. "Perhaps it's best if we don't talk about this."

"Then you are," he said more to himself. "I have to apologize for the last time we met, Hallie. I was too tortured with losing you yet a third time to be rational. It all seems like some cruel joke. I wonder how many times I will be caught in it." He sighed in resignation, smiling sadly, answering his own question. "I suppose as many times as fate chooses to play it on me. The rational part of my mind knows it is the best thing for you. I know you would never have been happy unless you fell in love with him. I know only too well the misery of pining for what cannot be. I doubt that he would ever have freed you, regardless of what he offered, so it is better that you chose to be with him."

"Please don't, Adam! I still care so much for you! I want you to be happy!"

He smiled kindly at her now, that grin she had seen as a child, that of an older brother. "I believe you do. Perhaps I will be in time. I'm glad that you at least are. You deserve to be. Does he love you?"

She swallowed the lump down in her throat. "I don't know. I'm afraid he doesn't."

"Has he given you reason to think he doesn't?"

"No, but he's never told me he does."

"But he stays with you and cares for you and obviously desires you." She blushed, and Adam laughed lightly. "You're a beautiful, desirable woman; no one knows that better than I. He'd be a fool not to want you. I suppose he's happy about the baby."

"He doesn't know. I was hoping it wouldn't be true."

"Why?" Adam's face showed his surprise.

"I'm afraid he won't want me afterward. I'm afraid he'll go back to Maeve Carson."

"You don't really believe that, do you? She can't hold a candle to you!"

"Oh, Adam, you know that's not so! She is beautiful and elegant and I can't help but think he loved her once and possibly still does."

"Then he's a fool, Hallie!" Adam's brows knitted with a new concern. "You won't do anything to rid yourself of it, will you?"

She shook her head. "No, I didn't do that before, though we never found who did the deed." She hesitated. "Actually, I want this baby very much. It's just that I'm so afraid of what will happen when he finds out."

"I don't suppose it offers you much comfort, but if it should not work out as you want, I'm still available."

"You wouldn't want some fat old pregnant lady, Adam," she teased, trying to ease the intensity in his eyes.

But Adam would not allow it. "I want you any way I can have you, Hallie, any way at all."

Michael raged, his voice booming at the coachman, "What the hell are you talking about, man?"

The nervous coachman shuffled his feet, repeating the message Adam Burgess had sent with him to Redland.

"You were to take her to her grandmother's house and for a drive in the park!"

"Yes, sir, I did, sir. But then she told me to go there. Maybe she got sick," he offered, feeling somehow responsible as he faced his employer.

"Dammit!" Michael paced like a caged animal. "See that my horse is saddled."

The black stallion was pushed to his full strength with the pace Michael demanded from him, racing like a man possessed to Dr. Hathaway's house. Why the hell would she have gone there if not to see Burgess? Michael knew his wife's health was fine, surely it was for no other reason. He called himself every kind of fool for letting his guard slip, for allowing himself to be vulnerable to her, for starting to love her.

The house was deadly still as he reined his horse to a halt. He saw the quarantine sign in the window, doubting Hallie's sincerity even more, for surely she would have seen it and not entered the place. Michael was determined, even if it meant exposing himself to the dread disease, to find out the truth. But before he reached the doorway the doctor's voice sounded from a room on the second level of the house.

"Don't do it, Redmond. This is not something to tempt."

"Where is my wife?" he demanded angrily.

"She is downstairs. I'm keeping her away from here. Maeve Carson is down with it, but I won't allow Hallie near her. Come back in five days. She can't come out before that."

"Then I'll come in!" he shouted.

"No, Michael, please don't do that!" Hallie's voice begged. She appeared at the door, her violet eyes wide with concern. "This is a terrible disease! I couldn't bear it if you came after me and contracted it!"

"What the hell were you doing here in the first place?"

"It's a long story."

"How is it that you didn't see that sign?"

"I was ill, Michael," she lied. "I simply did not notice it!"

"What's wrong with you?"

Now Adam's voice sounded again in answer, "It was something she ate. I've given her something for it. Now get the hell out of here."

"I'll keep her away from everyone, but she can't stay here!" Michael insisted, thinking he could not endure five days of her being alone with Adam, no matter what the reason.

"You know I can't do that, Michael!" Hallie answered him. "Think of Danny! It's even more dangerous for children. I have to stay. I'm sorry!"

"Not as sorry as I am." She barely heard his words.

Michael conceded that he could do nothing and was furious with that fact. "All right, dammit! But I'll be back in five days, not a minute later. And mark my words, Burgess, if you lay one finger on her I'll kill you!" Michael stormed off in frustration, knowing it would be the five longest days of his life and wondering if he could trust his wife. It was a baseless concern, for by the morning of the second day Adam had collapsed with cholera, leaving Hallie alone to tend both him and Maeve Carson.

CHAPTER FIFTY-SEVEN

It seemed to Hallie that the work was endless as she pushed her tired body to care for the two extremely ill people. Cholera was by its very nature a consuming disease to treat. The body first lost it ability to control the functions of the bowel, followed by severe vomiting. Within hours after the onset Hallie watched Adam's muscles begin to cramp in excruciating spasms, his face contorted against the pain as every bit of his body's fluids were purged from the tissues. His body seemed to shrink before her worried eyes, his skin drying and wrinkling until he seemed to age years in mere hours. His handsome features were pinched, his eyes sunken. His limbs were like ice, and to Hallie he looked as if he could not possibly live through this, and her concern turned to fear. There was an endless supply of linens or eating utensils or cups or clothing that all required burning or sterilization to ensure the disease did not spread. She carried blankets to warm both Adam and Maeve Carson, attempted to force liquids into them, cajoling and pleading patiently until she felt she would weep.

Maeve Carson was too weak to care who worked to keep her alive; she did not even speak to Hallie and did not acknowledge in any way that Hallie was nursing her back to health. Adam was placed in anguish by the thought that Hallie was meeting his most humiliating needs. But his greatest concern was the fact that his illness put her in peril. He hated this more even than the disease that threatened to steal his life, for he loved Hallie much more than he worried for himself.

By the time Adam had passed the danger stage Hallie was exhausted. She knew that he was reluctant to ask more of her, suffering rather than make more work for her. Maeve Carson was a different matter altogether as Hallie began to wonder how anyone in such a weakened condition could demand so much. She demanded constant attention—a fresh pillow, clean sheets, a lighter blanket and then a heavier one, her hair brushed, her face washed, more food, less food, no food now but some later, larger portions, variety, something to read.

As the June sun grew brighter the house seemed to bake beneath it; the rooms became stuffy and close with the stench of illness. Hallie thought she would collapse with fatigue; she pushed herself well past her usual limits, and the early stages of pregnancy meant she was not at full capacity. Always there was more to do. She prepared meals and scrubbed floors where chamber pots or buckets spilled, or washed and boiled sheets and blankets. By the morning of the fourth day she was barely able to drag her feet to Adam's bedside, her exhaustion obvious in her ashen face.

Adam lay weak and emaciated, but his eyes were clear. He saw the toll this was taking on her and was tortured by the sight. "Hallie," his voice was raspy in his parched throat, "leave it all! We're both past the worst part of it. Go downstairs and rest, sleep for a few hours."

"I can't, Adam. There is so much to do!"

"Think of yourself, of your baby. You have to get some rest. Now go on!" He used the last remnants of his strength, failing miserably in his attempt to sound forceful.

Still Hallie decided it was best. As she passed Maeve Carson's room she heard a weak request and went to do one more thing for the woman before she sought her own rest. Maeve looked better than Hallie did by now.

With each day of recovery her tone of voice had gotten more derisive.

"I want you to sit and talk to me for a time," she demanded.

Hallie tried to draw on her patience but found it lacking. "I can't," she said bluntly.

"It is important."

"Nothing is that important right now, Maeve. I am going to sleep, or you may have to get out of that bed and care for yourself."

"Then you had better come back afterward. I want to talk to you!"

It was midafternoon when Hallie reluctantly pulled herself from the deep, dreamless slumber, forcing her swollen eyes to open when she actually needed days of rest to recover. Her stomach was queasy and her head was spinning but she knew she had to ward it off and rise. She sat for a time on the edge of the narrow cot that served as her bed. A strand of hair fell to her cheek from the knot she had carelessly fastened atop her head. She peered down at her grimy yellow gown. She felt horrid. Her skin felt filthy and her bones ached with fatigue. She thought that if she and her baby managed to escape this disease they must both be blessed, but she was too tired to care. Her stomach lurched, but she knew there was nothing in it to come up, deciding that the emptiness was probably the cause. She forced herself to her feet, her head spinning for a moment and then nibbled a small crust of bread as she prepared a late lunch for her two patients. Before she lifted the tray to bring the food upstairs she ran the back of her hand across her forehead, wiping away beads of perspiration that had formed there, wondering how she would manage to carry even herself back up those stairs. It was a slow process, and once her feet touched the top Hallie breathed a sigh of relief.

Maeve was well enough to feed herself, though she resented it, but Hallie still had to spoon the thin broth into Adam's mouth, thinking each time how ravaged he looked. Where she had met with complaints about the lateness of the meal from Maeve, Adam merely smiled weakly, apologizing for the hundredth time for the need of her services.

"You don't look any better," he said weakly.

"I'll be all right, Adam."

"Did you send the message to Dr. Hathaway?"

"Yes. A boy came around this morning to see if we needed anything, and I told him. Surely he must be too busy to come here if this is an epidemic."

"I was hoping he would find someone else to send. I don't want you to stay past tomorrow."

"There isn't much choice."

"Maeve is well enough to go home and past being able to infect anyone else. By tomorrow I'll be able to care for myself."

She smiled thinly. "You know that isn't true, Adam."

"It is! I'm weak, but I can manage to feed myself and sleep. I don't need anything more."

"I won't leave you alone," she said firmly, rising to see to Maeve. "Let's not talk about it anymore."

Maeve Carson sat propped in bed, a shell of the beautiful woman she had been. She had eaten very little of her soup, but Hallie was not going to cajole her like a child. She was well enough to eat or refuse to, as she chose. "Are you going to talk to me now?" she asked sharply, leading Hallie to wonder how she could be so caustic in her present state.

She sat in the chair beside the bed, too weary to fight the woman. "What is it you want, Maeve?"

"You know very well what I want. Michael Redmond."

Hallie stared dumbfounded at the woman's audacity, then burst into hysterical laughter.

"I don't know what you find so amusing. I warn you I will use whatever I can to gain him, and this is the perfect opportunity."

Hallie shook her head, controlling herself now. "I'm afraid I am too tired to understand you."

"I intend to tell Michael of your little tryst in the room beside mine while I was ill."

"This is absurd. Adam is every bit as sick as you. Did you lose your senses with all of this?"

"Hardly. Being locked in a house with a man for all this time is quite enough to ruin you."

"Or you, if this ridiculous story were worth listening to." She stood, staring at Maeve Carson and seeing the desperation in her features. "I feel very sorry for you," she said and rose to leave the room.

"You know, of course, that he has been with me since your marriage." The words were lead on Hallie's ears. She stopped but refused to turn to face the woman.

Seeing she had gained ground, Maeve continued, "He has come to my bed more times than I can count. Of course, he is discreet, though it doesn't matter to me. I would have all the world know I am his mistress. I will relish the telling of this!"

Hallie left the room, hearing Maeve's laughter follow her. She was too drained to fight. As she neared the foot of the stairs, the front door opened to admit Dr. Hathaway. Hallie felt a new surge of strength at the sight of what she considered her savior. He looked remarkably well and rested, Hallie thought, putting her to shame. His old eyes widened in surprise to see her. "Why, Hallie! What are you doing here?"

She shrugged. "I came to see you and didn't realize the house was under quarantine. I've been here for four days tending to Adam and Maeve Carson."

He shook his head. "How are they?"

"Maeve is doing very well; Adam thinks she can go home. He is better, though he still needs care."

"And what about you? You seem the worse for wear, if you don't mind my saying so, my dear."

She blushed lightly, embarrassed by her appearance. "I'm afraid I'm not used to the work. It seems I've become quite soft in my married life."

"You're not ill, are you? Why did you come to see me?"

She sighed, remembering what had not been in her thoughts these past days. "I am fairly certain I'm going to have a baby. I wanted you to confirm it."

"Why, my dear!" he exclaimed, "it's no wonder you haven't borne the strain well! This is far too much for a woman in your condition! Come and sit down!"

"You look so well! How have you ever done it?"

"I feel quite guilty about it now. I thought Adam was here caring for only Maeve until I received the message this morning. I took one day simply to sleep. If I had known you were here caring for them I would have come right home! Are you sure you're well?"

She smiled at him. "I am now, though I hate to leave you alone with all of this!"

"I'm not alone. I have two nurses to help me, so I will have three people to do what you have done alone. When is your quarantine up?"

"Tomorrow. Do you think I will escape this?"

He patted her hand reassuringly. "After four days I would say the chances are very good that you will be free of it."

"And the baby?"

"Is well protected so long as you don't get it. I'm sure this exhaustion is not helping, but it's probably taking more of a toll on you than the baby. With a little rest and care you'll have a fine, healthy child, I'm certain." His gnarled hand lifted her chin to peer into her eyes. "That is what you want, isn't it?"

"More than anything, I think. After worrying about losing it to cholera I find I'm quite happy to have it still with me." Her features clouded with the thought of Maeve's words. "I only hope that Michael feels the same."

CHAPTER FIFTY-EIGHT

Hallie laid her head back and closed her eyes, basking in the steamy, scented water. She had rested for three weeks and was looking forward to her night out with Michael and Amanda and Jason. They were to dine at the Tremont House and then see *Hamlet* performed at the Tremont Theater. Due to Dr. Hathaway's orders, Hallie had spent the past three weeks in bed. She had feared at the time Michael had come to get her after the quarantine that Dr. Hathaway might tell her husband of the baby. But he had never mentioned it. Hallie meant to keep it a secret, for she wanted more time to lure him into loving her. Hallie's weakened condition and Dr. Hathaway's explanation of the work she had done had quelled any suspicions Michael might have had, so what she feared had never taken place. In fact, since her return Michael had been overly solicitous of her. After she had rested and her mind had cleared, she began to doubt what Maeve Carson had said to her. Hallie fought hard against her doubts, feeding a strong hope more than any real belief that it had all been a ruse.

She rose from the water, reaching for the warm towel that awaited her. Just as she began to dry herself Michael entered the room. She drew a quick, startled breath and shielded herself with the fluffy towel. She had been very careful of late not to present her body for his perusal. The change was slight, but she feared he would notice even that. Her breasts were fuller, their pink crests a bit darker, and her waist was not quite as narrow as it had been. She quickly donned her robe, but Michael's eyes and hands were too perceptive to be fooled. In this past week he had begun to think she was carrying a child. At first he found it odd that she so carefully avoided his watching her bathe. His hands had carefully explored that body he was obsessed with, and they had confirmed what was almost imperceptible to his eyes. Two things plagued him about the fact that she worked so studiously to conceal it. He was torn between worrying that she meant to harm it or that the baby was not his. Michael had never thought to calculate the time it would take for a pregnancy to become obvious, and so he worried that the child was a result of the time she had spent alone with Adam Burgess, either when she believed him to be dead or that past week at Dr. Hathaway's house, for why else would she not tell him?

Hallie's toilette was complete save for fastening her white satin gown at the back. She had stalled as long as she could, hoping Michael would wait downstairs, for she knew the effort it would take to cinch in her waist. But there he sat, dressed impressively in dark blue, his shirt stark white, his cravat black. He looked magnificent, his dark hair waving away from his handsome face, his moustache trimmed to perfection. There would be no escaping, she thought, for his piercing blue-gray eyes watched her intently. Hallie's hair was parted in the middle and pulled above each ear in bunches of long curls with clusters of purple wild flowers over each. She even fastened her beautiful brooch of silver and diamonds at the center of the low décolletage before having her gown buttoned.

Michael moved to her, sending Mercy to do other tasks and stepping to her back. His hands slowly began to button the tiny covered orbs, descending to her waist. Hallie's violet eyes widened, meeting his blue-gray ones in the mirror. He placed a soft kiss on her creamy bare shoulder. "You're beautiful, my love. Its been too long since we've made love, don't you think?"

She blushed becomingly, still unnerved by his open discussion of so intimate a matter. "I haven't been well, Michael," she reminded him softly, her senses reeling with his nearness.

"And now?" His voice was husky.

She smiled, wanting him as much as he did her. "And now we are about to go to the theater," she teased.

"We could always cancel it."

"No, we couldn't! You will have to contain yourself, sir. At least until later tonight."

He leaned against her, pulling her pressed tightly to his rapidly rising passions. "I don't know that the fabric is strong enough," he retorted, nibbling sensually at her earlobe while one hand reached down the low front of her gown.

Hallie laughed and pulled herself from his grasp. "I am looking forward to this evening far too much to be lured into your bed, sir. The fabric will have to be strong enough."

Michael groaned deep in his throat, a devilishly handsome smile curving his lips. "So long as it is only a matter of a few hours. I will never be able to concentrate on Shakespeare tonight!" He finished fastening her dress, noting the increased tightness at her middle but saying nothing.

Hallie and Michael joined their friends at the dining room of the hotel, an elegant place, luxuriant even in the lobby. Amanda fairly beamed with happiness, proudly turning so Hallie could view her thickening waistline. Jason watched his wife adoringly and Hallie felt quite envious of what was between the husband and wife as they joyously shared the coming of this child. She would have given anything to be in that same position, with Michael doting over their coming baby.

They dined on green turtle soup, salmon in hollandaise sauce, and chicken croquettes, and as if they were not full enough followed it all with wine jellies and orange water ices. By the end of the meal Hallie felt certain the seams of her bodice would burst.

At the theater Amanda and Hallie excused themselves to freshen up and sought the room meant for that. Hallie did not hesitate to apologize to her friend.

"Whatever for, Hallie?" Amanda asked in surprise, her joy too all-encompassing to have noticed her friend's lack of interest.

"I'm jealous of your happiness."

"Why? You and Michael seem to be getting along well."

She smiled pensively. "We are. But I fear it won't last. I'm going to have a baby, too."

Amanda grinned broadly, thrilled with this news. "But that's wonderful! Why will it be anything but good news to Michael?"

Hallie explained her fears, only to be met with Amanda's refusal to believe it. "Haven't you told him how you feel?"

"Of course not! He doesn't love me!"

"Don't be foolish, Hallie. I think he loves you a great deal. Certainly a baby will only let all of that out to the surface."

"We aren't like you and Jason, Amanda. He married me for other reasons, and once he finds out I'm pregnant he will go back to Maeve Carson. She told me that they have been having an affair since our marriage anyway!"

Amanda shook her head negatively, not believing that at all, but before she could speak, Belinda Scott joined them. "I saw you two come in here, and I just had to come tell you the news, Hallie."

"We must be getting back, Belinda," Amanda broke in urgently, obviously not wanting Belinda to continue.

But the green-eyed woman would not be deterred. "Oh, you can leave in a few minutes, there's time before the first act, and Hallie will want to hear my news!" She turned her red head to face Hallie, beaming victoriously. "Adam and I are to be married!"

Amanda watched the color drain from her friend's face.

"Wonderful, isn't it?" Belinda prodded.

"Congratulations. I hope you'll be very happy." Hallie's voice was surprisingly strong.

"We will, I'm certain of it." She turned and flounced from the room.

322

Hallie turned stricken eyes to Amanda. "Why didn't you tell me?"

She smiled sheepishly. "I didn't want to ruin your evening. Since it is out now, I might as well tell you the rest."

"Please do."

"They are getting married because she claims to be pregnant. It seems to be the time of year for it, doesn't it?" she added, feebly trying to lighten the blow.

Hallie sat heavily, her emotions in turmoil. Why should she feel so horribly jealous, so betrayed? She had no right, she knew that!

"Oh, Hallie, I'm sorry! It came as much of a surprise to Adam."

"It couldn't have been too much of a surprise!" Hallie said bitterly. "Oh, Amanda, why do I feel so awful?" she cried.

"Because you care for Adam, you loved him a great deal, Hallie. Its understandable."

But Hallie was not convinced. How could she love Michael and yet hurt so much at the thought that Adam would marry someone else?

CHAPTER FIFTY-NINE

Hallie did not utter a dozen words throughout the play or the ride home. Michael watched her but said nothing, knowing the evening had not been as pleasant as she had expected. Once inside their room his eyes still studied her, though she was lost in her own thoughts and did not notice the attention she was drawing. Michael drew her into his arms in bed, kissing the top of her head as he held her gently.

Hallie realized she was acting strangely, and searching for a way to seem normal, she tried small talk. "Did you enjoy the play?" she asked feebly.

"No. Did you?"

"It would have been better if there hadn't been such long intermissions to change all that heavy scenery. By the time it began again I had lost what had happened before."

"I'm surprised you were that aware of what was going on."

"What do you mean?"

"You haven't exactly been with me tonight. Shall I guess what's on your mind?"

"Nothing," she hedged.

Michael was unperturbed, his tone kind. "It wouldn't

be the fact that Adam and Belinda Scott are getting married, would it?"

She hesitated, judging his mood before she answered, "How did you know?"

"Jason told me. I saw Belinda Scott follow you and figured she came to gloat."

"Did you also know she is pregnant?"

"Yes, I did. Does that surprise you?"

"Of course it does," she said softly.

"He's only human, you know, love."

"You're being awfully understanding."

"Am I? Perhaps it's because he can't be pining after you if he's married and has a family of his own. It doesn't please you, does it?"

Hallie did not answer rather than lie.

"Do you still care so much for him?" he asked, an impersonal tone forced into his voice that belied the feelings raging in him.

Now Hallie did not pause, a reassuring fact to Michael. "I care a great deal for Adam, but not in the way you think. I love him much as a brother. I would not be pleased to see my brother entrapped into marriage by a scheming woman like Belinda Scott."

"And I suppose there is no jealousy whatsoever?"

Hallie pulled away from his embrace. "Would you feel no jealousy whatsoever to see Maeve Carson married to someone else?"

"I doubt that it would bother me."

"I don't think this is a good discussion for us to have," she said, moving farther away.

Michael stopped her, his long, powerful arm holding her within his reach. "Where are you going?"

"To sleep," she said peevishly.

"Oh, no—" A wicked grin showed in the moonlight.

"I don't want to argue, Michael."

"That is the farthest thing from my mind. You promised me a better ending to the evening than mourning Adam Burgess."

"I am not mourning him. I simply feel that this is not going to be a happy match for him."

"There's one way to prove it, Hallie."

His smile was too enticing to resist, and suddenly Hallie had a need to be loved and held and comforted

326

in the familiar embrace of her husband. He had been right, it had been a long time since they had made love. Michael pulled her back beside him, rolling to his side to kiss her, his lips warm and soft, eliciting a quick response as Hallie's yielded to the desires growing inside her. For just one fleeting moment she wondered how she could want him so much even when she felt so unhappy about something concerning Adam, but then she was swept into fierce passion. Her hands reached around to his back, one caressing the soft curls at the nape of his neck, her senses alive with the feel of him beneath her fingertips, his hard body pressed closely to hers. His tongue teased lightly at her and she met it, all thoughts lost now as her mind worked only on the pleasures erupting within her as his hand reached her breast, his thumb teasing gently at her nipple until it was taut with excitement. Now Michael realized the difference without a doubt, feeling the slight increase and firmness that was not present before, enjoying the added fullness. His mouth lowered to one breast, teasing, sucking, sending spasms of pleasure as never before, the sensations heightened with a new sensitivity. One powerful hand ran down her body, playing lightly at the small mound of stomach, this too more firm and rounder as he sought what he wanted to know.

Suddenly Hallie noticed a gentleness in Michael as his hands traveled her flesh, arousing, taunting, kissing, tasting, but all more slowly, more tenderly, driving her mad with desire for him. His hand explored her, rubbing the soft inside of her thigh and then drawing up until she moaned softly with pleasure, her spine arching up to him in a silent plea for his body to join hers. But again his mouth sought her breast, his hand playing in the silken hair below. Hallie drew her own hands from his back to his chest and then downward until she reached that portion of him that drove them both wild. She heard his indrawn breath as she held firmly, moving her fingers gently to the tip to arouse in him what he had brought to her, a need as great as her own. At last he raised above her, entering with amazing slowness, careful of the weight he placed on her as he held his upper half high above her, his arms straight. It lent a new dimension as he filled her com-

327

pletely, yet in a way that she could see his massive chest, his face held up to the silver moonlight, his features glistening with the intensity of his pleasure. She could see the muscles bulging in his chest and shoulders, his arms one massive play of hard power shadowed and highlighted as the skin stretched taut. Her hands ran to his chest as he moved slowly, with great tenderness until he could contain himself no longer, speeding his thrusts to bring them both to a sweet ecstasy that slowly lulled them into a perfect fulfillment of love.

Michael rolled from her without lowering his weight to her, fearful of harming her or the baby. He pulled her close to his side, his grasp tight, as if he thought she would leave him. For the first time he wanted to shout his love for her to the treetops, for in that instant of climax, he realized it was unique because of his feelings for her. Still he was too unsure of her response, and he did not. If only, he thought, she would tell him of the baby, say it was the product of his seed, then he could tell her, but those doubts held the words captive in his mind, and he merely kissed her head lightly.

Hallie was in much the same frame of mind. Her love for him exploded within her; her need to tell him of the child they had produced through just such a perfect act was strong. But she fought the words back, afraid of his reaction. Instead she raised deep violet eyes to him, savoring once more the sight of his handsome face. Her words were light, teasing, masking the emotion running rampant through her. "I trust this was more entertaining than the play?" She thought his smile held a bit of sadness in it but decided that surely it must be the light.

His voice was low, husky from passion. "It was almost perfect, my love."

CHAPTER SIXTY

Hallie lay close beside Michael as he slept, watching the breaking of dawn through the French doors. She could hear the sounds of the servants beginning their day, but she was reluctant to leave the comfort of her bed. Hallie felt tired still, but sleep eluded her as the sun broke the horizon, her thoughts filled with Michael and the baby she carried. After an uneasy night she decided keeping her pregnancy a secret had a second purpose behind it, for she had never discovered who had put that potion in her soup. She feared that the news of this baby might make the culprit strike again. She would not risk such a thing with this child, for she wanted it too much.

Hallie eased out of her bed to open the French doors and allow the early morning air to cool the warming room. The early days of July had been unbearable. Michael had risen in the short time since she had left the bed and rung for his bath. He was propped in bed watching his wife, thinking her exquisite even in the early morning hours. Her raven hair spilled free to her waist, her skin was creamy and her deep violet eyes returned his stare brightly.

"You didn't sleep well last night, did you, love?" he asked her.

"I'm sorry if I disturbed you. I was quite restless with the heat."

He smiled warmly at her. "You should nap in the afternoons," he suggested.

She returned his smile, thinking that Michael had been very good to her. In fact, he had also been extremely good to Danny and even Etta when the opportunity arose. He had treated Danny equally with Trent and allowed Danny a fair mixture of friendship and discipline. She was grateful for that, for if Emeline had been allowed to dominate him, Danny surely would have ended up with broken spirits.

Michael sank down into a cool bath, relaxing back against the brass tub, watching Hallie as she sat at her dressing table brushing her hair and fastening it into a knot for the sake of coolness. A smile gently curved his sensuous lips as she tried without success to catch these soft, curling wisps at her temples, knowing she wanted to control them, though Michael was quite fond of the feathery curls. His blue-gray eyes followed her as she moved to the low bureau to gather her undergarments and begin her dressing. She had just pulled a light cotton dress on over her chemise when without warning Danny burst into their room, waving a large snake proudly in the air.

"I got him, Hallie! I got him!"

Hallie shrieked in surprise and sudden horror, her hand pressed to her heart as if to slow its rapid beating from fear. Before she could speak, Michael's voice rang through the room in a loud burst as he rushed from the water without hesitation.

"Dammit!"

Danny's eyes grew wide with fear and confusion and he ran from the room without pause. Michael's handsome face turned to Hallie, tight with concern and anger. "Are you all right?" he demanded worriedly.

Hallie laughed lightly as she nodded her head, a quivering nervousness sounding in the aftermath of her fright.

She was more surprised still to see Michael throwing on his robe, his face a countenance of barely leashed rage. "He's gone too far this time!" he roared as he bounded from the room, leaving Hallie to stare after him in astonishment. Never before had he been so angry with one of Danny's morning invasions when the lock on their bedroom door was left unlatched. Hallie heard Michael's heavy, determined footsteps down the hallway to the room of her brother. Then the door to it flew wide, crashing against the wall behind it. The small boy stared with fear at the large, imposing man who seemed to stalk him, realizing that for some unknown reason he had ventured too far this time. The snake was held in one small hand, clasped to his chest as if he had forgotten its presence.

Michael's voice seemed to roar, and the boy quaked to be the recipient of such fearsome anger. "If you ever do something like this again I will beat your butt and then skin you alive and hang your hide out to dry! Never again to Hallie, is that clear?"

The gaping mouth bobbed up and down rapidly to leave no doubt that he understood.

Michael's scowl did not ease. "See that that damned thing finds its way back to the pond. Now!"

Danny scurried around the man, eager for any excuse to escape.

Michael breathed deeply, calming his temper before he left the boy's room to return to his own. Hallie stood in the center, having heard his tirade. She stared with wide violet eyes at him, her curiosity outweighing even anger at his harsh treatment of Danny. When their bedroom door closed Hallie ventured to speak for the first time. "What brought all of that on?" she said incredulously.

"Dammit, you know very well," he said, his anger further spurred by her refusal to acknowledge the danger he considered her to have just passed.

"I'm used to his interruptions and his tricks, Michael. If you didn't want him to come in, you should have left the door latched. You know how he is. The snake was unpleasant but hardly cause for what you did."

"It's not the goddamn snake, and you know it! When are you going to stop this farce?"

Hallie did not understand him, thinking he spoke only of Danny's joke. "I was not that upset by the snake."

Michael calmed his fury with an effort, not wanting

it to be this way. His voice became low but extremely serious. "It is not the intrusion, Hallie. It is the fright it caused you. I know what you're trying so hard to hide from me, and I worried that it would cause some damage to you."

The color drained from her skin as she stared at her husband. "What do you mean?"

He sighed in exasperation. "You know very well what I mean. You're pregnant and I was afraid you would lose it, though under the circumstances that might be best." This last was barely audible but enough to send her every fear soaring to new heights.

"How did you know?" she asked quietly.

"I'm not blind, Hallie. You're beginning to round in places you weren't before. Did you believe I would not notice your new voluptuousness?"

Her face flushed with embarrassment. "Why were you so angry with Danny if you would rather I lost it?" she asked, her words rising from pain.

He shook his head sadly. "I didn't mean that. Even if it isn't mine I wouldn't see you go through what you did before."

Hallie stared in awe. "You believe this baby isn't yours?"

"What else can I think? You believed I was dead those three months. You were to marry Adam. You could easily have turned to him for comfort. And you were alone with him for a time before he became ill, alone in a house without interruption or obstacles just last month. Either of those times allowed you the opportunity. If it was mine, why didn't you come to me with the news? Why have you been so determined to conceal it?"

Tears welled up in her eyes, the hateful weakness of pregnancy, but she fought violently to stem the flow. "You may not be blind, Michael, but sometimes you are dimwitted. I did not turn to Adam for that kind of comfort, as you put it. If I had and this baby were the result, I would be as large as Amanda by now, for that was the time she became pregnant. I am far from that! As for the other, I was with Adam only a few weeks ago. That was hardly long enough for any seed of his to be causing the signs you have noticed. This baby is due at the first of the year, nine months from a time when you and I were hardly ever out of our bed and certainly not a time when I had even met Adam on the street. I am not some whore who rushes to another man simply because there are no obstacles. I went to Dr. Hathaway's house that day to have this confirmed. It was far too late for Adam to do the deed."

"Then why did you hide it from me?"

She seized those thoughts that had been in her mind only this morning. "To protect the baby. I was afraid someone would try to harm it again."

"That doesn't make sense, Hallie. I can understand being afraid of that, but not enough to keep it from me—if, as you say, I am the father."

Now the tears fell as she saw the only way to convince him was with the truth, realizing that if laid bare, her feelings and fears would leave her all the more vulnerable to him. "I hoped that if I kept it a secret for as long as possible it might give me time to make you fall in love with me. I knew that it was all lost once you found out, that having gained what you wanted from me you would probably go back to Maeve Carson and I would become nothing more than the matron, mistress of your house, mother of your heir."

Michael pulled her into his arms, laughing lightly at her words. His voice was tender. "Why is it so important for me to fall in love with you?"

"You know why!" she wailed miserably.

"No, I don't know why."

"Yes, you do! You know I love you and have for a long time now. It was obvious!"

Michael's smile widened into a full grin of pleasure, hearing the words he had wanted to know for what seemed like ages. "I could listen to that forever, Hallie. I've waited long enough to hear it. In fact, that was the only thing missing last night to make it perfect."

"I don't understand," she said, her mind fogged with abject misery.

"You had no cause to keep the news from me, sweet; your fears were futile. I love you more than I can explain. I worried that you still cared for Adam, that you would never come to feel about me the way I do about you."

She stared up at her husband, the tears stopped though her eyes were wet, her black lashes forming dark spikes around the sparkling violet depths. "I've told you so many times that I don't love Adam anymore. I never loved him in the way I do you. It's not even a spark beside the flame inside of me."

"But you didn't let me know that. I've been tormented thinking how much I love you when you would never feel the same. Last night with Jason and Amanda I was so damned jealous I could hardly stand it, especially while I was fool enough to think the baby might be Adam's."

"You're very adept at hiding your feelings. I thought all along you were content for ours to be purely a polite marriage of convenience while you waited for the time to seek Maeve Carson again. She told me when I cared for her that she has been your mistress since our marriage."

"She lies, my love. I have not even an inkling of desire for her. That night before Christmas that you witnessed her kissing me was the last I have even seen of her. I was unrelenting in my stand against her. I thought by now she had accepted that. It is not true, I promise you that."

"Then you are happy about the baby?"

He laughed. "I could shout the house down with the news, but I think I've already done enough of that for one morning. I promise you it will be the most welcome, wanted baby in the world, until its dozen or so brothers and sisters arrive."

Michael's lips found hers in a kiss filled with passion, their emotions running free for the first time, and Hallie savored the moment as a memory to carry with her for eternity.

CHAPTER SIXTY-ONE

September dawned bright, a soft breeze whispering past the last traces of summer. The sun shone but had less heat radiating from it, leaving the air cooled just enough to make it comfortable. Hallie had dressed without a great deal of enthusiasm, wishing she could understand why this wedding raised such turmoil and jealousy in her. She was secure in her love for Michael, but the thought of Adam with Belinda Scott still had an intense power over her. She told herself it was irrational, yet she had some strange bond with Adam that she could not sever.

Her pale lavender gown deepened the violet of her eyes so that the pallor of her skin was not obvious. She wore her brooch, feeling oddly comforted with it pinned to her breast. The seams had been let out to accommodate her thickening waist, but her pregnancy was not readily apparent. Michael waited downstairs for her, dressed handsomely in a black broadcloth tail suit that accentuated his narrow waist and broad shoulders. Hallie was struck by his masculine beauty. She hoped her smile concealed her true feelings. Her life with Michael had been blissfully perfect these past weeks, and she did not want to jeopardize that in any way.

The Scott mansion was decorated gaily for the occasion, white flowers in a wild array throughout. The doorway under which Belinda would walk to meet her groom was wreathed in white roses.

Michael held Hallie's hand tenderly throughout the ceremony, seeing the pain and confusion in her lovely features as she witnessed the marriage of the man she had planned her life around only to have it abruptly altered without a consideration to what she wanted. Michael felt no pangs of guilt, for he loved her more, he was sure, than Adam ever could, and Michael knew she loved him. He was happy to see the wedding take place, for it removed Adam from Hallie's life. Though his feelings for Adam were not improved, Michael did have a little less animosity toward the man who had saved his life and that of his wife.

Hallie hardly felt like celebrating after the ceremony but could not leave out of respect and love for both Adam and Amanda. Hallie was at least grateful that Belinda Scott was well occupied and never had a moment to torment her. Hallie stood and watched Adam and Belinda dance the first waltz, realizing that what she felt could not even be a portion of the pain Adam had felt as she had danced that first time with Michael at their party. She felt such sadness, seeing Adam perform as he should, seeming to be a happy groom, though she thought his eyes held less than joy. By the second dance Belinda was whisked off by other male guests. Adam did not hesitate to walk to Hallie and bow gallantly.

He spoke to Michael, but his eyes never left Hallie. "I don't believe the groom can be refused. I would like this dance, if you don't mind."

Michael did mind but stepped back courteously.

Adam spoke as they waltzed, his brown eyes devouring her in a way he should not have let others witness. "You don't look happy. I hope it's because of all of this. I would like to think you're just a bit jealous."

"You know I am, Adam. But I'm also worried. You seem less happy than I."

His smile was sad. "I cannot have what would make me happy, so I must settle for a shotgun wedding. Polite, but forced nonetheless. Now, if it were you in that wedding dress, no one could claim to be happier. As she

336

stood in that doorway my eyes deceived me for a moment and I thought it was you, wished desperately that it was you. I can't tell you how many times I have wished that baby you carry were mine! Ironic, isn't it, that very wish has trapped me into marriage, only with the wrong woman."

"Adam, you mustn't do this to yourself or to Belinda. Don't you care for her at all?"

He shrugged, his well-defined features pulled with tension. "I can tolerate her. She was simply comfort, like a downy pillow or a bottle of Scotch. Except that I didn't avoid the dangers she also held."

"You could be happy if only you try a little, Adam. If nothing else, your child deserves that much. I can't bear to see you destroy your life by not making the best of this."

He laughed derisively. "I haven't your knack for that, Hallie. I never did have. You always took what came your way and twisted it and turned it until it fit into your plans. Amanda has that same ability, though she goes about it more subtly. But I never could. In fact, I took a bad situation and made it worse." The music ended and Adam bowed formally.

Hallie's hand rested on his arm beseechingly, her tone pleading. "Please try to be happy, Adam. Please!"

After that dance Belinda Scott Burgess refused to leave her husband's side, holding onto his arm with a possessiveness odd even for this day.

Hallie joined Amanda as Jason and Michael stood talking, Amanda's pregnancy quite apparent even in the loose folds of a high-waisted dress. "I saw you dance with Adam. He's miserable, isn't he?" Her concern for her brother was thick in her voice.

"Perhaps he will come to love her, Amanda. It worked for me, and surely he must have seen something in the woman to have turned to her in the first place."

"You know that isn't true, Hallie. She plucked him like a piece of ripe fruit. He didn't even have a chance of escaping her talons. She's made a disastrous mistake. Adam will never love her as he did you. Perhaps if he had found someone else and come to care for her more and more to ease his love for you out of his heart, it would have worked. But never like this."

337

At that moment Emeline and Lydia approached, the older woman's face a mask of disapproval. "I did not expect such a display at the man's wedding!" she reprimanded Hallie.

"Oh? Is a display of friendship out of place here, Emeline?"

"You know very well what I mean!"

Lydia's smile was pained. "Emeline, had I known you would do this I would not have accompanied you. Leave Hallie alone for just one day."

The withered lips pursed as she stared at Lydia, eyes wide. "It seems her impertinence is infectious!" And she stormed off in search of the other staid matrons of Boston society to harp on the impropriety of the young.

"Lord, Hallie, how do you ever tolerate that woman? I don't think I will come back to Redland until she has left!" Lydia said.

"If she ever leaves. This is proving to be a very long visit."

"Unfortunately. The town house is blissfully quiet. Even Oliver is hardly ever there. He's been quite busy with the work Michael is making him do. Ever since Michael's unfortunate reappearance he's an even harder taskmaster. I swear he has some vengeance against Oliver and me. I pity you having to live with Emeline and Michael both. I could never bear it! Now tell me," she continued, changing the subject without even a pause, "are you a bit thick through the middle?"

Hallie's features froze, for she and Michael had tried to keep this a secret out of fear of what happened the last time. She knew it could not go on forever and supposed that the time had come. "I'm going to have a baby, Lydia."

"Oh, how horrid for you!" Lydia wrinkled her nose. "You were so wise the last time to get rid of it! Why did you ever decide to let this one go on?"

Hallie sighed, thinking that Michael's family had a talent for grating on her nerves. "I want this baby, Lydia."

Lydia's eyes turned to Amanda, assessing her condition as well. "I suppose you girls know what you're doing, but I must admit it escapes me. Your figures will never be the same! Not to mention having a passel of sniveling brats at your skirts. No, thank you! Well, if you'll excuse me, I see someone I want to talk to."

Hallie and Amanda laughed as Lydia moved through the crowd. "Is she always like that?" Amanda asked in disbelief.

"Every minute. She does spare a person the problem of too many comments. She's a good match for Emeline."

The afternoon had drawn into evening and that into night by the time Belinda and Adam left amid handfuls of rice and wheat and cheers of good wishes. Hallie alone stayed at the rear of the crowd, not participating, her heart heavy with jealousy. She fought back pictures of Belinda in Adam's arms, tasting well of what Hallie had dreamed of for so long. Sometimes it was not easy to remind herself that her heart belonged to Michael.

CHAPTER SIXTY-TWO

"Standing there watching for that murderer, no doubt."
Emeline's grating voice broke into Hallie's thoughts as
she stood before the drawing-room window. She did not
turn to answer, having decided to ignore this attack
which had begun the day after Adam's wedding. Emeline made a sound that came near to being a snort and
continued on her way down the hall.

Hallie's eyes closed slowly. Gossip was so cruel! She
certainly understood Adam's need to escape. She remembered too vividly Amanda's visit and the horrible
news she had brought. Had it not been her friend who
told the story, Hallie would not have believed a word
of it.

Apparently Belinda Scott had wasted no time in falling upon Adam with her fury over his dance with Hallie
and his outward show of affection. In her wrath she had
flung in his face the fact that the child she carried was
another man's. Adam had left her then, but not before
assuring her of his intention to annul their brief union.
He had spent his wedding night in the home of his
sister, though the gossips held it differently.

Each of the servants left in Adam's town house that
night had related the same tale. Belinda had been wild
with anger, the temper of a madwoman having been

unleashed. She had virtually destroyed the master suite, breaking glass, chairs, windows, tearing the clothing from the wardrobe as well as the linens and mattress. No one ventured near the upper level of the house; even when the tantrum subsided, not one soul was courageous enough to go upstairs.

When Adam returned at noon the next day, he was the first to view the wreckage. He found his bride slumped in a chair—the only unscathed piece of furniture in the rooms. Adam's valet had verified his story. Amid the carnage sat Belinda, her life's blood pooled onto her torn white gown from deep, gaping wounds in both wrists.

Hallie shook her head to clear it of the pictures that tormented her. She saw too clearly how horror of the accusation had overwhelmed Adam, though the authorities at last had been convinced of his innocence. Hallie only wished the ever-ready tongues of Boston had been satisfied.

For Hallie October had been an unbearable month. Emeline had harassed her with every sensational tale she heard; she blamed Hallie for Belinda's death. By November Hallie was ready to seize any excuse to be free of the woman's prattle. Amanda's baby was long past due. Even though Hallie's pregnancy was well advanced, she begged to move to the Curtis home to help with the birth. Michael was dubious, worrying about his wife and baby, but he finally conceded. He realized that Emeline was taking a far greater toll on his wife's strength than the other would, and so they went to stay with Amanda and Jason.

For the first time in several weeks Hallie felt the tension leave her as she relaxed with her friend, talking about the coming of their children. Hallie felt that her protruding middle could not possibly grow more than it already had until she viewed Amanda. Her movements were so cumbersome as to make sitting or rising a burden. Hallie was not looking forward to becoming any more unwieldy than she already was. The stay with the Curtises also allowed Hallie to visit her grandmother and Michael to tend to some business at the docks.

Etta Riley was expecting her granddaughter. Etta

had set out her silver tea service, smoothing her gown with a gnarled hand. Her face seemed always to be in a smile, as if in these waning years she was quite pleased with every aspect of her life.

Hallie smiled warmly at her grandmother, exclaiming over how well she looked. Hallie moved awkwardly, pulling the loose folds of her gown away from the large mound of her stomach. She felt very self-conscious about her middle and always attempted to keep it as unobtrusive as possible.

Etta noticed the action and laughed. "You look very beautiful, my dear. Don't be ashamed of it. I must say that it quite pleases me to be a great-grandmother. I have worried that your marriage would not be a happy one, but I see plainly that it is."

Hallie blushed lightly. "I'm very happy, Grandma. I've come to love Michael a great deal."

"Then I made a good choice for you?"

Hallie laughed. "Yes, you did, though I feared you would be jealous. I thought you had your cap set for him yourself after that first day."

"Well, I will admit if I were a lot younger I certainly would have been. As it is, I will content myself with Dr. Hathaway."

"Are you becoming serious with him? Am I to have a new grandfather?"

Etta laughed joyously. "I'm quite serious about the doctor. But we will never marry. I will admit we discussed it, but then one of us would have to move to the other's house and we're both too old for that, or for changing our ways. It's better this way. He stays the night when we both feel the need for a little company, we dine together; its a perfect situation for us. We are never lonely, but we needn't have all the bother of marriage."

Hallie stared at her grandmother's matter-of-fact words. "You have Dr. Hathaway stay the night?" she asked incredulously.

"Oh, my dear, don't be upset! At our ages there is no reputation left to ruin. If tongues wag we would both be flattered! It's all quite wonderful. We're very compatible, and he is very tolerant of my quirks."

Now it was Hallie's turn to laugh. "You don't have any quirks!"

Etta's eyebrows rose amid wrinkles. "I certainly do have. We all do, dear. At any rate, it's rather nice to share his company at dinner and then enjoy brandy afterward over a game of checkers. As I said, at my age I don't have the time left to fret over a reputation."

Hallie rose ponderously, having delighted in this new revelation about her grandmother. "Well, Grandma, I certainly wouldn't begrudge you such a simple pleasure."

"Thank you, dear."

Hallie could hardly wait to return to Amanda to share this bit of gossip, knowing she would be as amused by it as Hallie was.

Across the city in the new office of Redmond Shipping Lines, Michael was far from pleased as he found Oliver Kent sitting regally behind the desk and dressed in chartreuse velvet with a pea green cravat tied so high his chin rested atop it. He was calm as he faced Michael's wrath, his thin brows raised in effrontery at being questioned but little disturbed otherwise.

"Where the hell is that other ship?" Michael demanded.

"It sailed three weeks ago for California."

"California?! What business did you have sending a ship there?"

"Lydia and I thought it a good idea."

"You know damned well that you weren't supposed to vary from the routes I set down!"

He shrugged his thin shoulders. "I saw no reason not to send a cargo there. I understand everything there sells for ten times our usual price."

"That's right, dammit, but Jason and I deal with that, and you know it!"

"Lydia and I saw no reason why we shouldn't be allowed a piece of the pie," he answered arrogantly.

Now Michael's tone was low, more dangerous than had he screamed. "Let's get one thing straight, Oliver. I own this business, and you work for *me!* It is not a matter of you and Lydia getting a 'piece of the pie,' it

344

is a matter of your following my orders. If you can't manage that, then you had damned well better get out!"

"Our mistake," Oliver said carelessly, unperturbed by the threat.

Michael reminded himself of his sister and her unrelenting harping on this subject and so drew back, putting a tight control on his temper. "Since the damage is done, let me see the list of what you sent."

Oliver Kent smiled evilly, pleased with himself. He shrugged. "I've lost it," he said simply.

"You lost it," Michael repeated, his jaw clenched while his hands ached to be around this insolent peacock's neck. "How did you manage that?" he asked sarcastically.

"I couldn't say. It simply disappeared."

"Was it a full cargo?"

"Yes, quite full."

"And you have no idea whatsoever of the contents?"

"None."

Michael strode toward the door, the muscle in his cheek working fiercely. "Don't push me farther, Kent. You tempt the fates."

A sneer greeted his words. "The same might be said of you, Michael."

CHAPTER SIXTY-THREE

November saw the full force of winter as the snow fell heavily for the first time. Hallie knew that unless Amanda's baby arrived in the next few days she would be forced to return to Redland. They had all decided that a miscalculation must have occurred, for the birth was almost two weeks overdue.

The *Boston Evening Transcript* was filled with news of the end of the cholera epidemic, which had taken the lives of one thousand citizens. Everyone breathed a sigh of relief to have the dreaded disease on the decline. Jason and Michael sat discussing it as Hallie and Amanda worked before the fire on baby clothes.

Hallie sighed contentedly, her hand moving to her protruding middle as the baby moved. "I dread going home," she said after a time, setting the blanket she embroidered in her lap and staring into the briskly dancing flames.

Amanda knew exactly what her friend meant. "Is there any hint as to when Emeline will end the visit?"

She laughed derisively. "It's too interminable to be called a visit anymore. Now she says she will stay until the baby is born, though I'm sure she will be no help. She probably just wants to start picking away at the poor little thing to prove how Michael is not the father.

I can hear her words before she even speaks them. There will not be even one thing that vaguely resembles a Redmond. Her nagging and harping has worn me thin. Sometimes I would like to hit her, she makes me so mad."

"Wouldn't Michael ask her to leave?" Amanda suggested.

"I don't know. I don't feel as if I can ask that of him. After all, she is his mother's sister. Besides, Trent is fond of her, and it would cause an enormous row between him and Michael."

"But it is your house too! You haven't had any time without that woman since Michael returned. I think it's time it was suggested that she visit someone else."

"For all I know, she has nowhere to go. She might have closed her house permanently, for she never speaks of going home. I did suggest to Michael that he might find some poor man to marry her."

Amanda laughed, then winced with the action. "I don't think there's a man on earth who would have her!" Amanda moved in discomfort, adjusting her position but finding that did not ease her.

"Are you all right, Amanda?" Hallie asked in concern.

"I don't know. I've been having these odd pains all day long."

"Do you think it's time for the baby?"

She shrugged. "I'm ready if it is. If I grow any larger I will be in danger of being harpooned as a whale."

Amanda's laughter ended abruptly as a sharp pain stabbed at her. Now Jason was alerted, moving rapidly to his wife's side, his face even redder than usual. "It's the baby, isn't it?" he asked urgently.

Amanda smiled, though fear showed in her features. "I believe it is. I'm suddenly all wet."

Jason helped her to her feet, her face flushed with embarrassment that such an intimate thing should happen with Michael there. As they climbed the stairs, Jason's voice rang through the house, screaming for someone to go for Dr. Hathaway.

Jason could not be contained as he paced the drawing room feverishly, muttering to himself unintelligibly.

Michael tried to calm his friend but after a time gave up, seeing that it was futile. Hallie was relegated to keeping the men company as Dr. Hathaway refused her admittance into the room, saying that her own advanced pregnancy was reason enough for her not to witness the birth, nor could she do any of the work that was involved. Instead she fidgeted nervously, for she feared that something would happen to this baby, and she knew well that Amanda could not live through it again.

The night drew into the early hours of morning as Amanda's forced moans and cries of pain echoed through the house. Michael watched his own wife, hoping this would not frighten her for her own ordeal to come, though he knew she was well aware of the perils of childbirth. He sat close to her, holding her hands in his large, powerful ones, comforting her in this way. He pressed her to drink the tea that the servants brought, but as he realized the extent of her trepidations he poured her a glass of wine.

Just as the grandfather clock in the entrance hall chimed three, a low scream sounded from the room upstairs as if torn from Amanda. All three people in the drawing room jumped to their feet. A long silence followed, and all three of them feared that Amanda had screamed in horror at having borne another dead child.

Seconds passed like hours until the high-pitched wails of a newborn infant were heard. Jason turned a tear-streaked face to Michael, pride and relief glowing from his face like a ruddy beacon. The two clasped hands first and then grasped each other in a sudden masculine embrace before Jason bounded up the steps to see his wife and child.

Tears streamed down Hallie's face as she breathed a deep sigh of relief and moved into Michael's warm embrace. The tiny baby girl they viewed only minutes later was the image of Jason. A shock of curly red hair crowned her head. Her eyes squinted against the light, and she wrinkled a flat little nose, turning her head into the blanket. Hallie and Michael each felt a growing impatience to hold their own child in their arms.

CHAPTER SIXTY-FOUR

The holidays passed pleasantly in spite of Emeline and her incessant harping. Hallie grew larger than she had ever expected, and she longed for her pregnancy to find an end. She felt ponderous and clumsy and knew that her waddling walk was comical. She needed assistance in rising and sitting. Michael insisted that to him she looked more lovely than ever, but she believed that to be only a kind gesture on his part. She could have cried in frustration when she opened her Christmas gift to find a filmy nightgown and wrapper inside, a bare wisp of lace and alluring veil, for it seemed that she would never be able to appear before her husband in it without self-consciousness.

Hallie resisted Michael's every attempt to study her protruding middle; she hid behind a silk screen to dress and usually moved his hand from her stomach when he tried to explore it. It was a bone of contention between them, for Michael complained of the separation it caused them, insisting that he was never allowed to hold her anymore and that since making love was out of the question at this point he should be granted at least this solace. Hallie adamantly refused, and so this argument never ended. After spending an enjoyable Christmas Day together, Michael would brook no resistance. He pulled her into his embrace gently but firmly, determined to experience some of this pregnancy before it ended. He also needed a bit of closeness to soothe his raging desire for her. Her feelings about her appearance were incomprehensible to him, for he found her to be even more desirable as she carried his child.

He held her tenderly, his mouth seeking hers in the darkness, a warm, loving kiss filled with a passion that could not be assuaged. Hallie reveled in his nearness, relaxing beneath his touch and realizing how much she had missed this aspect of their relationship. When the kiss ended, her head rested on the broad expanse of his chest, and she sighed contentedly. She was not even uncomfortable as his massive hand caressed her middle, following the baby's movements with fascination.

"God, you're beautiful," he said with passion. "I know you don't believe it, but I find you very lovely this way. I won't mind seeing you in this condition many times over as our family grows." He began to laugh. "That is such an odd statement coming from me."

"Why?" She snuggled closer to him.

"I was wild and unruly. I made Danny look like a mouse. I spent many years flaunting all that my father held dear. He believed in the family life, in high standards and a strict moral code, though he veered from that for your mother. He preached to me endlessly about duty always coming first, before pleasure. Yet I was as committed to satisfying my own desires as I was to defying him and all of his beliefs."

"Has that changed?"

Michael chuckled deep in his throat, kissing the top of her silken head. "In more ways than you will ever realize. A part of it began during the war. It was such an inhuman thing! As I watched men all around me die, I came to understand that men need to perpetuate their name. I began to care for those simple people, to feel their pain as they watched their loved ones die in battle. When I came home to find Trent so unhappy I thought what a failure I had been, that I felt so much for those strangers and yet my own brother was miserable, and he is a part of the Redmond line, just as Danny is. I suddenly felt that continuity was very important. Then I came to love you and want a baby of our own, to see the product of our love be given life and grow and prosper. It is ironic, for suddenly I find that my values are not so different from those I disdained in my father. So you see, it is so unlike the man I thought I must be to find this pleasure in the baby that you carry, in the whole process of its growth, to care so much for you and for having a family with you."

Silence filled the air for a time before Hallie spoke. "Thank you, Michael. I could not have asked for a nicer Christmas gift."

His hand lowered again to her stomach. "Nor could I, my love. Had he been born today it could not be a better gift."

Hallie put the finishing touches on the nursery, making certain that everything was ready for the baby. She opened the drawers of the small bureau, running a loving hand across blankets and clothing and all the necessities she had worked on so diligently.

"You're anxious for your child, aren't you?" Trent's voice sounded from the doorway. Hallie thought it an odd question but believed it was asked in innocent curiosity.

Hallie smiled at him warmly. "Yes, I am. Michael and I both are," she added, watching the mention of her husband's name turn the boy's features cold.

Trent moved into the room, standing before the small cradle, rocking it gently with his foot, his hands thrust into his pockets. He looked reluctant to admit his interest here. "This was mine, you know," he said after a time.

"Michael told me. It is a lovely piece." Hallie watched him as he remained staring down at it, saying nothing. "Do you remember your mother at all, Trent?" she asked conversationally.

Now his eyes raised to her curiously. "No, I never knew her as a child."

"I'm sure Danny doesn't recall our mother either. He was just a baby when she died. I've always been sorry for that." Her hands rested on her stomach as her thoughts wandered. "It would be a horrible thing for a mother not to be there to raise her own child."

Trent's eyes seemed to grow wise suddenly, as though he had given this thought. "I can think of nothing worse for the child or the mother. It is cruel indeed."

A moment of silence passed as Hallie watched him, seeing a deep sensitivity in him that she had not noticed before. "May I ask you a question, Trent?" she ventured after a time.

He smiled at her openly, and Hallie felt encouraged.

"Why do you shun all of Michael's attempts at friendship?"

His face hardened perceptibly. "He is not my friend," he said coldly, almost accusingly.

"He is your brother and he wants so much to be close to you, to help you, if you would only allow it."

Trent's posture grew straight, stiff. "I don't need anything from Michael." He turned and left Hallie to stare at his back, leaving no doubt as to his feelings for his brother.

CHAPTER SIXTY-FIVE

Michael and Hallie sat alone before the fire. It was New Year's Eve and they were alone in the house. Lydia and Oliver were giving another of their tasteless parties in the town house, and Hallie was grateful for the excuse not to attend it. Emeline had gone to visit a friend for a few days and was not to return until the following morning; Trent had accompanied her. Danny had gone to spend some time with Etta, and all of the servants except Farley and Mercy had long since gone home to their families. Beyond the large bay windows snow was falling heavily, the wind whistling the new year in with a violent force.

Hallie sighed and leaned back into Michael's arms. "It seems our baby will have a birthday in 1850," she said, a note of resignation in her voice.

Michael laughed lightly; his tone deep with an unsoothed passion from the weeks of celibacy. "I only hope he doesn't choose 1851 before he makes an appearance! Sometimes I don't think the little imp will ever vacate that spot and allow his father to ease his burdens."

Hallie's violet eyes widened in mock indignation. "I've noticed how difficult it is for his father to carry that heavy burden!" she said and laughed.

Michael's hand went to her enormous stomach,

stretched to its limits. "You know what I mean, my love. I give you full credit and all of my sympathy for the way I know you must feel by now. But you have to admit that I am long starved for your more intimate attentions."

"I suppose you believe that only you suffer in that respect as well?"

He laughed hoarsely. "I certainly hope not! I want you as eager as I am to return that element to our bed."

Hallie's voice was calm, quiet. She stood with a great deal of effort. "I believe your son was listening to your pleas," she said simply.

"Oh? Has he given you some sign that he will show me a little compassion?"

She smiled beautifully down at her husband. "As a matter of fact, that is just what he's done. If you don't mind, I think in consideration of the weather you had best send Farley for Dr. Hathaway."

Michael smiled, thinking she teased him. "Should we prepare him a room and keep him as our guest until the day arrives?"

Hallie laughed at his ignorance. "I certainly hope it doesn't take that long. He should be able to go home by morning."

Now Michael's features grew serious, his blue-gray eyes wide, the corners of his moustache pulled down over his sensuous lips. The color drained slightly from his face. "Don't joke about such a thing, Hallie! Is there something I should know?"

"Yes, I suppose there is. I am sopping wet. Unless I'm greatly mistaken, we are about to have a baby."

"Oh, my God!" Michael jumped to his feet, his pulse racing, beads of perspiration suddenly forming on his brow. He picked Hallie up into his arms and climbed the stairs two at a time.

"Michael," Hallie spoke reassuringly, "you must relax. These things take some time. There is no reason for you to be so agitated."

"You'll have to allow me that just this once, love. I've never had a baby before." His voice boomed through the empty house as he screamed for Farley, bringing the huge man in his nightshirt and cap, and Mercy in almost the identical garb. After sending Farley for the doctor, Michael helped Hallie shed her wet clothing, then placed her gently in their bed. Mercy left them to get dressed. Michael was perturbed with the old woman's calm, leisurely treatment of what he felt was an emergency, even though Hallie also seemed unhurried.

A sharp pain tore through Hallie that unsettled her calm demeanor. Her violet eyes grew wide, and she grasped her hard abdomen in shock until the spasm passed. "I thought they were supposed to begin mildly," she said gasping.

At last Mercy returned, pushing Michael out of the room to gather sheets and towels and to stoke a fire in one of the cookstoves. Michael was reluctant to leave his wife, but with Hallie's encouragement he did as Mercy requested. The tasks took some time to accomplish, and Michael wished fervently that Farley would hurry up with Dr. Hathaway. It had not occurred to him before that he would lose Hallie in childbirth, and as that thought struck him it sent a flash of fear running through him to chill his blood. He could not endure life without her.

Michael's past words flooded his memory, those he had spoken when he and Hallie had first come to live here together. If love was an illusion, it was a damn strong one. This had outlasted the moment he had expected and gone on to be ultimately enduring and worthy of his trust. He laughed derisively to himself, thinking of his well-thought-out plans for this marriage, telling Hallie that they would find other things to share that would fill their lives without love. What a fool he had been, he thought now. Hallie had been right then, that without love nothing was worth anything. What an empty life he would have had without her, or God forbid, if he had succumbed to Maeve Carson's ploys. Surely fate would not be so cruel as to seize what it had taken him so long to find.

Michael's attention was drawn back to his wife upstairs as he heard a low moan. He frowned, knowing that it was too soon for her to be in that much pain. It had been hours before Amanda had made a sound. He bounded up the stairs, overwhelmed with concern for his wife, the person who meant more to him than anything in the world. He saw that Mercy's casual treatment of the situation had altered as she worked frenziedly at the foot of the bed, discarding the quilts and blankets and anything that might hinder this birth.

"What's wrong?" he demanded.

"Nothing. But this baby is in a hurry to be born."

"But Dr. Hathaway isn't here yet!"

She chuckled lightly, "This baby didn't ask who was here. I'm going to need your help. Sit with her and hold her hands. When I say *push,* help her sit up a bit and brace her back."

Michael moved to the head of the bed, perspiration beading his forehead. He did as Mercy ordered, talking to Hallie encouragingly, calmly, belying his own apprehension. Though it was only minutes, Michael felt as if it were hours. He watched her agony with horrible fascination, wishing he could ease her in some way. The tension mounted as Mercy worked and coaxed, her own face red and damp with sweat.

"Just one more time, child, just one more!" she said, excitement ringing in her voice. A short scream of pain escaped as the baby emerged, and Michael saw the fear that erupted on Mercy's face. Still her voice sounded the same as she spoke to Hallie, "Once more, love. It's coming butt first. One more time and your baby girl will be born!"

Willing to do anything, exert any amount of strength to free her body of this misery, Hallie pushed as hard as she could, her face distorted.

At last the baby passed into Mercy's capable hands, and Hallie fell back in utter exhaustion. She listened intently for the first sound of her baby, fear rising in that instant as she thought of Amanda's dead infant in her hands. Eternity stretched on and on until finally the high-pitched, lusty cries of her daughter filled the room.

Michael held his daughter as Mercy tended to his wife. Looking down at the bloody, wet baby girl he thought her the most beautiful child ever born, her tiny mewlings a perfect accomplishment. After a short time Mercy took the infant from her father's muscular arms, and Michael went to sit beside Hallie. He kissed her warmly and then took her hand tenderly. "I love you, Hallie. Are you all right?"

She smiled weakly up at him. "I'm wonderful. Is she the most beautiful child you've ever seen?"

"Without a doubt!" He pulled his pocket watch out, opening the ornate lid to view the time. "You were right, love, she did wait until 1850 to arrive. It is nearly one o'clock. She is a New Year's baby."

"Are you pleased with her?"

"I couldn't be more pleased. She has already filled me with an indescribable feeling of love and pride, much like her mother."

"Poor Dr. Hathaway will have come out in this weather for no reason."

"I'm glad he didn't make it."

"Why?" she asked in surprise, her voice soft with fatigue.

Michael smiled sheepishly. "I was so damn jealous that Adam was with you the last time, that he should be there to help and comfort you while I paced the hall. I have worried ever since he left Boston that he might return and under some circumstances be the one to deliver the baby. It was a closeness I felt miserably excluded from and now, after being here with you, I will never allow anyone to leave me standing in the hallway. It was a moment I will always cherish, my love."

Mercy returned with the tiny baby girl, who was to be named Sara. She placed her in her mother's arms and left the room, seeing that this was a time for Hallie and Michael to be alone with their firstborn child on this wintry New Year's night.

CHAPTER SIXTY-SIX

Michael stayed close by Hallie's side until the beginning of February, never venturing farther than her voice could carry. He reveled in the baby and the closeness he shared with Hallie as they explored and enjoyed their child.

With the passing of January, however, Michael realized he must pull his attentions back to business. The first task he had set for himself was to rid Redmond Shipping Lines of Oliver Kent. Michael would no longer tolerate the man's cocky ineptitude. He would pay him not to work for him.

When Michael entered his office he was neither surprised nor happy to see that his sister had accompanied her husband in answer to his summons. Lydia sneered at her brother while Oliver examined his nails, obviously bored with this family squabble.

"I'm glad you're here, Lydia," Michael said as he took his seat behind the desk. "It will save me having to explain this twice." He lowered his gaze to Oliver, who did not meet his glance but stared at the wall. "You are no longer under the employ of this company, Oliver."

The man eyed Michael as if he were mad. "For what reason am I being dismissed?"

Michael heard Lydia's indrawn breath as she readied

herself to attack. Still he answered Oliver, "Do you mean other than the fact that you're an incompetent fool? Or that you seem incapable of following instructions? I cannot decide if your actions are criminal or simply inept. I have decided to give you the benefit of the doubt."

"I won't stand for this!" Lydia's voice boomed forth.

"No, Lydia," Michael returned calmly, "*I* won't stand for this. And I can't imagine what you think you can do about it. I have tolerated your whims and your foolishness for far too long, thinking that perhaps our father had been unfair to you. But he was right in his assessment of you and your husband. He left it to me to decide what would be done, and I have decided. This farce is at an end."

"You cannot do this to me! I demand what is mine!"

Michael sat back in his chair, peering over long fingers that touched only at the tips. "Demand all you want, Lydia, but this is what you are getting." He paused, savoring the end of this conflict. "As of this moment, you no longer have a home in Boston. Redland will not welcome you, nor will you be able to enter the town house. You may not make use of any Redmond property or accounts."

Lydia's face was a study in rage, but Michael ignored her and went on calmly. He handed an envelope to her as he spoke. "That, my dear sister, is your future. It is yours to take or leave."

"You bastard, you—"

He cut her off. "There are times when I wish I were a bastard, Lydia. It would free me from any relationship to you. Instead I am freeing myself. In that envelope are papers of passage for you both to San Francisco. The city should be to your liking; I understand it is quite bawdy there. There is a house in your name, Lydia; all the details are in those papers."

His glance fell on Oliver. "Do forgive me, Kent, but I felt a need to protect her. You will have to cultivate her for your livelihood." Kent's countenance was expressionless.

Michael shook his head as Lydia began to speak. "You will also find you have a substantial bank account and investments that will support you if you act with any

362

wisdom at all. But everything is in San Francisco, and your affairs are now arranged in such a way that all this will be yours only if you are a resident of that city. If you stay here, you are a pauper. The choice is yours."

"You think you will be rid of me, don't you?"

"Absolutely. I have taken all that I intend to from this thieving idiot. And should you be toying with the notion of remaining in Boston, you should also know that I will open a serious investigation into your husband's mismanagement of my holdings. I am patient but I am not a fool. I am choosing to drop the matter for the moment. Should you reappear in Boston, Mr. Kent, I think that prison will be your new home. Now make your choice."

Only a moment passed before she took the envelope and opened it. After a time she looked at her brother, a smirk of victory on her face. "It's I who have won, you know. Oliver and I will live in luxury while you work to support us."

Michael's visage was not that of the loser. "It will be my pleasure just to be rid of you both."

Lydia rose from her chair and swept out of the room. As Oliver followed her through the door he stopped and turned, a sneer further distorting his hawkish features, but he said nothing. He left the door ajar behind him as he moved with a studied lack of haste.

Hallie placed the sleeping baby in her cradle near the hearth in the drawing room. She stayed bent over the side, watching lovingly as Sara slept, still awed by the child's perfect beauty. Hallie did not hear anyone enter and was startled by the soft sound of the voice from the doorway.

"What I would give to be witness to that sight each day."

Hallie jumped and turned quickly in surprise, instantly recognizing the voice. "Adam! I didn't hear you come in!" she said, amazed that he stood in her drawing room. "I didn't know you were back!"

He smiled wearily at her. "I arrived only this morning. I couldn't hide from the wagging tongues forever, could I? How are you, Hallie?" His tone was tinged with sadness, and her heart went out to him as he stood before her looking so dejected.

"I'm well, Adam. You look tired."

"Do I? I'm really not. I haven't worked or done any-thing of value these past months. I've sat and felt sorry for myself. I suppose it shows."

"Will you have tea?" she said, fearful that Michael would return and be suspicious of even so innocent a scene.

"No, I won't stay long. I just needed to see you again, to see your baby. Amanda tells me you have named her Sara and that she is as beautiful as her mother. I told her that was not possible. Are you happy, honey? It's important to me that you are."

"I am, Adam, truly. I only hope you can find the same."

"That isn't likely unless you gain your freedom and we can ever be together. I won't make the same mistake I did with Belinda, Hallie. There is no other woman in the world for me but you. I knew it all along. Belinda was a feeble attempt at something that cannot be. Any woman would only be a sorry replacement for you. It wouldn't be fair. I know it's foolish, but I can do nothing but stay as I am, waiting for you, if that day should ever come." He smiled down at her, the lighthearted grin of her childhood. "Perhaps we will be as your grandmother and Dr. Hathaway, finding one another in the last years of our lives, when we can enjoy our-selves without worry."

Hallie smiled at the picture, but still she felt so sad to hear Adam speak this way. "I wish you wouldn't say such things. You mustn't refuse yourself a life, Adam. You must find someone to love, to give you children. I know it's important to you."

"I found someone a long time ago, Hallie. A little imp with raven hair and violet eyes who followed me through years and drove me to distraction with wanting her."

He moved to the cradle, staring down at the baby with a warm smile. He bent and picked her up gently, cuddling her close to his chest, a tiny white cocoon in his arms. He kissed the downy head, securing the blan-ket where a corner had come free. Hallie watched si-

364

lently, moved by the scene. "She should have been ours, Hallie." He rested his cheek against the soft pink head.

Hallie had no idea what to do. Why could Adam not accept the fact she was lost to him?

"But she isn't yours, Adam. She is mine." Michael's voice came from the entrance, deep but not harsh. Hallie was grateful for the compassion she heard. It did not ease the feeling she had of being torn between these two men, it merely helped her instincts of protectiveness to know Michael would not cause Adam more pain with an ugly confrontation.

Adam raised his eyes to Michael, hatred shining there. He reluctantly lowered Sara into her cradle, tucking her blankets about her to ensure her comfort. When that was done he moved to Hallie, taking her hands in his. She saw the love he held for her, and her heart ached. "I know I have said it a hundred times before, honey. I only mean for you to be certain I have not changed. I will always be here for you. Always." He kissed her chastely on the brow, then lingered as he seemed to memorize her features.

When he released her, his shoulders drew back and he faced Michael squarely. "I will hate you until the day one of us dies, Redmond, for what you stole from me."

Michael did not move, nor did he speak. He watched with pity as Adam left, happy that their positions were not reversed.

Hallie felt his arms come around her and turn her into his embrace. She rested her head against his massive chest, tears falling freely from the agony in her heart. When at last she had resolved her feelings, knowing she could have done nothing differently, her voice sounded small and far away. "I love you, Michael. Thank you for your kindness. I know it was not easy for you."

"It was easier than walking out of here with the knowledge that you were left the wife of another man."

Hallie stayed in the warmth of his embrace for a moment longer. When at last she could raise a dry smile to him, she did. "I do love you as no other, Michael."

"I'm glad to hear it, love. No words could be more welcome right now." He pulled her again to his broad chest and lowered his head to press a warm, lingering kiss in the sweet-smelling mass of curls.

CHAPTER SIXTY-SEVEN

The woods were quiet and peaceful, full of winter's silence. Michael raced through the night, pushing his horse to its greatest speed. It was far past the dinner hour, and he was tired from a long day of trying to set right what Oliver had come close to ruining.

A loud crack tore through the stillness. Michael slumped over the long mane of his chestnut stallion, barely grasping the pummel to keep his seat. Burning pain shot through his shoulder, an excruciating contrast to the cold air. Another shot rang through the silence, frightening the steed into a bolt that sent Michael to the frozen earth, knocking the breath from his lungs. He lay perfectly still, the side of his face pressed to the ice-packed road. The well-trained animal returned, nuzzling him as if in question, then lifting his velvety head as a rider approached.

Michael did not move, did not even breathe. He knew his best chances lay in letting his attacker believe the deed had been done. He sensed rather than saw the rider draw near and stop to study him from a small distance, then turn and spur the mount toward Redland.

Hallie fed Sara for the final time that night and

settled the tiny infant in her cradle. Mercy was tending an injured field hand with the assistance of Farley; Emeline and Trent had retired early to their beds. Hallie placed a last tender kiss on the baby's forehead and doused the candle as she left the room to seek her own. She yawned and stretched, hoping Michael would be home soon. She was surprised to see a light from beneath the doorway to her room, for it was Mercy's habit upon retiring to stop to light a candle so that she and Michael would not find their room in total darkness. No other servant remembered, and Hallie knew the old nanny had left the house hours ago. Still she felt no trepidation as she pushed the door open to enter.

Hallie's eyes grew wide at the sight that greeted her. Trent stood at the far side of the room, a gun in his hands. "My God, Trent, what are you doing!?" Her voice was soft, alarmed.

His hands shook as his knuckles showed white in the tight grip of the revolver. His mouth opened to speak, to give the order he needed, but closed again in nervousness. One thumb raised slowly to pull the hammer back.

Hallied saw the uncertainty in his eyes, the childlike questioning as though he begged for guidance. "Please, Trent!" Her voice was as calm as she could force it to be. "Put the gun down! Tell me what is wrong! Please!"

His hands shook wildly now, his brow creased in confusion, his body quivering. When he spoke, his voice was that of a child, not a young man, a frightened little boy. "I can't do it! Run, Hallie, get away! I can't save everybody! Run!" His hands opened though his arms remained extended, and the gun fell to his feet.

Hallie stared at him for only a moment, not understanding any of what was happening or of what he said. She turned and ran to the nursery, knowing that no matter what was going on in the house she must protect her child. The door stood wide when she reached it, the glow of a lantern lighting the hallway beyond. She paused only seconds, terror striking as her eyes took in the scene.

"Emeline!" she screamed as the woman stood poised above the cradle, a pillow ready to smother the tiny baby.

The older woman's eyes raised at the sound, a vicious snarl sounding as she pushed the pillow into the cradle. Hallie charged like an animal, knocking Emeline to the floor and falling with her. The much larger woman turned her energies to Hallie now, struggling to gain a grasp on her throat. Hallie struggled futilely; the other woman's strength far surpassed hers.

Trent's voice boomed to them, now hard and echoing with the strength of a man. "Enough, Emeline!" he shouted. "Release her!"

The older woman stopped suddenly, her gray-streaked hair falling in strands around her face. Reluctantly she withdrew her hands from Hallie, staring up at the slight youth who moved into the room. She stood, her gaze never leaving the gun Trent held. Hallie gasped for breath, her hands at her neck, where it bore the marks of the other's fingers. She fought her voluminous skirts to stand, wary of moving more, though she wanted to pluck Sara from her bed. Hallie stared from Trent to Emeline in confusion, not understanding, not knowing what madness had befallen them.

Emeline's voice came loud and grating. "Why didn't you kill her?" she demanded. "Do it now, Trent! Shoot her!" she commanded.

Hallie turned to Trent, seeing his new calm, as though his decision had been made; he was no longer a bewildered child. He did not remove the gun from its position toward Emeline. No one moved as the air crackled with tension.

"Drop the gun, Trent." Michael's voice sounded from the doorway now, drawing all eyes his way. Hallie's breath drew in a gasp as she saw him leaning heavily against the jamb, the shoulder of his jacket blood-soaked, his face pale, his eyes shining with pain. He held his own revolver leveled at Trent; there was no indecision in Michael's stance.

"No!" Emeline shrieked. "It can't be! You're dead! You're dead!"

Trent turned to Michael, never lowering the weapon he held. His expression was filled with hatred.

"Shoot!" Emeline commanded.

Trent's gaze lowered to the gun pointed at his own chest and then returned to the face of his brother. Trent

369

stared long, leaving everyone suspended, awaiting his decision in horrible fascination.

The barrel fell as he released his grip, his breath came in a sigh of surrender. He turned to Emeline. "I can't do this, Mother! I can't kill! I'm sorry! I couldn't go through with it when I set fire to the warehouse! I pulled him free then, and I can't shoot him now! I can't shoot anyone!"

A low moan of defeat escaped Emeline as she sank to the floor, her hate-filled eyes staring at Michael. "It isn't fair! It is my due!" Her arms curled around her own waist, she rocked in inconsolable misery, words tumbling out as if to herself. "I loved him! I always loved him! It was agony watching my sister marry him, seeing her with him! So many years I suffered it, the watching, the wanting! After Lydia's birth my sister was left an invalid, too sickly and weak to leave her bed. Michael turned to me then. It was I who comforted him, who loved him. He said he loved me, that we would be together someday. We knew she would not live long as she was. I gave him all I could, I never held myself from him! I loved him that much! Even when I found I would bear his child, I was happy! Happy!" She fairly snorted at the memory. "He took my baby. He took Trent and pretended she had borne him, my sister who could do nothing but lie in her bed. He said Trent would not be a bastard, he said I would be able to claim him again when she died. He lied to me." Her voice was soft as she wept now with old pain.

"When my sister died I came back here. I thought my life was just beginning. But he refused all I wanted. He was in love with that Wyatt tramp! Your mother!" she spat at Hallie.

Then Emeline stared at Michael again. "You never knew, did you? It was always 'poor Emeline,' 'poor spinster,' 'unwanted, unloved,' 'a nuisance to us all.' I knew how you hated my visits. I knew how you dreaded anything to do with me. No one wants a woman no man would have as wife. She is pitied! All I ever wanted was my son! To be near him! When you went to war, I came here. I took the place that should have been mine all along. I told Trent the truth, I claimed what was mine. But then you came back!" she accused, her hatred of

Michael plain. "Again I was the unwanted aunt, the spinster, the childless annoyance. How could I ever have my son, my home unless you were dead? Unless any heir or offspring died with you? What am I left now?" Her face dropped to her hands as her body was wracked with sobs.

Trent moved to her, awkward in his attempt to comfort her. His hand rested on her shoulder, where hers grasped it in desperation. He looked suddenly not like a slight lad but like a man who sees his responsibilities and accepts them. "It's all right, Mother. You will always have me. Nothing else matters. I'll take care of you."

Emeline's weeping filled the room as she fell against Trent's legs. Hallie picked Sara up, glad the child still slept. She saw the stain of Michael's wound had broadened and placed her free arm around him to offer her strength.

The house was suddenly alive with noise and activity as Mercy and Farley returned to find this scene, but the sound of Emeline's sobs echoed in the house for hours as her young son held her and offered what comfort he could.

CHAPTER SIXTY-EIGHT

Hallie stood alone in the ballroom, staring at the scattered remnants of their first party. It seemed odd to her that only a month had passed since that night that still plagued her, bringing her violently awake from terror-filled nightmares. Yet here she was, in a house that bore no hints of the painful events of that evening or of the people who had caused it.

Emeline had returned to New York a woman not even remotely the same as before. She had left seeming old and withered, her stiff, formal countenance having vanished, a broken, vulnerable woman who wore the scars of her wasted life in the deep lines of her face. It was hard for Hallie to believe that Emeline had actually attempted to kill both Michael and her baby. That the woman could have been so driven by her need for revenge actually to shoot Michael...that she had been prepared to smother the infant in her cradle. But Hallie pushed these thoughts away. Both she and Michael had agreed that Emeline was now a broken woman and that she posed no further danger to them or the baby.

Emeline had left the day after she had attempted to get what she felt was hers. Trent had asked to go with her, to become her son in fact. Michael had agreed to provide for them both financially, assuring Trent of his fair share of the Redmond holdings.

Michael had healed rapidly under Hallie's careful ministrations. Life had at last become normal as Oliver and Lydia departed at almost exactly the same time as Trent and Emeline.

To celebrate the fact that they were at last alone in their own house, they had given their first party. For the first time since her marriage, Hallie had felt free and uninhibited at Redland.

Amanda and Jason were asleep upstairs, having agreed to spend a short time visiting with them; their daughter, Alexis, was safely cradled beside them. It made Hallie feel good to think of them and the happiness her friend had gained at last. She appreciated the understanding Amanda had offered, as always, in Hallie's problems. Amanda had stood beside her friend when the gossipmongers had once again begun their tongue-lashings, and she quelled the rumors before they ran rampant. She had shared her strength with Hallie, offering comfort and solace when she most needed it. And Hallie knew the time would come, as it always did, when she would find cause to reciprocate. It was never a burden, and she supposed that was what made this friendship special.

Hallie's heart was not so light when she thought of Adam, for her last meeting with him had been painful. It was a sorrowful burden for her knowing she would never again love anyone in the way she did Michael and wishing Adam could find that same kind of fulfillment. She knew that she could do nothing more than hope that someone would come along who changed his mind and brought him all that Michael did her.

The candles had nearly all burned away; a few stubs remained to cast a soft glow in the large room. Hallie was not startled when Michael approached her from behind, his powerful arms enfolding her in a warm, tender embrace. His lips lowered to her hair, enjoying the sweet scent of her.

"What were you thinking, love?" His voice was deep, rich.

"Of the past, of all that has happened, good and bad."

Michael turned her in his embrace, holding her as

if to dance. Slowly they began to waltz in the large, empty room, needing only the music in their minds. "The first time we danced it was a waltz. Do you remember?" he asked, smiling down at her, his features extremely handsome.

Hallie laughed lightly. "Of course I remember! You were horrid to me."

Now Michael chuckled. "Was I? I don't doubt it. I had some very foolish notions about you."

"Oh?" Her curiosity was piqued. "What were they?"

"I thought you were merely a convenience for me, a necessity for that portion of my life. I was certain you would be no more than a woman to bear my children, to care for my house, to warm my bed when I wanted but never to hinder my pursuit of my own pleasure. I was absolutely positive I would never be trapped by that evil wile of women called love. I had myself convinced that I was different from my father, too wild and free-spirited to be caught and tamed. I told myself I would simply use you for my own purposes and never give you a thought afterward. You were to be my wife, and for pleasure I would seek my mistress." He laughed.

"I fail to see what is so funny about that!" she said in mock sincerity.

"It was ludicrous, love. I was wrong in all of it. I could never get you out of my mind. In fact, one night when I was very, very angry with you and so damned jealous of Adam I could barely stand it, I went to Maeve Carson. It was quite embarrassing, for I could not manage to be aroused by her. It was you I wanted, even then, before I had begun to realize all you meant to me. You are the most important thing in my life, Hallie. If you never provided any of what you do, of what I expected you to do, I would still love you, worship you in a way I thought was only for fools. If this is foolishness, I revel in it!"

Hallie smiled beautifully up at Michael, basking in the warmth of his glance. "Does that mean you don't resent being forced to marry me just for the sake of Danny?"

"It means that I am forever grateful for my good fortune."

"And I for mine. We have found something perfect for ourselves."

"Not quite. It will take a few dozen more children before it is perfect." He teased, "If you'll recall, I warned you that first night that it was my intention to fill this house."

She laughed. "I love you, Michael. I wonder if even now you know how much."

"I hope enough to keep you here, even when things are unpleasant and Adam beckons," he said more seriously.

"You know that! I will never run off with Adam. I care for him, but nothing to measure up to what I feel for you. You are my life, Michael. It is not even comparable to what I had with Adam."

"I hope that's true, Hallie, for I could not live if I lost you."

She kissed him passionately, her desire for her husband rising markedly. "Then I suppose you had better keep me satisfied. Do you think you're up to it?"

He swept her up into his arms, his laughter echoing in the large, empty space. "I believe I'm up to a week of nothing but romping with you in bed. Shall we see which of us begs for a reprieve first?"

Michael bounded up the stairs, eager to reach their room. Once there he swung her onto the bed and himself onto Hallie. It was a joyous moment, holding them both in the beautiful, cloudlike world of their desire for one another and leaving no room for intrusion. Hallie knew they shared a very unique passion, a perfect, unrivaled love. In that instant, entwined together as they reveled in joining their bodies, she realized that what they had found together would endure for all eternity.

THE NEW NOVEL FROM
MILLION-COPY BESTSELLING AUTHOR
Shirlee Busbee

The story of a violet-eyed English beauty, and a darkly
handsome arrogant Texan...and of the magic that happens
when their eyes first meet at a dazzling New Orleans ball and
awakens them to the magnificent passions of love.

82297-0/$3.95

ALSO FROM SHIRLEE BUSBEE:

LADY VIXEN   83550-9/$3.50

To escape the clutches of her greedy relatives, a lovely orphaned
aristocrat flees England and her beloved ancestral estate only
to discover adventure in the Caribbean and romance in the
arms of a dashing pirate!

GYPSY LADY   82859-6/$3.50

This fiery novel sweeps from England and France to Virginia,
New Orleans and the American frontier as a beautiful English
woman raised among gypsies is drawn into a tempestuous
romance with a handsome American adventurer!

AVON Original Paperbacks